Wild Need of Love

"Lone Eagle?" Abigail called out again. She walked into the darkness behind their *tipi*, for she had not seen him anywhere in the light of the fires. "Lone Eagle, where are you?"

She gasped as a strong arm grasped her about the waist and pulled her close. In the next moment his lips were on hers, kissing her savagely, a light odor of whiskey on his breath. She knew it was her husband, and yet somehow he was different, his soul torn by the fact that Swift Arrow loved her, his heart ravaged by the knowledge of what his son would suffer in the next few days, and his desire enhanced by the whiskey that he had drunk to try to forget the ache of what was happening to his people.

He released the kiss, but kept a tight hold on her so that it was difficult for her even to breathe. "I want you," he told her fiercely.

He came down on her, wrapping his arms around her and rolling over quickly so that she was on top of him. "Be free tonight, woman of Lone Eagle," he told her. "Do not be like a white woman. Be Lone Eagle's woman. . . ."

SAVAGE DESTINY

EMBRACE THE WILD LAND

#4

F. ROSANNE BITTNER

ZEBRA BOOKS
KENSINGTON PUBLISHING CORP.

With deepest gratitude to two of my most enthusiastic fans in the very early days of my writing, my sisters, Linda and Pat.

Each novel in this series contains occasional reference to historical characters, locations and events that actually existed and occurred during the time period of each story. All such reference is based on factual printed matter available to the public. However, the primary characters in this series are purely fictitious and a product of the author's imagination. Any resemblance of the author's fictitious characters to actual persons, living or dead or of author's fictitious events to any events that may have occurred at that time and of which the author is unaware is purely coincidental.

The major portions of this novel take place in present-day Colorado and its surrounding territory. Fort Laramie is in today's southeast Wyoming; Bent's Fort in Southeast Colorado. The Arkansas River (primary location of the Southern Cheyenne during this time period) is also in southeast Colorado. Fort Lyon is in northern New Mexico.

During the time period of this novel, the Sioux Indians occupied much of what is now Minnesota, the Dakotas, Montana and parts of Wyoming and Nebraska. The Cheyenne Indians were split into two factions—the Northern Cheyenne, who occupied most of Nebraska and parts of Wyoming and also mingled with the Sioux in the Dakotas; and the Southern Cheyenne, who occupied most of Colorado, parts of Kansas and the southern part of Nebraska, mingling very closely with the Arapaho Indians.

With grateful acknowledgment to authors and/or establishments whose books were inspiring and of valuable resource: St. Stephen's Indian Foundation, Wyoming, The Wind River Rendezvous magazine; the Language Research Dept. of the Northern Cheyenne, English Cheyenne Student Dictionary; Ronald P. Koch, Dress Clothing of the Plains Indians; the Time/Life series, The Old West and The Civil War; Donald J. Berthrong, The Southern Cheyenne; and various works by Dee Brown and Will Henry.

We are surrounded by war, my love.
The guns roar, and blood flows,
Dividing brother from brother
In the land where the sun rises;
And exploding the peace
Between red man and white
In the land where the sun sets.

But we will not let the guns and the blood
Divide our sweet love.
Neither war nor the different blood
That flows in our veins
Can separate us;
For our hearts and our spirits are one,
Whether we be together or apart.
Let others be
 By blood divided.
  Our love shall endure. . . .

Prologue

The call could be heard far off, a long, lonesome wail that moved out from the silent, granite Rockies, over the vast plains and prairies of Nebraska, New Mexico and Kansas Territories, and through the Dakotas. It was an odd, groaning howl, heard only by the animals and the Indians in the deepest part of the night—a chilling wail of sorrow that the Indians knew was the souls of their brothers, the animals, and their god, the land. For both were being destroyed, in the name of power, in the name of gold, in the name of wealth to the white man's shouted words of "Manifest Destiny." Such destruction could only bring on the extinction of the Indian himself. The weight of the oppressors was being felt, and the land and its children were weeping.

It was that weeping of those who are one in spirit that haunted the plains and prairies in the last days of freedom. Already the white man spilled his own blood in the mysterious East, where bluecoats and graycoats clashed in bitter opposition. But it would not be enough blood. For when matters were settled between North and South, there would be an even greater migration westward, and the red men of the plains would be in the way. The Indians felt this, felt the imminent danger, and their hearts were heavy with sorrow. The buffalo and the eagle felt it, too. And the land itself felt it with every gouge into its skin for mineral wealth, every polluted stream, every stripped forest, every game animal killed for sport and left to waste.

It seemed in those times that the land bled on every border and in all places in between . . . and there was much weeping. And so each night the lonesome wail of the land moved over mountain and plain and prairie. A painful change was developing. And life as it once was would never be again.

But two people would move through the change, two people who would be scarred and torn by the bleeding land but who would endure. For they lived, breathed and walked as one, and their love was so strong that it would rise above the pain, the warfare and their own personal sorrows. His name was Zeke, and she was his Abbie-girl. . . .

One

It stood out stark and jagged against the intense blue
sky, a puffy, white cloud softly drifting over the rusty
brown, flat-topped butte that jutted upward from the
mesa of pure rock. It was nothing more than a huge
rock, perhaps two miles in length and a mile in width,
like so many other molded hills of rock that were inex-
plicably scattered over the desolate, endless wasteland
that was New Mexico Territory. There seemed to be no
reason for their existence, as though the god of Nature
had thrown them carelessly around when He designed
the vast and beautiful West.

But the white woman who rode beneath the great
shadow of the butte challenged the beauty of the land
with her own beauty. Her hair was deep brown, with a
hint of red to it in the sunlight. Her skin was browned
from exposure, but supple from creams that her half-
breed husband insisted she use. Her eyes were a gentle
brown, and her stature was straight and proud, as
proud as the Cheyenne Indians with whom she now
rode, quietly making their way toward Fort Lyon, the
feet of their horses padded by the soft, green grass of the
valley they traveled.

The woman held a small boy in front of her and

a very young daughter sat behind, clinging to her mother's waist. The woman kept glancing back watchfully, keeping an eye on five more children who rode their own mounts, babbling back and forth, sometimes laughing, all excited over the trip they were taking with their mother and father to see the annual Navaho horse races.

Sometimes the white woman's gaze wandered farther back—to her husband, a half-breed Cheyenne. He was the biggest man among the Cheyenne men with whom they rode—the tallest and the most handsome. He rode behind the rest, herding along some of the grand Appaloosas he raised on their ranch along the Arkansas River in southeast Colorado—in the middle of Indian country. But the white woman was not afraid to live among the red men of the plains. They were her friends, her family—the only family she had since losing her own white family many years ago when first she came west.

Her husband waved to her and she smiled, waving back, then turned forward again, riding her own sturdy Appaloosa with agility and skill, for she had long lived in this wild land and had learned her riding skills from a man who knew all about horses and riding, a man who loved horses and raised them for a living.

They were the Monroes, Zeke and Abbie and their seven children. They rode together—a loving family, and one about whom others sometimes talked. The Monroes not only loved together, but they had also fought together against the forces of a savage land, both seen and unseen, their love made stronger by their battle scars. Both Zeke and Abbie knew the risk the future carried for those who lived in a dangerous land, but they were not afraid. They had each other, and from each other they received the strength and courage to face whatever life might bring their way.

Now as they rode casually through the valley beneath the majestic butte, a new danger lay waiting, for six men skulked in the shadow behind them, watching the small band of Indians with whom Zeke and Abbie rode.

"We could pick them off right easy," one called Blade told a companion with an evil grin. He spit out some tobacco, some of which landed on his smelly calico shirt, its colors long faded from being worn for many months without being washed. He brushed at it, then rubbed his grizzly beard where more had dripped from his lip.

"I thought you preferred using that knife," another answered, also eyeing the Indians, considering the fun he could have with one of the squaws. He'd pick the prettiest and youngest one.

Blade closed his hand around his favorite weapon, nervously moving it in and out of its sheath. It was the knife he used that had earned him his nickname. Few men were better at stripping the hide from a buffalo with a knife than Blade. But he much preferred opening up a man's hide; he took a hideous pleasure in watching someone else bleed.

" 'Course I prefer my knife," he answered. "But at the moment there's a few too many for that. We'll save one or two to cut up later. Maybe I'll just use it on the women."

They all chuckled, feeling pleasant urges at the thought of taking the squaws. They were buffalo hunters, the bare beginnings of the hundreds who would come in future years to kill the animal strictly for its hide. It did not matter that wiping out the buffalo would mean wiping out the Indian. In fact, it was being looked upon as a very convenient way of ridding the West of its rightful inhabitants—much cheaper than war. But the idea had not fully caught on yet, and would not until the infamous Sharp rifle, which would

13

be nicknamed "The Big Fifty," came into the picture, making it much easier for the hunters to casually shoot their prey while seated at a comfortable distance, picking off the great beast of the plains at the rate of one hundred per day.

Still, these men with their weapons were already doing enough damage to the buffalo herds to create a mild panic in the Indians and to keep the troubles between Indians and whites bubbling and steaming. And these particular men were like so many more to come— careless and cruel, with no regard for life and beauty, no room for love or concern in their hearts. They were there for the excitement and for whatever monetary gain they could wring from the bounty of the West; some of them were also there to avoid the law in the East. In this lawless territory they could enjoy the fruits of their evil without fear of imprisonment. Still, there was little worry about prison when one killed an Indian. It was expected and accepted; sometimes for soldiers it was even an order.

"Where do you expect they're headed, Carl?" Blade spoke up again.

"Fort Lyon, most likely," Carl answered. "The Navaho gather there about this time every year to trade and have a powwow with the soldiers. I heard they have a horse race every year, too. The redskins usually win. Mighty fine horsemen, them Indians."

"And mighty fine horseflesh they ride," one called Bowlegs added. "I'm thinking that small herd of horses bringing up the rear down there would bring a pretty price from the army at the fort."

"Look like Appaloosas from here," Carl replied. "We can pick off the men, then get what we need from the women and take the horses on to the fort."

"What about their little lice-covered kids? There's plenty of them down there," another put in.

14

Blade shrugged. "Kill them or let them go, which-ever suits your fancy. Them we don't get, the wolves and snakes will take care of. This might turn out to be a damned profitable day, boys—warrior scalps, women and horses." He spit again. "Damned profitable."

"Only thing is, they don't look like Navahos to me," one called Moose spoke up. "Look more like Chey-enne, and the Cheyenne are good warriors. There must be a good fifteen men down there."

"So what?" Bowlegs sneered. "We all take aim and eliminate six of them right off. I'll bet they ain't even got guns. And with women and children along they'll try to make a run for it. We can get the rest of them in the back. We're wasting time, boys." He dismounted and dropped to one knee, taking aim. The others fol-lowed, positioning themselves and aiming carefully. "Left to right," Bowlegs warned them. "Tilly, you take the one farther back in line and so on, so's we don't all aim for the same man. Get that big one herding the horses back there."

There was a moment of silence while the small band of Indians moved almost silently through the tall buf-falo grass. Painted ponies ambled casually, many of them dragging travois with needed supplies. Some chil-dren walked, as did some of the women. Then six shots rang out, nearly all at the same time. But only one man fell: the big one who had been herding the horses. It was Zeke.

"Goddamn it! They're out of range! They're out of range!" Blade swore.

"I thought they was close enough!" Bowlegs grum-bled.

There was general confusion below. Abbie's horse whirled and reared, her little girl clung in terror to her mother, and her son, who Abbie held onto with one hand, began to cry. Abbie's horse galloped back toward

15

her fallen husband while the buffalo hunters began to bear down on their prey, in too much of a hurry to even notice the woman with skin much too fair to be Indian.

"Come on! Let's chase them down!" Carl said excitedly, mounting up. "With them women and children along we can overtake them easy!"

The others followed suit, their brains too overheated by lust and excitement to consider anything other than victory. Leather squeaked and horses whinnied as the six big men who smelled worse than their animals swung themselves into the saddles to chase after the confused Indians.

Zeke was back on his feet, shouting something to Abbie and smacking her horse into motion. She rode forward again, herding several children with her. Other children were whisked up by warriors and still others by their mothers, and they all headed for a cluster of rocks nearly a mile away. None of the six men noticed that Zeke and one other warrior stayed behind, ducking into the buffalo grass for cover amid the confusion of the scattering Appaloosas they had been herding.

The buffalo hunters came thundering down from the mesa, their horses' hoofs echoing until they were several yards away from the rocky monolith. Now Zeke could feel the ground shaking, both from the fleeing Indians and the approaching hunters. There was a tense moment as the hunters finally came close, then galloped right past the two warriors, their eyes and senses riveted to the Indians and the herd of Appaloosas ahead of them.

Sod and rocks flew as the hunters passed. Zeke and his companion rose from their hiding places. Blood flowed from Zeke's right arm as he took aim with his rifle; the other Indian raised a bow and arrow. A sharp report followed, accompanied by a silent arrow, and the ones called Tilly and Bowlegs fell, both mortally

16

wounded in the back. The other four men whirled at the sound behind them, shocked, their hearts pounding with fear now that they were the hunted rather than the hunters.

Another shot rang out before they could gather their bearings, and the one they called Moose fell, a hole between his eyes. Carl grunted and sat momentarily transfixed with an arrow in his throat and blood spurting over its shaft.

Blade was already in motion, leaning forward and galloping hard in a sideways direction away from both the two warriors and the Indians farther ahead, leaving behind his friends. The sixth man, called Stu, swore at his mount, which was snorting and rearing in confusion, out of control. Carl finally tumbled from his horse, the arrow shaft shoving even deeper into the already dead man's throat when he hit the ground. By then a huge knife had landed in Stu's lower back, just as his horse turned again in frightened prancing. The man cried out and fell, and the horse ran off after Blade, who was already too far out of range for rifle or arrow.

Zeke tossed his rifle onto the grass and walked up angrily to Stu, who lay writhing on the ground, facedown. He yanked out his knife, no remorse or pity in his dark, vengeful eyes. He kicked the white man over onto his back and held him down with his foot.

"Appears you had in mind murdering some innocent people, mister!" he hissed, surprising Stu with his clear English that even carried the hint of a Southern accent. "Trouble is, my woman and my children were among them. You picked the wrong victims this time!"

The last thing Stu thought before his death was how strange the words sounded coming from a man as dark as an Indian, his hair long and black and straight, his dress pure Cheyenne. But that curiosity lived for only a

17

very brief moment before Zeke whisked the big, ugly knife across Stu's throat and ended his thoughts for good.

Zeke wiped blood from the knife and turned to face his companion, shoving the knife back into its beaded sheath. His companion grinned. "You have not lost your touch, my brother."

Zeke smiled but looked out at the disappearing sixth man with worried eyes. "But one got away. That could be a problem, Black Elk."

"We did nothing wrong," the Cheyenne warrior replied.

Zeke looked back at him. "Since when does that matter? White men can attack and kill Indians, but Indians had better not do it to the white man, remember?" He bent down to pick up his rifle.

Black Elk's eyes clouded. "Your white brothers have a strange way of saying what is justice," he answered.

Their eyes held. "Just because half of me is white doesn't mean I call them my brothers. The Cheyenne are my true brothers, and those with whom I share the blood of our mother—you and Swift Arrow." He turned and whistled to his mount, a sturdy and faithful Appaloosa that was already heading back to its master. "Let's get going. I'm worried about Abbie and the kids, and we have some horses to round up before we go on to the fort."

Black Elk nodded. "We will leave the bodies for the wolves."

"No," Zeke answered. "We'll have to bury them, much as I would prefer not to. But if this thing is thrown back at us later, the soldiers will believe us more if we show enough compassion to bury the bodies. I know how the white man thinks, Black Elk. If we leave the bodies they'll say it's just proof of how savage the Indian is. We'll bury them the white man's way and we'll ride right into that fort and tell them exactly what happened—show them we have nothing to hide. Abbie's along. She's white. They'll listen to her.''

Black Elk nodded. ''Your woman is much help sometimes. You chose well when you chose that one, Zeke.''

Zeke nodded, feeling a pleasant urge inside at the thought of her, his love for her intensified by the way she loved his people, and the way they accepted and honored her as one of their own in spite of her white skin. He mounted his horse in one quick movement, and Black Elk sprang up behind him. The two men headed for the rest of the band, who had already noticed that the fighting was over and were riding back toward them. Abbie was right in front with some of the men, anxious to make sure her husband was all right.

''Zeke!'' he heard her shout from a distance. He trotted his horse faster and rode up to meet her, thinking to himself how beautiful she looked astride her spotted horse. She wore a newly painted and beaded tunic, and her lustrous, dark hair was blowing in the west wind, strands of it brushing over her lovely face. They halted side by side and their eyes held while Black Elk dismounted. How she wanted to embrace her husband and weep with joy that he was all right. But when they were with the Cheyenne, she behaved as a Cheyenne woman, refusing to shame him by displaying too much emotion in front of the rest of the men. Zeke knew her thoughts and grinned, loving her for wanting to hold him, and for understanding the Cheyenne way.

''I'm all right,'' he told her, reaching over and squeezing her hand. ''It's only a flesh wound.''

''You're still bleeding,'' she said, her voice shaking. ''When I saw you fall—'' Her voice broke and she swallowed as their eldest son galloped up beside his mother.

"Father! You are all right?"

Zeke nodded, his heart swelling with pride at the sight of his teen-age son, who rode as a Cheyenne and practiced the Cheyenne way, already an accomplished warrior for his age.

"What your mother still can't get through her head, son, is that I'm too damned mean to die. I've just added another scar to my collection, that's all." He looked back at Abbie, who was quickly wiping at unwanted tears.

"We should . . . clean and wrap the wound," she said quietly.

Zeke nodded. "Agreed. Dig out what you need and I'll get my shirt off while the men here bury the bodies." He looked at his son. "Wolf's Blood, you and Black Elk get going and round up the Appaloosas. If we hurry we can make the fort by sundown."

The boy nodded, obvious relief in his eyes, for he worshipped his father with great passion, and Zeke in turn worshipped his son.

Zeke looked back at his wife. "Fix me up good, woman. I don't want this to interfere with the knife-throwing contest when we reach the fort. I intend to line my pockets with some bets."

She sighed deeply and sniffed. "I doubt any of them who know you will bother even entering in any knife contests with Zeke Monroe," she answered.

Zeke shrugged. "We'll see." He stared out at the horizon. The one called Blade had disappeared into the distance, headed for Fort Lyon to report the terrible "Indian attack" on him and his men, angry that he had been unable to use his knife that day on the "dirty redskins." Blade gripped his knife tightly and cursed his luck.

Two

Soldiers stared. Some in awe, some in contempt. Yet as they watched her ride past, her lovely chin held high, her back straight and proud, her face showing the strength and courage of a woman who must battle all the adversities of a hard life in an untamed land, most of the contempt turned to respect. Abbie could hear the whispers, could feel the eyes staring at her back. But it didn't matter. She had come to Fort Lyon with her half-breed husband simply as a wife and a mother who wanted to enjoy the festivities of the yearly gathering of these soldiers with the Navahos and Cheyenne and Arapaho Indians.

Her youngest son, Eoveano (Yellow Hawk), called by his white name, Jason, was perched in front of her on the gentle Appaloosa; his four-year-old sister Lillian (her Indian name Meane-ese, Summer Moon) still sat behind, holding onto her mother. Abbie clung tightly to little Jason, her "baby," the last child she would have. She had nearly died at his birth, and an operation in Denver three years earlier had ended her child bearing. But little Jason was special for another reason. He was turning into a replica of her own little brother, who had died when Abbie first came west with her family.

All of them had died. There was nothing left of her family, or of the Abigail Trent who had grown up in Tennessee. That was another time, another Abbie.

The other five children rode, biggest to smallest, behind their mother, a touching and somewhat amusing picture. In the distance, three Cheyenne men kept Zeke's Appaloosas in check; the rest of the band waited for a signal to come into the fort. Zeke had told them he would ride in first, with his half-brother, Black Elk, and two other braves, wanting to discover if any trouble had been stirred over the incident with the buffalo hunters. White bandages around his upper right arm stood out in stark contrast to his dark skin as he rode shirtless in the late afternoon heat. The summer had dragged into autumn, and this September day of 1861 had grown warmer rather than cooler.

Soldiers and traders alike watched the small procession enter the fort, some gathering and following as Zeke led his family up to officers' quarters, where already he had spotted the horse that had been ridden by the fleeing buffalo hunter in the skirmish several miles back. The man had come straight to the fort, just as Zeke had suspected.

The Indians halted their horses and waited silently, all of them sitting straight and proud, ready to defend their position. Soldiers and traders gawked at the white woman with the Indian men. She wore an Indian tunic, as did her four daughters. Her three sons sported buckskin leggings and shirtless backs. The men did not doubt the fierceness of the big man beside the woman, for in addition to his bandaged arm, his dark skin bore several scars—scars that could only belong to a man accustomed to doing battle, scars of a man who had known violence all his life. His chest and upper arms showed signs of having suffered the torturous Sun Dance ritual to prove his manhood; on his lower left side was a scar from an old bullet wound, a bullet Abbie herself had dug out of him many years ago; another faint scar in his left chest bespoke another bullet wound; and there were faint traces on his back from a whipping many winters ago. Yet the man remained strong and fierce, his tall, broad stature silently defying anyone to challenge him.

At forty-one, Zeke Monroe remained as hard and strong as any man twenty years his junior. His hair hung long and unbraided, a beaded band around his forehead with four coup feathers tied at the back and pointing downward. A copper band circled the hard muscle of his left bicep, and the wide leather belt at his waist sported a tomahawk, a hand gun and two knives, one of them the huge blade he had used on the buffalo hunter, its menacing, curved blade and buffalo jawbone handle the source of bloody tales among Indians and white man alike for many years.

"What do you make of that?" one soldier said quietly to another. "That woman is white."

The second soldier nodded, both men's eyes studying the curious family that had just ridden in. "That she is," the second man replied. He scratched at an ugly scar on his left cheek that stood out pink and bare, surrounded by a grizzly, dark beard. No hairs would grow there where an Indian's tomahawk had once sliced off part of his skin, barely missing splitting open the soldier's skull. The man grinned. "Looks like this year might bring us some extra entertainment. Any white woman who rides with an Indian has to be either captive or a woman who'll sleep with any man."

The first man glanced at him sidelong. "From the looks of that buck she rides with, I'd think twice about even looking at his woman, Cole. And look there on her horse. She carries her own rifle, and I'll bet she knows how to use it!"

Cole ran his tongue over his lips. "Maybe. But how often does a white woman ride in here—and one that looks like that besides? She's the best looking thing I've seen in many a moon, friend."

It was then that an officer came outside, accompanied by a slovenly man in a faded calico shirt, brown moisture at the corners of his mouth from tobacco, a blade nearly as big as Zeke's strapped to his belt and a rifle in his hand. They studied the small group of Indians silently for a moment, their eyes resting on Abbie for longer than necessary, both men astonished to see a white woman with them. Zeke glared back at them with hard, angry, dark eyes, a soft evening breeze blowing strands of his jet-black hair across the finely chiseled face of the half-breed, a face that the lines of hard living and even a thin scar on his left cheek from a Crow warrior's knife did little to detract from a handsomeness that seems to come only to those of mixed blood.

"I'm Zeke Monroe," he spoke up curtly, his quick defensiveness on behalf of his white woman rising to the surface as the two men stared at Abbie. His voice drew their attention back to him, and their eyes showed surprise at his good English. Zeke turned threatening, vengeful eyes to the man in the calico shirt. "I've come here to report an attack on my family and some of my Cheyenne friends by some buffalo hunters." He shifted his eyes to the officer. "Thought maybe the one that got away would come riding in here to try and make trouble for my brother and his people."

"That's them!" the man in the calico shirt growled. "They attacked us, Lieutenant. Killed all five of my friends! They should all be put in irons!"

The officer frowned and shifted nervously. "I'll not jump to any conclusions, Blade," he answered, looking back up at Zeke. "I'm Lieutenant Perkins. This man here says you and your warriors attacked him and his

24

men for no reason. Now you come riding in here telling me just the opposite. Suppose you tell me the whole story. And how is it you speak such good English?''

''My father was a white man. I was raised in Tennessee. My mother was Cheyenne.'' He turned to the man beside him. ''This is Black Elk. We share the same mother. He is my half-brother.'' He looked back at the officer. ''If we had done something wrong, Lieutenant, do you think we'd ride right in here like this and risk being arrested? Look around you. I have my whole family with me, and so do some of the other braves. Why would we go attacking this man and his friends? We aren't a war party. We were simply coming here for the annual celebrations with the Navaho, to take part in the horse races and other contests. Back on the hill are some of my horses. I have a ranch on the Arkansas River where I raise Appaloosas. I've brought some here to sell to the army and to trade with the Navaho for some blankets. I'm telling you that this man here is lying. It was they who attacked us. And my guess is they were after our women—and my horses.''

''You stinking half-breed!'' Blade hissed, taking a step forward. The lieutenant grasped his arm and held him back.

''Hold on there, Blade!'' he ordered. ''I'm inclined to believe this man. This is no war party, you fool! And we're having enough trouble without men like you stirring things up!'' He looked back up at Zeke, glancing across to Abbie, then back to Zeke again. ''That your wife, or is she a captive slave?''

Zeke broke into a handsome grin, glancing over at Abbie, who smiled back at him. He looked back at the officer. ''She's my wife, legal, and we have papers to prove it. We've been married for sixteen years.'' He wanted to add that it was he who was the captive slave, for little Abigail Trent had captured his heart years ago

25

and had chained it to her own. The lieutenant turned to Abbie again.

"That true?"

"It certainly is," she replied in a soft but determined voice. "I am Mrs. Zeke Monroe, and these are all our children. And what my husband told you about the buffalo hunters is true. They ambushed us, for no reason whatsoever. You can see my husband was wounded. I and the others fled to some rocks, while my husband and Black Elk fell back and waited for the buffalo hunters who pursued us."

"You gonna believe a white whore who sleeps with a half-breed?" Blade stormed.

Quickly, Zeke was off his horse, his big blade drawn in challenge. "Any man who insults my woman had best be ready to defend himself!" he growled, his dark eyes blazing. Blade's eyes lit up.

"Gladly!" he answered, drawing his own knife.

"Hold it!" the lieutenant ordered. He whipped out a side arm and two other soldiers moved in, holding rifles to both Zeke and Blade. "Blade, you apologize to the lady."

"I'm not apologizing to anybody! I'd rather have it out with this stinking half-breed!"

"You're crazy!" a trader spoke up, moving in on the argument. "I've heard about this half-breed. Some call him Cheyenne Zeke. The Indians call him Lone Eagle. All of us in the hunting and trading business have heard of him. He's got a reputation from the Missouri clean out to California with his knife. Anybody that challenges him with the blade is looking to die!"

"How do you think I earned *my* nickname!" Blade sneered, still watching Zeke.

"I don't give a damn how you earned it," the trader replied. "I'm just being fair in warning you about this man. You'll never win a knife fight with him!"

Blade straightened a little, sizing up the fine physique of Zeke Monroe, gauging the expert way with which Zeke grasped his big knife. But Blade had a reputation of his own, and he was not about to back down. Perhaps winning a knife fight against this half-breed would bring him fame and envy and make him a more important man.

"I ain't impressed," he told the crowd. "And since we both tell a different story and the lieutenant here has no way of knowing the truth, I say we solve the whole problem with a duel. If I win, these Cheyenne get arrested." His eyes shifted to Abbie for a moment, as he thought hungrily about the situation she would be in without her man to protect her. He looked back at Zeke. "He wins, it's over. I'll be dead and it won't matter."

Black Elk grinned, as did the other two Cheyenne men and Zeke's eldest son, Wolf's Blood. All knew Zeke's skill with the blade. Abbie remained silent. Her husband was Cheyenne, a proud warrior. He would not back down from a challenge, nor would he let an insult to his woman go unanswered. She would not complain and try to stop him.

"This white man is a fool!" Black Elk told Zeke in the Cheyenne tongue. Zeke's eyes danced with eagerness as he straightened and shoved his knife back into its sheath, a vicious smile on his lips.

"You warm my heart with your offer, white scum!" he answered. "I welcome a duel. We'll make it exciting for the others here and set a time. As long as the soldiers and Indians are here for games and betting, you and I will be one of the games!" He reached back and untied a piece of leather from his horse's bridle. "We'll duel the Indian way, unless you're too yellow!" He held out the leather, and Blade knew what he meant. He had fought that way before. He would do it again against

27

this infamous Cheyenne Zeke.

"However you want it, half-breed!" he answered. "Your insides will greet the sunshine same as every other man's that's gone up against me."

Zeke stepped back, keeping his eyes on Blade. "Wolf's Blood, go stand by the support post by the lieutenant there," he ordered his eldest son. The fourteen-year-old boy dismounted, a tall, strong, handsome boy, the replica of his father except for the age difference. He walked up to the support post, putting his back against it. "Make a mark right where the top of my son's head comes," Zeke told the lieutenant.

There were mumbles from the onlookers, and Blade scowled. The lieutenant frowned and took Blade's knife from its sheath, walking up to Wolf's Blood and cutting out a little piece of wood to mark the post. Wolf's Blood's eyes held his father's steadily. Once called Little Rock, the boy now used the name he had chosen after having his first vision and living alone in the mountains in a cave with wolves at the tender age of twelve. At times it seemed to Abbie that the boy had never been a child at all, for he had always been mature for his age. There was no evidence of the boy's white blood, except that his skin was more of milky brown than the reddish darkness of his full-blooded relatives. His black hair hung well past his broad shoulders, shiny and straight, and even in his early teens he gave the appearance of a fine warrior in the making. His lips were set hard and unsmiling now, for he, too, was anxious to see his father mete out the proper punishment to the buffalo hunter. He faced his father without fear, knowing what Zeke would do but never doubting his father's abilities. Cheyenne Zeke would plunge his blade into his own breast before he would harm his favorite son. The scarred soldier called Cole scratched at his cheek again, considering that between the father and the son, it would be difficult getting to the lovely white woman.

Zeke removed his knife again and backed up a little more. Wolf's Blood took a deep breath and held it, keeping his eyes on his father as Zeke raised back his hand with the knife in it. With a quick flick he flung the menacing blade. Wolf's Blood did not blink when it landed square in the spot the lieutenant had marked, one side of its blade resting against the part in Wolf's Blood's hair, literally touching the scalp but not harming the boy. Gasps arose from the crowd. Blade swallowed but hid his fear. Zeke walked up to his son and their eyes spoke of their love. Then Zeke yanked out his knife and turned to Blade.

"Every man meets somebody just a little better one day, Blade. Now it's your turn."

Blade threw his shoulders back and glared back at him. "Maybe it's yours, half-breed! Knife throwing and knife *fighting* are two different matters."

Zeke grinned again. "Trouble is, I'm better at fighting than I am at throwing," he sneered. "You'll find that out tomorrow noon." He walked to his horse and mounted up again. "I'm bringing in the rest of those with us to make camp among the Arapaho," he told the lieutenant. "We'll talk later about my horses. I want to get my family settled first."

The lieutenant glanced at Abbie and back to Zeke. "Your wife might want to stay here in a more comfortable facility."

Zeke looked at Abbie with humor in his eyes, and Abbie rode up closer to the lieutenant. "I have lived in a *tipi* before, Lieutenant," she told the man. "They're quite comfortable; and I don't doubt I'll be much safer camping with the Cheyenne than I would be within the walls of this fort." Wolf's Blood laughed lightly at his mother's remark as he mounted up, and Abbie turned her eyes to glare haughtily at the buffalo hunter.

29

"Once your husband is dead, you'd best sleep with your eyes open, bitch!" he sneered.

Zeke charged his horse forward just enough to make the man stumble backward and fall. "If not for our agreement to meet tomorrow, you would be dead right now, you fat, yellow-bellied snake!" he growled. "I don't want to see your face until noon tomorrow, or the deal is off and I'll kill you on the spot!"

He turned his horse and headed out of the fort, followed by the woman who had belonged to him since first he claimed her virgin body and heart. At fifteen, she was ten years younger than he, but looked much younger even than that, for she had the enviable inherited trait of not aging as rapidly as some women in this rugged Western land. She was a woman very pleasing to look upon: her complexion was clear and smooth, with hardly a line of age on her beautiful face; her large, soft brown eyes were provocative; her dark hair was lustrous and enticing. She had borne seven children from Zeke's seed, and he had been the only man to ever plant his life in her womb. All of the births had taken place on the harsh plains, with no one to help but Zeke himself. Yet the hard living and heavy workload she carried had kept her body firm and agile, and her breasts were still full and pleasing. There was no fat on Abbie, just firm muscle and sun-browned skin, slim thighs and a body quite pleasing to hold in the night. The intensity and passion of their lovemaking had not lessened over the years; rather, it had become even more exciting and satisfying with their ever-deepening love, a love that had grown out of the sharing of pain and hardship. She knew his heart as well as he knew himself, and he in turn had given her the love and security she had needed after losing her family in a strange land.

Abbie held tightly to little, dark-haired, hazel-eyed

Jason as they left, and gave her little Lillian a pat to re-assure the child that everything would be all right. Lillian held tightly to her mother's waist with frail arms. She had always been the sickly child, and the past week had been the first time the little girl had seemed to be free of the cough that had plagued her for months. Her coloring was a flat medium, her hair and eyes a dishwater brown. She was a gentle, unselfish child, always ready to help her mother, a child that brought Abbie comfort with her loyalty, but also the pain only a mother understands at seeing a child almost always sick.

Wolf's Blood rode proudly behind his mother. He grinned at Blade victoriously, halting his horse in front of the man for a moment. "You had better eat well tonight, my friend," he gloated. "I have seen my father fight with the knife. A man's last meal should be a good one, so fill your belly!"

"Wolf's Blood!" Zeke barked.

The boy laughed lightly and urged his horse forward again. He was the only child who had refused a white name, and his heart carried the eager pride of his full-blooded Cheyenne friends, the young men anxious to prove their own manhood. A large, menacing gray wolf trotted alongside the boy's mount, its thick fur standing up on its neck, the animal sensing that it was also a part of the family's protection. The wolf's saliva flowed heavier, its claws tense, its fierce loyalty to the young man who was its master planting an instinctive readiness in its savage heart to charge and lunge at the throat of any man who dared try to harm a member of the Monroe family.

Behind Wolf's Blood rode his sister, number two child, Margaret, her Indian name Moheya (Blue Sky). At twelve, Margaret was a budding beauty, provocatively dark like her brother, with just a little wave to her black hair hinting that she bore white blood. She was followed by another sister, child number three, LeeAnn, whose Indian name was Kse-e (Young Girl). LeeAnn was nine, and her passing drew even more stares and whispers, for she carried the genes of Abbie's blond mother and sister, both now dead. LeeAnn's almost white hair and her vivid blue eyes and fair skin kept her from fitting in with the rest of her family, and Zeke watched his blond daughter with a fierce protectiveness. Not only would she be a beautiful woman, but he feared that soldiers or citizens would come along and try to take her from them, refusing to believe she was not a captive.

Behind LeeAnn rode Jeremy, called Ohkumhkakit, or Little Wolf, by the Cheyenne. The eight-year-old boy was slender and small, bearing little resemblance to his older brother, either in build, coloring or spirit. His eyes were a pale blue, his hair medium brown. Unlike Wolf's Blood, Jeremy was afraid of weapons and had only learned to ride in order to please his father. He was learning to use a rifle now, but was sure he would never get used to its loud noise. And also unlike Wolf's Blood, Jeremy liked books and reading.

Abbie had taught all her children to read and write when they were old enough to learn, for there was no school in the untamed land where they lived. Wolf's Blood had quickly grown restless and had lost his interest, preferring to be out riding free, feeling the wind in his face, to sitting with the rest of the children for the daily two-hour lessons. Abbie had finally given up, for the boy's brooding spirit and sulking attitude had only distracted the other children.

There had been some tense words between Abbie and Zeke over the eldest son, but Zeke understood his first-born's spirit, which was kin to his own. He remembered the days back in Tennessee when he'd suffered the torture of hard school benches, forcing himself to sit still for fear the teacher would whip him. But his Indian soul had overpowered him many times, and little Zeke Monroe had suffered many whippings before the teacher finally told his white father that the boy's presence in the classroom would no longer be tolerated. His father and stepmother had been very upset with him, and his father had given him a good thrashing. But Zeke had enjoyed it, for being free of school was worth the price he'd paid. He'd been cast off as an "ignorant savage" who had no respect for "proper whiteman's ways" and whose heathen soul would surely burn forever in hell. But for Zeke, hell had been the classroom and the stiff white man's clothing. Heaven was freedom, the feel of the wind on his face, the smell of the earth and the sharing of spirit with the animals. He well understood how Wolf's Blood was feeling, and he had convinced Abbie to understand and let the boy go.

But Jeremy was a complete opposite, and his quick learning was almost more than Abbie could keep up with, his appetite for reading was voracious. He was a good boy, but he did not have an Indian's spirit; and although Abbie knew Zeke loved each of his children with great passion, she knew there might one day be fierce friction between Zeke and his second son.

Child number five followed Jeremy, a third daughter named Ellen, six years old. Her Indian name was Ishiomiists (Rising Sun), and she was a grand mixture, with skin that soaked up the sun easily, eyes as blue as the sky, and dark hair but not truly black like her sister Margaret's. Ellen's nature was quiet and friendly, a calm, dependable child who seemed to accept both her Indian and white blood with equal pride.

Ellen was the last in the long line of Monroe children, with numbers six and seven riding in front with their mother. Her horse disappeared through the gate, and then the fort came alive. There was suddenly movement everywhere, with officers trying to keep order while men began eagerly betting on the next day's knife duel, as well as getting bets organized for the horse races, which would take place on the second day. In one corner of the fort a side of beef was being roasted over an open pit, being prepared for that evening's celebrating. Each Indian tribe there would give a demonstration of one of their dances of celebration to the soldiers, and campfires would burn well into the night. The next day would bring the contests—wrestling, running and shooting, and then, of course, the duel between the one called Blade and the half-breed called Cheyenne Zeke.

Abbie watched the broad shoulders of her husband's back, her heart tightening at the thought of the challenge. She had not expected the fight to take place the Indian way, with the left hand tied behind the back and each man taking the end of a leather strap in his teeth, forcing their bodies to stay close together.

"Zeke?" she spoke up, moving her horse up beside his but staring out ahead rather than looking at him. "You're wounded, you know. You'll have to use that right arm."

He caught the fear in her voice. "I'm aware of that. If I thought I couldn't handle it I wouldn't have made the challenge, Abbie-girl."

She turned to meet his eyes, and he saw the misty tears in her own. "I need you," she said quietly.

They rode for a few feet saying nothing. "We're setting up two *tipis* while we're here," he finally spoke up. "One for this brood of ours—and one for you and me. Wolf's Blood can watch over the others. I want you to myself, Mrs. Monroe. We haven't had any privacy since we left the ranch to come down here."

She smiled a little then and actually blushed. "How

34

can you speak of such things when tomorrow you'll be risking your life?'' she chided.

His eyes moved over her curved body, longing to strip off the white tunic she wore and feel her bare skin close to his own, hear her whisper his name in the ecstasy they both shared when they were one. ''Woman, when you look like you do right now, I can always speak of such things.'' He gave her a wink and kicked at his horse, riding out in a circle to signal the rest of the Cheyenne to come in and bring the Appaloosas.

The one called Cole stood at the gate of the fort, watching the white woman ride toward the Navaho village with her children in tow. He scratched at the pink scar again and felt an urgency in his groin. Somehow he had to get her alone. Surely she would rather be with a white man. Surely she was a captive at one time who had been beaten and humiliated into staying with the Indians. Surely she would never tell her husband if a white man invaded her. Her husband was a savage. The man would beat her and cast her out, and Cole would be ready to make her his own woman.

Three

Danny Monroe stepped up onto the familiar wooden porch and stomped mud from his feet. Thunder boomed around the old farmhouse, and he noticed when lightning brightened night into day that the house seemed more dilapidated than ever. The porch boards creaked under his weight as he walked to the door and pounded on it. He waited a moment, sure he detected slow footsteps inside and wishing his father would hurry and open the door, for the autumn rain chilled his bones with a cool dampness that came down off the Tennessee mountains.

The door finally opened, and his heart ached at the look in his father's mournful eyes.

"I'm here, Pa."

The old man nodded, blinking back tears. Danny quickly stepped inside and closed the door. He embraced his father, noticing how some of the meat on the tall, once-powerful man had seemed to melt away. Hugh Monroe was still tall and broad, but somehow more frail, and he had developed a slight stoop.

"Thanks for coming, Danny-boy," the elder Monroe said brokenly. "I'm so lonely."

"Soon as I got your letter about Lenny being killed

at Wilson's Creek, I quit the Union, Pa." He pulled away and blinked back his own tears. "I've left Fort Laramie. I'm joining up with the Confederates."

Their eyes held, and Hugh Monroe's saddened more. He patted Danny's arm. "It's good your Tennessee blood hasn't left you, son. But you had a good career out there with the Indians. You've been out there a long time, Danny, a long time. That's your life. And you've got Emily, and my little grandaughter—"

"Emily and Jennifer are safe in St. Louis. They're living in Emily's father's house. It's a grand house. She's sharing it with other women whose husbands have gone off to war. They'll be all right." He pulled out a wooden chair from the kitchen table and motioned for his father to sit down. "You look tired, Pa."

The old man sighed. "I am tired. With Lenny gone, there's nobody to help with the farm anymore. We were a partnership, you know." He shook his head and rubbed at his eyes, sinking wearily into the chair. "With his wife and my two little grandchildren gone to live with her mother, and with your brother Lance off to war himself, God knows where, there's nobody but me to run the place."

Danny sat down across the table from the man. He reached out and took his father's hand. "I'm sorry, Pa," he replied sincerely, frowning with sympathy.

Hugh Monroe met his handsome son's intense blue eyes. Danny's face was deeply tanned from years of duty in Indian territory, his blond hair bleached even whiter from the Western sun. Dan Monroe looked much younger than his thirty-five years for he was a big, strapping, healthy man, with a quick, bright smile. "You sure Emily and my little Jennifer are safe in St. Louis?" the older man asked. "You should have brought them, son. I haven't seen them in two years."

"Things are too dangerous in Tennessee, and you

know it, Pa. And here in the country is where a lot of the fighting will take place; out here there's no help for them if Union soldiers should come. There's a lot of unrest in Missouri, that's sure, what with the Jayhawkers and Border Ruffians going at it all the time. That state's really torn, but they haven't officially picked a side, and St. Louis is a big city, not remote and dangerous like the countryside. The house Emily's father left to her when he died is a fine house, and she has lots of company. She'll be OK.''

The old man nodded. He squeezed Danny's hand and then let go of it, reaching across the table to a half-empty bottle of whiskey. ''So you've quit after all them years with the army to come over to the graycoats, have you?''

''Yes, sir. I guess my Tennessee-born pride just kind of boiled over when I got your letter about Lenny. I figured if my brother could die for Tennessee, I guess I ought to be here, too.''

Hugh Monroe took a swallow of whiskey. Danny noticed how much whiter his hair had become. He was a lonely man. Danny's mother had died years before, and Danny had served duty in the West for many years. The youngest son, Lance, had been somewhat of a drifter himself, and now had also joined the Confederates. Lenny had been the only son to stay close to his father and help with the farm. Now Lenny was dead. The ugly war between North and South had killed him. Danny took no particular issue on slavery, but did take issue with the fact that the Federal government wanted to tell Tennessee citizens and other citizens of the South what they could and could not do. Southerners didn't like taking orders from outsiders. Molehills had grown into mountains, and now the country was exploding. Hugh Monroe turned dark eyes to his son and studied him for a long, silent moment.

"Every time I look at that blond hair and those blue eyes, I think of your ma," he told Danny. "She sure was pretty."

Danny smiled softly. "I remember."

The old man smiled and blinked back more tears. "You look so much like her, except for being so big."

Danny laughed lightly. "I got that from you. I guess out of all four sons, Zeke and I were the two biggest. I remember—" He stopped short, seeing the terrible pain in his father's eyes and wondering what had possessed him to mention the oldest son, the half-breed brother who was seldom discussed: the meanest, the most rebellious, the one who had left home over twenty years ago, never to return. Hugh Monroe shifted in his chair and frowned, slowly twisting the whiskey bottle in his gnarled hands.

"Have you seen him since the last time you was home?" he asked quietly.

"I haven't seen him for about four years, Pa. Fact is, he and his wife have never even met Emily, or seen Jennifer. With my duties at Fort Laramie and always running Emily back and forth to St. Louis for one thing and another, there just never seemed to be a good time to travel all that way down to the Arkansas River to Zeke's ranch. But as far as I know he's still doing right well. He's got seven kids, Pa. You have seven more grandchildren by Zeke."

The man grunted a sarcastic laugh. "A lot of good it does me. I'll never see them."

Danny sighed and ran a hand through his hair. "Pa, you can't blame him—"

"Damn him!" the old man blurted out, slamming a fist against the table. "Why doesn't he come back, at least for a visit! He's been cleared of all those murder charges! He's a free man now in Tennessee, and still he stays out there with the damned Indians!"

"Pa, you don't understand him. Zeke *needs* to be out there. He's so much more Indian than white, Pa. If he came back here, he'd suffocate on civilization. And it isn't the murder charges that keep him away. It's the *memories*, Pa! All the bad memories of finding Ellen raped and murdered and their little son killed by those men. *White* men, Pa! Friends of Ellen's who turned on her and tortured her just because she went to bed with a half-breed. A man doesn't forget those things, Pa. They burn in his gut for all his life! Even though he's married again and has all those kids, he still remembers. He hates Tennessee!"

The old man waved him off. "You always did stick up for him. Even after he murdered all those men so ruthlessly and showed his savage Indian blood."

"Pa, he can't be blamed for that! I might have done the same thing if someone did that to my wife and son! Now at last he's been cleared from the Wanted posters. Be glad for that much. It was a long time ago and it's over. He's happy now. He's got a good woman, a damned good woman. She's even from Tennessee herself."

The man turned hopeful eyes to Danny. "What about her? She's Tennessee born and bred. Surely she'd like to come back for a while."

Danny shook his head sadly. "Not if Zeke doesn't want to come. Abbie wants only what her husband wants. She knows how painful it would be for him to come back here. If he needs to be with his people, then she'll put up with the hardships of that life. That's the kind of woman Abbie is. There aren't many like her." He took his father's hand again. "But she has told Zeke a time or two that he should come and see his blood father, Pa. She's a good woman. She knows a man ought to have things right with his father. Zeke's never coming back has nothing to do with Abbie."

40

Hugh Monroe nodded and rose, walking to a window and watching raindrops glisten against the glass, lit up by the lantern light. "It's me, Danny. It isn't the bad memories that keep him away. It's me, and that's the hell of it. He'll never forgive me for dragging him away from his Cheyenne ma all them years back. He's hated me since he was four years old. That's a lot of years of hating."

Danny studied the once-powerful man from whom he and Zeke got their commanding physique. "Why'd you do it, Pa?"

The old man kept watching the raindrops, studying them silently for several quiet seconds. "I missed home," he replied. "I missed Tennessee. Gentle Woman could never have survived here among white people. It was common, Danny-boy, for a trapper to take a squaw. Not many men like me had feelings for their Indian wives. They were more of a necessity than anything else. When I got hungry for Tennessee, I knew I had to leave her behind. But—" he shook his head and swallowed—"I couldn't leave my boy behind. I couldn't leave my *son*, Danny! I loved him. I wanted him with me. But he never understood that. He thought I just brought him back out of meanness, to prove I'd had a squaw. I don't know how many times I tried to explain to him that wasn't so. But he'd look at me with them . . . dark, accusing eyes, and I knew he never believed me. I . . . never meant for him to suffer like he did. I never thought . . . people could be so mean. And I guess I never took notice how bad he was really being treated. Your own ma never loved him, I admit that. He knew it." The man sighed deeply and sniffed. "When I think on it now, I realize how lonely he must have been." He wiped at his eyes. "You're right. I can't blame him. I can't blame him for going back there soon as he could handle himself and looking

41

up his ma. He was always mixed up about whether he was white or Indian. I reckon now he's found his place. I should be glad of that. But I did love him, Danny. Still do and always will. I just . . ." He sighed again. "I'm not getting any younger, Danny-boy. I'd like to see Zeke once more before I go to my grave."

Danny picked up the whiskey bottle and took a swallow himself. "Well, I hope you get your wish, Pa. But I wouldn't count too much on it, even though his Indian mother is dead now. His stepfather, Deer Slayer, he died, too, just last year. His oldest half-brother, Swift Arrow, rides in the north with the Sioux. I have contact with him at times, or at least I did before I defected. I may never see the West again." He rose himself from his chair and came over to stand beside his father. "His other half-brother, Black Elk, lives among the Southern Cheyenne not far from Zeke's ranch. The third brother, Red Eagle, is dead—shot himself after selling his wife for whiskey money. Red Eagle was the black sheep of the family, I guess you'd say. Swift Arrow and Black Elk are fine, proud men, good warriors. They stay away from the firewater."

Hugh turned to face his son again, his eyes shocking Danny with their sorrow. "And Zeke? Is he a fine warrior?"

Danny grinned and nodded. "One of the best. He's highly respected among the Cheyenne and other tribes, even though he's a half-blood. Half-bloods aren't always accepted readily into the tribe, but Zeke proved his courage in the Sun Dance, and he's been proving it one way or another ever since."

Hugh Monroe nodded sadly. "Well then, I sure had a flock of fine sons, didn't I?" He patted Danny's arm. "Life is strange. I had me four sons, yet as soon as you march off to war, I'll have none. Who knows if you and Lance will ever come back. And God knows Zeke won't." He shook his head. "I'm a tired old man, Danny-boy. A tired old man full of regrets. But then I reckon there's few men who live to my age who don't have a lot of regrets." He walked back to the table and sat down again. "So . . . where will you go, Danny?"

The younger man walked back to the table into the brighter light of the lantern, and Hugh Monroe was impressed and proud by his son's handsomeness. He wondered how handsome Zeke was. He'd been a fine-looking lad, and that was the only way Hugh Monroe could picture his eldest son, for he'd been a very young man when he left Tennessee for good.

"I'm headed for Nashville. I'm told that's where all the Tennessee Volunteers are headed, to meet up with General Sidney Johnston. The plan is to hold Tennessee, especially Bowling Green and Nashville, where all the industry and supplies are. And we have to keep the supply routes open—the Green River, the Tennessee and Cumberland Rivers. That's why I think this whole state will be a powder keg, Pa. The North will try to take Tennessee as fast as they can, cut off our supplies. I've got years of experience behind me. I want to volunteer my services to General Johnston as an officer."

Hugh Monroe felt his heart tighten at the thought of anything happening to Danny. "There will be no comforts in this war, son. I have a feeling it will be worse than any duty you served out West. I'm told the volunteers out here get the short end of the supplies. President Davis keeps all the good stuff farther east and lets those in the border states make do with what's left, which sometimes is nothing at all. This war won't be a short one, son, and it will be damned bloody. I've heard some pretty sad stories from stragglers who've already been involved in the fighting. Your brother was lucky to die at Wilson's Creek, the way I hear it. He was bad wounded in the leg and they'd . . . they'd had

43

to . . . cut it off." The old man's voice trailed off and he bent his head and covered his eyes. "Lenny . . . could never have been happy that way . . . if he'd lived."

Danny frowned and put a reassuring hand on his father's shoulder as the rain pattered gently against the window pane. It seemed incredible to him that the roar of cannons could come to the peaceful hills that he'd known in his boyhood. Perhaps his father was wrong. Perhaps this war would end quickly. He hoped so. He missed Emily already. For some strange reason he suddenly thought of another woman, a lovely young Sioux girl he had loved once. But Small Cloud was dead now, a casualty from a different kind of war. It still pained his heart to think of it. So many Indians were dead or dying. It suddenly struck him how ironic it was that the Federal government was participating in a war to free the slaves, while at the same time it seemed everything was pointing to putting Indians on reservations as just one of many ways to rid the western lands of the "bothersome" Indians.

But none of that really mattered. He was a Tennessee man at heart, and Lenny had died for a cause. The cause was Tennessee's right to make its own laws and decisions. Right now he would simply fight for Tennessee and the South. What happened to the slaves once they were freed would be another matter. And what happened to the Indians was out of his hands now, at least for the time being.

"At last we are alone!" Zeke said with a sigh. He added more wood to the small fire inside their *tipi* to ward off the chill the autumn night would bring. "We always seem to be surrounded by children."

Abbie smiled and sat down on a bed of robes. "You don't really mind all those children, now, do you?"

He glanced over at her, at first saying nothing, only thinking how much he loved this woman who had come into his lonely life so many years ago and had brought him so much love and joy. He smiled softly. "You know I don't. They're my pride and joy, every one of them special in his own way."

She began brushing her thick, dark hair. "Are you sure they'll be all right, Zeke?" she commented, her strong motherly instinct making her want to gather her children at her feet where she could watch over them herself.

"Of course they are. Wolf's Blood and that wild animal of his are better protection than six men. You know that. Smoke wouldn't let anyone with evil intentions get within a hundred yards of those kids," he added, referring to his son's pet wolf.

"I guess," she answered, putting down the brush. Their eyes held. At their cabin on the Arkansas River in Colorado Territory, they had the privacy of their own bedroom. But on this journey they had either camped under the stars or erected only one *tipi;* either way, seven small Monroes had slept beside them.

"One Indian custom you've never learned is to quietly make love under the blankets even when your children are sleeping nearby," Zeke teased. "Most all Cheyenne children have heard or even seen their father and mother mating at one time or another. It's as natural as the animals."

Abbie reddened deeply. "Those children's parents grew up the same way," she answered. "I did not. There are some things about me that will always be white, my husband, and one of them is making love in private."

He grinned and moved over to kneel in front of her, unlacing the shoulders of her tunic. "Well, you have privacy now, Mrs. Monroe." Her heart quickened as

45

he let the tunic drop to her waist and he lightly kissed the fruits of her breasts.

"Zeke," she said softly, touching his hair. He moved his lips to her neck and gently layed her back, caressing her cheek then with his lips.

"What's bothering you?" he asked quietly. "You're as tense as a frightened deer."

"I am frightened," she answered. "Are you sure you can handle that man tomorrow? I mean, you're wounded, and—"

His mouth covered hers tenderly, cutting off her words. The kiss lingered hungrily until he felt her relax and she breathed a soft whimper. This big, fierce man who was her husband and the only man who had ever done these things to her never failed to bring forth great passion from her soul, never failed to be gentle, conscious of her woman's needs, never failed to bring excitement and satisfaction to their lovemaking. The coming together of their bodies held the special beauty and total pleasure that comes only to those who have shared lives for many years, those who have suffered and wept together, struggled and worked together, played and laughed together, those who know one another's thoughts, fears, haunting memories and needs.

"Don't worry about tomorrow when we have tonight," he whispered passionately. He moved back down over her breasts to kiss her flat belly and pulled the tunic down farther. His lips moving down over secret places known only to Zeke Monroe and over slim thighs, he removed the tunic completely.

He sat up on his knees and just looked at her a moment, drinking in her beauty. Here lay the woman he had invaded when she was hardly more than a little girl, the woman who had turned to him for love and protection so many years ago when she had lost all her family on her journey west, the woman who had sacrificed everything, even most of her white identity, to be the wife of a half-breed and live among his people.

"I don't think you'll ever age, Abbie-girl," he told her with a teasing smile, as she curled up slightly when his eyes lingered on her nakedness.

"That is only because you see me every day," she told him. "I've changed since I was fifteen years old, and I certainly wasn't getting younger in the process."

He shook his head. "If you've changed at all, it was only to become more beautiful and to fill out in all the right places," he told her, removing his clothing. She felt the same old tingle at the sight of his broad, dark shoulders that glowed bronze in the firelight. The many scars did nothing to detract from the virile handsomeness of this rock-hard man who would soon fill her with his life again.

Again he saw the traces of worry in her eyes. "Zeke, I—"

He stilled her worry with a kiss, his strength and power and manly needs, combined with the gentle touch of his big, familiar hands on her bare skin, making her submit as she had always submitted to this man. She whimpered as his fiery kiss drew forth her own desires, and his gentle hands moved over her body, taking in the texture of her silky breasts, the soft skin of her belly and bottom, the welcoming moistness in sweet, warm places reserved only for Zeke Monroe.

Her breathing was deep, her eyes closed as her man took liberties with her body. In spite of the years, the children and the terrible struggles they had suffered together in this harsh land, they still had this. Their powerful love had kept them together and had kept this expression of their love always sweet and beautiful.

"My little virgin child," he whispered as his lips brushed teasingly against her ear and his hand explored and caressed, bringing forth wonderful passions. *"Ne-*

mehotatse," he moaned, voicing "I love you" in Cheyenne. Always he had ways to taking her back over the years . . . back to that first time he had claimed her in the foothills of the Rockies before she was even truly his wife . . . back to the frightened, lonely woman-child she was that fateful night when she gave herself to the half-breed scout.

That one act had sealed the destiny of Abigail Trent forever. At times it seemed a savage destiny, with all of its hardships and cruelties, and because of the savageness of the very man she had married and of his people. But when they were together this way, there was nothing savage about him, except perhaps his dark skin and fiery eyes and the wanton savageness he drew from her own soul, forcing her to give and give, to arch up to him and cry out for him and grasp his arms tightly, sometimes almost bruising them with her grip when his manliness surged inside of her, filling her almost painfully, claiming again that which belonged only to Zeke Monroe.

He sat up slightly as he took her, running his hands over her breasts and ribs and belly. "You are still so beautiful," he told her softly, his excitement enhanced by the way she still blushed when he looked upon her nakedness. He came closer again, and she ran her hands over the broad, dark shoulders, touching the gauze still wrapped around his arm. How thin was the line between life and death! He saw the renewed fear in her eyes, and he pushed deeper, telling her with his own eyes and with his body that she must not worry or be afraid, that she should enjoy the glorious, private moment at hand.

Her eyes became glazed with passion and her breathing quickened, and a moment later she cried out with the wonderful explosion his lovemaking brought to her insides. He came close then, enveloping her in his

48

arms, holding her tightly until their passion was finally spent and their bodies close but limp. It had been a long, tiring day, the strain of the buffalo hunters' attack quickly taking its toll. Zeke was soon asleep, but Abbie slept fitfully, worried about the knife fight that was to take place the next day, and on which some soldiers were still placing bets.

Four

Winston Garvey traced a fat finger along the map that hung on his wall, following the North Platte, then south through Denver and down to the Arkansas River, east into Kansas Territory and back up to the Platte.

"That used to be Indian treaty land," he explained to his son. "But thanks to the Treaty of Fort Wise, it's all been cut down to just a little chunk—here, right here." He pointed to a tiny square of land in the southeast portion of Colorado Territory, bordered on the south by the Arkansas River. "That's all that's left to the bastards. Most of the Cheyenne don't agree to the new treaty and refuse to abide by it, but it's been made law, nonetheless, and all that land is open to settlers now. I'm buying up all I can, son. I want you to know all about my affairs. I'm getting on in years, and my empire will one day be yours."

Charles Garvey's eyes lit up hungrily. He wanted to know everything there was to know. He wanted to be the richest and most powerful man in Colorado Territory one day, and he wanted a hand in Indian affairs; namely, he wanted a hand in eliminating the Indians completely from Colorado.

"I want to understand, Father," the gangly and rather homely teen-ager told Garvey. "I want you to be proud of me."

"I'm already proud of you, son. Soon you'll graduate high school and go east to college. But I don't want you getting mixed up in that damned Civil War. If you're ever going to go to war, it will be against the Indians, not your own kind. Our interest lies out here, son. You remember that. I'll help you make it to the top some day, Charles. I have the money and influence to do it. Don't forget I used to be a senator, and some people still call me that. I have a lot of connections in Washington, and some day you'll be up there helping make the laws—laws that can be designed to rid this territory of every last redskin that stands in the way of settlement and mining!"

Charles grinned. He hated all Indians. They had killed his mother when he was a small boy, and his father had taken advantage of the boy's memory by instilling in him an ever-growing hatred for every red man of the West. Winston Garvey's reason was not a desire for vengeance for the death of a young and spoiled wife he had never loved; his reason was purely a desire to possess as much land and power in the West as he could obtain. He had used his son's fear and hatred of the Indian to further his own plans of conquest. He wanted to be certain that once he was dead, the Garvey empire would live on through his son. It was best to nurture the boy's hatred of the Indians. No matter that Charles thought it was Cheyenne who had killed his mother, even though his father knew it had been Comanches. It was Cheyennes who were the most numerous in Colorado, so let his son hate them. It would only aid to ensure Charles Garvey would one day design laws to eliminate the bothersome natives of Colorado from their homeland.

"I don't understand why we can't just set a bounty on the Indians," the boy complained, studying the map again. "They are no different from wolves or coyotes or skunks. One is the same as the other."

"You're young and eager, son," Winston answered, patting the boy's shoulder. "One thing you have to remember if you're going to be a congressman some day is to always appear to be a great humanitarian. There are ways of fooling the public, Charles, and I will teach you how it's done. But never voice such emotions in public. Always wait until the *public* voices such feelings to *you*. If the general outcry is to kill the Indians, then you can be safe in declaring open season on them. But it must never be your own idea. Otherwise you'll get branded as too radical. Do you understand what I'm saying?"

The boy nodded. "I understand, but I wish it wasn't that way. It would be more fun to ride through their camps and rape the women and run a sword through all their damned maggot kids and shoot the men on sight."

Winston chuckled. "Patience, my boy! It isn't that easy."

The boy shrugged. "It would be if I were in control." His eyes gleamed, and his cold smile gave even his father a chill. Winston walked around behind his desk.

"You been making any headway with Jim Danhart's girl?" he asked, suddenly feeling he'd better change the subject.

Charles made a face. "She's too stuck up."

"Her father is a big rancher. Owns a lot of land."

The boy walked to look out a window. "So what? I don't need her kind. Besides, her kind gets serious, and I'm too young to get serious. I have an education and a career to think about first." He knew in the back of his mind the real reason Susan Danhart wouldn't look twice at him, yet he could not bring himself to admit it, for he was Charles Garvey, rich and able to have whatever he wanted. So what if he was homely? Girls should want to be with him just because of who he was. "I prefer the whores at Anna's place," he added.

Winston chuckled. "Can't blame you there, son. Those ladies can show a young boy a real good time."

The boy turned. "All except Anna. She's the one I want, but she won't sleep with me. I don't think she likes me."

Winston lost his smile. "I'll talk to her. She shouldn't shun you that way. Who does that bitch think she is?"

Charles grinned. "That's the way I look at it. I want her more than the rest of them. She's the prettiest. But just because she's the boss of the place, she says she doesn't have to sleep with me if she doesn't want to."

Winston frowned. There had been a time when he all but owned Anna Gale. He had brought her west years ago, all the way from Washington, D.C. He had set her up first in Santa Fe, then moved her to Denver when gold was discovered there and the men flocked to the Rockies. Anna Gale was rich now because of him. But she knew the secret—the terrible secret that had released his power over her. His son must never know what Anna knew: Winston Garvey had a half-breed son. Garvey had tried to find out who the child was and who the mother was, for unknown to his son or second wife, the man had slept with several different Indian women over the years, most of them by force. But Anna swore she knew nothing more but that the child existed. Whoever had told her about the child had given her no details, and she would not tell Garvey where she had received her information. Garvey did not doubt that the child existed, and if Charles found out his father had layed with a squaw and had produced

53

a half-brother that was part Indian, the already slightly demented boy would go crazy with the horror of it.

"Damned bitch!" Garvey muttered to himself over Anna Gale. If he ever found out who and where the boy was, he'd have him murdered. He looked up at Charles, his hope for the future. "I'll talk to her," he told the boy. "Anna and I go back a long way." He rose. "I hope you understand why I visit that place, son. You'll do the same even after you're married. Your stepmother isn't very—well, some women don't understand a man's needs, Charles. So I go to Anna's place on the side. Lots of men do that. Most times their wives know about it, and they don't care because it keeps their husbands out of their own beds, where they aren't wanted. That's what prostitutes are for—to show a man the good time he can't get at home."

Charles grinned. "I understand better than you think, Father. A wife for appearances, and a whore for sex."

Winston guffawed, his huge stomach shaking and his fat face reddening. "Son, you're a gem! A chip off the old block! You'll do fine, my boy—just fine." He returned to his desk chair, still chuckling. "Sit down, son. We have some studying to do about Indian legislation."

"Can I have some whiskey first?"

Winston shrugged. "Why not? If you're man enough to go to Anna's place, you're man enough to drink."

Charles hurried over to the buffet where drinks were always kept on hand. Winston watched him pour a shot for himself. He was pleased with his son, and he had a feeling Charles Garvey would be more ruthless in obtaining what he wanted than even Winston himself had been. Watching Charles Garvey grow in power was going to be a very interesting pastime. He lit a fat cigar, then offered one to Charles.

"Light up, my boy. Today you've talked and acted like a man. I'm proud of you."

Charles grinned and took the cigar, thinking about Anna Gale. He was accustomed to his father getting him anything he wanted. Perhaps now that he had complained about Anna, his father would make sure she was made available to him. No one refused Charles Garvey and got away with it!

Indian and soldier alike circled around Blade and Cheyenne Zeke, emotions high, as were the bets. Many of the Indians, especially the Cheyenne, had bet everything they owned on Zeke, for they knew well the stories about the great knife warrior. But Blade had earned his own reputation, and he would soon learn whether he had met his match.

The tension mounted as a soldier walked up and handed the leather strap to the two fighters. Indians let out war whoops and shrill cries of excitement as Zeke grabbed the strap and put one end in his teeth, his dark eyes on fire with the excitement of the challenge, his huge frame now a hard, powerful fighting machine. He had prayed all morning, drawing strength and courage from the depths of the spirit world with which he was close, from *Maheo,* who had saved him many times before. He looked as fierce as any warrior could look, with streaks of yellow paint across his forehead, one red streak down his nose and three black streaks on his chin. He was painted for war, even though this battle would be against only one man. His hair hung long and loose, parts of it twisted around eagle feathers, which were believed to bring courage and power to their owner. He wore only a loincloth, with two Crow scalps hanging at his waist, along with the big, menacing blade that had earned him a reputation throughout the West.

55

Wolf's Blood watched with a pounding heart as Blade put the other end of the strap into his own teeth, while two soldiers strapped each man's left hand behind his back and the two opponents glared at each other eagerly. Blade was nearly as big as Zeke, but his belly was paunchy, not hard and flat like Zeke's. Yet Zeke had told his son many times never to judge a man by his appearance. Blade looked soft, but Wolf's Blood knew Zeke would not take it for granted that the man was not as fast or as strong. The reputation he bore should not be taken lightly. But Wolf's Blood knew that if Blade should prove to be as skilled as his father, Zeke Monroe had one advantage. The man called Blade had attacked the Cheyenne and Zeke's family for no reason. Zeke Monroe's wife or one of his children could have been killed. That was all the provocation Zeke needed to give him an edge over his opponent, for vengeance was as important to Zeke as breathing.

The lieutenant gave a signal to start, and the circle of onlookers widened but grew noisier as the two opponents pulled on the strap in their teeth and circled, both simply eyeing one another the first few seconds. Wolf's Blood wondered what was going through his mother's mind as she waited back at camp with the rest of the children. Surely she could hear the crowd. Surely she was terrified. Yet she had said nothing to Zeke. She had not argued against the fight, even though to a white woman it must seem barbaric, as some whites described the Indian ways.

But those people simply did not understand the Indian code of ethics, the Indian man's need to prove his strength and skill, or the Indian's compelling need for revenge. Somehow his mother understood all of that and accepted it. She understood that what Cheyenne Zeke was doing at this moment was only one part of the man, an extension of his Indian religion and his Indian instincts. And Abigail Monroe had seen her husband use his knife before.

"Rip him open!" a soldier shouted to Blade as the man took the first swipe. Zeke sucked in his belly and arched backward, barely escaping the tip of Blade's knife. The strap they held in their mouths was about three feet in length, giving both men enough room to dart back, yet close enough that the heat of the challenge was intense. Both men knew the rule. If he let loose of the strap he would automatically lose, and the opponent had the right to end his life. The left arm could not be used in defense.

Zeke bent forward slightly then, his dark eyes boring into Blade and planting a cold fear in Blade's soul. As the two men again circled, Zeke's long hair and its eagle feathers danced with the movement of his lean, supple body, his broad, dark shoulders tensed into balls of muscle. Everything about him was savage then. There was no Tennessee man there, no gentleness there, no part of the man Abbie knew in private, no sign of the lonely, abused little boy that still lurked deep in his soul.

He took three quick slashes, and Blade could not keep away from the third one, which drew a red line across his chest that quickly grew darker as blood met sunlight. The crowd grew wild at the sight of it, and beads of sweat broke out on Blade's forehead. Blade came back quickly with a kick to Zeke's ribs. Zeke grunted, and Blade came at him again, slashing wildly.

"Keep back, Father!" Wolf's Blood yelled amid the roar of the onlookers, his fists clenching as his own tension became almost unbearable. Zeke avoided the blade after the first swipe, which slashed across his lower abdomen. Wolf's Blood's eyes widened in horror at first, but it looked as though the cut was not deep. Still, opening Zeke's skin had given Blade more faith.

He came at Zeke again. Zeke pulled back while he slashed at Blade's arm, putting a deep cut into the muscle of the man's upper arm and ending Blade's momentary flurry of swipes.

The crowd was delirious with the excitement of the fight, the Indians screaming out war cries and jumping up and down, slapping one another on the back and laughing, the soldiers yelling at the top of their lungs for Blade to "Kill the damned breed," their fists shaking in the air. Zeke and Blade circled again, both regaining their breath and planning their strategy. Wolf's Blood was glad Abbie was not there to see Zeke bleeding. She would want to stop the fight and fix his wound, but this fight could not be stopped. Only the death of one of the combatants would end it.

Blade kicked at Zeke's stomach where it had been cut, then grinned wickedly at the look of pain on Zeke's face. But Zeke instantly and surprisingly kicked back, several well-aimed, acrobatic movements from a man who was born loving to wrestle and fight. Wolf's Blood found himself screaming at the top of his lungs along with the others as both men darted in and out, waving knives, gauging one another more than actually trying to do physical harm. The secret was to wear down the opponent, cut him enough to cause the loss of blood, work him enough and bruise him enough to make him weak, then take advantage.

Back at her *tipi* Abbie occupied herself by sponging down little Jason. The naked baby boy stood in a little tub of water, giggling as water trickled down over his ribs. Little Lillian sat to the side practicing beadwork. She was afraid of all the shouting in the distance, and she preferred to be near her mother. The other four children played in the village, obediently following orders that they were not to go near the fort or the place where their father was challenging the man called

Blade. The children were somber but joined in the games with their Indian friends, somehow sure that their big, fearless father would escape unharmed from the fight he was in. After all, it was just one of the games. At least that was how Abbie had described it to them.

"Your father will be fine," she told them. "It's just like wrestling and the shooting of arrows. But there are nothing but loud, excited men over there, so only Wolf's Blood is allowed to go and watch."

The children had accepted the explanation. Now Abbie's heart raced and her throat hurt from choking back tears as the yells and war whoops rang in her ears. Her mind screamed a silent demand to know if Zeke was all right. Half the village was empty; even some of the Indian women had gone to see if they could get a peek. Tall Grass Woman, Abbie's close Cheyenne friend, watched the children guardedly in a nearby grassy meadow where she kept them occupied with games.

Abbie trickled water over Jason again, needing to hear his laughter, wishing it would drown out the men in the distance. She smiled, pretending to be casual for her son's sake. But her smile vanished when a large, dark figure loomed at the entranceway to the *tipi* and quickly darted inside. She sat staring dumbfounded at first at a burly, bearded soldier with a hideous scar on the side of his face. In the middle of a Cheyenne camp in broad daylight, with all the men supposedly involved in the fight and the betting, Abbie had not thought about having to protect herself.

She rose, wrapping a towel around little Jason and lifting him from the tub. "Who are you and what do you think you're doing!" she demanded. Lillian stopped her beadwork and stared at the soldier with wide, frightened eyes as the man removed his hat, grinning hungrily and looking Abbie over as though she

59

were standing there naked.

"Name's Cole, ma'am," he answered. "Randolph Cole. I, uh, I come here to see if you was OK . . . find out if you was maybe a captive or somethin'. That breed steal you from your folks years back, maybe?"

She held Jason closer. "I married Zeke Monroe willingly, Mr. Cole!" she snapped. "We were legally married almost sixteen years ago at Fort Bridger, and I have papers to prove it. Now I will thank you to get out of my dwelling! You have no right to be here, and to enter without announcing youself was crude and callous! You had better leave before that fight is over and my husband comes back and finds you here!"

The man only stepped closer, and she held Jason protectively. "There ain't a man left in this camp," he told her. "And that knife fight has a few minutes to go. They'll feel each other out first." His eyes roved over her again. "And even when it's over, there will be lots of bets to be paid off and some celebratin' to do. Your man won't be back for a bit." He grinned. "Then again, Blade might win, and your man won't be back at all, and you'll be left a widow." He reached out and touched a breast with the back of his hand. "A pretty thing like you shouldn't be wasted like that. You got a lot of good years left in you."

Abbie's eyes blazed and she jerked back from his touch. "You get out of here!" she hissed. "You've no idea what my man is capable of doing to someone who threatens his family!"

The men's shouts grew to a roar again, and Abbie felt crazy with wonder over her husband and fear of this man who stood near her now with rape in his eyes. "You're near a fort, lady," the man reminded her. "Your man attacks me and you'll see a lot of dead Indians layin' around, includin' him. You know what happens to Indians when one of them dares to kill a settler

60

or a soldier. Now why don't you just put that kid down and take off that tunic. We can do this real quick and quiet, and nobody will know the difference. Besides, any white squaw who will spread for a breed will spread for any man. Maybe you, uh, maybe you're curious about what a white man is like, especially one that hasn't had a woman for a while. You ever been with a white man?''

She turned her thoughts from Zeke now. She had to think straight. This man was right in what could happen if she screamed and got the Indians or Zeke involved. She knew the kind of trouble soldiers could make for her people. Things had been bad since the Treaty of Fort Wise and were getting worse. She did not want to cause trouble, yet neither would she allow any man but her own to touch her. She must somehow take care of this situation herself. She feigned desire and gave Cole a faint smile.

''Just don't harm my children,'' she told him.

He nodded, his face reddening with passion. She turned and handed Jason to Lillian, who looked at her mother with tear-filled eyes.

''Don't be afraid,'' she told her daughter. ''Keep Jason with you.'' She turned back to face Cole, allowing him to come closer and unlace her tunic. She remained still as the tunic fell and exposed one breast. Cole jerked her close, grasping at the breast while he kissed her roughly. She felt ill at the taste of tobacco juice and the horror and humiliation of his hand on her breast, but she wanted to lead him on for the moment. She reached up around his neck, and just as as he was lost in the ugly kiss, she quickly dug her nails deeply into his skin, from his forehead, down over his left eye to the upper part of his cheek where no beard grew.

Cole cried out and pulled away, putting a hand over the already bleeding scratches, and Abbie used the moment to bring her foot up hard into his groin. He grunted and bent over, and she used her foot again to push against his shoulder and send him sprawling backward, his rear end landing square into the tub of water.

Jason laughed at what he thought was a funny trick and Lillian began to whimper as Abbie quickly rushed to the side of the *tipi* and grabbed up her Spencer carbine. The rifle was old and had once belonged to her father, but it still worked, and she aimed it now at the groaning Cole, who struggled to get himself out of the tub of water.

"I've killed three Crow bucks with this gun, Mister Cole!" she told the man with cold determination. "I've never used it on a white man, but I'll use it on you if you don't get out of here right now!"

The man pulled himself out of the small tub in which he was close to being stuck. He sat hunched on his knees for a moment, catching his breath and fighting the pain of her kick. Blood ran from the deep scratches on his face as he managed to get to his feet and turn to glare at Abbie, his legs wobbly.

"You white squaw bitch!" he growled. "You'd shoot one of your own kind?"

"I don't call the likes of you my own kind, mister!" she replied, keeping her voice firm to hide her own terror. She held the gun steadily. "Now get out of here!"

"If you shoot me, you'll make big trouble for yourself and the rest of these red buggers you call friend."

"Perhaps I would!" she spat back. "But either way, you'd still be *dead*, wouldn't you, Mr. Cole?"

Their eyes met in challenge, and he decided that if she had truly killed three Crow men she was not a woman to argue with when she had a gun in her hands. He bent down and picked up his hat, pain still ripping through his groin, his breathing labored, his pants dripping wet. He sought her eyes once more.

"You better hope your husband wins that knife fight today, white squaw woman! Because if he don't, you won't have nobody around to protect you!"

"I'll have my son—and the entire Southern Cheyenne nation to protect me, Mr. Cole. Your threats mean nothing to me! Now get out of here!"

The man glared at her another moment, on fire with desire at the sight of her bared breast. He turned and stormed out.

Abbie closed her eyes and breathed deeply for composure, setting the gun aside with shaking hands. She quickly retied her tunic and rushed to Lillian. She grabbed Jason into her arms, meeting Lillian's terror-filled eyes.

"You must not tell your father, Lillian, or your brothers and sisters! Do you understand? It's very important they don't know about that man who was just here. He could cause big trouble for your father! Promise me, Lillian!"

The little girl nodded and sniffled. Abbie hugged Jason close and could not prevent a sob from escaping her own soul. The crowd in the distance had grown louder, but she was more afraid of Zeke finding out about the soldier's visit than of the knife fight, which must now be close to over. The way the men were shouting, perhaps it had already ended.

"Sweet Jesus, bring him back to me!" she whispered. "And don't let him find out about this!" She opened her eyes and looked at Lillian again, giving her a reassuring smile, although tears spilled down her cheeks. "Help Mama clean up, Lillian. That man spilled water everywhere."

Five

At the fort everything was pandemonium. Wolf's Blood fought tears as he watched blood pour from three wounds on his father: the one on his stomach, one on his right forearm and one on his right thigh. But he seemed neither weak nor tired. Blade suffered from four slashes: the ones on his chest and upper right arm, a third across his chest again and one deep gash through his cheek and lips. Both men were panting and sweating and covered with dust, circling, waving their huge blades menacingly. Now was the time. Now was when instinct must dictate the right moment to move in! It was only a matter of which man would be first to grasp the advantage.

"Now, Father, now!" Wolf's Blood quietly hissed through gritted teeth. "Hurry before you weaken!" The roar of the crowd around him was almost deafening, and the onlookers closed in, leaving the opponents less room in which to move.

Zeke suddenly let out a blood-curdling screech through gritted teeth, taking advantage of a misstep by Blade that made the man stumble slightly. A quick thrust ended with Cheyenne Zeke's blade deep in the abdomen of the one called Blade. Blade froze in place, his eyes bulging, while the crowd of onlookers suddenly went almost dead silent. Wolf's Blood grinned through tears as the two opponents stood there for one tense moment, until Zeke, using his own brand of ending a knife fight, jerked upward with his knife, opening Blade's torso before pushing the man off his knife and letting him fall backward, the leather strap ripping from his mouth.

Everyone gawked in astonishment as Blade lay writhing for a moment before his body finally went still in death.

"Damn!" someone muttered.

Zeke spit out his end of the leather strap and walked up to Blade, wiping blood from his own knife onto Blade's pants, then shoving the weapon into its sheath. He turned to face his Cheyenne brother, Black Elk, who grinned; then he faced his son, seeing the relief on Wolf's Blood's face and the love in his eyes. Zeke raised his free arm and let out a Cheyenne yell of victory, and the rest of the Indians suddenly broke into howls and cheers, while Wolf's Blood ran up to hug his father. The boy quickly began untying the strap that held Zeke's left arm, while the Indians began collecting on their bets and making new bets on the horse races that would take place the next day.

"Father, you are hurt!" Wolf's Blood was lamenting.

"The only bad one is my arm," Zeke replied. "Tie that strap around above the cut, Wolf's Blood. Get the circulation stopped until Abbie can pour some whiskey in there and wrap it good and tight. The other two are just surface cuts."

Their eyes held, and the noise of the crowd seemed far away as they looked at each other lovingly. "I am glad you are all right, Father," the boy told Zeke. "I hope one day I will be as great a warrior."

Zeke nodded. "You will, son. You'll be better."

"I will try."

Zeke put an arm around his shoulders. "I need to go back and rest. Tonight I'll collect for the Appaloosas I sold. Tomorrow are the horse races, then we head for Santa Fe before we go home. I want to bring your mother to the Navaho camp tonight to trade for some of those blankets she's been wanting, the ones with all the colors in them."

"She will like that. Right now she will be worried, though. You should hurry and tell her you are all right." He quickly secured the strap around his father's arm to slow the bleeding.

They walked toward the Cheyenne camp, Zeke's wounds stinging and his arm beginning to ache fiercely. But he would hide the pain as much as possible for Abbie's sake. Their progression was slow, as Indians and even some soldiers stopped Zeke to congratulate him and offer him whiskey. Zeke ignored most of them, wanting only to get back to Abbie and assure her he was not badly wounded.

It was several hundred yards to the camp. In the distance Zeke could see children playing, and Abbie's plump and faithful friend, Tall Grass Woman, waved at them, letting out a screech of joy at the sight of Zeke returning. Several Cheyenne men were quickly following them, cheering about the great knife warrior, Black Elk leading them, relieved that his half-brother had not been badly hurt. There would be much dancing and celebrating and feasting that night. The Cheyenne who were present would take advantage of the moment to forget about the illegal Treaty of Fort Wise and the fact that they were now expected to survive within a chokingly small piece of land the Great White Father claimed was all they had left. They would forget the fact that often some of them were shot on sight by settlers

66

for no reason. They would forget that when just one of them disobeyed the Great White Father, all of them were punished. This was not a time for dwelling on deprivation and disease. It was a time for celebration, time for the annual trading and betting and horse races at Fort Lyon a time to enjoy their women and to enjoy the warmth of the autumn sun before it stopped giving off enough heat to keep away the bitter winter snows.

Abbie emerged from her *tipi*. Her eyes locked onto Zeke's, and he instantly sensed something wrong, something more than the fact that he'd been in a fight and wounded. Her eyes dropped quickly, too quickly. He could see her shaking even from the distance. He walked faster, quickly enveloping her in his arms while the rest of the men joked about the victorious warrior enjoying his woman that night as part of his prize. There was something about being victorious in war that made a man desire his woman. Abbie blushed at the other men's gentle teasing but kept her face buried against Zeke's chest, not caring that he was getting blood on her, caring only that he was alive and had walked back to her on his own two feet. Most of all she hoped she could hide the incident with Randolph Cole from him.

They ducked inside the *tipi*, while outside drums began beating and men's hoots and laughter filled the air.

"Get out the whiskey!" Abbie ordered Wolf's Blood. "And the alcohol. Zeke, you drink down some whiskey for the pain. I'll douse the wounds with alcohol. It will burn terribly, you know."

"I know," he answered quietly, watching her closely. He noticed Lillian sitting quietly to the side, her body jerking occasionally as though she had been crying, her eyes wide as she watched him, her mouth sealed tightly. Jason ran around the *tipi* babbling about water but making no sense. Abbie was bringing things

67

over to him to treat his wounds: gauze, scissors, alcohol, a pan of warm water to wash out the wounds. She was nervous, not the kind of nervousness that came from someone she loved being wounded, but more the kind that came from wanting to avoid something. She would not meet his eyes directly, and she moved too quickly, tried too hard to be casual.

"We should sew this arm, you know," she told him as she gently washed the deep cut on his right forearm.

"I want to try just wrapping it tight as hell," he replied.

She sighed. "If you say so. But I think I should sew it." She shook her head. "You won't have any room left for scars pretty soon, Zeke Monroe. The day is coming when you'll have to stop all this, you know."

"I'll never stop. The day I stop defending my honor and my family is the day I stop being a man."

She glanced at him, then quickly looked away, turning and rinsing out the rag. The water turned red. "I suppose Blade is dead."

He snickered. "Would I leave him any other way?"

She gently washed the wound once more. "I suppose not." She reached for the alcohol while Zeke took a bottle of whiskey from Wolf's Blood with his left hand and put it to his lips. He took a long swallow, then set the bottle down and watched Abbie with all-knowing eyes while she doused the wound with the alcohol. He jerked at the pain, but made no sound. For several quiet minutes he let her work, loving her, feeling apologetic, wishing he could have given her a better life, even though she had never asked for more. But strangely, she was not his Abbie now. Something was amiss.

Wolf's Blood watched also, thinking there was something different about his mother. Perhaps she was just upset with Zeke for getting into the fight in the first place. But that would not be like her. Yet she was too

68

quiet.

"I've made you angry," Zeke told her, trying to discern her quiet aloofness.

She shook her head. "No. I've lived with you too many years to be angry over something like this."

He frowned, noticing an odd red puffiness at the corner of her lower lip. His chest tightened with apprehension.

"What's wrong with your lip?" he asked.

She met his eyes too quickly. "My lip?" She put her fingers to the spot, disgusted with herself for being unable to control the blush that rose to her cheeks. She had not realized Cole's brutal kiss had left a mark. "I . . . must be getting some kind of sore," she answered, returning to wrapping his arm. It was then he noticed the shoulder of her tunic was laced crookedly, and a pale bruise, like that of a finger or thumb mark, was appearing on the inner side of her left arm. He reached out and grasped her wrist firmly but gently.

"Suppose you look me in the eye and tell me again about your lip," he told her. "You've never had a blemish or a sore on your face since I've known you, Abigail Monroe!"

She swallowed and met his eyes hesitantly. "I said it was a sore," she told him quietly.

His eyes flashed. "Like hell!"

"Zeke, we are at a fort! A *fort!*" she said in a shaky voice. "We're surrounded by soldiers, and you know what that can mean! Let it go, please!"

He studied her eyes, gentle brown eyes that pleaded with him now. "Let *what* go?" he asked carefully.

She looked at her lap and shook her head. He grasped her chin firmly and forced her to look back up at him. "Answer me, woman! Let what go?"

She squeezed her eyes shut. "Beat me if you want! But I'll not tell you!" she replied, a tear slipping down

69

her cheek.

There was a long moment of silence as she waited for an angry reaction. But he only spoke her name softly.

"Abbie-girl." She opened her eyes to meet his loving ones. "I've never laid a hand on you and you know very well I never would, no matter how angry I might be. You're talking foolish, which only tells me there is something terribly wrong. You've never lied to me and you've never hid anything from me. So don't play games with me now. Trust me, Abbie."

"But . . . the soldiers!" she whimpered.

"You let me worry about that. I brought my woman along on this trip because I thought it would be good for her to get away from everyday hard work, away from the loneliness of living on a ranch in the middle of nowhere with never any company and no place special to go. I brought her along because I hate being apart from her and I wanted her with me—wanted to show her things, buy her things. We haven't even been to Santa Fe yet. You'll like Santa Fe, Abbie-girl. I want to buy you something nice there—anything you want. And I don't want anything that's happened here to spoil your good time. Now you tell me what happened and let me handle it."

"Someone has hurt her!" Wolf's Blood hissed. "I'll bet it was one of those white soldiers. It was, wasn't it?" the boy demanded, his fists clenched.

Her eyes were still on Zeke's, and he saw the pain and humiliation there, mingled with an almost apologetic look. "No apologies, Abbie-girl," Zeke told her. "Just the truth, plain and simple."

She watched him for several silent seconds. He was still painted for battle, his handsome face fierce but his dark eyes gentle. His presence was powerful. He always had a way of making her do his will in such matters. She could not deny him.

"A soldier . . . came into the *tipi*," she told him. Her body jerked as she sniffed in a sob. "Oh, Zeke! Don't do anything foolish!"

He sighed and pulled her close with his good arm, then looked up at Wolf's Blood. "Go outside, son. Take Lillian and Jason with you."

"I want to get that soldier!" the boy growled.

"I'll take care of it. Go on outside so your mother and I can talk."

Wolf's Blood sighed impatiently, then walked over and picked up Jason. "Come with me," he said to Lillian, who quickly obeyed her older and much revered brother. The boy stopped and looked at his mother, who wept quietly against his father's chest. "I should have left Smoke with her!" the boy lamented with a mixture of anger and sorrow.

"It's all right," Zeke answered. "I'm the one to blame." Both Wolf's Blood and Abbie could already sense the rage that seethed beneath Zeke's calm exterior, for although he gently stroked Abbie's hair, he was tense, his eyes showing a need to kill. Wolf's Blood left, and Zeke ran his hand over Abbie's shoulders. "I'm afraid you've got to finish my arm, Abbie-girl," he told her gently. "Why don't you tell me what happened while you wrap it."

She sniffed and nodded, pulling back and taking a handkerchief from the beaded belt at her waist where she'd put it after crying earlier. She blew her nose and wiped at her eyes, and Zeke's heart ached at the thought of her warding off the soldier alone, just to keep her husband and the Cheyenne out of danger.

He reached out and touched her cheek with the back of his hand. "Who was it?" he asked.

She turned to finish wrapping his arm. Blood had already soaked the gauze she had used so far, and she began wrapping faster. "I still say I should sew it!" she fussed.

"I heal fast," he replied. He sighed impatiently, and the entire *tipi* seemed filled with his power and thoughts of vengeance. When he was this way, Abbie always thought she could hear drums and bells and distant war cries, for he was pure Indian, his thoughts filled only with revenge and murder. "I want an answer, Abbie," he told her gently but sternly. "I asked you who was here."

There was no arguing with him. "He called himself Randolph Cole." She swallowed. "He's . . . a big man . . . with a beard and an ugly scar on his left cheek where no beard grows. And he . . ." She hesitated and glanced up at him. If he were not her own husband, she would have been afraid of the dark warrior look in his eyes, the thin scar that ran down one side of his handsome face showing whiter than usual. The scar had been put there by a Crow Indian's knife years earlier, and the Crow Indian had not lived. This man had known nothing but violence all his life, and she often marveled that he could be such a gentle and loving husband and father. She returned to dressing his wound, wondering when the day would come that one of his wounds would kill him. "He will have scratches over his left eye," she continued. "I put them there."

He winced with pain but made no sound as she wrapped back upward again from his wrist to his elbow. He wanted to smile at the thought of his Abbie putting marks on Randolph Cole. She had spunk and courage—two of the things he loved about her. But his heart hurt too badly at the thought of her attack, and what could have happened, for him to be able to smile about any of it.

"What did he do?" he asked in a low hiss. "Tell me all of it, Abigail."

She wrapped downward again. "He wanted to know if . . . if I was a captive." She smiled a little. "I should have told him I was." She looked up at him. "A captive of love," she added, trying to humor him. But there was no humor in his eyes. "When I told him I was most certainly not a forced captive here he . . . said things." She looked away again.

His breathing quickened, and she knew he was reliving the horrible memory of his first wife's brutal rape and death at the hands of Indian haters. She, too, had been white, and had died at the hands of men she had once called friend. But Zeke Monroe had found her murderers, one by one, dishing out a horrifying vengeance that had left him a wanted man for many years in Tennessee.

"Did he hurt you?" he asked in a near whisper. "Touch you?"

She tied off the gauze and looked at her lap. "I . . . I needed an advantage, Zeke. I wanted to get rid of him without any trouble, and I was afraid for Lillian and Jason. So I . . . I let him . . . unlace my tunic." She swallowed and crossed her arms over her breasts almost defensively. Zeke thought he might explode any minute. "He . . . touched me . . . and I let him . . . kiss me. I . . . wanted him to think I was willing." She blinked back tears of shame and her face reddened. "Then I scratched his face and eye as deeply as I could. He let go of me and I kicked him where it would hurt the most and then kicked him backward. He fell into Jason's little tub. It gave me time to grab my Spencer." She wiped at her eyes. "I told him I'd shoot him if he didn't leave, and apparently he believed me." She covered her face. "I was so scared! Not for me, but for the baby and Lillian. And then for you if you found out. I . . . wasn't trying to lie to you, Zeke. I just don't want trouble. Not here! All I could think of was what those soldiers did to the Sioux at Blue Water Creek. I don't want that to happen here!"

He grasped her wrists and pulled her hands away, forcing her to look at him. He bent close and kissed her lip where it was bruised. "Abbie, my Abbie," he said softly. "Forgive me. This is my fault."

"No. It isn't anyone's fault but that man's."

He kissed her tears and gently unlaced her tunic, letting it fall. He traced his fingers lightly over a bruise near her breast. She well knew the rage that would have to be unleashed from his soul for the wrong done to his woman, but he held himself in check for her sake, as he gently kissed the bruise. His eyes met hers, and his glittered with remorse and determination as he pulled the tunic back up and tied it again. "Tell me that's all he did," he told her, fear of something worse in his voice.

She nodded. "It is. I've told you all of it, Zeke."

He closed his eyes and sighed as though greatly relieved. But when he opened them again the cold look of rage was surfacing. "He'll pay, Abbie. I'll find a way to do it without making trouble for the others. But he'll pay, one way or another!" He caressed the thick tresses of her hair. "No man touches Zeke Monroe's woman without wishing he hadn't! The fact that he abused you in front of poor little Lillian makes it even worse! After being sick so much, I wanted her to have a good time on this trip." He moved his hands to the sides of her face. "I'm so damned sorry, Abbie-girl. I keep you buried on that ranch because I'm always afraid of how you'll get treated whenever I take you to settled places. You're the best damned woman west of the Mississippi. You don't deserve those insults. And you deserve a hell of a lot better life than I've been able—"

"I have exactly what I want," she interrupted, reading the little boy look that always came into his eyes when he thought he might lose her because of the different blood in their veins. "I have everything a woman could ask for in a husband, and I have my children.

And I love the ranch and that little cabin. I love the beautiful horses we raise and the mountains in the distance. I love baking for my husband and children and I love being near your brother and the people. Tall Grass Woman is the most loyal friend a woman could have. I love the days with the children—and the nights with my husband. I have never wished for more, Zeke Monroe, and you know that. When I married you my eyes were wide open. I well knew what some people would think, but I didn't care. I was Zeke Monroe's woman, Lone Eagle's woman, and nothing else mattered."

His eyes were misty, and he pulled her close against him. "Sometimes I love you so much it makes me want to weep," he told her. "Once I was very weak, when I could not make love to you for fear of another pregnancy. Do you remember?"

"Of course I remember. I was so lonely I was ill."

"You are my strength, Abbie. Being one with you gives me power. Knowing you love me keeps me alive, heals my wounds, makes my heart leap with joy. But when I fear losing you—"

"I wish you would never say that, Zeke. You know better than to say that."

"It would serve me right, for leaving you alone to go and fight so that men can win their bets."

"You weren't fighting for bets. You were dealing out justice. That man deserved to die for what he did. His kind would shoot an Indian for no reason whatsoever—man, woman or child." She pulled back and looked into his eyes. "Be careful, Zeke. Randolph Cole is the same kind of man."

A sneer curved the corner of his mouth. "Randolph Cole made a grave mistake coming into my lodge and threatening my woman and children." He caressed her cheek gently. "You are not to worry any more about Randolph Cole."

Six

Before the really big race of the day, there would be several smaller races. The upper level of Fort Lyon was packed with soldiers who strained against the wall, leaning out to watch the races from their high vantage point. Outside the fort gates the path of the races was lined with Indians on both sides, and Abbie was among them, all of her children but Wolf's Blood lined up beside her. Wolf's Blood would race one of Zeke's Appaloosas and was among the contenders who milled about the fort gates as one by one the challengers rode to victory or defeat.

Tall Grass Woman, Abbie's close friend of many years, stood near Abbie, shouting out her support for each Indian who rode by, whether he be Cheyenne or Navaho. Abbie had to laugh at the woman's excitement, for the plump, jolly Tall Grass Woman was like a child at such occasions, screaming and jumping up and down.

Their friendship had been strong and fast, beginning with the first time Abbie arrived with Zeke to dwell among the people. Tall Grass Woman had presented Abbie with a white tunic, and had offered friendship at a time when Abbie had no one to turn to, alone among a people who were foreign to her. Later that first summer Abbie saved Tall Grass Woman's little girl from drowning. The little girl had since died from cholera, but Abbie's brave deed had made her honored among the people, and had won Tall Grass Woman's love and loyalty for all time.

"There he goes! Your son!" the round-faced, giggling woman told Abbie now. She raised a fist in the air and screamed as Wolf's Blood beat out the soldier by barely a nose. He had ridden what Zeke considered his fastest horse, and all the Indians cheered at the victory.

Tall Grass Woman yipped and yelled as loud as the men, squeezing Abbie close and laughing. But Abbie's own happiness was marred by the realization that before this day was over, her husband would find some way to avenge her attack of the day before. It was a nagging worry at the back of her mind, for not only were they in the midst of soldiers, who would surely have Zeke arrested and shot, but Zeke himself was in considerable pain from his wounds suffered in the knife fight. He had not voiced his pain, but she knew her husband too well by now to not be aware of when he was suffering silently. The pain was written on his face; he had slept restlessly, perspiring through the night.

Now he was with the soldiers and those Indians who were racing, pretending for her sake that he was fine. But she knew the reason he walked among the soldiers and spoke freely with them was because he was searching for the one with a beard and a scar on his face where the beard would not grow, a man with deep scratches over his eye. It would then be a simple matter to ask one of the other soldiers what the man's name was to be sure it was Randolph Cole. He had told Abbie not to worry, but it was impossible not to, for she knew her husband's temper and the utter destruction he could wield against another human being who had wronged

77

someone he loved.

Another pair of horses thundered past, and this time the soldier won. All of these races were just a buildup to the biggest race of the day, an event that had been taking place over the years between these soldiers and the Navaho. It was a standing challenge. Every year the Navahos came here, bringing their best rider and their fastest horse to race against the soldiers' pick of their own best rider and mount. The Navahos always won, and they considered it a fine joke to beat the soldiers every year. They expected no less this year, and they had bet heavily on another Indian win. But the soldiers seemed convinced that this year would be different, and as Zeke had voiced to Abbie the night before, the soldiers seemed almost too sure they would win. He suspected something was amiss, but could not imagine what it might be.

"Look!" Tall Grass Woman told Abbie, grabbing Abbie's hand. "Your husband is challenging someone." The woman used the English she had so proudly learned from Abbie's patient teaching.

Abbie's heart tightened, and she leaned out to see Zeke standing face to face with none other than Randolph Cole. The blood drained from Abbie's face and she felt light-headed.

"Keep the children here," she said quietly to Tall Grass Woman, moving past her to walk closer to Zeke.

"Where you go?" the woman asked. "What is wrong, little Abbie?"

"I'll explain later," Abbie replied, patting Tall Grass Woman's arm reassuringly. She hurried toward the confrontation, staying behind other Indians so Cole would not see her.

"Fifty dollars says my Appaloosa can beat out your black mare," Zeke was telling Cole. The Indians cheered, while Cole met Zeke's challenging eyes, trying

78

to discern whether or not the man knew Cole had been to his *tipi* the day before and had tried to attack his wife. Cole decided Zeke probably didn't know, for Zeke kept a friendly look to his eyes. Besides, no Indian man's wife in her right mind would tell her husband that another man had touched her. Cole had always heard that Indian men beat and scarred their wives for such things, accusing them of leading the other man on in some way and inviting the intrusion.

"When I seen that Appaloosa race with your son on it, mister, I knew my mare could beat her," Cole replied. "I've never lost a race yet with this mare, but I'll not race you unless you ride, not your son. Your son's much lighter, and I aim to ride my own horse." He scanned Zeke's tall, broad physique, secretly burning with envy at the thought of this half-breed bedding the pretty white woman. "You and me are about the same size, I'd say," he continued. "If you ride the Appaloosa yourself, I'll race you."

Zeke struggled to keep a friendly look on his face. It was important that Cole not suspect, but his blood burned with vengeance at the sight of the scratches on the man's face.

"I'll ride," he told Cole. "Intended to in the first place. Lay your money out, mister, and kiss it goodbye."

Abbie watched in terror as Randolph Cole handed a sergeant who was in charge of bets fifty dollars. Zeke did the same. They shook hands on the deal, and Zeke forced himself not to squeeze too hard when he took Cole's hand, though inside he was raging. He would have his revenge, and he would have it in this race. He had decided.

Both men moved back, waiting their turn. Two races would take place ahead of them. Abbie wiped sweat from her brow and blinked as dust from the next race

79

billowed through the cheering crowd. She watched Zeke carefully but could not read him. He stood next to Cole, calmly smoking a pipe and watching the races, as though nothing were wrong. Yet in their emotional closeness he felt her eyes on him, and he suddenly turned to scan the crowd, catching her standing behind Black Elk and some others. He gave her a nod and a wink, seeing the terror in her eyes. She could not imagine what he had in mind, and there was no time for him to explain. Their eyes held for just a moment, and he turned back to the races.

"That is the bastard who hurt you, isn't it?" She heard a voice beside her. It was Wolf's Blood. He had spoken to her quietly and moved closer to put a hand to her waist. She met her son's eyes, already having to look up at him because he was taller than she.

"What is he going to do?" she asked the boy, her eyes tearing. "The soldiers will—"

"Ho-shuh," Wolf's Blood told his mother, putting two fingers to her lips. "Father always knows what to do." He smiled, a teasing gleam in his eye, and in that moment he looked more like his father than ever. Her heart quickened at the resemblance. This son of hers would be a replica of Zeke, and it was good to know that Zeke would live on in such a way.

"What is he going to do?" Abbie asked the boy.

"I do not even know myself," he answered. "But he has something in mind. Of that I am sure. He knows the danger, Mother. He will not risk leaving you unprotected by getting himself arrested. You will see."

Their eyes held. "You have great confidence in your father."

The boy grinned again. "And you do not? After all you have been through with him? All you have seen him do?"

"But . . . the soldiers—"

"Do not worry," he interrupted.

She turned back to see Zeke, but he had mounted his Appaloosa now and was waiting next in line. Wolf's Blood stayed beside his mother, and his pet wolf sat on its haunches beside its master, eyes and ears alert as always.

The next race ended, and Zeke and Cole moved up to the starting line. The course took the riders a half mile straight from the fort gates to a dip in the landscape, where for about one minute the riders disappeared before reappearing for the return ride, ending at a point just short of the starting line, a total of about one-and-one-half miles.

Zeke sat straight and sure on his Appaloosa, talking softly to the animal and patting its neck. The horse snorted and pranced, ready for a good run. Abbie felt ill. She knew Zeke Monroe all too well. He most certainly did have something in mind, and God only knew what it was. The cheering of the crowd around her grew dim. She no longer heard them or even saw them. Her eyes rested only on Zeke, for perhaps after today she would never see him again, never hold him again.

Wolf's Blood moved behind her and put his hands on her shoulders reassuringly. He was himself full of rage over the thought of the bluecoat putting his hands on his mother. Abbie was to him nothing less than something to be worshipped, and she was the property of his brave and honored father. He knew in his heart that if he ever witnessed another man touching his mother he would kill the man on the spot and would enjoy it, especially if that man was white, for he had good reason to hate most white men. He had been the brunt of their prejudice and cruelty more than once.

A soldier held his gun in the air and called out to Zeke and Randolph Cole to make ready to ride. Zeke leaned forward then, as did Cole. In the next second the gun went off, and both riders kicked their horses into a fast gallop.

At first so much dust was stirred by the already worked-up dirt of the racing lane that no one could tell who was in the lead. But as it settled, it appeared that Zeke was slightly ahead. Abbie ran back down toward the children to try to get a better look, and Wolf's Blood ran with her, holding her arm. The crowd cheered and shouted, but to Abbie everything was silent and black. Her chest hurt from anxiety and her throat felt tight. The two horses disappeared over the crest where the raceway dropped down and circled around the small hill that hid the riders until they reappeared over the crest again for the final run back to the fort.

It took several minutes for the crowd to realize the two riders had not reappeared when they should have. Abbie felt as though she might faint from dread as the crowd began to quiet and just watch, wondering what could have happened to the two men. It seemed that suddenly all eyes were glued to the horizon—waiting.

Abbie clung tightly to her son's arm, and he could feel her shaking. "Do not worry, Mother," he told her.

She looked up at him with eyes wide from fear. "What is he doing?" she squeaked.

Wolf's Blood shook his head. "I do not know. But he said he would make things right, and he will. Father is not a foolish man."

She blinked back tears as Black Elk walked over to her side. "The other rider—he was the one?" he asked. Abbie nodded, and Black Elk just looked at his nephew and grinned. "I wonder what my half-brother has planned," he told Wolf's Blood.

"You know my father well, Uncle," Wolf's Blood replied, also grinning. "That man touched my mother."

Black Elk folded his powerful arms in front of him

and nodded, turning his eyes back to the horizon. Neither Zeke's brother nor his son seemed overly worried about what might happen.

Another minute went by, and still there was no sign of them. LeeAnn turned wide blue eyes to her mother, then ran to her, her blond curls bouncing. "Where is father, Mama?" she asked. "Did he lose?"

Abbie patted her head. "We . . . have to wait and see," she replied. The other children began walking back toward their mother, little Lillian's pale brown eyes showing her fright. She had recognized the other man as the one who had invaded their *tipi* the day before and had tried to hurt her mother. Surely her big, strong father would try to hurt the other man. "It's all right, children," Abbie tried to reassure them all.

The crowd was almost silent by then. Two soldiers mounted up to ride out and investigate the problem. But just then something appeared over the crest, and Abbie's grip on Wolf's Blood's arm actually pained him because she clung so tightly in her anxiety. He put a hand over her hands and both watched the two figures approach at a slow walk. Soon it was evident that there were two horses coming, but only one rider. The direction of the sun made it difficult at first to see who was returning. The rest of the crowd watched quietly as they came closer, and finally Abbie could see that the rider was Zeke on his own Appaloosa. He led the black mare behind him by the reins. The mare was limping, and Randolph Cole's body was slung over the horse's back, his head dangling strangely.

Abbie gasped and let out a little whimper of fear.

"Hush, Mother," Wolf's Blood told her quietly. "Do not let on that you knew this might happen. The other soldiers do not know what happened yesterday. Do you not see? That is father's advantage. They must not know he had any reason to harm Randolph Cole."

She sniffed and nodded, her heart pounding so hard she was certain all must be able to hear it.

The two horses came closer then, as people just stared in surprise and curiosity. Not even any of the Indians, other than Black Elk, knew of the encounter between Abigail and Randolph Cole. Zeke rode right past his family without looking at them, sitting tall and determined, leading the limping black mare. He stopped at the point where the race should have ended, his eyes on Lieutenant Perkins. The lieutenant marched forward, with several men behind him.

"What happened?" he asked Zeke.

"His horse stumbled," Zeke replied, his voice sounding true and sure. "This man was thrown—broke his neck."

Wolf's Blood and Black Elk struggled not to grin. Both knew what had really happened. The lieutenant and the others walked over to Randolph Cole and inspected both the horse and the dead body it carried.

"This leg looks bad, but I don't think it's broke," one man commented. Zeke turned his head slightly and looked sidelong at Abbie. Their eyes held, and his glittered with secret victory. Her heart swelled with love, but she also felt consumed with guilt for the terrible risk he had taken just to defend her honor. One of the soldiers grasped Cole's hair and moved the man's head slightly, then jumped back in revulsion.

"Neck's broke, all right." He scratched his head and looked at the lieutenant. "I don't understand it. Cole was a damned good rider."

"Happens to the best sometimes," Zeke commented, shifting his eyes to the lieutenant. Their eyes held for a moment, and the lieutenant smelled foul play, yet it would be impossible to prove, and he could not imagine any reason why the half-breed would want to bring any harm to Randolph Cole, except that Cole had the scratches on his face. The men had teased him that morning about messing with Navaho squaws. Perhaps it had not been an Indian woman who put the scratches there. Perhaps . . . He glanced at Abbie, who looked away. The woman radiated a goodness that commanded respect. The lieutenant did not want to make trouble for the white woman and her family.

Soldiers mumbled and scowled, eyeing Zeke suspiciously, more of them coming to mill around Cole's horse and the man's own dead body. Two men pulled the body from the mare and another man walked the horse carefully toward the fort.

"I guess you have to be declared the winner," the lieutenant told Zeke.

"You can't do that!" one of the soldiers shouted. "It wasn't no race."

"What else can I do? Cole didn't finish and this man did," the Lieutenant barked. "And I might remind you that you're talking to an officer, Private!"

The other soldiers began to grumble and Zeke dismounted, wincing with pain from his knife wounds. "It's all right, Lieutenant," he told the man. "Just give me my own money back and divvy Cole's up among those who bet on him. I can't call it a race either."

The lieutenant frowned. "You sure about that? It's yours, fair and square."

Zeke glanced over at Abbie, then faced the lieutenant again and shook his head. "Just scratch this one and do what you want with Cole's money. Get on with the rest of the races."

Lieutenant Perkins turned to the sergeant holding the money and ordered him to give back all that had been bet on the race, as well as to divide up Cole's fifty dollars. The decision seemed to ease the men's grumbling and suspicions, and Abbie wanted to cry with relief. But she kept her composure as Zeke approached, warning her and the others with his eyes that they should show no particular emotion that might give away what had really happened. He reached out and gently touched the little red mark on Abbie's lip, and she saw the sweat on his brow. However he had managed to kill Randolph Cole, it surely had taken a great deal of physical strength, and he had already been weak and in pain that morning. His bandaged arm had begun bleeding again.

"Zeke—"

"I'm all right," he told her quietly. "But it might be a good idea to be on our way. To hell with the big race. Let's pack our gear."

She nodded in agreement, then put a hand to her throat as the lieutenant approached them. Zeke saw the look in her eyes and turned to greet the man, nodding politely. "Lieutenant?"

"Mister Monroe, I wanted to ask you something," the lieutenant spoke up. "I keep wondering if you might be related to a Lieutenant Daniel Monroe, who served up at Fort Laramie. I knew Danny, and he once told me he had a half-breed brother."

Zeke grinned. "Danny's my brother, all right. How's he doing? I haven't seen him for about four years."

The lieutenant frowned, glancing from Zeke to Abbie and back to Zeke. "Your brother deserted the Union, Mister Monroe. Went back home to Tennessee to fight for the Confederacy."

Zeke's smile faded and Abbie paled in surprise. "Danny?" she asked. "But . . . he was so dedicated to his work at Fort Laramie. He's been in the army for many years, earned a medal in the Mexican War for bravery."

"I know all that," Perkins replied. "I was surprised,

too." He looked up at Zeke. "I liked Danny, but he was a Southern boy at heart, I suppose. I just thought maybe you knew what he had done and had heard from him. He had a wife and a little girl, you know. I think he left them in St. Louis."

Zeke sighed. "I'll be damned." He looked at Abbie. "I figured he'd been out here so long he'd forgot about being a Tennessee man."

Her eyes showed the slightly chiding look she sometimes used when they argued about Zeke going back to see his real father. "Tennessee is in his blood, just like you are drawn to the Cheyenne in your own blood."

Their eyes held, and she saw the pain in his that she always saw at the mention of Tennessee. Zeke turned his eyes back to Lieutenant Perkins. "How long ago did he leave Laramie?" he asked.

"It's been a couple of months at least. He's home by now—probably joined up with the graycoats already." The man's eyes narrowed. "I can't say I'm happy about it. I liked Danny. We lost a good officer. I'd hate to have to face him in battle. There's brother fighting brother back east, Mister Monroe, friend fighting friend. It's going to be an ugly war."

Zeke nodded. "I reckon it will. But it's not my war, Lieutenant. My war is right here, on the side of the Indians against the whites who come out here and kill them off with their diseases and by slaughtering the buffalo and trying to pen my people up like cattle."

Their eyes held and the lieutenant studied the tall, dark man before him, whose very manner bespoke courage and meanness. He still had a nagging intuition that Randolph Cole had not fallen from his mount and broken his neck. "You ride a dangerous road, Mister Monroe," he replied. "You're either a Southerner or an Indian. Either way you're on the losing end."

"I'm no Southerner," Zeke replied. "I make no

claim to that part of me. I'm just Indian, Lieutenant, and if that's the losing end, then at least I'll go down fighting and go down proud."

The lieutenant glanced at Abbie. "God be with you, ma'am," he said quietly. He turned to Zeke once more and stared briefly. Zeke realized the man suspected something and was letting it go.

"Thank you, Lieutenant," he said, his eyes grateful.

The lieutenant sighed and nodded, then left. Zeke watched after him a moment, then turned to Black Elk with a gleam in his eye.

"I think maybe I'd better start packing, Black Elk, before somebody puts two and two together, and while Lieutenant Perkins is in a generous mood."

Black Elk nodded. "You go to Santa Fe?" Zeke nodded. "I stay for big race," Black Elk added.

Zeke looked around at the frenzied crowd, as more racers took off and the young Navaho and young private who would ride the big race of the day stood to the side, talking to their mounts.

"Watch yourself, Black Elk," he told his brother. "I don't like the mood of the soldiers, and I have an uneasy feeling. I can't name it. I just smell trouble."

Black Elk shrugged. "We will see." He put a hand on Zeke's shoulder. "It is a good job you did on that man who touched your woman." His eyes gleamed. "I knew you would think of a way."

Wolf's Blood stood aside, watching his father with pride and feeling his own revenge through his father's deed. He reached down and petted Smoke. "It is a good day!" he told the animal softly. Smoke's tail wagged, something the animal rarely did. The vicious but loyal pet seemed to sense that proper vengeance had been meted.

Zeke put an arm around Abbie. "Let's get out of here," he told her. She swallowed and nodded, still shaking from worry.

"Agreed," she answered quietly. She bent down and picked up little Jason, and they headed for the village, the rest of the children running and skipping beside them, the little ones trying to keep up with their father's long stride.

"What do you think about Danny leaving Fort Laramie to join the Confederates?" Zeke asked Abbie, himself troubled by the news about his favorite brother.

"I don't know what to think," she answered. "I'm only worried. Everyone we talk to keeps saying what a terrible and bloody war it's turning out to be. I only hope you don't get mixed up in it, Zeke."

He kept a hand on her shoulder and gave her a squeeze. "Don't worry about that. I've no cause or desire to get involved. There is enough happening right here with my own people."

"But you also have people in Tennessee, my husband, much as you wish to deny it."

He stopped walking, and she went on a few steps before turning to meet his eyes. "I'll not say it again, Abigail. I have no people in Tennessee!" His eyes flashed with anger, as they always did when she mentioned his white father, which he knew was what she meant by her remark. She reddened slightly and nodded, saying nothing. It was a subject they rarely spoke about, mostly because it was the only subject that caused painful feelings between them. She turned away and started walking again.

"Abbie!" he called out. She stopped, holding little Jason close and keeping her back to him. "I'm sorry, Abbie."

She blinked back tears. "I know, Zeke. I'm sorry, too."

He walked up to her and put his arms around her. How he hated hurting her, or being demanding in any way. The subject of his father always seemed to stir his anger and make him speak harshly to her. "It's been a trying day, and I'm in a lot of pain, Abbie," he told her gently. "Let's go pack and head out for Santa Fe. We have a few hours of riding time left."

She looked up at him and their eyes radiated understanding and forgiveness. He kissed her lightly, suddenly wanting more. But there was no time for more.

They walked together toward the two Monroe *tipis,* but there was a new heaviness to her heart. The news about Danny had stirred an old fear in her heart: the fear that the distant and confusing Civil War would somehow separate them. They had been separated before by the hands of fate, and the fact remained that Zeke Monroe now had a favorite brother involved, and he still had a father in Tennessee, even though he made no claim to that part of his heritage. It was the first time in many years she had thought of Tennessee with any kind of worry or nostalgia. She had long ago decided Tennessee was a part of her own life to be forever buried, for she was not the same person as that young, dreaming Abigail Trent who had left that state with her father, brother and sister. Her family was dead, and that part of her life was dead. This was her life now, here in this land that she loved, with this man that she loved. Yet suddenly Tennessee had unexpectedly and without invitation loomed back into her life.

Zeke tied the last rawhide strips that secured the travois to Abbie's horse, wincing with the pain in his arm.

"Zeke, we should stay here and rest a day first," she told him. "You never should have done what you did. There's blood on that gauze again. You started it bleeding."

He shook his head. "I did what had to be done. I couldn't leave here without making sure that man

90

regretted touching you." He walked to his own mount and her eyes teared. But her worry was interrupted by gunshots and distant screams. They all looked in the direction of the fort. Navahos seemed to be scattering everywhere, mixed with some Cheyenne and others who had stayed for the final big race.

"What the hell?" Zeke mumbled. He quickly mounted his Appaloosa. Abbie and the children sat frozen and confused on their horses, Abbie clinging to little Jason, and Lillian holding tightly to Wolf's Blood, with whom she would ride on this trek of their journey. They were prepared to leave for Santa Fe. Black Elk and the rest of the Cheyenne would head back home to the Arkansas River.

"Zeke, what's happening?" Abbie asked, her heart pounding at the sound of more gunshots and more screaming. Some Indians, including women and children, were falling.

"Be ready to get the hell out of here," he replied sternly. "I knew it! I've smelled something foul all day. Randolph Cole wasn't the only reason I didn't want to stay for the last race."

Black Elk was running toward them now, dragging his young wife, Blue Bird Woman, and their son with him. "We go! We go!" he yelled to Zeke. "You leave now! Get children away! *Hopo! Hopo!*"

"What's wrong?" Zeke asked. "Why are they shooting the Indians?"

"Race! Somebody cut the bridle of Navaho's horse. He fall. Lose race! Navahos say soldiers cut the bridle. Soldiers say it is not so." He hurriedly gathered his own horses, and Zeke quickly dismounted, helping his brother knock down his *tipi,* gathering only part of their belongings and throwing them onto Abbie's travois.

"There's no time for more!" Zeke shouted to Black Elk. "Get your family out of here! We have enough to keep you supplied back to the Arkansas.''

Abbie watched in terror as more Indians fell in the distance. Would the soldiers ride out of the fort and chase more of them down? Lillian started crying.

"Navahos say soldiers should give them back their money. But soldiers keep it," Black Elk was shouting. "Slam the gates on the Navahos and tell them to get out. Navahos started pounding on the gates and trying to climb over, and soldiers started shooting. I do not understand what is happening!''

Zeke stared at the fort a moment longer. "I do,'' he replied coldly, his eyes tearing. He mounted up again, grunting with pain. "Get moving!" he ordered all of them. "Get to those hills to the north. We'll hole up there for a time and see if there are any stragglers that need our help. Get the children out of range in case they start shooting in this direction!''

Zeke slapped some of the children's horses on the rear and got them going. Black Elk followed, with his wife and child, but Abbie hesitated. Zeke circled his horse around and galloped up to hers, grabbing the bridle. "Get going, Abbie!" he ordered.

She looked at him with desperate tears in her eyes. "Tall Grass Woman!" she sobbed. "Where is Tall Grass Woman? I won't leave without her!''

"You have to," Zeke told her gently but firmly. "You have Jason and the other children to think about. They need their mother, Abbie-girl. Now get going. *Nonotovestoz!*''

She stared at the fort and the fleeing Indians, as some soldiers came out, running Indians down and shooting them point blank. "Why?" she whimpered. "Why are they doing that?''

"Do you really need to ask that?" Zeke asked bitterly. He turned his horse and pulled hers along with him, feeling faint from the pain in his arm. She finally got the horse into motion herself and headed for the northern hills. It was frightening to know what the soldiers and settlers could do to the Indian and get away with. She had been at Blue Water Creek when soldiers had slaughtered so many Sioux. Now it was happening all over again, and it hit her with all its horrible realism just what kind of hell lay ahead for the Cheyenne. What had happened to the Sioux and the Navaho would most surely happen to the Cheyenne and all the others. It was only a matter of time. It was open season on the Indian, as though he were no more than a wild animal on which a bounty had been placed.

She rode hard then, following Zeke three miles back into the hills, where they waited until dark. No soldiers came. The Navaho had scattered in every direction, having to leave their dead loved ones behind. Most of their own Cheyenne clan were also missing, but few had been at the final race, so they held out hope for them, figuring many of them had already headed for home.

Abbie sat on a hillside with the younger children around her. She wanted to be strong for them, but she could not control her tears. She felt especially ashamed at being of the same race as the men who had slaughtered the Navahos with no feeling and no regret. Wolf's Blood stood at a distance, his face hard set, his eyes cold. This was only more proof that the white man was no good. He wanted no part of being white. His decision to be Indian and nothing more was now forever sealed. He too still had memories of Blue Water Creek, even though he had been much younger then. Now there was this new massacre. Nothing had changed. The soldiers who had acted friendly to the Navaho all these years had suddenly turned on them, cheating on the horse race and then shooting the Indians down for no reason.

"E-have-se-va!" the boy hissed.

Zeke walked up to Abbie, kneeling down and putting his arms around her from behind, hugging her tightly. "I'm so sorry, Abbie-girl. I didn't want it to be like this for you. This whole trip was a disaster for you. I'm so goddamned sorry."

She gently grasped his arms and placed her head back against his chest. "You couldn't have known," she replied quietly. "The first part was wonderful. I enjoyed it, Zeke. You couldn't help what happened here." She sighed deeply, breathing in the cool night air and looking up at the stars. "I'm so ashamed that it's my own people who are doing this. And I feel so . . . so helpless." New tears came and he kissed her hair.

"Please don't cry, Abbie. It just makes me regret even more that I brought you into this damned mess by marrying you."

She sniffed and kissed his arm, turning her body then to face him. "I wish you wouldn't say that," she told him. "If I had it to do over again, I'd do the same. You know I'd suffer anything to be with you, Zeke Monroe. That hasn't changed."

Their eyes met in the moonlight and he bent down to kiss the tears on her cheeks. *"Ne-mehotatse,"* he whispered. "May the spirits always bless you and keep you safe—for me."

It was then they heard a warning call from the darkness. Someone was approaching. Zeke left her and hurried to get his rifle from his gear, but then Falling Rock, Tall Grass Woman's husband, called out.

"Cheyenne!" came the voice from the darkness. He walked into the dim light of the small fire Zeke had built. "It is I, Falling Rock." Tall Grass Woman approached behind him, and Abbie leaped up and ran to the woman. They hugged tightly, and Zeke's heart

94

ached, both with joy at the fact that Abbie's good friend was all right, and with agony at the suffering she would surely endure for being married to him and loving the Cheyenne. He set his rifle aside and grasped Falling Rock's shoulder.

"It is good to see you, friend. Abbie was worried about Tall Grass Woman."

The man nodded. "And Tall Grass Woman was worried about Abbie," he replied in the Cheyenne tongue.

Tall Grass Woman carried on in Cheyenne for several minutes, wiping at constant tears and lamenting the fate of the poor Navahos. Abbie gave her another hug, then turned to Zeke.

"Zeke, would you mind if—" She swallowed.

"You want to go home," he finished for her. "You don't want to go to Santa Fe first."

She blinked back tears. "I just want to be in our own little cabin. I feel safe there," she told him. "Would you mind terribly?"

He smiled sadly. He had wanted so much to make this trip a nice one for her—to buy her things in Santa Fe and let her live like a white woman ought to live. He wanted so much for her. And yet she expected none of it. She was satisfied with the simple things in life, satisfied with her little house and her many children—satisfied to live among the Cheyenne. She had never asked more of him. It was just that he had wanted to give more.

"I don't mind," he replied. "We'll head out come sunup. If home is where you want to go, Abbie-girl, then that's where we'll go."

She smiled, and he loved her more than ever.

Seven

Anna Gale sauntered toward Winston Garvey, handing him a drink. She scanned his rotund body with derision as he took the glass, and he in turn drank in the voluptuous body that was provocatively shrouded beneath her thin robe.

"What is it you want to know this time, Senator?" she asked the man, using the pet name most people had given him, even though he was now retired from the office he once held in Washington. "You seldom come here without a purpose, and that purpose usually involves some shady business dealing." She watched him with wide, blue eyes, her beautiful face framed by thick, lustrous black hair, her shape still firm and perfect in spite of many years of prostitution, her only method of survival.

Garvey sipped his drink, then smiled at her with fat, red lips. "What do you know about Silverthorn?" he asked. "He ever done business with you?"

She smiled slyly through painted lips, coming back over to the love seat and sitting down beside the man, crossing her legs and letting the robe fall away from her so that her legs were bare to her naked hips. "What if he has?" she asked cautiously.

Garvey studied the slim, velvety thighs and wondered how she stayed so well preserved. "The man wants to borrow some money from me. He has a ranch about twenty miles north of here, on the South Platte. He's using it for collateral—wants to mortgage it in return for money he'll give to the Union to support their cause."

Anna shrugged. "So? Lend it to him."

"It isn't that simple. I'm for supporting the Union, partly because I know they'll win the war, and partly because the sooner we get this war over with, the sooner we can turn our attention to the Indians and put them in their place. But if the man's a Union sympathizer, then he's also anti-slavery. And if he's anti-slavery, he might also have a soft spot for the Indians. I'll not lend money to any man who might fight for Indian rights."

She grinned and shook her head. "You're really an Indian hater, aren't you?"

"You know anyone in Denver who loves them?"

She looked away, thinking with a flutter of desire about one Indian she knew. But Zeke Monroe was happily married. Men like Zeke were not for the likes of Anna Gale. No decent man wanted a woman who had slept with so many men she had long ago lost count. "There might be a few," she replied wistfully.

"Then they're stupid!" Garvey sneered. He took another sip of his drink. "And I won't lend money to one. If Silverthorn ever comes here to sleep with you, try to find out his feelings. And ask around. I want some answers as fast as I can get them. I don't have much time."

She arched her eyebrows and looked at him. "What are you worried about? If he proves to be an Indian lover, you can always foreclose on him and take his land. Lord knows you've done worse to others."

Garvey chuckled with satisfaction over his own evil.

"Anna. Anna," he replied with mock admiration, running a hand along her bare thigh. "Only you really understand me. Only you know my deepest secrets." He untied her robe and pulled it open, exposing her nakedness. "Perhaps I should have you disposed of, my pet." He ran the back of his hand over her breast. "You know too much."

She only smiled. "You won't get rid of me," she purred, moving closer and slinging her legs over his lap. "I've never betrayed you, Senator. I could have ruined you years ago back in Washington, but I didn't do it. Now I'm a free woman, with no more debts to you. But I still do your spying for you, you devil. You'll lose a valuable source of information if you get rid of me."

He sighed and nestled his puffy face between her breasts, unable to see the sneer of revulsion on her lips at his touch. "Ah, but you have betrayed me, sweet Anna," he answered. "You won't tell me where I can find my half-breed son."

"Why should I tell you? So you can kill the poor child? He's doing you no harm. I may be a lot of bad things, my darling Senator. But I won't be a part of harming children."

He raised his head and looked at her through the slits of his puffy eyes. "I told you once I won't kill him."

She ran a lovely, slender finger around his face. "I know you too well," she answered. "You would most certainly get rid of him. If your son ever finds out you slept with Indian women and sired a son by one of them, he'd probably shoot you himself. I swear, that boy is slightly crazed when it comes to Indians."

Garvey shrugged. "You can't blame him. Indians killed his mother."

"And I don't suppose you've had anything to do with feeding the boy's hatred, have you?" she answered sarcastically. She layed back, stretching out across the love seat and resting her head on the arm. "Besides, I've told you before that I only know the boy exists. I have no idea where he is, and I'll not tell you how I even got that much information." She thought again of Zeke, and her body felt on fire. There were men like Garvey, and then there were men like Zeke. There was no comparison.

The senator ran his hand over her milky white skin. "I'll get it out of you some day, you little vixen."

She bent one leg and dropped it to the side, exposing herself for him. "Perhaps. But I doubt it. Treat me right, and I'll treat you right, Senator. By helping each other, we both remain very rich. That's all that matters, isn't it? Forget about the boy." She tried to sound casual, but she always dreaded the fact that he might press the matter. She did not ever want to have to tell this evil man how she had got the information that she now held over him—information that kept him in her power. For to tell him would be to lose her hold on him, and worse than that, it would mean betraying Zeke Monroe.

"Then I'll find out some other way," the senator grumbled.

She shrugged. "Go ahead and try."

The man toyed with her in places now familiar to him and she closed her eyes. "Anna, I want you to do something else for me. I'll pay you a great deal of money."

She eyed him warily. "What's that?" she asked.

"I want you to go to bed with my son. Charles is very fond of you. But he tells me you won't do business with him."

Her stomach churned with revulsion. There was something repulsive about Charles Garvey. It was not just his looks, which were finally just beginning to improve as he grew older. It was his manner—a sadistic evil in the boy's eyes. There was something not quite right about him, and it frightened her.

"He's a child," she replied. "I don't go to bed with children."

"He's trying to be a man!" the senator snapped. "He needs to learn about women."

"He's already learned!" she answered with a sneer. She sat up and pulled her robe closed. "This is my business, Winston, and I'll run it my way. I'm the madam of this house, and I'll sleep with whomever I choose! I do not choose to sleep with your son!" She rose and walked to the window. The senator got up and lumbered over to stand behind her, pulling her robe from her shoulders.

"Don't push me, Anna. You might be important to me, and right now I have no wish to bring you harm. But my son is more important to me, and the fact remains that I could and should get rid of you for my own safety."

Her blood chilled. She had no fear of Winston Garvey. Theirs was a long and infamous relationship. But now someone more important had come into the picture, someone who could convince Winston Garvey he could get along without Anna Gale. Charles Garvey was a shrewd, demented, spoiled boy who always got what he wanted. Now he wanted her. She turned and looked up at the senator.

"How much?" she asked.

He grinned. "A thousand dollars?"

She stared back. "Make it fifteen hundred," she replied boldly. "Your son, so I'm told, has not quite 'matured.' It won't be a lot of fun for me, if you know what I mean."

The senator chuckled. "Whatever you say. I just like to keep the boy happy."

She moved away from him, not wanting him to see the revulsion in her eyes for his son. She walked to a night table and picked up a long, very thin cigar. She lit it and puffed it for a moment. "Send him up tonight," she told him quietly. "And as far as Silverthorn, I'll see what I can find out."

"Thank you, Anna dear," he replied, feeling powerful and important for having broken down her proud resistance. Anna Gale was still at his command, even if he didn't technically "own" her any longer. She had long ago become rich enough to pay off her debts to him. But some debts were not tangible, and each owed the other in many ways. "I'd stay myself for another round with you, but I have a business engagement. Take care, my sweet."

He trudged out of the room, his breathing heavy from carrying so much weight. She heard the door close and she shuddered. In spite of all the men she had slept with, she chilled at the thought of Charles Garvey putting his hands on her. Her thoughts moved again to Zeke. How many times over the years had she thought of him? And why, out of all the men she had known, did Zeke Monroe nag at her heart and her memories?

Thunder rolled as a late autumn storm rumbled over Nashville. Danny headed for the biggest tent in the Confederate encampment in that city, where he knew from his own army experience the commanding officer would be stationed. The thunder and impending storm seemed a foreboding of the storm coming to the South, and he tried to shake off his dark worry, praying again that his wife and child were still safe in St. Louis, and that his father would still be alive when he returned to the farm. God only knew when he would see any of them again.

He reached the tent, and a first sergeant eyed him

warily, taking in Danny's cotton pants and plaid shirt, suspicious of any man not in a uniform. These were times of deceit and mistrust.

"Speak your piece." the sergeant drawled.

"I'm Daniel Monroe, from down near Shelbyville. I rode in with some of the other Tennessee Volunteers this morning," Danny replied sternly, a man accustomed to giving orders rather than taking them. "I want to speak to General Johnston and offer my services. I was formerly a lieutenant in the United States Western Army and I also served in the Mexican War."

The sergeant ran his eyes over Danny again. Even after several years of service in the West, Danny carried a hint of his Tennessee accent, and he had a strong, wholesome country boy look to him. He was a handsome man, with a tall, commanding physique. His face was tanned from his years of duty in the western sun, and strands of his blond hair that dangled from beneath his floppy leather hat were bleached even whiter by that same sun. His intense blue eyes showed honesty, and the sergeant lowered his rifle. "I'll tell the general you're here." The man disappeared inside the tent.

Danny waited impatiently. He was tired and hungry. He forced himself to stop thinking about his distraught father and his own aching loneliness for Emily. Moments later the sergeant reappeared. "Go on in," he mumbled.

Danny removed his hat and entered, finding the large, gray-haired Gen. Sidney Johnston sitting at a makeshift table inside. At fifty-eight, Johnston was one of the oldest men to join in the battle between blue and gray, but he was a competent and well-liked leader. His hairline was receded but thick at the edges, and his mustache was equally thick. His blue eyes were firm but tolerant as Danny came to stand before him. The man looked Danny over, already liking what he saw.

102

"The sergeant tells me you were a lieutenant in the Western Army," the man spoke up with a satisfied smile.

"Yes, sir. I've come to join the Confederates. I'm a Tennessee man. I think I can be of some use to you, General Johnston."

The general leaned back in his chair. "Perhaps you can. You also served in the Mexican War? That was a long time ago. You don't look that old."

Danny flashed a handsome grin. "I'm thirty-five, sir. But I was just a kid in the Mexican War. Went west to search for a half-breed brother of mine and ended up in the army. I saved an officer from a bullet down in Mexico and found myself promoted to first sergeant while I was still wet behind the ears—then before I knew it, lieutenant in command at Fort Laramie." He ran a hand through his thick, blond hair. "Right now I know more about Indians than I do about this kind of war, sir. But I am accustomed to commanding men and keeping them in line." He shook his head. "From what I've seen, you have a mess on your hands—a bunch of backwoods farmers ready to go to war with nothing more than shotguns and old muskets."

Johnston frowned and rose, putting out his hand. "Exactly right, Monroe." They shook hands. "It is Monroe, isn't it? That's what the sergeant said."

"Yes, sir. Dan Monroe. Born and raised in Tennessee."

"Have a seat, Monroe," Johnston told him, motioning to a crate nearby. "Sorry about the accommodations."

Danny shrugged. "I've lived away from civilization too long to worry about such things," he answered.

"Good. Because I have a feeling in this war there will be no comforts, Monroe. You look like a strong, well-trained man. And I'm glad you've noticed the problem

103

we have. It's compounded by the fact that President Davis can't help me much with supplies. All the good stuff stays in the East. Out here in these border states we have to make do. It's a mess, just like you said.''

Danny sat down on the crate. ''Give me a gray uniform and let me help clean up the mess, General. I lost a brother at Wilson's Creek. He was a good man—a simple man. I promised our father I would exchange my blue uniform for gray and avenge my brother's death. I have another brother serving with the Confederates. But I don't know where he is right now. And a half-breed brother, too.''

Johnston frowned, but his eyes bade Danny to continue.

Danny leaned forward and turned his hat in his hands thoughtfully. ''His name is Zeke. Before my pa married my ma, he lived with a Cheyenne woman out west. They had a son. My pa got homesick for Tennessee and came back. Brought Zeke with him.'' He shook his head. ''But life was rough for a half-breed. He was bad abused, and white men raped and murdered his first wife and killed their little son. The woman was white.'' Danny sighed. ''Zeke went a little crazy after that. Some of that Indian blood came to surface, I guess. He hunted down the men—one by one.'' He looked at Johnston sheepishly. ''Needless to say, he left Tennessee a wanted man. He headed west to search for his Cheyenne mother and his people. He's been out there ever since. Through some connections of my own I managed to finally get him removed from Tennessee's wanted list a couple of years ago. I see him now and then. He has a wife and seven children now. Still lives among the Cheyenne. He's happy there.''

''Married an Indian woman then?''

Danny smiled softly. ''No, sir. Married another white woman.''

Johnston's eyebrows arched. "And he lives among the Cheyenne?"

"Mostly. They do have a cabin down on the Arkansas River. But it's right smack in Cheyenne country. Abbie is quite a woman, a very lovely person, in looks and character. She's one brave lady."

Johnston fingered his mustache. "This Zeke sounds like the kind of man we could use on the Confederate side," he commented. "Is he as big as you?"

Danny grinned. "Bigger! But Zeke would never take sides in this war. He has no ties with Tennessee—no desire to ever come back. His only concern is the Cheyenne—and his own family."

"Too bad." Johnston studied Danny thoughtfully, liking the young man right off. "So, you went west to find this Zeke and ended up in the army. A lieutenant at Fort Laramie. Takes rugged men to last out there on the frontier. I admire your courage and strength, Monroe. I most certainly can use you." He leaned forward across the table. "We've got to hold Bowling Green, Mr. Monroe. And Nashville. The Green River, the Tennessee and the Cumberland Rivers are our supply routes. We've got to keep them open. Nashville is important because of its industry. Here we get our uniforms from clothing factories, arms and equipment from other factories. Several railroads lead to Nashville. We must secure Tennessee and keep all of these routes open. The area on the Green River around Bowling Green, all the way down to Pittsburg Landing on the Tennessee is vital. Vital! The Federals know this, and they're already building forces under Generals Grant and Sherman. I intend to be ready for them! The Confederates can and will win this war, Mr. Monroe." He rose again. "And fine young men like yourself will help us win it!"

Danny rose and put out his hand again, shaking the

general's vigorously. "Thank you, sir."

"I'll consider your former service and let you know in the morning what your command will be, Mr. Monroe." Their eyes held in mutual love for the South and the Confederacy. Then Johnston let go of Danny's hand. "Tell me, son. You served out west apparently for a long time. Do you miss it?"

Danny sighed, his eyes softening with a special love. "Every man who goes out there misses it, sir. There's something about it that kind of grabs at a man, keeps pulling him back toward the setting sun. I expect I'll go back out, once this war is over."

Johnston nodded. "You love it. I can tell." He searched Danny's eyes again, wanting to be certain of the man's loyalty. "But you still love Tennessee more, don't you?"

Danny swallowed and nodded. "Tennessee will always be home, sir. It's in my blood."

Johnston smiled softly. "Good. Welcome to the bloody war, Monroe. May God keep you safe."

Winter winds howled outside, but Zeke and Abbie sat by the hearth, warm and comfortable. Abbie sewed on a new pair of winter moccasins for her husband, made from the shaggiest part of a bull buffalo hide. The thick hair would be turned to the inside, creating a natural insulation that made for much warmer footwear than the conventional boot.

The house was quiet, with only the sound of the crackling fire and the soft strumming of the mystic mandolin, an instrument Zeke Monroe played very seldom now, but one he played well. The music he made with the instrument was always a source of fascination and excitement for the children, and this night it had lulled them all to sleep as they lay in their beds listening to their father play and sometimes sing songs he had learned back in that mysterious place called Tennessee.

Abbie held a particular love for the old and beautiful mandolin, for when first she met Zeke Monroe on a wagon train west, he had played the instrument for her, helping soothe her fears and loneliness with his music. When he played and sang, he presented a picture that was in stark contrast to the vicious and vengeful man Zeke Monroe could be. There was nothing Indian about him when he strummed the mandolin strings. His mellow voice and the Tennessee mountain songs he sang turned him into a purely Tennessee man, and Abbie treasured those moments, for she felt as though she could own and control that side of him. She loved everything that was Indian about him, yet that was a part of him she could never fully share, for no matter how well she understood the Cheyenne religion, customs and language, the fact remained that she was white. There was a side to him that belonged only to Zeke—the side that was called Lone Eagle, the side that had visions and drew power from the spirits of the earth and the elements. But when he played his mandolin and sang for her, he was a man she could share fully, and he gave her, willingly and lovingly, a little part of the world from which she had come so many years ago—a world she had given up for him.

He stopped strumming and sat watching the flames for several silent minutes. She put down her sewing and watched his dark, troubled eyes, as he flexed his right hand.

"Is your arm bothering you again?" she asked. The knife wound Blade had inflicted upon him four months before at Fort Lyon had not healed quite right, and at times his arm felt numb.

He shrugged and flexed his hand more. "Just a little. I want to keep working it. This occasional numbness could mean my death if I'm using my knife in self-defense. I think if I work it enough all the strength will come back.'' He sighed. ''Guess my old age is making me so I don't heal so fast any more.''

Abbie laughed. ''Zeke Monroe, there is no such thing as age with a man like you. You'll never be old. All the years do to you is make you more handsome. You're as hard and strong as the day I met you, and you know it. Soon as I laid eyes on you I decided I'd not let you get away, because I'd never again see a finer specimen of man, and you had those gentle eyes on top of it. I thought my heart would jump right out of my mouth when you volunteered to scount for my pa's train.''

He snickered and looked at her with a twinkle in his eyes. ''Now you sound like the little girl you were then, always pouring gushy, flattering words over me. Remember that time you blurted out to your sister all those fine compliments about me, all my wonderful attributes, trying to defend me because she tried to discourage you from being interested in me? Everybody on the train heard you, you crazy kid, and there I was trying to keep the others from knowing you had an interest. I was afraid they'd look down on you.''

She raised her chin defiantly. ''I didn't care one whit what they thought! And any woman who tells me I shouldn't be with you is just jealous!''

Zeke chuckled and shook his head. Then he sobered as he studied the scar on his arm again. ''I sure have my share of these. Sometimes I wonder how I can still walk on two feet. I should have been dead about thirty times over. I've been close to death so many times I try not to even count.''

She began stitching on a moccasin again. ''Men like Cheyenne Zeke don't go down easy,'' she commented. She sewed quietly for a moment, then raised her eyes to his again, herself sobering. She had noticed the scar on her own left hand, put there by a jealous Arapaho woman who had once wanted Zeke for herself and had attacked the white woman he had married. And there was the scar on her back and breast, where a Crow arrow had penetrated her body. How many years ago was it? And yet it seemed like yesterday. Zeke had saved her life then, draining a terrible infection with his own knife.

"We both have scars," she commented. "Inside and out. It's the wounds on the inside that hurt the most, Lord knows."

Their eyes held and then he suddenly looked away. "God, Abbie, you never should have married me," he said quietly.

She caught the little boy tone again and refused to let him feel guilty for anything. "Look at it this way, Zeke," she told him. "What other man would have put up with a strong-minded woman like me? I'm too independent and fiesty for the ordinary man. As some men put it, I have too much spirit. I needed a man as strong and mean as you to keep me in my place."

He met her eyes again and saw the teasing look in them. Then he broke into a grin. "Abbie-girl, I believe you're probably right."

She nodded. "Of course I'm right."

He picked up a heavy rock he kept near the hearth and began bending his arm to exercise the stiff muscles.

"I'll bet I'm right about something else, too," she added, this time more serious.

"What's that?"

She pulled at a strip of rawhide. "Oh, the way you played that mandolin tonight—your music was kind of sad." She met his eyes. "You're worried about Danny, aren't you?"

He stopped lifting the rock and leaned back to study her. "Woman, the way you read my mind, I swear I'd better be careful not to think about some other woman, or you'd be coming at me with a skillet aimed at my head."

She laughed lightly. "You're exactly right."

Immediately both of them sobered. For one night there had been another woman—the prostitute called Anna Gale. But that had not been out of desire. It had been out of necessity, for Zeke Monroe had never desired another woman but his Abbie since the first day he'd set eyes on the virgin child he knew he must claim for himself. Anna Gale was something that had happened a long time ago, a brief, forced interlude to gain vital information. It was something they had long ago decided to never again discuss.

He sighed and leaned forward, turning his eyes back to the crackling fire. A mantle clock above the fireplace ticked peacefully. It had been a gift to her from Zeke many years ago; "something from the world you should be living in," he had told her. They still lived in a *tipi* when he first bought it for her. The cabin had not yet been built. She used to set it on an upturned log before she had a mantle to set it on. Now she had one made of stones Zeke had dug from the bed of the Arkansas River and put together with earthen clay. He had lamented at the time that the mantle was not made of fine marble, but Abbie loved it just the way it was, for loving, hard-working hands had built it.

"What made you start thinking about Danny again?" she asked.

He moved his eyes to hers. "Talk of the war," he told her. "I've been meaning to tell you. Black Elk came to see me today while I was out in the north pasture. He said runners had come to their camp telling them a General Albert Pike was enlisting the services of Indians to help the Confederates. Seems the Confederates, hopefully with the help of Indians, plan to attack

110

every fort along the Arkansas and maybe even move on into Denver.''

She stopped her sewing and paled. ''Oh, dear Lord! They shouldn't get involved in that, Zeke!''

''That's what I told him. He said William Bent had given them the same warning. I told Black Elk that to join up with the Confederates would only make things worse for the Cheyenne, no matter how many guns or whatever else the Confederates offer them. I don't see the South winning this war, Abbie. The Union is too many and too strong and too industrialized. The government will one day come down hard enough on the Indians without having the excuse that the Indians aided the Confederates. That's all the remaining fuel they need to wipe out every red man west of the Mississippi. The worst part is that if there is even a hint out in these parts that the Indians are joining the Confederates and planning to raid along the Arkansas, Colorado will arm itself full force. You know how scared and crazy the settlers get at the mere hint of Indian trouble. I don't like it. I don't like any of it. It's easy enough to shoot an Indian as it is, without the excuse that he might be aiding the rebels.''

''What did Black Elk say he would do?''

''He's a wise man. He listens to men like me and Bent. I think he intends to stay out of it.''

She sighed deeply. ''I should hope so.'' She frowned. ''Why would the Confederates want anything out here anyway? I thought the concern was between North and South.''

He rose and paced. The confines of a cabin in winter always made him restless, like a bobcat in a trap. She knew that in the morning he would go riding again with Wolf's Blood, no matter how cold it was.

''You forget that there is no longer just North and South, Abbie. ''We're surrounded now. There's Cali-

111

fornia, and that state is pro-Union. They'll surely send troops east to help the Union, and the South knows it. Their only hope to stop that is to bottle them off by cutting off their ability to get through the West on their way. Besides that, there's gold out here, and the South needs that gold.''

She felt a chill. "I don't like to think about it. I just pray that Danny is all right—and his family. And I pray that none of it comes here to our peaceful little ranch."

She looked up at him and they were both consumed by the sudden premonition that the war, no matter how much they tried to stay out of it, would somehow come to their doorstep and try to separate them. He walked over to her, bent down and placed his hands on each arm of her rocker. He came closer and kissed her hair, her eyes, her cheeks, her chin, her mouth, suddenly needing her. She returned the kiss hungrily, as tears slipped down her cheeks. He released the kiss and moved his lips over her cheek and to her neck.

"Zeke—" she whimpered.

"Don't say it," he groaned. "Just don't say it, Abbie-girl. I'll not let us be separated again. I can't stand to be apart from you."

"Oh, Zeke, why does there have to be war and fighting everywhere? Why can't we live in peace? I don't want any part of the fighting."

"Hush, Abbie." He covered her mouth again with his own, moaning as he kissed her almost desperately. When his lips left hers she saw the terrible need in his eyes. She rose and set her sewing aside, and he lifted her in his arms and carried her into their small bedroom. He set her on her feet again and removed first the knitted sweater she wore, then her tunic. Neither of them spoke as he drank in her nakedness in the dim light that filtered through the curtains at the doorway of the room. His own earthy provocativeness and rugged power seemed to fill the small room, and again she marveled that her small self could please such a man. He ran his hands over her body, touching nipples that were taut from the cold air, for they were not near the hearth now, and the temperature was bitter outside the log walls.

"You'd best get under the covers," he told her. She could see his dashing, handsome smile in the dim light. "I'll warm you up soon enough."

In spite of the darkness he knew she was blushing, and it excited him as it always did, for in so many ways she was still the little girl he had claimed and married those many years ago. And in spite of his own strength and power, she had a hold over him, this small woman whom he could easily break into little pieces with his bare hands. Yet those big hands held nothing but gentleness for his woman, and she had a way of making him feel weak.

She climbed under the robes, which they preferred to regular blankets, for in winter they were much warmer. In moments her body heat warmed the soft fur of the skins that made their bed. She watched him undress, taking in the hard muscle and commanding physique. In the next moment he moved in beside her under the robes and naked bodies touched in familiar but still exciting moves, for each knew exactly how to please the other now. He moved over her with expert hands and lips, whispering words of love, their lovemaking synchronized to perfection over years of touching and loving and sharing bodies in the ultimate expression of that love. She soon felt the rippling pulsations of intense desire, and her body cried out for him.

He moved on top of her, his lips lingering on her breasts, then her throat, as he moved between her slim thighs. She felt his long hair brush against her bare skin

113

as it hung over his shoulders while he bent over her. In the next moment her Cheyenne warrior was surging into her, taking his pleasure in her and giving her pleasure in return. They moved in perfect rhythm, loving, sharing, giving and taking, each under the other's power, each feeling weak from it. This was her man, and she had chosen well. When she was with Zeke Monroe, she never had to be afraid.

She arched up to him in sweet abandon, whispering his name and grasping his arms tightly, and he drank in the beauty of her small form beneath his body, always amazed that he could invade her this way without hurting her.

"Abbie, my Abbie!" he whispered. He came down close against her, enveloping her in his powerful arms as his life poured into her small body. "Abbie," he groaned again, suddenly feeling a terrible fear of his own and feeling like a small boy who was going to be left all alone. He had been too lonely all his life. This woman was his only refuge from that lonely world, his only link to love and happiness.

She felt the urgency of his embrace and she kissed his chest. "We have this moment, Zeke," she told him softly. "Let's lie here in each other's arms and not think about tomorrow."

She felt him shudder, and he pulled her close against himself as he rolled to his side. He layed his cheek against hers, and she felt a wetness. And she knew this was one of those moments when even Zeke Monroe was afraid. He was a man of fierce pride and courage and strength, a man of vicious vengeance and superb fighting skills. It was not man or the elements he feared. Rather, it was the things he could not see, the intangible, the element of fate that frightened Zeke Monroe. He feared where destiny and his Indian blood might lead him, pulling his loved ones with him. It was that

114

secret side of him that only Abbie had seen and understood—the fear of the lonely little boy that dwelled within the man. And it was that tiny, vulnerable part of him that she loved the most. No one but Abbie knew this hidden part of the man who was called Lone Eagle.

They lay in each other's arms, each drawing strength from the other, each praying to his and her own gods. Soon they were asleep, as the treasured mantle clock ticked softly and the unfinished snow moccasins lay in the rocker. Abigail Monroe would not return to her sewing this night.

Eight

Sweet-smelling smoke wafted into the air, as Zeke held the sacred pipe out to the four directions, offering it in the sacrifice called *Nivstanivoo*. He drew on the smoke, then held the pipe up to *Heammawihio*, God of the Sky, the most powerful, and down to *Ahktunowihio*, God of the Earth. He puffed it again and breathed deeply, raising the pipe again while his eyes were closed.

"Oh, great *Maheo*, our father spirit, bless my first-born son. May his life be long and healthy, and may you fill him with courage and take from him his pain when he offers his flesh at the Sun Dance in this his fifteenth year."

He opened his eyes and handed the pipe to Wolf's Blood, who sat near him. "Offer the pipe in the same way," he told the boy. "The spirits will know your heart is pure and your courage is great. They will help you bear the pain of the Sun Dance sacrifice, for in spite of your white blood, they will know you are a true Cheyenne."

The boy took the pipe reverently, offering it as his father had done. Father and son sat alone on a hillside that overlooked Zeke's ranch and the Appaloosa herds

116

below. Both were painted in their prayer colors, Zeke's face striped in white, Wolf's Blood's in blue. They wore only loincloths that warm spring day of 1862, and their bodies were also painted in prayer colors, as well as bedecked with strands of bone and bead necklaces. Zeke's hair hung long and loose, the eagle feathers he had earned for his own courage tied into one side of it.

This was a special moment, a weekly ritual now between father and son, as Zeke prepared his first-born for the upcoming Sun Dance celebration and sacrifice. It would not be easy to watch his beloved son suffer, yet he would do so with pride and love and would not stop Wolf's Blood from doing that which was in his heart to do. The boy handed the pipe back to his father.

"You are probably the only son I have who will be all Indian in his heart," Zeke told the boy. "You were raised among my people in your early years, taught the warrior ways by your uncle, Swift Arrow, as is the custom. But things are changing, Wolf's Blood. The people are being forced into ever-shrinking territory, and I fear that one day, as we lose the freedom to ride and hunt and join our brothers to the north, we will also lose a part of ourselves and our old ways. It will be up to ones like you to preserve the language and the customs and the religious ceremonies."

Zeke looked into Wolf's Blood's eyes, which shined with worship. "I will not let such things be forgotten, Father. There is something . . . inside of me. Something that cries out to be free . . . to ride and hunt and feel the wind in my face, to open my arms and hold the whole universe, to laugh and sing and sacrifice my flesh to the spirits so I will know that I am one with the whole earth and with the animals. This thing inside of me—it cares nothing for books or for white man ways. It longs only to . . . I don't know . . . only to . . . be. Just to be."

117

Zeke smiled softly. "You don't have to explain to me, son. I know what you're trying to say."

"It is hard, having this white blood in me."

Zeke's eyes saddened. "Yes. It is hard. It was harder for me, for I was forced to grow up among whites who hated me, forced to sit in their schools and wear their clothes, told I was worthless and ignorant. I knew that wasn't true, but I was alone. I hope you never know that kind of loneliness."

"You wish this, but I, too, will know such loneliness, Father. I feel it in my bones—see it in my dreams. The life I choose to live will create the loneliness, for I will one day have to leave this home—and my mother." He swallowed. "And I shall have to leave you, for your place is here with my mother."

Zeke nodded, his eyes full of pain. How he loved this son, already tall and muscular for his age, with a handsome, finely chiseled face framed by shiny black hair that hung straight and long, nearly reaching his waist. His dark eyes already made the young Cheyenne girls steal flirting glances at the makings of a fine husband. To look at him made Zeke think of his own youth and all its tortures. At least Wolf's Blood had grown up away from the cruelty of white rejection, yet now white encroachment would surely bring some of those same problems to his son's doorstep.

"It will be very hard for me to watch you go, Wolf's Blood," he spoke up, his voice tender with emotion. "I love you. And I love being with you. My heart glows with pride in you. But soon you will be fifteen, and you will make your sacrifice. And not many winters after that you will be a man and go your own way, the way of the people. You will take a wife and have your own family."

"I am not sure that I want a wife," the boy mused, taking on an air of manliness. "My uncle, Swift Arrow, says taking a wife can make a man weak. He is a great Dog Soldier. The best Dog Soldiers do not take wives. I cannot be a Dog Soldier because of my white blood, but I can still be a good warrior and prove I am as good as the Dog Soldiers.''

Zeke suppressed a smile. "You can be a good warrior *and* have a wife, Wolf's Blood," he replied. "Swift Arrow speaks as a man full of bitterness. He lost his first wife to the white man's disease and his second wife to the soldiers' guns. That is why he does not marry again. He is full of hatred. He stays in the North with the Sioux, where the Indians still ride with more freedom, still hunt where they choose and do as they please. But now the soldiers ride hard against those in the North also. It will be bad for them.''

The last words were spoken sadly and quietly as Zeke took out his knife and began sharpening the huge blade against a rock that he held in his other hand.

"There is a new kind of war coming, son," he went on, scraping the blade against the rock almost angrily. "You will have to understand this kind of war if you want to survive. It won't be a war fought with guns and lances. It is a white man's kind of war—one fought with power and riches, laws and the pen. And it's part of the reason your mother thinks book learning is important. In that respect, she is right.''

The boy frowned. "I do not understand. How can a man fight without weapons?''

Zeke sighed, seemingly lost in thought. "There are all kinds of weapons, Wolf's Blood, and sometimes there are ways to get what you want without breaking the white man's law and getting into trouble. And there are some men who will look at you and smile and shake your hand, but who can do you more damage than the fiercest warrior you might face in physical battle.''

Wolf's Blood reached over and petted his wolf, who

119

lay lazily on its belly beside its master. He ran his fingers through the animal's thick fur. Zeke stopped sharpening the knife and eyed the boy and wolf for a moment. The two of them fit together well, both wild, a part of the earth and things that are untamed. Wolf's Blood met his father's eyes then, seeing pain there.

"There is something you wish to tell me, Father," he said. "It is about this other kind of war."

Zeke nodded. "I want you to understand your enemies, Wolf's Blood. Know who they are and be ready for them. Your worst enemies will be men like Winston Garvey, scheming, selfish, power-hungry animals. They'll smile at you and shake your hand, but on the inside they are considering just how they can kill you and get you out of their way. They are men who will stop at nothing to get what they want, and they use white men's laws and courts to back them. They are educated and clever, and you must always be prepared to outwit them."

"Winston Garvey is the man who kept my aunt, Yellow Moon, as a slave? The one who is the father of her half-breed son?"

Zeke nodded. "You are the only child old enough to remember what happened to the child after Yellow Moon was killed by soldiers. The baby was badly crippled, his foot and leg twisted, an affliction the white man calls clubfoot. Abbie, who loves everything that walks, wanted to take him, but she already had four children of her own, and your brother Jeremy was only a baby himself at the time. I thought the burden of a crippled baby would be too much for Abbie. Besides that, the child needed help, the kind we couldn't give him. We took him to missionaries north of Fort Laramie. Remember that?"

"*Ai*. The woman's name was Bonnie."

Zeke returned to sharpening his knife. "Yes. Bonnie

Lewis. Her husband, Rodney, is a preacher up there, and her father, who is also there, is a doctor—a good one. A year before that I had saved Bonnie's life when I rescued her from a band of outlaws. We became good friends. That was down near Santa Fe. She had told me then that if there was ever anything she or her father could do for me, that I should tell them. So Abbie and I took Yellow Moon's crippled boy to Bonnie.'' He smiled softly. ''Bonnie is a good woman. Soon as she set eyes on that poor crippled baby, she wanted to take him and see if her father or one of the fine doctors they knew back east could help him. Abbie and I agreed. Bonnie's father knew all the right people who could help the boy. So we left him there. As the months went by, Bonnie grew to love him more and more, until finally she wrote and asked us if she and her husband could legally adopt him. Bonnie can't have children of her own—at least it appears that way. She's been married several years now and still hasn't conceived. That makes the boy even more special to her. She's a kind, loving woman, and Abbie and I decided it was best for the boy to remain with Bonnie and her husband.''

He set down the knife and leaned forward, resting his elbows on his knees.

''I'm telling you these things, son, for a reason. You knew we left the boy with Bonnie, but we never told you we received letters after that regarding the boy's progress, operations he has had to help correct his crippled foot, or the fact that Bonnie adopted him. We haven't said much about it because for one thing we want the other children to forget about their half-breed cousin. We don't speak of him, and it's best they forget him and know nothing about where he is. But you remember enough that you should know the rest so that you are prepared.''

The boy frowned. ''I do not understand. Prepared

for what?''

"Prepared for the fact that the boy's real father, the one who kept Yellow Moon as a slave and fathered the child, might one day discover the boy's identity. If he does, he will have the child murdered. The last thing Winston Garvey wants is for anyone to know he slept with Indian women or worse than that, fathered a half-breed son. You know enough that it's dangerous for you not to know it all. If you know the whole story, you won't be as likely to spill something that you shouldn't. You and I and Abbie are the only ones who know of the boy's whereabouts. Bonnie and Rodney and Bonnie's father know the story behind the boy and will never reveal his origins to anyone west of the Mississippi. My white brother, Danny, also knows, because he helped us find Bonnie when we first took the crippled boy to her. But Danny knows he must never tell anyone. Even his wife knows nothing about it.''

Wolf's Blood sighed and shook his head. "You are confusing me, Father. Why should Winston Garvey care that he had a half-breed son? Many half-breeds are born—to the trappers and mountain men. A man should want his son.''

Zeke thought for one painful moment about his own white father, but quickly pushed the thought away.

"Of course a man should want his son," he told the boy. "But not men like Winston Garvey. If Garvey ever finds the boy, he'll murder him. I'm sure of it, because I'm sure of the kind of man Garvey is. I found that out when I rescued Yellow Moon from him in the first place. He lived down in Santa Fe then. I've seen men like that before, Wolf's Blood. He's just like the kind of men who chased the Cherokees out of Georgia, rooting the Indians out of their rightful homes and sending them on a long walk of tears and death to Oklahoma. It was one of the most pitiful things I have ever witnessed, hundreds and hundreds dying along the way, all because the whites decided they wanted the Cherokee land. That's the kind of man Garvey is. He hates Indians. He made that obvious when I went after Yellow Moon. He tortured Yellow Moon and kept her purely for sexual pleasures. The only way I got her out of there was to threaten to expose his sexual involvement with Indian women as well as the fact that I knew he consorted with a well-known prostitute. Garvey takes pride in his fine citizen reputation. He didn't want that ruined. Besides that, I threatened to return to his ranch with all the Indians necessary to wipe the man out, and that I personally would take Garvey's scalp. He apparently believed me. He handed Yellow Moon over to me. I couldn't take her through violence because the man had a virtual army protecting his ranch. So I used white man's tactics—threatening to expose his fine standing as a righteous, God-fearing ex-senator. Few people know what the man is really capable of doing, or that he is scheming at this very moment to own as much of this territory as he can get his hands on, and to rid Colorado Territory of most of its Indians—all of them if he can do it. The last thing he wants is for anyone to know he has a half-breed son. Hatred and resentment toward the Indians are being nurtured by schemes of men like Garvey, and the man has a son who is going to be worse than the father. That is what I mean about understanding the trickery of the white man, Wolf's Blood—about being prepared for men like Winston Garvey and his son, Charles. And because of the danger to the life of Yellow Moon's half-breed son, you must be aware of all the details. The boy Yellow Moon gave birth to was fathered by Winston Garvey. And because Yellow Moon was first the wife of my brother, Red Eagle, she is considered a sister-in-law. After I rescued her from Garvey, your uncle, Swift Arrow, took her for his wife, because Red Eagle was dead. It is often the custom for a Cheyenne man to take in a dead brother's wife. Then Yellow Moon gave birth to Garvey's son, and even though he was not fathered by Red Eagle or Swift Arrow, we consider him your cousin, because he was born to Yellow Moon and she was a part of the family. Now the boy lives with the missionaries, Bonnie and Rodney Lewis. His name is Joshua, and he's a cripple. He's eight years old now."

Wolf's Blood picked up a stick and poked at the fire. "I think I understand, Father. But how would Winston Garvey know about the child? Joshua was not born until many months after you rescued Yellow Moon, and he was born far to the north, in Sioux country, after Yellow Moon went there to live with my uncle, Swift Arrow."

Zeke picked up his knife and turned it in his hand. He knew he must explain the connection between Winston Garvey and Anna Gale, and how and why Anna Gale knew of the existence of Garvey's half-Indian son. But to tell Wolf's Blood that much would mean telling him that Zeke himself had slept with the notorious prostitute. How could he make a fifteen-year-old boy understand why he had done so? The thought of his infidelity still brought pain to his own heart, and now he must try to explain it to his son. He rose and walked to the edge of the hill, looking down at the little cabin far below and watching the younger children playing tag. It was such a peaceful picture. How he loved his family, and the love he had found through them.

"It's possible Garvey would find out," he answered his son quietly. "Because one other woman knows the boy exists—not his name or where he is, only that he exists."

Wolf's Blood looked up at his father. "Who is the woman?" he asked.

Zeke sighed. "Do you remember when we were in Denver, son, when we took your mother there because she needed to see a doctor badly?"

The boy's eyes turned colder. "How could I forget Denver?" he hissed. "I hate Denver! The people there were cruel to us! That ugly white boy came down the street and called me dirty names! I jumped on him and beat him up good, but then a white man pulled me off and beat me and threw me in the street, where that horse rode over me! And when you tried to help me those men all jumped on you from behind and hurt you and took you to their jail. They were bad men, and that boy was evil! I saw the evil in his eyes."

Zeke turned around and faced his son. "That white boy was Charles Garvey, Winston Garvey's son."

Wolf's Blood's eyebrows arched in surprise. "He was? Why did you not tell me this before?"

Zeke looked down at his knife. "Because I didn't know how to explain it all to you, Wolf's Blood." His voice was strained and distant. He walked back to the small fire and knelt down across from his son. "When we went to Denver four years ago, I had no idea that Winston Garvey had shifted his interests to Colorado Territory. I thought he was still in Santa Fe. At the time you got in that fight with his son in the street, Garvey himself was away in the East, which was a lucky thing for us. If he had known I was in town, he'd have had me hung. He knows I can expose a lot of things about him, one of which is that he is very closely connected with the prostitute called Anna Gale."

Their eyes held, and he saw the curiosity in Wolf's Blood's innocent gaze. "Anna Gale is the woman who helped to get you out of jail," he mused. "And she got a doctor for me and gave me and my mother shelter."

"That's right," Zeke replied. "You never questioned why Anna Gale helped us, son. And I never offered a reason. But I had known her before. When I was searching for Yellow Moon, I had traced her to Anna's place back when Anna was still in Santa Fe. It was Anna who told me where I could find Yellow Moon, but she wanted a price for the information. I couldn't beat it out of her because I was in a civilized town and she was well guarded. I had to think about Abbie and my family and getting back home to them. I couldn't risk a noose around my neck or being labeled as a wanted man, which is what would have happened if I had made trouble in Santa Fe. I was a half-breed. I never would have got out of that town." He gripped his knife tightly, frustrated by the times when he could not use it to get what he wanted because of the white man's laws and trickery. "Anna Gale wanted only one thing from me, son. So I gave it to her."

He met the boy's eyes again, and the boy's heart began to race a little faster as it suddenly came to him what his father was telling him. "You . . . slept with her?"

Zeke saw the desperate disappointment in the boy's eyes. "It isn't what you think, Wolf's Blood. I'm only telling you all of this so that you understand the connection—between Winston Garvey and Anna Gale, and me."

The boy blinked back tears. "But . . . you love my mother!"

"Of course I love your mother! I'd cut out my eyes for your mother! But I'm trying to explain to you about the other kind of war, Wolf's Blood! The *white* man's war!"

The boy shook his head. "Women like that—they are filth!"

Zeke threw down the knife. "Damn it, Wolf's Blood, I'm trying to explain something to you!" Their eyes locked for a moment in both love and anger. Then

126

Wolf's Blood looked down at the flames.

"Tell me what I should know, Father," he said quietly, his voice dejected. Zeke's heart ached with a longing to have the boy understand.

"I was desperate by then to find Yellow Moon, son. I had rescued Bonnie and got her back to safety, but I'd been shot in the process and my wound still wasn't healed. I was tired and I was lonely for Abbie and my family. I had already come close to losing my life more than once in my search for Yellow Moon and had killed a lot of men to get that far. I was close, Wolf's Blood! So close! All I had to do was sleep with Anna Gale to get my information and I could find Yellow Moon and go home. There are many things about men and women you don't understand yet, but some day you will discover that there can be sex without love. There is no beauty in it, no pleasure, no satisfaction. I did nothing more than provide stud service to a scheming whore. But it was my only weapon at the time. I played the white man's game to find out what I needed to know. Anna Gale used me, but I also used her. And there wasn't a moment when your mother was not on my mind. What I did tore at my soul, but I had to find Yellow Moon, and I could only pray your mother would understand that, because I knew I could not and would not hide it from her."

"She . . . knows?"

"Of course she knows! And she knows how it pained me to be untrue to her, because I made myself suffer. I made my own atonement, punished myself physically so that she would understand, so that I could offer some sign to her that I did not sleep with Anna Gale for the pleasure of it. When I left Anna's place to go after Yellow Moon, I made a sacrifice. I turned to the Indian ways and chose to make myself suffer physically so that the pain on the inside would not be so great." He held

127

up his left hand; most of the little finger was missing. "I did this."

Wolf's Blood's eyes widened. "You . . . you said that was an accident!"

"It was no accident, son. I've never known quite how to tell you. But now maybe you're old enough to understand, and it's our secret now. Yours and mine and your mother's. It took more courage than I've ever needed to do this, Wolf's Blood. But I knew it was necessary. I found a quiet place alone and I cut off my finger. And then I wept, Wolf's Blood. I wept for a long time—and prayed to the spirits that Abbie would understand and forgive, for such things are hard for a white woman to understand. And I hope you, too, will understand. This is my sign, Wolf's Blood." He held the finger closer. "This is my atonement—proof of how much I love your mother."

Wolf's Blood studied his father's eyes. He knew the true heart of this man he worshipped and admired, and he knew how strong was the love between Zeke and Abigail Monroe. Of that love he had no doubt, nor did he now doubt his father's reasons for sleeping with Anna Gale. He grasped Zeke's hand.

"If my mother could understand, then I, too, understand," he told Zeke. "This Anna Gale. She is the link, then, between you and Winston Garvey, a way he might find out about Joshua?"

Zeke nodded and squeezed the boy's hand lovingly, then rose, walking to his horse and retrieving a small pipe from his parfleche. He began stuffing it with tobacco. "Anna knew Garvey years before, back in Washington," he explained. "Garvey would find clients for her, and she managed to get information from them that Garvey could sometimes use later against them." He lit his pipe. "Then Garvey set her up in business in Santa Fe during the Mexican War, where

128

he planned to come out himself after he retired and get himself set up—buy up land, establish banks, and in general increase his wealth tenfold by getting out here before the whites began surging west to settle. Garvey more or less owned Anna for years. She hated the man, but she was at his beck and call. When gold was discovered in Denver, they both headed north to reap the benefits from the miners and new settlers. That's how Anna ended up in Denver at the same time we were there. And then when she saw us in trouble she decided to help us." He puffed on the pipe quietly for a moment. "I guess in spite of what she was, she had developed fond feelings for me after the night I spent with her. I don't know why, for she was a woman who took in men and cast them out like you cast away nutshells after eating the meat, but she considered me special, and for some reason she had fond memories of me. So she helped us when you got hurt and I got thrown in jail."

He puffed on the pipe again and Wolf's Blood watched him. "Did that woman love you?" he asked curiously.

Zeke thought for a long moment. Anna Gale was exceedingly beautiful, a wasted woman who might have turned out differently if not for her childhood. "Perhaps," he replied. He puffed the pipe again and turned to face the boy. "At any rate I wanted to do something for Anna for helping us out of a bad predicament. She'd been kind to Abbie at a time when Abbie was helpless and alone in a strange city, her husband in jail and her son badly wounded and lying in the street. If not for Anna, God only knows what might have happened to Abbie that day, or to you. So I gave Anna a weapon to use against Winston Garvey, because she hated the man, and I hated him, too. After seeing his son again and hearing from Anna how demented the boy was, I knew the last thing Winston Garvey would want would be for his own son to discover he had a half-brother who was part Indian. So I gave Anna a weapon to use against Garvey and free her of her indebtedness to the man. I only told her enough to threaten Garvey. I told her that he had a half-breed son. I told her nothing more, and since Garvey has no idea I was in Denver and that the information could have come from me, it isn't likely he would ever make the connection. But there is always the possibility, which is why you and I and your mother must never reveal we know anything about a half-breed boy born to Yellow Moon. Yellow Moon is dead, and as far as we are concerned, never had the child. If anyone should ever ask about it, you know nothing of it. Understood?"

Wolf's Blood nodded and rose. "I understand, Father. I understand many things now. I am glad you told me of this so that I will never deceive my cousin, Joshua. And more than that, I understand better about men like Winston Garvey."

Zeke took the pipe from his mouth and walked closer to the boy. "Always remember the warnings I give you this day. Men like Winston Garvey don't know the meaning of love. They have no heart. They marry for power and money, and their children are nothing more than something to be nurtured in the ways of evil so that they can carry on the father's empire. The Winston Garveys of this world think they are better than other people, destined to rule and own; and if he thinks someone like myself is in the way of his climb to glory, he'll try to cut me—or you—down. He uses people for his pleasure and then disposes of them. His kind will cry out publicly against the Indian and then turn around and sleep with slave squaws. He pretends to be pure and pious, but he is filth on the inside. Such men know nothing about being one with God and the

130

elements—about the joys of being free, of hunting alone, watching an eagle, talking to the animals, sleeping close to the earth with the smell of grass and wildflowers in your nostrils. Such things are riches to us. But they are nothing to men like Garvey. He hungers only for wealth and power. And I predict right now that his son, Charles, will be worse than the father. Remember that—and remember his name."

Wolf's Blood nodded. "I will remember all these things, Father. I hate such men. I remember that day in Denver. It burns in my stomach! I hate such men the way my uncle, Swift Arrow, hates them. And if they ever come and try to take me away to their world, I will kill them! And if those I do not kill still want me, they will have to catch me first. Just let them try to catch Wolf's Blood!" He smiled haughtily, even though his eyes were watery. "They will never catch me. And I will never go to that world, Father. Do not ever make me go there!"

Zeke reached out and put a hand on the boy's shoulder. "I'll never make you go there, son. You aren't made for those places. You're made for freedom, and because you are the way you are, your heart is pure and your soul will be free, and the wind will always be at your back." He bent down and picked up the infamous knife, holding it out to the boy. "Grab hold, son, and get a feel of the balance."

Their eyes held in a new understanding. Wolf's Blood slowly reached out and grasped the buffalo jawbone handle of his father's notorious weapon.

"I want you to get your mind off that other world, son," Zeke told him. "This is your time—the year you have chosen through your own vision to become a man and suffer the Sun Dance ritual. Because of what you know about your enemies, you are even stronger now—wiser. It is good that you know these things so

131

that when the celebration comes, your eyes will be open to good and evil. This is important. Evil lurks in all of our hearts, Wolf's Blood. It is up to each man to decide which side shall win his soul—the good or the evil. The evil side is the easy way. To truly be strong, to truly be a man, means standing up for what is right, against all odds. It means fighting a power worse than all the evil that surrounds us. It means fighting the evil inside ourselves and being strong from within. It is my own inner strength that has pulled me through many bad experiences and saved me in all the times that I came close to losing my life in battle. And when a man finds his own inner power and strength, then he chooses a weapon as a warrior, a weapon that represents his strength, an extension of a man's power. For me this weapon is the knife. Now you yourself have been practicing with it. I have watched you. In so many ways you are like me. Perhaps you also will choose the knife as the extension of your power.''

The boy looked at his father again. ''I want to learn more,'' he said, his eyes suddenly strangely cold. ''I want to be as good as you with the knife. I am good with a lance, but a man cannot easily carry a lance every place he goes. A knife can be taken wherever I go.''

Zeke nodded. ''Exactly.'' He closed his eyes and breathed deeply, drinking in the fresh air of a land that was still relatively virgin. Yet he knew that even on this very spot where he stood, whites would one day stand and claim the land for themselves. Where would he be then? Where would Wolf's Blood be? It was too painful to contemplate. He could only hope such a thing was a long time in the future. Perhaps his son would be an old man by then. Yet he knew it was a foolish hope.

''Come, Wolf's Blood. We'll do some knife throwing,'' he spoke up. ''Get a feel of the knife, son. Always remember that whenever you sharpen your blade, it changes the balance of the knife. Always get a feel of it again after you've sharpened it."

The boy nodded, gripping the knife eagerly. Smoke looked up at them from his comfortable position, not bothering to get to his feet. He was too comfortable, lying stretched out in the soft grass with the Colorado sun warming his back. Let the two men practice with the knife. That was man's perogative. Today was a good day for an animal to stretch out and sleep.

Somewhere a bird sang, and Zeke's and Wolf's Blood's horses stood nearby nibbling on tall grass. It was one of those rare moments that Zeke suddenly drank in with his eyes, a moment he realized would for some reason hang in his mind forever, a sweet morning when the air made him drunk, and his nostrils were full of the smell of grass and the sun heated his skin—a moment when for a brief time it seemed his life was standing still, and he and the animals nearby, the grass and the sun and the air and his son were all one entity. A moment when the spirits walked with them.

Nine

It was called the Homestead Act, and Congress could not have enacted a more devastating bill for the Indian. The act officially opened the West to thousands of hungry settlers, offering land tracts of 160 acres to anyone over twenty-one who would live on the land for five years and farm it, or for $1.25 per acre outright. The Indians were neither warned nor even consulted in the matter, even though thousands of them already occupied the land and survived on its natural offerings. Suddenly, with no aid or advice, no explanations of any kind, the Indians found themselves inundated by thousands of new settlers who diminished hunting territory and who considered picking off Indians at random just one of the "necessary" means of settling "their" land, just as one would shoot a nest of foxes or skunks they might find when clearing their property.

Indian reaction was to be expected. They were frightened, starving, dying of white man's disease. They were desperate, and desperate men do desperate things. To the Indians' logical thinking, the whites did not belong there. It was as simple as that. There was only one way to make them go back home, and that was to show Indian strength and power, to literally "scare" the whites into getting out. Of all Indians, the Sioux were the most successful at accomplishing their objective—raiding, raping, burning, taking captives, and in general, sending most new settlers fleeing back to where they came from. The worst raids were in Minnesota, but many spread to the Dakotas and into Nebraska.

A wind rushed down from the Black Hills, a hot summer wind that blew sand against the bare back of Swift Arrow. He was sure he could hear the strange moaning again that he often heard in the wind: the land crying out; his people crying out. Yes. The land and the people and the animals were all weeping. The white people who lived in the little house below the hill where he sat would also weep—before they died. He watched with a hardened heart as Sioux and some Northern Cheyenne rode hard toward one of the hundreds of new soddies that had been built on the Dakota plains. These people had to be stopped. He did not always like hurting them. But he, too, had been hurt. He had seen his own people shot down like animals, his women raped, his villages ravaged—all in the name of the white man's progress and settlement. There had been no reason for any of it. It was criminal and illegal, and the white man seemed to listen to none of the Indians' pleas. This was the only thing the white man understood. Brutality. Violence. If that was what the white man wanted, that was what he would get.

Swift Arrow was a handsome man, but a lonely man. His lips were pressed hard together in bitterness, his once-warm brown eyes now glazed with hatred. The screaming below only made him smile. His deep brown skin was painted vividly for war, and in his hair he wore many coup feathers and other grand decorations. He was an honored Dog Soldier of the Cheyenne. Many women wanted him, but he wanted none of them. There had been only one woman he'd wanted since his first wife had died of the white man's disease. But that woman could never be his, for she came from the world that he hated.

He urged his painted pony into motion and headed toward the already burning settlement. Indians circled below, waiting for the settlers inside to come out of their smoke-filled soddy. Flaming arrows had been carefully aimed and shot through the windows, which had no glass or even any boards to cover them, for the soddy had been freshly constructed. By the time Swift Arrow reached the bottom of the hill, several Sioux were riding off with the settlers' livestock, and a woman and little girl came running out of the soddy, screaming, followed by a man with a rifle. In the next moment the man was dead, an arrow in his chest.

The woman fell to the ground and covered her little girl. Swift Arrow was very close by then. One of the other braves rode up to the woman and raised his lance, but Swift Arrow had noticed her dark hair, and the red glint to it in the afternoon sun. In that brief moment it reminded him of another white woman's hair.

"Stop!" he commanded, using the Sioux tongue when he did so. The Sioux warrior with the lance looked at him in surprise.

"Why do you tell me to stop? They must all die!"

"Wait!" Swift Arrow again commanded. He motioned for the man to see what else he could find to steal, especially any food. The people were starving to death. Little children cried with stomach pains.

The Sioux warrior scowled and rode off, and Swift Arrow looked down at the weeping, shivering white woman. "Get up," he told her quietly.

She slowly raised her head, shocked by the fact that this savage Indian standing before her had spoken to her in English. They stared at one another for a moment, and he was struck by how much she looked like another woman—like Abbie. How many years had it been since he had seen the wife of his half-brother? It was easier living here in the north, where he did not see her often, for Abbie was too easy to love, even for a Cheyenne warrior. He studied the white woman before him haughtily. He could rape her. He could kill her and scalp her. He could take her back and make a slave of her and the little girl, or use them as ransom to get supplies from other whites. There were many options. "I told you to get up!" he repeated.

She rose, pulling her little girl close to her and staring at him with wide, terrified eyes.

"I speak your tongue," he told her. "My mother was Cheyenne. But once, before she married my Cheyenne father, she was the woman of a white man. She learned the language. And so I learned it also." His eyes moved over her. Then he reached out and lightly touched her cheek. She closed her eyes and shivered, sure that he would do something horrible and degrading. But he only touched her gently. "Why is it that you whites cannot just leave us alone?" he asked, surprising her with the strange question. "Why do you make us hurt you?"

She opened her eyes and tried to speak, but the words would not come. Her throat was tight and dry with fear. Another brave galloped up to them.

"We go now!" he told Swift Arrow in the Sioux tongue. "We must kill the woman or take her captive. Which shall it be?"

"She is mine!" Swift Arrow stated flatly. "All of you can leave! I will stay and take my pleasure with her— and with the girl. Then I will come."

The other warrior smiled. "As you wish, Swift Arrow. We go now." The man rode off and the others followed, yipping and yelling and shooting off rifles. They had taken many horses and had found food. It had been a good raid. Swift Arrow watched until they disappeared over a hill. Then he turned dark eyes back to the woman, who still stared at him. Again he was struck by how much she reminded him of Abbie.

"I told them I was going to stay here and rape you," he told her matter-of-factly. He saw more color drain from her face, and her lower lip trembled. Then to her utter astonishment he smiled, not evilly but warmly. "But I lied," he added. "I will bring you no harm. The best I can do is take you to the nearest settlement and let you off. You can go there for safety. But I cannot guarantee what will happen to that settlement after that, or that you will not be attacked again. You would be wise to go back where you came from, white woman. This is a bad place to be. A very bad place."

He reached down and grasped the little girl, lifting her and plopping her onto his mount. Then he turned to help the woman up.

"Why?" she asked, stepping back a little. "Why would you help me?"

His eyes moved over her again. "Because you remind me of someone. Another white woman. She loves the Indians. Understands them. She is gentle and full of goodness. She reminds me that there are some whites who are good, some who can be trusted. But their numbers are few."

He reached out for her again and she stepped back once more. "My man. I can't . . . leave him lying there."

"You have no choice. When I get you to safety you can send men back to bury his body. We must go. If the warriors come back and catch me helping you bury your man, they will not only kill you and your child, but they will kill me also, for being weak. Even I am

138

ashamed of my weakness. But I cannot harm you. The spirits tell me it would be bad for my soul. Your God is with you this day."

She began to tremble, and tears spilled out of her eyes. She suddenly covered her face and broke into frantic sobbing. In the next moment she felt strong hands grasping her about the waist and she was being hoisted to his horse. Then he jumped up behind her and the little girl, reaching around her to grasp the reins of his mount. Her hair brushed his face and smelled sweet.

"Go ahead and weep, white woman," he told her. "There will be much weeping in the years to come. Our women weep also. They weep over their little dying children who are starving because the braves can no longer find game, dying also of white man's diseases. They weep because they are raped and humiliated by the white man, and because their own men are shot down like dogs. They have many reasons to weep. Once we lived in peace, happy to be just as we were. But the white man will not let us have peace any longer."

She wiped at her eyes and held her little girl close, praying this savage man would not change his mind about helping her. "My God . . . will bless you . . . for helping me," she whimpered, hoping the words would keep him calm. He only laughed lightly.

"I do not need the blessings of your God. I have suffered too much to ever think I can be happy again." He got his mount into motion and smiled at the realization that what she had said was very much like something Abbie would say. "I do not help you out of the goodness of my heart, white woman. If you did not look so much like another, you would probably be dead now."

If there were such a thing as hell on earth, Danny Monroe had found it. It was as though the devil had come to this place called Shiloh and was laughing, for as Danny lay in agonizing pain and surely dying, surrounded by the groans of Confederates and Federals alike, he could see the outline of the little Methodist Church against the sky whenever the lightning flashed. Surely God had deserted Shiloh this night.

He tried again to crawl, but in his confused state he didn't even know which way to go, and so much blood had left his body that he had no strength. The torture of the pain in his side and the terrible thirst that always follows a gunshot wound was only enhanced by the terrible screams and groans of the men around him. The Federal stronghold, called the Hornet's Nest, had been taken: but Danny wondered if it had been worth the price in human bodies that had been paid. The Federals were still holding out farther back, and Danny lay with the hundreds of other wounded, Federal and Confederate alike, in "no man's land," a vast area between the two factions that the remaining fighting soldiers would not enter. No help had been sent for the wounded of either side, and to add to the misery of the wounded, a cold spring drizzle started at nightfall, turning to a harder rain mixed with sleet as a cold wind from the north whipped the storm into a more brutal attack on the wounded.

They lay there helpless, the cold rain soaking their clothes at a time when they should have been kept warm because of shock. All through the night screams for help tortured Danny's ears, made worse by the sounds of grunting hogs that began licking at the field of blood and feasting on some of the dead bodies. When lightning flashed, Danny could see bodies everywhere, some heaped one upon the other, blue and gray uniforms lying side by side. Some men sobbed. Most only moaned, unable to find the strength for anything more. There would be no help. This place called Shiloh would go down in history as one of the bloodiest battles of this brutal war, and Danny wondered how he had let himself get involved.

He closed his eyes, trying to do something Zeke had once told him about, trying to find his inner soul, a secret, peaceful place inside of man to which he could turn whenever his outside world was filled with pain and heartache. He suddenly wished he had the special spirituality that Indians seemed to have, that feeling of "oneness" with the universe. He could not find that "inner self" Zeke had tried to explain to him, and his only result was a siege of terrible convulsions that brought screams from his lips until his body finally stopped jumping and shaking and he could lie still again.

How he wished he could see Emily and Jennifer! How would poor fragile Emily survive without him? He was all she had now. And his father! What about his father? What if he and Lance both died in this bloody war and never returned to the farm? There would be no sons left but Zeke, and Zeke would never go back. Hugh Monroe would die a shriveled, lonely old man. "Pa," Danny moaned, wishing there were some way he could just crawl home. This horrible battleground near Pittsburg Landing was only a few miles from the old farm. So close and yet so far! If only Hugh Monroe knew his son lay wounded and freezing just miles away. If only he knew, he could come when this battle was over and take his son home. But there was no way for him to know, and Danny Monroe resigned himself to believing he would never see his father again, or Emily and Jennifer, Lance and Zeke.

He suddenly thought of Fort Laramie and the rolling hills of eastern Wyoming. He tried to envision the warmth of the Western sun, pretending it was shining down on him now. Why had he ever left that place? He missed some of the Indian friends he had made, and he thought about Swift Arrow, Zeke's full-blood brother who rode with the Sioux. He actually smiled at the thought, for in spite of Swift Arrow's haughty hatred of the white man, he was a likable man, mostly because he was an honorable, proud man. Swift Arrow could be fierce and menacing one moment, and joking and teasing the next, with that special kind of humor the Indians had that came out in wry statements of blatant truth that could sometimes make a white man feel foolish. Swift Arrow had a way of tripping up a man's statements and turning the words around. Then he would look at the man with that teasing twinkle in his dark eyes, and the man would realize it was only a joke. Yet Swift Arrow was most certainly not a man to be taken lightly. He had lost two wives, one to white man's disease and one at the battle at Blue Water Creek, a senseless soldier raid on peaceful Indians. Swift Arrow's heart was hard as a rock and his goal in life set—to ride with the Sioux and keep the white man out of the Sacred Black Hills, no matter what the cost.

Suddenly Danny wished he were riding against the Indians. Anything would be better than this brutal battleground with the sounds and smell of death all around him. He forced back an urge to openly sob. General Johnston was dead. He had been a grand leader and had died valiantly. Danny had respected and admired him. He would miss the man. There were many others he would miss. But that didn't matter, for soon he himself would die. Lightning flashed again, and he saw that a few others had managed to crawl together for warmth. But what Danny wanted more than warmth was water. He opened his mouth so that some of the rain would fall into it, but it wasn't nearly enough to quench the excruciating, burning thirst he had. He was certain there was a pond not far away. He remembered it being there earlier when first he fell. If only he could get to the pond!

He turned onto his belly and tried crawling again, his overwhelming need for water giving him incentive to try harder. Lightning flashed again and he could see the little body of water, not so far away it seemed. But his progress was slow and painful, and what should have been a three-minute walk turned into an hour's crawl. He finally reached the edge and doused his face in the water, then put some to his lips.

"Oh, God, God help me!" he cried out as he spit the water back out and began to vomit. The water was undrinkable, for hours earlier the pond had turned pure red from blood. Many others had crawled there to drink and bathe their wounds. He did not know it then, but the place would be named Bloody Pond, in memory of that night of hell.

Everywhere the rain fell, cutting washouts in the softened earth. Each time a washout filled with the flow of rain water, it quickly turned red, for everywhere the ground was saturated with the blood of the wounded.

Danny tried to crawl away from the pond to find some kind of shelter, but his hand sank into the muddy, bloody bank, and he could go no further. He gasped and let his face drop against the mud, his tears mixing with the rain and slime. He thought again of Zeke, wondering what he would do in such a situation, knowing Zeke, too, had been wounded many times. Where was that special power men like Zeke drew on to survive?

"Zeke," he muttered.

"Ho-shuh," he seemed to hear a voice telling him. "Be still, my brother. Be confident."

Zeke moaned in his sleep, and Abbie was stirred awake, her subconscious mind sensing her husband's pain. She opened her eyes and sat up, reaching out to him. His body was soaked with sweat and he groaned again.

"Zeke?"

"Help me!" he whispered.

Abbie quickly got up, alarmed at the apparently painful nightmare he was having. Nightmares were common to her husband, whose past was filled with abuse and violence. Abbie wrapped herself in a home-made flannel robe, then climbed back onto the bed of robes beside Zeke as he groaned again and tossed.

"Zeke?" she said louder, pushing on his shoulder gently.

"No!" he shouted, suddenly sitting up. Abbie jumped back, and he sat there a moment just staring at her. In the dim light of the fire in the outer room his dark eyes looked wild and menacing. She was almost afraid of him, not sure if he was truly awake.

"Zeke, it's all right. You were dreaming."

His breathing was heavy, and he wiped at the sweat on his brow with a shaking hand. He said nothing as he suddenly turned and stood up, walking to the window and throwing open the wooden shutters, oblivious to the chilly night air on his naked and sweating body.

"Zeke, you'll be sick. Please close the shutters."

He stood there breathing deeply, his head back, his hands clinging to the shutters. "Something is wrong," he said in a choked voice. "Check on the children."

"Zeke, the house is quiet. They're all asleep."

"Check on them!" he barked.

She sighed and left the room, returning moments later to walk up close to him. "They're all fine," she told him. She folded her arms and rubbed at them. "Please close the shutters, Zeke."

He sighed and nodded, bolting the shutters closed again and putting an arm around her shoulders, leading her out to the fireplace. He picked up his deerskin leggings from a chair on the way out and began pulling them on while Abbie poked at the coals in the large stone fireplace. The flames flickered higher. She put another log on and hung a pot of leftover coffee over the hearth.

"What is it?" she asked him. She turned and met his eyes, alarmed at the pain and terror there. Zeke Monroe was a man of vision. He had sensed things before, especially in his sleep.

"Someone . . . is hurt," he told her. He began to pace. "Someone needs me . . . and I don't know who it is. Maybe . . . maybe soldiers have raided Black Elk's camp."

"Then you'll have to ride out tomorrow and see."

He ran a hand through his long hair and shook it out. "Maybe it isn't Black Elk. Maybe Swift Arrow has been raiding with the Sioux. They say the Sioux have been getting stirred up again lately, and you know Swift Arrow. He'll be right in the thick of it." He waved his hand. "I wish to hell he'd come back down here to live." He turned to face her, remembering why Swift Arrow stayed in the North. In that first year he had brought Abbie to the Cheyenne and to his brothers, Swift Arrow, nearly the same age as Abbie, had found himself falling in love with his half-brother's white woman. Zeke did not blame his brother. Abigail was easy to love.

Abbie blushed lightly under Zeke's eyes, herself suspecting Swift Arrow's feelings but never speaking of them. Zeke ran his eyes over the soft curves of his wife's body, made more enticing beneath the fluffy softness of her flannel robe. He wanted to touch her breasts, to run his hands over the roundness of her hips, suddenly feeling as though that privilege might be taken from him. This woman must never be touched by anyone but Zeke Monroe, who had been first to claim her, the man

145

who had stolen her virginity when she was not yet even his wife the white man's way. No other man had ever laid hands on her.

He came closer, and she read his thoughts. He embraced her, and she rested her head against the broad, dark chest, the familiar wonderful scent of him bringing her comfort, his strong, loving embrace always erasing her fears. He kissed her hair. "Perhaps it's Danny," he said quietly. "We keep hearing about how terrible the Civil War is." He closed his eyes. "God, I hope it isn't Danny." He squeezed her tightly. "Damn, I hate not knowing, Abbie! I feel like there's something I should be doing, but I don't know what it is."

"Unless you get word from someone, Zeke, there's nothing you can do. Perhaps it was just something from the past that haunted you and made you wake up."

He ran a hand gently over her hips and relished the feel of her full breasts against his chest. "I wish it were. But it's something more than that. I'm sure of it. I've had these feelings too many times before."

She leaned back and looked up at him. "They we'll just have to pray that if you're needed, God will let us know. We can't do any more than that." She pulled away from him and walked to the mantle, picking up an old Bible she kept beside the ticking clock. On the other side of the clock lay Zeke's sacred pipe. She turned to face him and he glanced at the Bible. Religion was probably the biggest difference they had in their marriage, but something that had never come between them. He looked at her with the little boy look again.

"Do you miss it, Abbie? Do you miss dressing up and going to a real church and singing hymns?"

She held his eyes steadily. "This house—this land—these things are my church, Zeke. And the love I have for you and my family is my hymn. I can sing to my

God whenever I please. He couldn't care less if I'm sitting in a pew or bending over a washtub." She turned and took his pipe from the mantle, handing it out to him. "I've told you before, I'm not so sure we don't both pray to the same being. I've seen how your prayers work, Zeke Monroe. They're very powerful. They have saved me from death—more than once."

He took the pipe, then sat down cross-legged on the floor in front of the fire. Abbie glanced at the table, where the big menacing knife that belonged to Zeke Monroe still lay where he had put it the night before. She stared at it, a tingling sensation creeping through her blood. It represented the wild, savage side of him, the side he seldom showed inside the confines of their cabin.

She tore her eyes from the knife and sat down in her rocker, closing her eyes and clinging to her Bible, praying silently, smelling the sweet smoke of his prayer pipe. For some reason she could not help being drawn back to the knife, as though it were almost alive. The tingling sensation would not leave her, and she suddenly realized his prayers and the knife seemed linked. The blade was as much a spiritual part of Cheyenne Zeke as was the sacred pipe. His prayers and spiritual strength only gave him the power and skill he needed to face his enemies. The knife was the extension of that strength, the instrument used to deal out proper justice. She rose and walked back to the table, setting down the Bible and touching the handle of the instrument that had brought a savage death to so many men.

"You're going to leave me," she suddenly blurted out, her voice calm and sure, interrupting his prayers. He frowned and lowered his pipe, turning to look at her.

"What?"

She held his eyes steadily. "You're going to leave
147

me. Something is going to take you away again. I know it as surely as I'm standing here now, Zeke.''

He slowly set down the pipe and rose, walking closer. ''I have already felt it. I just didn't want to say anything.'' He reached out and touched her face. ''I hope to God we're both wrong, Abbie-girl. I promised you once I'd never go away again, that I'd let nothing make us have to be apart again.''

She took a deep breath, fighting tears. ''Hold me, Zeke!'' she whispered.

He pulled her tight against him and suddenly they were kissing, desperately, both wishing they could stop time and keep this quiet, private moment together. He left her lips and moved down to her neck, and suddenly it didn't seem as though they had just done this earlier in the night, for this was a different need, a different hunger, both of them already feeling lonely because they sensed something was going to pull them apart.

''Zeke! Zeke!'' she whimpered.

''*Ho-shuh,* '' he murmured. ''You know that distance can't really part us, Abbie-girl. *Ne-mehotatse!*'' He picked her up in his arms, and she wrapped her arms around his neck. He buried his face in the opening of her soft robe, nuzzling the soft whites of her breasts, as he carried her back to the bed of robes, and gently laid her down. In the next moment he was naked beside her, his hands moving inside her robe and pulling it open. ''I need you, Abbie,'' he told her gruffly.

His lips covered her mouth hungrily and her robe fell open as his fingers moved lightly over her breasts and nipples, down over her belly and into the little hollow where her thighs met hidden places. She groaned as he moved his hand to that secret part of her that he owned and found that it was moist for him. How many times had they done this? Always she was willing and responsive. It would seem these movements would be so familiar to them that the excitement would be gone. But it was not that way for them. Their love was too strong, and the hardships they had shared had only enhanced this part of their love, for each knew that to predict tomorrow was a foolish game, and they had been apart enough to know the pain of separation and the glory and joy of simply being together. Moments like this were not to be wasted.

Abbie's own fear of being apart again only heightened her desire for this man that all women desired but only one woman could own—her own small self. Always she wondered how she had ever captured such a man to begin with. She could only thank God that she had, for to live without Zeke would have been like not living at all. She felt dwarfed beneath him, and basked in the thrill of his manliness, the wonder of being able to please this man who needed so much in a woman, and who gave so much in return.

She whimpered with a mixture of desire and fear of separation. In the next moment her insides were exploding with the ecstasy that only Zeke Monroe could bring to her soul. Her fingers dug into his skin, and she returned his kisses like a wanton woman.

"Tell me it won't happen," she whispered as he moved between her legs. "Tell me we won't have to be apart again, Zeke."

He kissed at her eyes, her cheeks, tasting the salt of her tears. "My Abbie-girl," was all he said. He kissed her lips again, searching with his tongue while his hands moved beneath her hips. Every moment like this must be savored. It must be gentle and easy and slow. Perhaps somehow they could stop time from moving at all. In the next moment that part of him that was most manly was moving into its nest of love, consumed by her passion, warm in the soft embrace of her womanhood. All the children she had borne had not changed

149

this part of their lovemaking, for it was the beautiful love they shared that made it so sweet, and each gave unselfishly and received gratefully. It was not just their bodies that were one, but their very souls. They were finely tuned to one another, each knowing what gave the other the most pleasure, moving rhythmically and in beautiful unison.

She opened her eyes and drank in the dark form above her, some of his long hair brushing lightly against her full breasts as he pushed deeper, almost violently in a sudden need to make sure this moment would not be taken from them. She knew that he was just as afraid as she that he might have to leave his family and his woman again, something Zeke Monroe did not like to do. She grunted when he thrust himself deep and hard in his sudden urgency to cling to her and keep the moment, and quickly the harsh movements vanished as he eased back slowly and then gently moved inside of her again.

"I'm sorry, Abbie," he whispered.

She traced slender fingers over his lips. "Do what you must do," she answered quietly. "The pain you give me is beautiful, just like that first time."

He thrust harder again, moving rhythmically, and Abbie tried to muffle her gasps of pleasure so that the children would not be disturbed. In the outer room the coffee hissed quietly over the fire. There was no one to drink it.

At dawn men came to pick up Danny's nearly dead body. He was unconscious by then, unaware of being carried to the little Shiloh church, which had been made a temporary Confederate hospital. But still he lay untreated, for the doctors had no time for internal wounds. All of their time was occupied with those who were the worst, those with legs and arms half blown off.

They had to come first, and all around Danny's unconscious ears there was the rasping sound of saws cutting through bone, and the pitiful groans of barely conscious men who knew they were losing limbs, men who begged and screamed with doctors not to cut them. Few of those who felt the saw ever lived to know what it would be like to survive with a leg or an arm missing.

Danny was oblivious to it all, and oblivious to the fact that Generals Grant and Sherman were preparing for a new onslaught. The Confederate victory at Shiloh would be a short-lived one.

Ten

Bonnie walked quietly to the door of her husband's small study, where he sat bent over a Bible on his desk, a nightly ritual. Rodney Lewis poured many hours into his sermons, for the settlers of the vast Dakota Territory that he served as a circuit preacher were hungry for good sermons, and Rodney Lewis was a sincere, devoted man.

"Rodney?" she spoke up softly.

He continued reading and scribbled something onto a piece of paper before turning around. "What is it?" he asked, almost impatiently. He was a spindly man, rather nervous in his actions, a wiry bit of energy with only one true desire—to spread the word of the Lord as far and wide as possible. In that greater love and passion he had for his work, there was little of those same emotions left for his own wife, and even this night, when he knew they would soon part, he did not seem to see the loneliness in her eyes.

"Are you sure you don't mind my going back East with father and Joshua?" she asked him, her blue eyes begging him to just once say something passionate, to ask her to please stay at his side—that he couldn't live without her beside him in the night.

"Of course I don't mind, darling," he answered, seeming almost irritated that she had interrupted him for such a question. "Your father is a doctor, and a good one. And the two of you have worked together for many years. God knows how badly medical help is needed for that bloody, sinful war. I'm sure the Lord wants you to go. And it's right that you take Joshua. At his age he should be with his mother. Besides, perhaps you can get him back to that specialist and get a progress report. The boy seems to be doing quite well with his new brace, don't you think?"

She swallowed her disappointment that he was not the least inclined to beg her to stay. But that was Rodney, and she did not hate him for it.

"Yes, he seems to be doing well. I'm proud of him."

They look into each other's eyes for a moment, he wondering if he would ever have a son of his own and if this woman he had married was barren, she wanting to scream at him that if he would make love to her more often, perhaps she would have a better chance of conceiving. But for a busy, dedicated man like Rodney Lewis, making love was more of a duty than a pleasure, and between his late hours and being gone for days and sometimes weeks riding the circuit, the physical aspect of their marriage had suffered greatly.

"Well," he said, turning back around, "It is settled then. Doctors are needed back East, and your father will go. And with your medical skills and the boy needing to see the specialist again, it's best you go with him. I would go too, Bonnie, but I'd be of no use to wounded men. The best way for me to serve the Lord is by preaching. So you go East and help those who hunger for medical help, and I shall stay here and serve those who hunger for the word of God."

She hesitated at the doorway. "I . . . I shall miss you, Rodney," she told him sincerely. "I wish when I get back that . . . perhaps you will be able to build a church and stay right here.''

He turned again, frowning. "I've told you many times, Bonnie, that I don't see that happening for many years. The settlers are spread too thin. There is no way they can all come to one place. Until this land is more civilized and this spot where we live becomes a city, I will have to go to the people, rather than their coming to me.'' He sighed and shook his head. "Now with the Indians getting restless again, the settlers will need the word of God even more. They're frightened. And you, my dear, will have to be very careful going through the Platte River area. You should be fine once you reach Illinois.''

She smiled softly. "All I have to do is mention Swift Arrow," she told him. "There aren't many Plains tribes who do not know that name. Swift Arrow knows we keep Yellow Moon's son.''

The man shrugged. "Yes. Well the fact remains that you can't be sure just using his name will keep your hair on your head. Joshua might be part Cheyenne and under the protection of Swift Arrow, but the fact remains that you are white and Joshua looks white, and a raiding Indian isn't going to stop to ask questions. In fact, you're probably safer right now back East in the middle of civil war than you are here in Sioux country for the time being.''

"And what about you—riding all over creation with hostile Indians around you? I'll worry, Rodney.''

He smiled faintly. "The Lord is with me, Bonnie. If He chooses to take me, and uses the Indians to do so, then I will just have to go. If He wants me to preach for a good many years yet, then I have nothing to worry about.''

She sighed resignedly. "I'm going to finish packing.''

He nodded and returned to his studies, and Bonnie walked to the bedroom. She took a flannel nightgown from the dresser, reminding herself as she packed that she must not get too upset with her husband or be too disappointed in him. He had many attributes, and his lack of warmth and tenderness toward her did not mean that he didn't love her. It was simply a part of his personality. He was kind to her and had never raised his voice or been demanding of her. Yet even that would sometimes be welcome.

She fussed with the arrangement of clothes in the old leather suitcase. Why did she always go around and around in her mind about her husband? It was as though two voices were speaking to her, one in his defense, and one telling her it had been wrong to marry him. The defensive voice reminded her he loved her in his own way. He was a dedicated man, a man of faith, and in that respect he was a brave man for going into dangerous country to spread the gospel. Yet the other voice asked if he would be brave enough to defend her person if necessary. And surely if he did, he could never win a fight, for he was slight of build and not a man to be aggressive.

The defensive voice told her this in itself was an attribute, a man who fights with words and the power of his faith; and she fully agreed. But there was something missing, and that was what caused the constant turmoil in her heart. The strength and courage, love and passion that Rodney Lewis poured into his preaching seemed to be totally spent on just that, with none left over for her. And she knew in her heart that she would always come second in his life. Again she felt the odd loneliness and the guilt she always suffered for not appreciating the good man that she had married. But she would keep these feelings to herself and suffer alone, for she was his wife and had married him willingly. Or had she?

"Lord, keep these sinful thoughts from my mind," she whispered in prayer as she returned to the dresser. She shrugged off her aching heart, but the pain returned in full force when she picked up a slip from the dresser drawer and saw it—the Indian necklace given to her by Zeke Monroe.

It was strange what the necklace did to her. She very seldom dared to look at it because of the awful ache in her chest and the rush of heat through her blood at the thought of the man who had given it to her.

Zeke. Just the thought of his name brought strange desires that Rodney had never created, desires forbidden to a Christian woman of proper upbringing. And yet they were there, and she knew in all her shame that it was her thoughts for a man she could not have that made her most dissatisfied with her own husband.

She blinked back tears as she carefully picked up the necklace. How many years ago had he given it to her? Eight or nine? Nine it was, for it had been a year before he had come back to her with the little crippled half-breed boy and asked her and Rodney to take the child.

It was a bone hairpipe necklace that was special to Zeke because his Cheyenne mother had made it for him. He had given it to her in friendship, a sign that he respected her love for him, a love she had been unable to hide. He respected it, but could not return it, for he loved another, a woman who would own his heart forever. How kind and understanding he had been over her embarrassment the day he had realized she loved him—the day he had saved her from Apaches and she had clung to him not out of fear, but out of a desperate yearning for the man himself. Never had she seen so much man, or a man of such skill and courage. If not for Zeke Monroe, she would surely be dead by now, but not before suffering the horrors of rape and slavery at the hands of outlaws. Zeke Monroe had saved her from all that, and she had been overwhelmed by his raw power and the tender, protective way he had treated her while taking her back to her father in Santa Fe.

She squeezed the necklace in her hand and closed her eyes as tears slipped down her cheeks. For Zeke, saving her had simply been a matter of duty, a necessary thing to do after seeing her a prisoner of outlaws. But for Bonnie it had been much more than that. It had been an awakening to the violent side of life that she had never witnessed before—and an awakening to a kind of man she had never known before, a man who was as much a part of the earth as the animals, a man whose power came from his inner self, who knew exactly what he wanted at all times and took it, whose law was survival of the fittest and whose God had a different name: *Heammawihio*. He had patiently taught her so many things about the Indians that she had not understood before. Now she loved them. But she loved one Indian in a special way. Zeke Monroe . . . Lone Eagle.

She wiped at her tears and walked over to place the necklace in the suitcase. She would take it with her, for she couldn't bear to be without it. If she could not have the man, at least she had this special gift of friendship from him—and she had the boy, little Joshua. He was a joy and a treasure, a sweet child who had never questioned all the painful operations he had undergone, and who seldom cried. He wore his new brace with courage and pride, eagerly demonstrating how well he could walk with it. Joshua had never questioned his origins. For the moment he only knew that Bonnie and Rodney Lewis were not his true parents. But he also knew that they loved him as a son, and he in turn loved them as his parents. She prayed that the evil man who was his real father would never discover Joshua's existence.

Some day she would have to tell him that his father

was a wealthy but disreputable white man and his mother was an Arapaho woman who had been married at one time to a Cheyenne man, Red Eagle. She would tell him the whole story of his mother, Yellow Moon, and how when Joshua was born Yellow Moon lived in the North with Red Eagle's brother, Swift Arrow, and that she was killed by soldiers. She would try to explain why the grieved Swift Arrow felt it was best that the little crippled half-breed boy be given to someone who could take better care of him. And then she would tell him about Zeke—Swift Arrow's half brother—whose loving white wife had taken the child out of pity before bringing Joshua to missionaries so he could get medical help.

It would be a long story, one that would have to wait for years, for the boy would have to be much more mature before he could understand and accept all of it. For now it was easier just to love him and receive his love in return.

She covered the necklace with clothing. Telling Joshua about his background would have to be buried for now, just as she must bury the necklace. But it was much harder to bury her love for the wild half-breed Indian who had so valiantly saved her nine years ago from a fate worse than death, and she secretly envied Abigail Monroe, a woman who must surely be totally fulfilled.

The little procession moved quietly over the soft summer grass of the Kansas plains. Between the unrest the Civil War brought into even the western lands, and the fact that Comanches and Sioux were again raiding, Zeke decided it was too dangerous to try to take his family all the way north for the Sun Dance. In the old days they would have joined a progression of thousands of Cheyenne in the summer, migrating north to follow the buffalo and to join with the Sioux in the Dakota hills for the great religious celebration. But war, and a false piece of paper called a treaty, made such migration difficult if not impossible now. The Southern Cheyenne were not even supposed to be wandering this far into Kansas, now officially a brand new state. But most of the Cheyenne still did not recognize the most recent treaty, and for them the Sun Dance was as important to sustaining their lives and well-being as eating and breathing. It was a time for celebrating, and they would celebrate. This was the year that Wolf's Blood, Zeke's first-born son, would partake of the ritual and sacrifice his flesh to the spirits.

Abbie rode beside Tall Grass Woman, who held seven-year-old Ellen in front of her. The plump Indian woman took great joy in helping the white woman who was her good friend care for her children. Tall Grass Woman's own little girl was long dead from white man's spotted disease, and her son was now full-grown and married. Tall Grass Woman had only Abbie to turn to for comfort, and Abbie let her dote on her little ones. Many, many winters before, when Tall Grass Woman's own little girl was still alive, Abbie had saved the child from drowning. The Indian woman had all but worshipped Abigail Monroe ever since.

Now the two women chattered, sometimes in English, sometimes in the Cheyenne tongue. Abbie rode with little Jason in front of her, and Lillian rode with her big brother, Wolf's Blood. The other children all rode their own mounts, and all of them were excited and curious about the ritual their brother would suffer to become a Cheyenne man.

Black Elk's wife, a slender, pretty Cheyenne girl called Blue Bird Woman, rode on the other side of Abbie, pulling a travois with her five-year-old son, Bucking Horse, happily sitting atop their supplies. On her back she carried a cradleboard with their new baby daughter inside.

Abbie watched Zeke lovingly. He rode ahead of her, Black Elk on one side of him and Tall Grass Woman's husband, Falling Rock, on the other. Now again there was nothing white about Zeke Monroe. His long, shining hair blew in the wind over the bronze skin of his bare back. A wide, brass band decorated the hard muscle of his upper left arm, and a beaded leather band decorated the other arm. He wore a beaded leather headband with eagle feathers at the back of it. A wide belt of ammunition was slung crosswise over his back and he wore a handgun and the infamous knife about his waist. His only clothing was his leggings and a pair of light moccasins. One wide stripe of white paint was spread across each cheek beneath his eyes, his prayer color. He had painted himself days before he needed to, but it was his son who would make the sacrifice this time, and Zeke prayed daily to the spirits to give his son courage and above all to erase the boy's pain at the ritual.

Abbie knew the ritual itself would be hardest on Zeke, for he had suffered it himself and well knew the agony of it. Watching his son make the sacrifice would be a terrible thing for him, yet his heart would also swell with pride. Already she could see the pride, as he sat straight and tall on the big Appaloosa he rode, riding among his people, almost haughty in the fact that all were going to the Sun Dance celebration to witness Zeke Monroe's son take a bold step into manhood. They would forget about wars and treaties and white encroachment. They would be Indians and they would celebrate in the old ways. Soon their small party would meet up with a much larger delegation of Cheyenne, and together they would ride to a place along the Smoky Hill River, where even more Cheyenne waited, among them some Cheyenne from the North, who had dared to come into territory the government had for-bidden them to enter. All of them took great amuse-ment and excitement in daring to go where they pleased. They knew such days were numbered, but they would cling to them as long as possible. The Chey-enne made no trouble for the whites. They could not understand why the whites wanted to make so much trouble for them.

They crested a hill and saw in the distance below a small wooden farmhouse, something that had not been in this particular pathway in years before. They drew their mounts to a halt and Zeke studied their surround-ings. Between themselves and the farm was a creek, heavily wooded.

"We'll go around a ways," he told Black Elk. "Keep to the creek and the trees. There's no need to cause trouble for whoever lives there, but if they spot us, they may be the ones to start something."

Black Elk said nothing as they headed toward the stream, but his chest hurt at the sight of the farm that had not been there before. More and more it seemed that wherever they went they saw yet another white set-tlement. There seemed to be no end to the numbers of white people from the mysterious East.

They guided their mounts into the shallow stream, and Bucking Horse laughed as water splashed on him.

"Be still, son," Blue Bird Woman ordered her little boy, her heart aching at the fact that her child could not even laugh as a child should laugh, for fear the whites might hear him.

They followed the stream for nearly a mile, then moved onto the opposite bank and into the trees. But they were greeted by fence posts and could not con-tinue.

"Damn!" Zeke swore. "We'll have to go back into the stream and go even farther down."

"No!" Black Elk snapped, angry at these constant interferences with his free travel. "We will go over the fence!" He headed his mount for the fence before Zeke could say a word, and to Zeke's horror, he realized the fence was barbed wire. Black Elk kicked his horse into a jump, but the animal did not see the topmost line of wire. A back leg caught on it and the animal came crashing down, pulling the wire and two posts with it. Blue Bird Woman stifled a scream and Zeke quickly dismounted.

"Everybody stay put and be quiet!" he ordered. "Wolf's Blood, come and help me. You, too, Falling Rock."

The women sat helplessly, watching the men hurry over to to Black Elk, who was quietly cursing in his own tongue as he crawled away from his struggling, badly injured mount. He got to his feet, his eyes blazing with anger at the idea of the fence being there at all, blood streaming from a bad cut on his arm.

"Katum!" he hissed, wiping at the blood and staring at his horse, its flesh badly torn. "What is this terrible thing?" he asked Zeke, looking at the man with horror in his eyes.

Zeke's chest hurt for the man. "It's called barbed wire, my brother. From now on when you see a fence, take a closer look before you try to leap it." Their eyes held in a new and torturous understanding, and he saw the pain in Black Elk's. "We'll have to kill the animal, Black Elk," Zeke spoke up. "I'll do it with my knife. That way we won't make any noise."

Black Elk blinked rapidly. It was not easy for a Cheyenne man to kill a horse. Horses were their most precious possession, and they were loved and cared for like good friends. Abbie could hardly stand the pain in Black Elk's eyes, and Blue Bird Woman looked away as Zeke pulled his knife from its sheath. Black Elk knelt down and gently stroked the animal's forehead, saying something softly to it in Cheyenne; in the next moment Zeke's big blade found the animal's heart.

Black Elk turned and walked a few feet away. Zeke wiped blood from his knife onto the grass, then shoved it back into its sheath and approached his brother, while Wolf's Blood stood staring at the dead horse, a new hatred and determination in his dark eyes.

"I'm sorry, Black Elk," Zeke told the man.

Black Elk only nodded, staring into the distance at the farmhouse. "Is this the way it shall be then? We shall be pushed into one small corner of this land, and there we shall stay and starve to death?"

"I can't answer that, my brother," Zeke told him. "I wish that I could. We can only pray for the best."

Black Elk shook his head. "I am beginning to understand why some of the other tribes fight harder—why they raid and steal and kill. One day the Cheyenne will also find it impossible to be peaceful. A man can bear only so much."

"That is true, Black Elk. But you must also keep in mind that some whites are going to force your hand. Some want you to feel as you are feeling now. They want you to raid and make war. Because then they can point their fingers and yell about how they were right all along. They can talk about how bad the Indian is— how ruthless and cruel. You must be careful not to fall into their trap and do the very thing they expect you to do. It would be easy now to ride down to that farmhouse and burn it and kill everyone inside. But there are those who would be glad to have you do so, my brother. It would give them the OK to kill every Indian they see."

Black Elk sighed. "I do not understand this kind of fighting, Zeke—with words and barbed fences."

"Of course you don't," Zeke replied, turning away,

himself filled with rage and a need to kill, his Indian blood screaming for the freedom his people deserved. His heart wrenched at a quiet sob, and he looked up to see Blue Bird Woman crying and Abbie also wiping her eyes. His children all stared at the horse with frightened eyes. Surely they wondered where their future lay, and he suddenly realized that each of them would have to make a difficult choice one day.

"Zeke, someone comes!" Falling Rock spoke up, running back to his mount to retrieve his rifle. Black Elk whirled, his dark eyes blazing, and he hurried to his dead horse and yanked his own rifle from the animal. Seven men approached from the other side of the creek, some in buckskins, some wearing what looked like an attempt at fashioning a uniform, a couple of them in the regular cotton clothing of white men. All were white, some sporting grizzly beards, all well armed. Abbie's heart froze. She had seen such men before, one terrible night when they attacked her and Wolf's Blood when the boy was just a baby. And on that night, Zeke Monroe had wielded his knife in a bloodbath of defense of his family.

Zeke stepped into the stream to face the approaching men. "You women get into the trees!" he ordered. "Get the children into some cover."

They moved quickly, Abbie's heart fearful now, for surely there would be trouble. "Black Elk, keep your senses!" Zeke was telling his brother. "You're angry. Let me do the talking. And whatever happens, don't kill anyone. Try to only wound them if they make trouble."

In the next moment Wolf's Blood was standing beside his father, his rifle in hand. He had dismounted and left Lillian on his horse, handing the reins to Abbie, who had taken the girl with the others to shelter.

"Get back out of the way, son," Zeke said quietly.

"No," the boy replied in a determined voice. "I will not obey you this time, Father. You should not stand alone in defense of my mother and brothers and sisters. I can fight and shoot now."

Zeke wanted to argue, but the boy was right, and Zeke could not help but be proud of the way he stood there, obviously unafraid, eager for a challenge. Yes. He was very much like his father.

The white men splashed into the creek water, and Black Elk moved up behind Zeke, while Falling Rock stood off to the side, rifle in hand, glaring at the strangers.

The seven men halted their mounts and stared at the three Indian men and the young boy. All had caught sight of the women moving into the trees.

For a moment nothing was said by either party, as the white men lined their horses in a straight row in front of Zeke and the others. The man directly in front of Zeke glanced at the bloody, dead horse still lying over the broken fence. Then his eyes moved to Black Elk's bleeding arm and he grinned. "Appears you Injuns is learnin' it don't pay to try to jump a white man's fence," he sneered.

"E-have-se-va!" Black Elk hissed, moving around to the other side of Zeke. *"Zetapetazhetan!"* he swore, raising his rifle into the air.

The white man who had spoken watched Black Elk carefully, his own hand resting on a gun he wore in a holster on his hip. The other six men sat in stony silence, all with rifles in their hands, ready to use them on a signal. One of them was very young, a rather homely boy with glittering, evil eyes. Wolf's Blood spotted him right away, and he stared at the boy, meeting the white boy's hateful glare with his own unafraid eyes. The white boy looked familiar, but he couldn't quite place him.

"You redskins is a little out of your territory, ain't you?" the apparent leader spoke up. "You look like Cheyenne. Cheyenne belong down on the Arkansas River."

"We're doing harm to no one," Zeke spoke up, surprising the man with his English, spoken too well for a full-blood. "We are going to meet others for the annual Sun Dance. Leave us, and we will be on our way."

The white man shook his head. "No way. I don't know who you are, mister, and I don't care. Appears you're a breed, else you wouldn't be so tall and you wouldn't talk like a man who's been around white folk a lot." He shifted in his saddle, relaxing more. "Now to men like us, a breed is even slimier than a full-blood Indian, and there ain't one of you who belongs here. You're all going with us to the nearest fort—and we'll see that your, uh, women . . . get back where they belong safely."

Some of the others snickered, and the younger boy looked down a haughty nose at Wolf's Blood.

Zeke gripped his knife more firmly. "We are going farther north," he replied coolly. "And our women will go with us. Who the hell are you, anyway? You own this property?"

The white man spit out tobacco juice and pushed his hat back off his forehead. "We're Colorado volunteers, just doin' a little scoutin' to see what Indians is strayin' off their allotted land." He glanced at the younger one. "And we're givin' the young one here some training. His pa is a real powerful man. Wants to raise the boy the right way—give him school learnin' and also give him some real live experience in the field, so to speak." He spit more juice as the younger one sat grinning proudly, and Wolf's Blood's heart raced. He had seen this one someplace. But where? Where? "The boy's pa has a lot of influence in Indian affairs," the white man went on. "Wants to raise the son to know all the ropes." The man snickered and looked at the boy again, then back at Zeke. "At any rate, we saw your tracks way back in Colorado Territory. We could tell by the travois you was draggin' that it was most likely Injuns, and since our job is to keep an eye on the movements of you straying bastards, we figured we'd follow and see what you was up to. Give the boy here some experience in trackin'." He leaned farther forward, as though to make a point. "The boy's pa intends for him to get a fine education and come back out here and be an officer in the Colorado army." He wiped some tobacco juice from his lip. "You Injuns ought to remember this boy's name. I reckon' you'll have a lot more run-ins with him in years to come. Name's Garvey. Charles Garvey. And he hates Injuns read good. His pa is Winston Garvey. Ever hear the name?"

Abbie stifled a gasp, and Wolf's Blood almost blurted out a string of hateful words when the man said the name, but he checked himself, remembering his father's warning about Winston Garvey. Zeke remained amazingly calm, showing no reaction at the mention of the Garvey name. But he cast a quick, sly glance at the young man, realizing the importance of remembering what Charles Garvey looked like. The boy glared back at him, finding both Zeke and the younger Cheyenne boy familiar. But he also could not place them.

"I never took much stock in a man's name alone," Zeke replied, looking back at the apparent leader of the motley group of men. "And if you're really Colorado volunteers, then you're out of your territory, mister. You've got no right tracking us into Kansas."

"We can track you anyplace we want!" the Garvey boy spoke up. "And you'd best remember my name, redskin, just like the man said. My father has a lot of influence in Colorado Territory, and men like you had

167

better have respect for your superiors!''

Wolf's Blood stiffened with a need to punch the boy, and Zeke scanned the group of men scathingly. "I don't see one man here who is better than I," he glowered. "A name doesn't make a man better. It's his courage and skill and honesty that makes him a man, and I doubt any one of you can boast of any of those things. Now I'd suggest you all leave, because we're going where we damned well please!"

"You Indian filth!" the Garvey boy growled. "We will show you who is the better man when we take you to the fort with us under arrest and throw you in the stockade! And we will show your women what their purpose is for existing!"

"You aren't taking us anywhere!" Wolf's Blood warned. "Nor will you touch my mother or sisters, white trash!" He could not control his youthful anger then; his finger squeezed the trigger of his rifle and a bullet ripped across the shoulder of Garvey's horse, just grazing the boy's right thumb enough to sting badly and startle the lad. Wolf's Blood had deliberately missed, taking great pleasure in Garvey's wide, frightened eyes.

After that, everything began happening fast and all at once. Charles Garvey's horse began rearing in startled pain from Wolf's Blood's bullet, and the Garvey boy struggled to keep the animal in control, his own heart pounding with fear. Zeke dodged a bullet fired by the leader of the men, then dove at the man, physically ripping him from his horse and quickly picking up the man's own dropped rifle and smashing the butt across the man's face, while another of the men aimed his rifle at Zeke.

In the next moment Wolf's Blood's own knife was out and thrown, landing in the shoulder of the man who intended to shoot Zeke. The man cried out and fell from his horse, and in that moment Zeke realized his son had just saved his life, but there was no time to think about such things now.

A fourth man, whose gun had jammed, leaped onto Zeke's back, and they tumbled into the creek. Abbie gasped as the man raised a knife while holding Zeke's face in the water, but Zeke arched up, turning quickly just as the knife came down. It glanced off Zeke's lower jaw, drawing blood. A split second later Zeke wrested his own knife from its sheath and rammed it into the man's hip. He would rather have ripped open the man's hide, but he felt it important that none of the men be killed, if possible, so that the Cheyenne would not be blamed for murdering these white men.

Everything was happening at once, and Black Elk had shot a fifth man in the foot. A sixth man made ready to shoot Black Elk, but his shot went astray when a great gray wolf he had not even noticed before suddenly leaped onto him, knocking the man from his horse and sinking vicious fangs into his chest, neck and arms.

Zeke shoved the man he had stabbed into the water, viciously jerking out his knife from the screaming man's hip. The seventh man had already shot at Falling Rock, but his own frightened horse was too unsteady and the bullet only grazed Falling Rock's head. Tall Grass Woman was screaming and Abbie deposited Jason onto Blue Bird Woman's mount, then pulled out her own Spencer. She moved forward out of the trees toward the confusion as the seventh man made ready to shoot at Falling Rock again and finish him off. Abbie raised her rifle, but Zeke's wicked blade flashed through the air and landed with a thud under the man's right arm as he raised his rifle. The man screamed and whirled, dropping his weapon and yanking the knife out of his flesh. He threw the weapon to the ground and rode off, while Wolf's Blood went after the Garvey boy, who still struggled with his wounded horse.

"White scum!" Wolf's Blood hissed. "I will show you who is the better man!" He yanked the Garvey boy from his mount.

The leader of the soldiers groaned and rolled over, one side of his face shattered from Zeke's blow and already swelling badly. The man's horse was gone, frightened off by the confusion. Zeke yanked the man out of the creek water and threw him onto the bank, while Abbie moved closer and held her rifle on the man being attacked by Wolf's Blood's wolf.

"Smoke! No, Smoke!" she shouted, holding her Spencer on the wounded man. "Get away now!"

The animal backed off, its lips curled and its teeth red from the man's blood. The man lay moaning and gave no more fight, while the man Wolf's Blood had wounded in the shoulder with his knife began to come around after falling from his horse. He began begging for someone to get the knife out of him, and Zeke obliged, enjoying the man's cry of pain when he jerked it out. He pushed the man into the muddy bank with his foot.

"I'd stay put if I was you, mister!" he growled.

The man Black Elk had shot in the foot feared for his life and whirled his horse, galloping off after the seventh man who had ridden away after pulling Zeke's knife from his armpit. A trail of blood followed both men as they disappeared. Falling Rock got to his feet, holding his hand to a scalp wound, and then everyone's attention was focused on Wolf's Blood and the Garvey boy.

The two of them wrestled in the shallow creek, as horses whinnied and scurried out of the way. Zeke picked up his own rifle and backed up, standing near Abbie. Black Elk and Falling Rock both joined them, all holding rifles on the injured white men, none of whom seemed inclined to interfere anymore.

Wolf's Blood dodged Charles Garvey's fist as the white boy tried to get the Indian off of him, but Wolf's Blood was much stronger, his muscles much more developed from living a rugged, outdoor life. He held the white boy pinned on his back, while water splashed over his face, making him choke. Again the boy tried to swing at Wolf's Blood, but Wolf's Blood arched back and only laughed.

"I think I will let you up, Mister Charles Garvey, sir!" he sneered. "This is no challenge!" He jumped off the boy and Garvey leaped up, tears of hatred and embarrassment on his face. He came at Wolf's Blood again, calling him every dirty name he could think of and swinging wildly, but Wolf's Blood only kept backing up and laughing.

Abbie watched anxiously, but knew Zeke would never stop the fight. This was Wolf's Blood's battle and the boy would feel insulted if his father tried to stop it.

Wolf's Blood finally stopped backing off and let the Garvey boy plow into him, his head butting into Wolf's Blood's middle. But Wolf's Blood only let out a quick grunt, then bent over and grasped the Garvey boy about the middle, picking him up and holding him upside down before flinging the young man back into the creek. He charged into the creek after him, kicking the boy in the ribs as he tried to get up out of the water. The boy fell face down, and Wolf's Blood quickly reached down and jerked him up, crooking a strong arm tightly around Garvey's neck from behind. Garvey pulled at Wolf's Blood's arm with both his hands, but could not budge the Indian boy's arm, and his face reddened as he began to choke.

"Now who is the better man?" Wolf's Blood sneered, giving the boy a jerk. "Tell me, white trash!"

"Y-you," the boy choked in reply, beginning to cry.

Wolf's Blood jerked him around and pushed him back into the water, and Garvey just sat there looking up at him and crying in fear for his very life.

"It would be so easy now to kill you!" Wolf's Blood hissed. "I have not killed a man yet. I would like to make you my first, but you are not a man!"

Their eyes held, both boys breathing hard, and suddenly Garvey remembered. "You!" he panted. "You are the boy I fought with in Denver! I remember you!"

Wolf's Blood quickly looked at his father, who warned him with his eyes not to react. Wolf's Blood looked back at the whimpering Garvey boy. "I do not know what you are talking about," he answered, sounding sure of himself. "I have never been to that place called Denver."

"You have! We fought in the street."

Wolf's Blood snickered. "You are not only a coward and a weakling, but you are also crazy!" He bent closer and yanked the boy to his feet. "Do you not know that all Indians look alike? Is that not what you and your white friends always say? You mistake me for another, white scum!"

He jerked the boy over to his mount, which had finally settled down, its wound only superficial. "Get up on your horse, coward!" Wolf's Blood ordered. "You will leave us now and let us be on our way, now that you and your friends know which of us are the better men."

The Garvey boy sniffed and angrily wiped at tears, one of his lips swollen and bloody. Zeke bent down and grasped the leader of the volunteers by the collar, dragging the half-conscious man to Garvey's horse. He picked the man up and slung him over the mount.

"Climb up," he growled at Garvey. "Take your great leader here and find a doctor for him at the nearest fort. His jaw is badly broken, and so is the rifle I broke it with!''

Garvey's lips puckered as he stared up at the tall, powerful looking Indian, his hatred for the dark skin well-nurtured by his scheming father. But the boy's haughty hatred was for the moment replaced by a shuddering fear that these ''wild men of the Plains'' would torture and mutilate him if he did not leave quickly. He turned and mounted up.

''Zeke!'' Black Elk called out. Zeke turned and Black Elk tossed him his wicked knife. Zeke caught it by the handle, his chest tightening at the fact that Black Elk had called him by name. He glanced up at Garvey, who sat pouting and bleeding, his clothes torn and muddy.

''My father will know about this and you will all be sorry!'' the boy hissed.

''We'll be long gone before you ever get back to your father and civilization,'' Zeke answered. ''Forget it, Garvey. You'll never see us again.''

The boy stared at him, his mind groping to remember where he had seen this man. Was it in Denver also? Perhaps. But he had seen him before that, when he was a very small boy. He was sure. He would remember the name and ask his father about it.

Garvey turned his horse without another word and trotted off. The man Wolf's Blood had wounded with his knife was on his feet then, his shoulder painful and bleeding. Zeke walked over to him and removed the rest of the man's weapons, telling Black Elk and Falling Rock to load the last two men onto their horses, one still lying badly wounded from Smoke's attack, and the other groaning from the knife wound to his hip.

''Get the hell out of here!'' Zeke ordered the man with the shoulder wound. The man scowled and mounted up, and Zeke put the reins of the last two men's horses into the conscious man's hand. ''You'd

173

better ride after that boy whose hide is so precious to you!'' he told the man. ''Winston Garvey wouldn't be too happy if you let something happen to his son. In fact, if this Garvey fellow is as powerful and wealthy as you say, I don't doubt your own hide isn't too safe, seeing as how that boy could have been killed today.''

He smacked the man's horse and it galloped off. Zeke turned and looked at Abbie, who still sat mounted, rifle in hand. He grinned to himself. Abigail could use a rifle if she had to. He'd seen her use it on three Crow warriors. He reached up and took the rifle from her stiff fingers. ''You all right?'' he asked her.

She nodded. ''What about you?'' she asked him with a shaking voice.

He wiped blood from the deep gash on his lower right jaw. ''Just another one of those damned scars,'' he tried to joke, seeing the terror in her eyes. It was not easy for a woman to watch her husband and son being shot at and attacked. Tall Grass Woman ran to her own husband, wailing and carrying on about the wound on his scalp.

Abbie moved her eyes from Zeke to Wolf's Blood and held out her hand. ''You saved your father's life today when you threw that knife,'' she told him proudly. ''In that moment I saw how much you are like your father.''

The boy reached up and took her hand, and Zeke folded his own big hand over both of theirs, again turning from vicious fighter to gentle husband and father.

''I'm more proud of you than I have ever been,'' he told Wolf's Blood. ''What else can I say, son?''

''Nothing,'' the boy replied. ''You have saved my life and that of my mother and the others too many times to remember. It is time for me to do my share of protecting our family. But I am worried, Father. Black Elk spoke your name. That Garvey boy will remem-

174

ber.''

Zeke squeezed his hand. ''Let him remember. It was a long time ago. We will not waste our waking hours worrying about it. This is your time, Wolf's Blood. We will put all of these things behind us.'' He looked up at Abbie. ''They'll be a long time getting to help and taking care of their wounds,'' he told her. ''We'll be far from here if and when they send others back, which I doubt they will do. But to be on the safe side, we'd best get out of here.''

''I agree,'' she answered calmly, blinking back tears. ''I . . . I hope that boy's father doesn't figure out—''

''Forget it, Abbie-girl,'' he told her. ''I don't want anyone fretting over it.'' He patted her arm and left her and his son and approached Black Elk, who was removing his belongings from his dead horse. ''I brought three extra Appaloosas to trade at the Sun Dance,'' he told his brother. ''Put your blanket on one of them.''

The man nodded. ''I will pay you,'' he said sullenly.

''It isn't necessary, Black Elk.''

The man turned sad eyes to Zeke. ''I have learned much this day. I have learned we are followed wherever we go, and I have learned about the barbed wire fences. I have learned there is no future for my son and daughter.''

Zeke put a hand on his shoulder. ''There is always a future, Black Elk. We go now to the Sun Dance celebration, and you will see.'' He scanned each of his children, walking up to them and patting each one on the arm or the bottom, making sure each one was unharmed and reassuring them that all was well. But he saw questions in the eyes of the older ones, a confusion as to why white men should hate them. He walked up to his eldest daughter, a budding young girl just entering her teens, a girl with the rare, provocative beauty given only to those of mixed blood. He recognized already the strikingly beautiful woman she would some day be, and felt a sudden possessive jealousy, as well as a hidden fear of how men might treat her.

"What is your name?" he asked her.

She frowned. "Father, you know my name. It's Margaret."

"But what is your Indian name?" he asked her.

She thought for a moment. "It is Moheya," she replied, "Blue Sky."

"That's right." He stepped back and spoke to all of them. "Each of you has a white name, and an Indian name. You are the best of both worlds, and there is no reason to ever be ashamed of either blood that runs in your veins. Do you all understand that?"

"Yes, Father," they answered almost in unison, all of them carrying a high respect for their father, and sometimes in absolute awe of him, especially when they saw him fight as he had fought this day.

"Good," Zeke replied. "For the next few days you will be Indians, and you will help your brother celebrate his manhood. It will be an exciting time for all of you."

He walked over and took little Jason from Blue Bird Woman, hoisting the child to his shoulders. The boy laughed as his father walked him over to Abbie and plopped him in front of his mother.

"Let's ride!" he announced. He leaped up onto his own horse with ease. "We'll ride on down to where the fence ends." He moved his mount forward and the others followed, Falling Rock holding a cloth to his still-bleeding scalp. Smoke trotted along beside Wolf's Blood, enjoying the taste of blood in his mouth.

Behind them lay Black Elk's mount, tangled in the wicked barbed wire, a sad symbol of a dying way of life. And Zeke buried his own haunting worry over the fact that Charles Garvey had seen him again—and knew his name.

176

Eleven

There had been many days of celebrating while the huge medicine lodge was erected in the center of the Sun Dance camp. The gathering of nearly all the Southern Cheyenne made camp on the south bank of the Smoky Hill River, in a circle close to a mile in diameter, the opening of the circle facing east, as was the custom, to face the rising sun. The Sun Dance lodge was surrounded by the *tipis* of the lodgemaker's warrior society, and outside of that circle were the lodges of the rest of those who had gathered for the great celebration.

The first few days had been good ones, a time to forget the disaster that seemed to be coming to claim the Cheyenne. This was a time to live the old way, a time to hunt buffalo for the tongues and hides needed for the ceremony, a time to gather brush and timber for the Sun Dance lodge. It was a time to paint the bodies of those who would participate in the ritual with many colors and designs that signified life—the sun, moon, flowers and plants, or animals.

Wolf's Blood would be painted with his sign, the wolf, and with his father's sign, the eagle. Tall Grass Woman did the painting, a job she accepted with great honor. It would be tedious and time-consuming, but she would do it with great joy, for this was the white woman's first-born son, and this moment was very special to her good friend, Abbie, and to the boy. But Abbie knew it was most special to Zeke, who saw in his son the Indian blood he knew would not run as strong in any of his other children.

Abbie wore her best tunic, one bleached white and painted and beaded in bright colors. It was a gift from Tall Grass Woman many years before. Her cheeks and arms were painted with flowers, and to Zeke she was a vision—a goddess—an Indian with white skin, for when she was with his people this way, she was an Indian at heart. She understood his need to live this way, at least some of the time, and she never objected.

About her waist she wore a leather belt with two eagle feathers, a gift from an old priest when first she came to the Cheyenne—a gift he had given her in honor of her courage and strength for what she had suffered on her way West, and for living through the wound of a Crow arrow. She had been more like a little girl then. Now she was a woman, and to Zeke she was more enticing then ever.

For days the drums beat and the dancing continued, and the air was filled with sweet smoke from campfires and roasting meat. Wolf's Blood sat patiently outside his parents' lodge day in and day out while Tall Grass Woman painted with painstaking care—his chest, arms, back, face and legs. Abbie exclaimed that her son would be the most beautifully decorated young man at the ceremony, but each day Zeke grew more quiet, in spite of his pride and eagerness for the ceremony. This was his son. And his son would suffer.

On the night before Wolf's Blood's fasting and three-day-long ordeal of constant dancing around the Sun Dance Pole, the entire family sat quietly in a circle in their *tipi*, Zeke and Abbie on either side of Wolf's Blood. Abbie offered her son another piece of the venison she had cooked for him that evening. She cooked it his favorite way, flavored with pork and special herbs. This would be the last meal her son would eat for many days, for not only must he begin fasting, which would last for three days, but after that he would suffer wounds to his flesh. He would lie in pain while recovering and eat little.

Zeke sat quietly, not eating anything, his face painted in his prayer color. He seemed totally removed from what was going on around him, and Abbie knew he was concentrating all of his faith to beg the spirits to save his son from too much suffering. Some participants would cry out and give up, and some would die. He prayed that neither thing would happen to Wolf's Blood.

Outside the drums beat rhythmically. Wolf's Blood didn't seem worried at all. He was excited and ready, for not only would he show the other warriors he was a man, but he would also show the young maidens, many of whom had been watching him slyly. Never had he been so disturbed by the soft curves of their bodies as he was in this his fifteenth year, and he was beginning to change his mind about never marrying. He had grown up with parents who were happy in their love, strong in their love, whose very strength seemed to come from the bond they shared. His father was a skilled and powerful man, a man of spiritual faith and magnificent courage. Taking a woman had not weakened him. In fact, Zeke had told him once that being with Abbie gave him more strength—that it was when he had to be separated from her that he felt weak.

Yes. Perhaps taking a wife would not be so bad. But first he must be a man. He would show the young maidens who would watch and who would encourage him with their songs as he suffered just how much of a man he was.

The boy bit into another piece of meat when Smoke suddenly leaped to his feet, his ears perked straight and his lips curling. He growled low and looked at the *tipi* entrance.

"Someone strange is near," Wolf's Blood said, quickly getting to his feet along with his father. Zeke whipped out his knife when someone rattled the bells and buffalo hoofs Abbie kept strung outside the entrance for people to announce their entrance.

"Zeke. It is I. Swift Arrow," came the voice.

Abbie gasped and broke into a smile, and Zeke was instantly throwing back the flap of the lodge entrance, while Wolf's Blood ordered Smoke to lie back down. Swift Arrow ducked inside, dressed in his most brilliant warrior regalia. Zeke grasped his wrist instantly, grinning broadly, his eyes watery.

"Swift Arrow, my brother! You came to witness my son's sacrifice!"

Their eyes held in brotherly love, and Swift Arrow placed his other hand on Zeke's shoulder. "The runners told me the Cheyenne to the south would not come north this summer for the ceremonies. I knew this was Wolf's Blood's fifteenth year, the year that he was told in a vision he must make the sacrifice. For the first six years of the boy's life I helped raise him, taught him the warrior ways. He was like a son to me. I wanted to be here."

Zeke's jaw flexed in an effort to control his emotions, and Swift Arrow saw how difficult the ceremony would be for him. "I . . . am glad you came, Swift Arrow," he replied. "It will be easier with you here. And it's been so long since we've seen you. I had a vision several weeks ago . . . a bad dream. I thought perhaps something had happened to you."

Swift Arrow grinned. "I am fine." They squeezed

each other's wrists, and Swift Arrow dared to move his eyes from Zeke's to look at Abbie, something that would be difficult, for he must not show his emotion. Zeke knew the moment Swift Arrow saw her standing there, beautifully painted, her long, lustrous hair brushed out thick and loose, her white skin painted with flowers, that it was still difficult for his brother to look at her. He squeezed Swift Arrow's wrist again in a gesture of gentle warning mixed with quiet understanding.

Abbie smiled and blinked back tears. "Swift Arrow," she said quietly. "It was . . . good of you to come. It's been such a long time. We were worried. And Zeke needs you."

His eyes quickly scanned her beauty, his body rigid with cold control. Did the woman never change? Did the elements never age her? Why did she have to be cursed with such beauty?

"So . . . you live like the Indian again . . . like that first year you came to the Cheyenne with your new husband," he spoke up.

"You taught me many things that year," she replied.

He nodded, then tore his eyes from her to face Zeke. "I learned that there are some whites with the same strength and courage as the Indian." Their eyes held. Zeke knew it was difficult for his brother to come at all, for out of honor and to ease the pain in his own heart, he had vowed to stay in the North with the Sioux and never set eyes on Abigail again. "I . . . came only to give you support, my brother," he told Zeke. "And to witness my nephew's sacrifice." He grinned. "You must be very proud."

Zeke nodded, and Swift Arrow turned to Wolf's Blood, grinning more and walking up to the boy, placing his hands on Wolf's Blood's strong shoulders. "My nephew—look at you! You are a fine, strong, handsome young man. The young girls, they watch you eagerly, do they not?''

Wolf's Blood grinned and actually looked embarrassed. "I am glad you came, my uncle! My heart is happy. Now you will all be here—you and my father and my uncle, Black Elk. My father and his brothers will be together. It is good! I can bear the pain with all of you there.''

Swift Arrow put a hand to the side of the boy's face. "My Little Rock. This is how I remember you, by the name you were called when you were small—before you had your vision and slept with the wolves. You are the son I lost. You and your family are my family. I have no other.''

Abbie looked at Zeke, wanting to weep at the words. She walked over to Zeke and he embraced her.

"Swift Arrow, there is food left,'' Zeke told his brother. "Sit with us and eat. Did you come alone?''

The man turned, forcing back the ache of seeing Abbie standing in Zeke's embrace. *"Ai,"* he replied, "I have come alone. It is dangerous to travel the country in large bands now. Whenever the stupid whites see more than ten Indians together, they think it is a war party.'' He laughed sneeringly, then marched around the circle of Monroe children and studied each one as Abbie named them for him. The children looked back at their estranged uncle with wide eyes. He looked very much like their father, only slightly darker, a handsome Indian man, but not the same handsomeness Zeke had, for Zeke carried mixed blood, the harshest Indian lines toned down by his white father's blood into the best of both. Swift Arrow was not quite as tall and broad, for Zeke got his size from his father; but Swift Arrow was bigger than most Cheyenne men, and was a powerful man in his own right, a highly respected Dog Soldier.

Swift Arrow was a superb specimen of a Cheyenne warrior. Zeke was the best of two bloods, and it was obvious Wolf's Blood would inherit his father's height and breadth, for already he was as tall as Swift Arrow, and was not finished growing.

Swift Arrow's eyes rested on LeeAnn, and he reached down and touched her golden curls. "The soldiers will think you have stolen this one," he told Zeke. "You must be careful with her." He moved to Margaret, struck by her provocative beauty. "You are Moheya," he said softly. "Such beauty I have never seen!" He looked at Abbie, then Zeke. "She has the soft beauty of her her mother, and the fine lines of her half-breed father. The warriors will give you many horses for this one."

Zeke grinned. "I have horses of my own. The warriors will have a hell of a time proving to me they're good enough for my daughter," he replied.

Swift Arrow grinned. "I do not think I would want to be the young man who must come to you for her hand," he answered. He glanced at the big knife strapped to Zeke's waist. "And how many men have felt your blade since last I saw you, my brother?"

Zeke smiled more. "I've lost count."

Swift Arrow laughed and Wolf's Blood grinned. "You should have seen him last summer, my uncle," the boy spoke up eagerly. "He was in a knife duel with a white man who was the best white man with a knife. They fought the Cheyenne way, with a leather strap in their teeth and one hand tied behind their backs. You have never seen such a duel!"

Swift Arrow scanned his tall, powerful brother. "I have seen him use the knife, Wolf's Blood. No warrior that I know would consider fighting him with the blade."

"And then later—when he found out a white soldier

tried to hurt my mother, father raced him, and when no one could see them, he knocked the man from his horse and broke his neck with his bare hands!'' The boy laughed lightly. ''He came back and said the man fell from his horse and was killed, but all of us knew what really happened. He was a big man, Swift Arrow, and my father broke his neck.''

Swift Arrow looked at Abbie again, enraged at the realization of what the boy was telling him. A soldier had insulted her—perhaps even . . . His eyes darted to Zeke. ''She was hurt?''

Zeke read his eyes, understanding the meaning of the words, and Abbie reddened. ''No,'' Zeke answered.

''She scratched him!'' Wolf's Blood spoke up. ''She scratched him good on the face and kicked him into a tub of water. She told us. She held her rifle on the man and chased him away!''

Swift Arrow watched her eyes for a moment, remembering the brave, fiesty young girl Zeke had brought to his people those many years ago. She had not changed. He grinned and then started laughing. ''I can see it!'' he exclaimed.

Zeke smiled himself, pulling Abbie close again, and the other children smiled, some of them giggling. Swift Arrow sat down and Abbie scurried to get him some meat.

''What is happening in the North, Swift Arrow?'' Zeke asked his brother.

Swift Arrow sobered then, and the air was suddenly heavy. Abbie handed the man a tin plate full of meat, and he felt warm at her closeness. He knew the next few days would be very hard for him. There was a rich womanliness about her that filled a man's nostrils and stirred his insides. Zeke Monroe knew what he was doing when he claimed this woman. He looked at Zeke.

''Things are bad,'' he told his brother. ''The Great

White Father in the East has passed a law that gives land away to new settlers. They come by the hundreds, Zeke. By the thousands! They swarm about the land like bees. They shoot at us whenever they please, but if we shoot back we are called savage. Whole villages are punished for what one or two men do. Many more Sioux and Northern Cheyenne have died from disease. Our children starve. And it is only the beginning!''

Zeke sighed and closed his eyes. ''I know, my brother. On the way here Black Elk's horse got caught up in a barbed wire fence. We had to kill it. I'll never forget the look on Black Elk's face—the hopelessness in his eyes.''

''In the North we fight!'' Swift Arrow answered. ''Our brothers in the South think that by continuing to be friendly, they will be treated better, given more land and rights. And for now it is so. The Great White Father has declared that more food and supplies should be given to the peaceful Indians. My brothers in the North are angry over this, because the Southern Cheyenne have lead the whites to believe that we all agree to the Treaty of Fort Wise. But we do not! It is not a legal treaty. There are only a few signatures, and the primary chiefs have never signed it. And I tell you this, my brother. Those Indians who remain peaceful will one day suffer just as much as those who choose to fight. It is not just the warring Indians the soldiers will come for. It is *all* Indians! For the white man wants his land—north and south, east and west. There will be no place for us.'' He bit off a piece of meat and chewed quietly for a moment, and Zeke stared at the flames of the small cooking fire. He knew his brother was right. ''We in the North have decided that if the white man sees fit to kill us off like so many flies, then we shall do the same,'' Swift Arrow continued between bites. ''If violence is the only thing they understand, then they will discover what a violent people we can be. We have raided many farms, burned the houses and stolen the horses! They plant fields and we burn them.'' He moved his eyes to Abbie. ''It is not a safe place for white women,'' he added.

Their eyes held. ''And you? Have you killed white women?''

He studied her for a long, quiet moment. ''No,'' he replied. ''Only the men.''

She looked down. She knew why he would not kill white women.

''I remember when we would go out on the hunt,'' Swift Arrow continued. ''And all we would see for miles and miles would be rolling plains, sometimes black with buffalo. Such visions are gone forever now. You remember those days also, my brother, when first you came out here and found our mother and lived among the Cheyenne. Those were good days.''

Zeke nodded. He missed his mother, and the thought of being torn from her when he was very small renewed his hatred for his white father.

Swift Arrow sighed and bit into the meat again. ''No more of this talk,'' he declared. ''We are together again. And this is Wolf's Blood's time.'' He put a hand on Wolf's Blood's shoulder. ''It is good to be here. When I finish eating I shall go and see Black Elk and his family.'' He set his plate down and faced Wolf's Blood fully. ''Tomorrow you begin to fast. Make your father proud, Wolf's Blood. Remember that the spirit of the wolf is in you. The wolf is strong and rugged. And remember that if you cry out you will bring much pain to your mother's heart and you will frighten your brothers and sisters. When they pierce your flesh, think only of the wolf, and of your honor. Blow on the bone whistle. Remember that. This is why a whistle will be put to your lips. Blow it—hard. Breathe deeply and blow and

186

blow. It helps the pain. It is made of the eagle bone and will carry your prayers to the spirits."

Wolf's Blood nodded. "I shall remember, my uncle."

Swift Arrow turned and looked at Zeke, who sat wearing only a loincloth. He studied the many scars on his brother, some of them from his own sacrifice at the Sun Dance. "In spite of your white blood, you proved your courage at the Sun Dance," he told Zeke. "Your son will do the same. Watch him with pride, my brother. Look at him as a warrior, not as a little boy." He turned his eyes to Abbie. "And you must do the same. It is hardest for the mother."

He suddenly leaped to his feet. "I go now. I will come back in the morning." He bent down and picked up the remaining meat. "Thank you for the food, Abigail. You are a good squaw."

The remark brought a smile to her lips again and Swift Arrow grinned back. He nodded and quickly left, suddenly needing to get away from her.

In the deep of the night all was quiet. The children slept soundly, but Abbie lay awake, staring at a star she could see through the hole at the top of the *tipi*. There was so much to think about this night. It was good that Swift Arrow had come, but the joy of it was broken by his sorrow over what was happening to the Indians, and by the fact that her son must begin his ordeal the next day. She stirred and realized Zeke was not beside her. She sat up.

"Zeke?"

"I saw him go out, Mother," Wolf's Blood spoke up. "I think he took whiskey with him. Perhaps you should find him."

She frowned and held a robe in front of her. "Your father almost never drinks," she replied. "I think you're right, Wolf's Blood. I had better go find him. Turn around so that I can put on my tunic."

The young man turned over and she quickly put on a plain tunic, wanting to save the white one for the ceremonies that would begin in the morning. She went outside, where many campfires still burned. In the distance, at the center of the circle of hundreds of *tipis,* was the Sun Dance lodge. The pole at the center of it, which was the center of the sacrifice, cast an odd shadow created by a fire that burned inside the sacrificial lodge.

"Zeke?" she called out again. She walked into the darkness behind their *tipi,* for she had not seen him anywhere in the light of the fires. "Zeke, where are you?"

She gasped as a strong arm grasped her about the waist and pulled her close, and in the next moment his lips were on hers, kissing her savagely, a light odor of whiskey on his breath. She knew it was her husband, and yet somehow he was different, his soul torn by the fact that Swift Arrow loved her, his heart torn by the knowledge of what his son would suffer in the next few days, and his physical needs enhanced by the whiskey that he had drunk to try to forget the ache of what was happening to the people.

He released the kiss, but kept a tight hold on her so that it was difficult even to breathe. "I want you," he told her flatly. "I can't take you inside because my need is so strong that the children would hear."

Her heart pounded with a desire that was close to fear, for this was a rare moment when he was much more savage than white, when his needs would be feasted on her in more of a rage than in love. But this was her husband. She would not fight him, even though he had been drinking.

"Then take me where no one can hear," she answered. "After tomorrow neither of us will want to do

188

this for a while. Our time and our hearts will be spent on Wolf's Blood.''

He picked her up in his arms and carried her into the darkness, where already he had a blanket ready. Somehow he had known she would come searching for him and would go with him. He laid her gently on the blanket, then removed his loincloth, looking even bigger and more powerful in the soft moonlight. He bent over her and pushed up her tunic, and she was naked beneath it. She let him pull it over her head, and then he was bending close, tasting her body with his lips, claiming her as though he needed to prove she belonged to him. It was not necessary, but she knew that for him it was. In this moment he could also forget about his son and what the next day would bring.

He lay down beside her in the opposite direction, nestling his face against her belly, then moving down to taste her sweetness, his strong hands gently pressing her thighs apart. This always brought a blush to her skin but fire to her blood, and tonight especially it felt so right, for she was his woman and he had a great need this night.

She cried out in an ecstasy he forced from her, for to be totally claimed by this man meant an awakening of great passion. He moved back up her body, lingering for a moment on her full breasts before moving to the curve of her neck. His lips were moist with her own sweetness and she trembled with a mixture of lust and invaded modesty, a modesty this man had ways of sometimes breaking down completely. He realized it was still there, in spite of all the children and all the times they had made love, for this was Abbie, and she was really no different than the first time he had taken her. That was what always made it exciting, and still the challenge was there to get her to totally let go of her inhibitions and give to him her most secret parts.

189

"My Abbie-girl," he whispered, moving between her legs. "You lie here on the grass like a squaw, and tomorrow your son will begin his suffering because you have let him be Indian. What have I done to your life?"

"You have made me happy," she replied. "Nothing less."

He rested on his elbows, grasping the hair at each side of her head, and in the next moment he surged inside of her, his long hair brushing across her lips. She grasped his powerful wrists in her hands and arched up to him in return, tingling with the extent of his power and the knowledge that she had been chosen to be the woman on whom he spent his passions. She gasped at the savageness of his thrust and moaned his name. He wanted to be more gentle, yet somehow he could not. The whiskey made him want to take her and take her, consume her, ravage her. He was almost angry with her for being so damned sweet as to marry him and love him, forcing him to do that which he had wanted most not to do—marry another white woman. He loved her, and yet sometimes he hated her for making him love her by her own goodness and unselfish love.

He came down on her, wrapping his arms around her and rolling over quickly so that she was on top of him. "Be free tonight, woman of Lone Eagle," he told her. "Do not be like a white woman. Be Lone Eagle's woman."

She had never done such a thing, yet somehow this night she felt strangely uninhibited, and for the next few moments she was wild and alive and so much in love with this man that it hurt, remembering the times he had risked his life to save her, more times than she could even count over the years. With this man she was never afraid, and with this man she was more alive than at any other time in her life. She leaned down and he tasted her breasts, then rolled her over and poured his life into her as a cry of spent passion exited his lips.

He lay there limp then, sorry for his savageness, sorry for the whiskey, and suddenly overcome by his concern for Wolf's Blood. "Hold me, Abbie," he groaned. She put her arms around his powerful shoulders, and when he rested his face against hers, she felt a wetness on her cheek.

"He'll be fine," she told him gently. "He's the son of Lone Eagle."

Twelve

The special herbs that the shaman put on the fire created more sweet smoke, which the man then fanned over Wolf's Blood's face. The boy groaned slightly, and Zeke's fingers dug into the earth, where he lay face down praying for his son.

"Zeke, it has to be done," Abbie told him again. "Just like it had to be done when I nearly died from the arrow wound."

"I can't," he moaned. "Not to him."

"You can and you must!" she pleaded.

He raised his head, looking at her with red-rimmed eyes, his face showing his torture. "No."

She sucked in her breath, wanting to scream at him. She glanced at her son again, her heart wrenching at the sight of his hollow cheeks and sunken eyes. How courageously he had suffered the Sun Dance! For three days and nights he had danced constantly around the central pole with the others, without eating or drinking. On the fourth day he had stood silently while the skewers were placed through the flesh of his breasts, the back of his shoulders, his upper arms and his thighs. And again he had danced, dragging the weights that were attached to the skewers, until the flesh weakened and the skewers tore through and he collapsed. He knew then that he could endure all things.

His father had proudly carried the boy to their *tipi*, and both he and Abbie nursed him. But something had gone wrong. Infection had developed in one thigh. If not for the boy's already weakened condition, perhaps he would have healed more readily, but the infection had brought him so much pain, on top of his other wounds and his lack of nourishment, that Wolf's Blood could not bring himself to eat, which acted as a vicious circle, making him weaker. It had been five days since the ordeal had ended. The other wounds were healing, but the one in his thigh had only gotten worse, and the boy was failing rapidly.

"I don't see where there is a choice," she told Zeke sternly. "The infection must be drained. The shaman's medicine is doing him no good. And you are the best man with a knife. It's your duty, Zeke Monroe!"

"Leave me, woman!" he growled. She flinched as though he had hit her. Never had he spoken to her in such a tone. For a brief moment an apology swept through his eyes, but then he turned away and put his head down again. Abbie blinked back tears and left the shaman's *tipi*, where Wolf's Blood had been taken. She shuddered with confusion. If Zeke did not do something soon, she would have to do it herself. But she would be clumsy at such a thing and perhaps only make the boy worse. She walked to their own *tipi*, where Swift Arrow sat outside, keeping guard over the rest of the Monroe children, who slept restlessly, all of them worried about their brother. Black Elk sat with Swift Arrow, both men gravely concerned.

Abbie approached them, her face strained, obviously forcing herself to stay calm. "Come and walk with me a moment, Swift Arrow," she told the eldest of Zeke's Cheyenne brothers.

Swift Arrow looked up at her with terrible sorrow in his eyes. He loved Wolf's Blood as his own son, and he loved this woman. How tired she looked! How drawn and lonely. He rose and nodded toward the darkness. Abbie turned and he followed her as she walked away from the *tipi*, so that the other children would not hear her concerns. Swift Arrow walked up close behind her, and the scent of her hair was pleasant to his nostrils.

"The boy?" he asked.

"I need your help, Swift Arrow. Sometimes you can talk to Zeke when I can't." She turned to face him. "If Zeke doesn't cut out that infection, our son will die. It's as simple as that."

"To do such a thing would be impossible for Zeke. It is his son. He cannot take the knife to his son."

"If he doesn't take the knife to him, it's the same as killing him!" she almost growled. "Please . . . help me, Swift Arrow!" she added, her voice turning to more of a whimper. "Talk to him! Make him understand he has no choice. He won't listen to me." Her body jerked as a sob caught in her throat. "If Wolf's Blood dies, Zeke dies also, Swift Arrow. Don't you . . . see? I will lose them *both!* Please. If for no other reason, then do it for me."

He felt as though lightning had struck him. She knew! She knew that he loved her. He stepped back slightly, mortified that she should know, suddenly ashamed and embarrassed.

She swallowed and reached out to him. "Zeke . . . told me once . . . that to be loved by a Cheyenne Dog Soldier was the greatest honor that could be given to me, for it shows that I have truly become one of the people. There is no shame in loving someone, Swift Arrow, not when it is done with the honor and respect you have given me. And I know that your love for Wolf's Blood—and for Zeke—is also strong, strong enough

194

that perhaps you will find a way to màke Zeke understand, words that I have not yet found. I beg you to try,
Swift Arrow. I . . . I feel so guilty. I've heard some of
the others whisper . . . saying my son has too much
white blood in him . . . and that is why he did not
heal." Her voice began to break. "I . . . can't bear to
hear them say that," she whimpered. "And . . . if
Wolf's Blood dies . . . Zeke will blame me . . . because I am the one who is all white. He never . . .
should have married me!" Her shoulders shook in a
sob and she hung her head, and in the next moment
Swift Arrow was standing close, pulling up her chin
with his hand.

"This is not the proud, strong young girl my brother
brought to the people those many winters ago," he told
her gently. "Your white blood is strong, Abigail, as
strong as any Cheyenne blood. My brother loves you
much more than his own life. It is not you he would
blame, my sister. It is himself. Always he has feared
that side of himself. And always he has blamed that side
of himself whenever tragedy comes to him. I have seen
this in him, the child in him that sometimes still hears
the voices of those who insulted him back in that place
called Tennessee—those who almost convinced him he
was not worth spitting on. Now he feels helpless. He
has told himself that he does not deserve the beautiful
woman he married, or the fine son she gave to him. He
has given up the fight before it even began."

She reached up and took his hand. "Talk to him,
Swift Arrow," she said quietly. She sniffed and
squeezed his hand. "Please. You think it isn't your
place to interfere, but I do. I'm asking you to do this
. . . for me, and because of your love for Wolf's
Blood."

Their eyes met, and he reached up to put a hand to
the side of her face. How easy it would be now to steal

her away and do what he wished with her. But Abigail Monroe loved just one man. There was no room left for anyone else.

"I don't want to lose my son," she whispered. "And I don't want to lose my husband. I'm scared, Swift Arrow."

The words pierced his heart, for still she did not truly understand the extent of his love for her. But perhaps that was best for everyone. She looked at him now the way she would look at a brother, turned to him as a brother, and that was, after all, all that he was to her—a brother. He had called her sister since the day she had bravely saved Tall Grass Woman's daughter from the deep waters.

"I will see what I can do," he told her.

She hugged him spontaneously, and he hesitantly put his arms around her for a moment, giving her the support he knew she needed. Then he quickly pushed her away, reminding himself that he was not only just a brother, but also a warrior, with no interest left in life but to kill and raid. He turned and left her and headed for the shaman's *tipi*.

Abbie quickly followed, and Black Elk looked up curiously as Swift Arrow walked rapidly and determinedly toward the *tipi*. He got up and followed behind Abbie.

Abbie gasped and stepped back when Swift Arrow suddenly emerged from the *tipi* dragging Zeke with him. He kept pushing at him, but Zeke was not fighting back, and he stumbled and fell, the fight strangely gone from him, his eyes red and wild.

"Why are you not doing what you can to save that boy?" Swift Arrow yelled at him. "What is wrong, white belly?" he sneered, deliberately insulting Zeke's white blood. "Has your cowardly side finally shown itself?"

196

Zeke blinked, as though someone had just awakened him. He rose slowly to his feet, frowning in confusion. "What the hell is wrong with you, Swift Arrow?" he asked quietly.

Swift Arrow stepped closer. "I am telling you I am ashamed of my half-blood brother for the first time! Always he has proven himself a true Cheyenne. Always he had nothing but courage and honor. Now you show neither! Your stinking white blood is bringing death to your son!"

More Indians had emerged from their dwellings at the sound of the shouting, and Zeke stiffened, still somewhat confused. He wore only his loincloth, with the infamous knife at his waist as always. Swift Arrow wore only leggings, and the two of them stood there with muscles taut, eyes gleaming, both grand specimens of Indians but Zeke a head taller than his brother.

"Why do you speak to me this way, Swift Arrow?" he asked. "I don't need you to tell me it's my white blood that is killing my son."

Swift Arrow's fists clenched. "You fool! At this moment I cannot call you brother! Always I thought you the better man, but now I wonder." He deliberately grinned. "Even your wife wonders."

He had found the right words. New fire seemed to whip through Zeke's dark eyes, and he straightened more, glancing from his brother to Abbie, who stared at him wide-eyed, unsure of how to react. The words were cruel and untrue, and yet they had sparked something in Zeke and shaken him from his stupor. She looked away, wanting him to think she was ashamed of him.

Zeke looked back at his brother, his eyes wild.

"I was just with your wife," Swift Arrow taunted, his own heart pounding. To tempt Zeke Monroe into a fight was asking for death and he well knew it. "I think

perhaps she is too much woman for you, white belly!"
he sneered.

Abbie screamed as Zeke charged into him then, and
both men rolled on the ground. Black Elk pulled Abbie
back farther when she started to reach out and try to
stop the fight.

"Let it be," he warned. "You would get hurt. Swift
Arrow knows what he is doing."

Others who had gathered began to get excited, taking sides and urging on their favorite, as the two powerful men struggled in the dirt, wrestling violently. For
the first few minutes it seemed almost even, for Zeke
was weak from lack of food, as he had been unable to
eat ever since the ritual. He had only anger and pride to
go on, and those two factors were building inside of him
every moment as he rolled in a tangled heap with his
brother. One voice told him it was foolish to think Abbie would ever look at another man; but another voice
reminded him that Swift Arrow did, after all, love her.
And although Zeke knew few women could be more
trustworthy and honorable, the thought of his brother
even looking at her suddenly brought a raging jealousy.

The fight continued, each taking a turn at slamming
the other to the ground, twisting an arm or a neck, one
pinning the other down only to be suddenly flipped to
find himself on his own back. The crowd cheered excitedly, and Abbie clung to Black Elk's arm tightly. Both
men were covered with dust and mud, and each man
bled from cuts and scrapes suffered from wallowing on
the gravelly ground.

Suddenly the fight began to turn more one-sided, as
Zeke's strength returned with every second that his
jealousy grew, combined with the desperate fear that
his son might be dying and perhaps it was his fault for
urging the boy to participate in the Sun Dance.

Zeke arched up like a grizzly, releasing himself from

another pin, then whirled and kicked out, landing a foot in Swift Arrow's ribs. Swift Arrow grunted and jerked back, and Zeke kicked out again, sending the man sprawling backward into the screaming crowd. The onlookers scattered out of the way, and Zeke dived into Swift Arrow, jerking him up and viciously yanking the man's left arm behind him, while whipping out his huge blade and reaching around to hold it against Swift Arrow's throat.

"Zeke, no!" Abbie screamed.

He hesitated, and the two men stood there panting and sweating, Swift Arrow pinned with his back against Zeke and the big knife at his throat. He reached up with his right arm to try to pull Zeke's knife hand away, but could not budge Zeke's powerful arm.

"Now who is the better man?" Zeke hissed. He bent Swift Arrow's arm more. "Tell the others who is the better man!" he growled.

Swift Arrow only grinned. "I have never doubted who is the better man," he said calmly. "Nor did your woman. You, my brother, are the one who doubted. The Zeke I called brother would be in the shaman's *tipi* now draining his son's infection and saving his life, just as he once saved his woman's life, even though it brought him great sorrow to bring her such pain."

Zeke softened, suddenly beginning to see the reason for Swift Arrow's cruel words. He whirled Swift Arrow around and the two men glared at each other.

"Perhaps you would rather let your son suffer until he must lose his leg!" Swift Arrow added. "Or perhaps he will get so bad that you will have to end his life for him, as you had to do for your wife's small brother many winters ago when first she came west."

Abbie covered her face and wept quietly, remembering the terrible decision she had had to make when asking the scout, Zeke Monroe, to end her little brother's life for him, for the boy was suffering a horrible, slow death from a crushed, infected body. The mercy killing Zeke had agreed to was the most difficult thing he 'had ever done, an act of love that still sometimes haunted him. The reminder brought the terrible pain of it to Zeke's heart again. He lowered his knife and shoved it into its sheath, then reached out and grasped Swift Arrow's wrist. "Help me, my brother. Talk to Wolf's Blood. Help hold him down and give him courage. It will be . . . so painful for him."

Swift Arrow nodded. "Pain is better than death. At least when you feel pain you are still alive."

Zeke moved his eyes from Swift Arrow to Abbie, suddenly realizing how difficult the last several days had been for her. He walked up close to her, remembering her brave act of love when she asked him to put her little brother out of his terrible misery those many years ago. She was still that same strong, determined little girl, and he suspected she had had much to do with Swift Arrow's attack on him. He pulled her into his arms and held her tightly as she wept against his chest. She felt weak and relieved, realizing the arms around her were strong again, sure again. He would be all right, and suddenly she knew her son would be all right.

"Boil some water, Abbie-girl," he told her. "Let's make our son well and go home. Ole Dooley must be wondering what has happened to us. I hope Comanches haven't come and stolen the horses from the ranch."

Seven days later Wolf's Blood emerged from the shaman's *tipi*, walking on his own two feet. His right thigh was heavily bandaged, and he limped slightly, but he refused to use a cane, and he insisted that he would ride his own mount when they departed. After all, he was a man now. He would not lie on a travois like a woman. He wore a necklace of wolf's claws around his neck, a gift from the shaman for his courage. In his hair he wore two eagle feathers, given him by Swift Arrow, and at his waist was strapped a new knife from Zeke, one Zeke had secretly bought at Bent's Fort as a gift for his son at the Sun Dance sacrifice. It had a beautifully carved horn handle, with a tempered steel blade that was razor sharp. The knife was fifteen inches long from tip to the end of the handle. It was called a bowie knife, and it was the boy's most prized possession, the finest knife he had ever set eyes on. It rested in a leather sheath, beautifully beaded in brilliant colors, the handiwork of his mother.

His little brother, Jason, grinned at the sight of his big warrior brother and ran in circles around him on chubby legs and feet, sometimes falling, but giggling when he did so. Thirteen-year-old Margaret, to whom Wolf's Blood was the closest, walked up and hugged him, and nine-year-old Jeremy just stared in awe. Jeremy had never liked the things Wolf's Blood liked. He only rode a horse because it was necessary. By the age of nine, Wolf's Blood had been much bigger than Jeremy, and already knew how to use a bow and lance. But Jeremy didn't like weapons and still hated the noise of a rifle. He was not wild and aggressive like his brother. He preferred to sit quietly by himself and learn his letters, or listen to his mother tell him a story. He didn't hate Wolf's Blood. He simply knew already in his young heart that he would never be like this older brother of his. He admired Wolf's Blood, but he had no true desire to be like him, and in that respect he always feared the father that he loved would somehow love him less.

Zeke caught the way Jeremy watched Wolf's Blood, and he immediately walked over to the boy and whisked him up to his shoulders. "Each man proves himself in his own way, Jeremy-boy," he told the child as he carried him to his horse. He plopped him onto the animal's back. "Your day will come, Jeremy," he reassured the boy. "You will prove yourself in your own way. Be proud of your brother, but don't think you must be just like him. Be yourself, Jeremy."

The boy grinned as Zeke left him, a man and a son worlds apart. But the love was there.

Zeke loaded up the rest of his children, taking Lillian with him this time so that Wolf's Blood could ride alone. Most of the hundreds of others who had gathered for the celebrations had already left the camp, heading back to Arkansas River country in southeast Colorado Territory, a few going north to join the Northern Cheyenne and the Sioux, and all wondering if they would find enough freedom the next summer to gather for another celebration, none aware yet that in Minnesota, two hundred whites had been massacred by the Sioux and the entire frontier was in a panic, with governors of western territories screaming for Washington to send out more troops to obliterate the red man from the plains and prairies. But there were no troops to send, for the best men were involved in a bloody civil war, and there was nothing left to do but form a western army from volunteers—people who were already Indian-haters. And the cry in the wind and the groan in the land seemed to be getting louder with each passing winter.

But for the moment, those things did not matter. Wolf's Blood was healing. He would not lose his leg or his life. Zeke mounted up and rode up to Swift Arrow, who sat on his mount several feet from the rest of the family, a man who hated emotional partings.

"Thank you, my brother," Zeke told him.

Swift Arrow glanced over at Abbie, who was hugging

and talking to little Jason. "Thank your woman, not me," he replied, returning his gaze to Zeke. "Tell her goodbye for me. I go now. Always, because of her kind heart, she cries when I leave. I do not wish to see the tears."

Zeke nodded and reached out to grasp his brother's wrist. "I understand, Swift Arrow."

The man nodded. "Watch her closely, Zeke. The people grow restless. Bad times are coming, and the day may come when even the ones like Abbie are no longer trusted. The wind weeps, my brother."

Zeke nodded. "May the spirits ride with you, Swift Arrow, and save you in battle. I will worry about you."

The man just grinned. "Do not worry about Swift Arrow." He frowned. "And where is your white brother, the one called Danny? He was a good soldier, a friend. The people trusted him. I no longer see him at Fort Laramie."

Zeke sighed. "Danny left the Union army to go back to Tennessee. He joined the graycoats in the Civil War."

Swift Arrow looked confused. "I do not understand that white man's war."

Zeke sighed. "Not many of us do. But it's one I intend to stay out of. I just wish I knew what has happened to Danny. There hasn't been any word."

"I hope that some day he will return to our country. He was the only soldier that I trusted."

Zeke picked up his horse's reins. "I have a feeling he'll be back, Swift Arrow."

Swift Arrow moved his mount away a little. "I go now. I have had many long talks with Wolf's Blood and said my farewells. Keep the wind at your back, my brother, and your face to the sun. You will always be *Kehilan*, drinker of the wind. And so will Wolf's Blood."

He turned his horse and rode off at a gallop. Abbie turned her mount and called after him, but he kept riding. She watched him for a moment, realizing without being told why he had left so quickly. Zeke rode up close to her and said, "Let's go home, Abbie-girl."

She studied the handsome face, the high cheekbones and dark eyes. This was Lone Eagle. She had her man back again, the man she had fallen in love with the moment she first set eyes on him. For a moment she saw him as she had seen him when he stepped into the light of her father's campfire to volunteer his services as a scout. His provocative power seemed to fill the night air, and that same power still emanated from his very being. He had not changed. The wind blew the dark hair over the shoulders of his buckskin shirt, and the fringes danced at his broad shoulders. He seemed unusually handsome this day, beads and feathers entwined in thin braids that mixed in with the rest of his hair, a turquoise stone at his throat, in the center of a bone necklace that he wore, the lines of his face and even the scar on his cheek and chin only adding to his handsomeness.

He tore his eyes from hers and rode ahead, little Lillian clinging to his waist.

Abbie's heart pounded with joy as they crested the hill and looked down on the little cabin below. Everything looked peaceful. The Appaloosas grazed lazily in the tall grass of the north field, and Dooley was waving, having spotted them from below. The faithful ranch hand and Zeke's good white friend urged his own horse into a gallop and called out a hello as he rode up toward them. Abbie noticed as she rode more to the left and got a better view of the cabin that a carriage sat outside, as well as three horses she had not seen before. She turned to Zeke.

"Zeke, someone is at the house. I don't recognize the horses."

He frowned and rode over to look, then urged his horse toward Dooley, who was approaching the top of the hill by then.

"Zeke!" he called out. "What happened? I expected you a good ten days ago."

"Wolf's Blood developed an infection. He had a bad time of it, but he's all right now."

Dooley glanced at the young man. "You came through the ritual just fine, I'll bet, didn't you, boy?"

The boy nodded. "I did not cry out. And look at this!" He held up the bowie knife. "From my father."

Dooley grinned. "You learn to use that like your father, and you'll not have to worry about your enemies, Wolf's Blood."

The boy grinned.

"Dooley," Zeke interrupted, "what is that carriage doing below?"

The man's smile faded as he faced Zeke again. He moved his eyes to Abbie, then back to Zeke. "Your sister-in-law is here, Zeke. Danny's wife. Emily."

Abbie and Zeke looked at each other in surprise. They had never even met the woman.

"Why on earth did she come here?" Abbie asked.

Dooley sighed. "You'll have to get the whole story from her. All I know is she said she'd wait it out here until you folks got back. Says Danny needs help and Zeke here is the only one who can help him."

Abbie's heart sank. "Oh, my God," she whispered, meeting Zeke's eyes. "I knew it! I thought . . . perhaps I was wrong . . . about you leaving again."

He reached out and grasped her shoulder. "We don't know yet for sure what she wants, Abbie-girl. Don't jump to conclusions." He squeezed her shoulder then let go and rode forward, but Abbie watched him as though he were riding right out of her life.

"Zeke," she whispered. She felt fate grasping at her again, their destiny being guided by elements that could not be controlled. She urged her horse forward to meet Danny Monroe's wife.

Thirteen

The young woman who stood on the cabin porch to greet them was frail looking, with auburn hair and sea-green eyes and a silky white complexion. She was a woman of exceeding beauty, and Zeke's first thought was that she looked like a piece of fine china that might break at any moment. He knew that when Dan first married this woman there had been problems with getting her to leave the luxuries of St. Louis to come and be with him at Fort Laramie, and the marriage had almost ended before it had a chance to begin. It was easy to see now why Emily Monroe doubted her ability to survive in the West. She was obviously not of strong constitution. A man could tell that at first glance. She was rich and slightly spoiled when Dan had met her, but Zeke could see how his brother might have over-looked those things in return for the chance to hold such exquisite beauty and call her his wife. She was not the kind of woman Zeke would want to marry, but he had to smile at the thought of Danny being taken by the girl.

He rode closer and slid from his horse, reaching up and taking Lillian down, while Emily stood staring at him as though he were some kind of grizzly coming to attack her. Zeke Monroe was not only bigger than she had even pictured, but also much meaner looking. He was pure Indian in appearance. She had not expected that, in spite of all the times Danny had tried to explain to her what Zeke was like. He wore only leggings this day, and his bare chest displayed a belt of ammunition, while the menacing knife was strapped to his waist along with the handgun. His arms were decorated with copper bands and his hair hung loose.

The rest of the Monroe family rode closer, and Abbie was struck by the exquisite beauty and frail countenance of Emily Monroe. So this was the spoiled young girl she had once written to, trying to explain that it was possible for a woman to survive in the West, trying to convince the girl she should come out and be with Danny, who in the early days of their marriage was a very frustrated, unhappy and lonely man, to the point of having an affair with a Sioux woman. But things had finally improved, and much of the credit for that went to the beautiful letter Abbie had sent to Emily, a woman she had never met, until now.

The rest of the Monroe children stared at the woman and Wolf's Blood immediately disapproved, deciding right away he would never marry something as breakable as this woman looked to be, although she was very pretty—like a flower. But flowers wilted, and this woman looked like she could wilt very easily.

Zeke mounted the steps and towered over the sister-in-law he had never met. She stepped back, her eyes wide. He grinned and put out his hand. "So you're Danny's wife, are you?" he spoke up gently, seeing the fear in her eyes. She had no choice but to offer her hand, and she was surprised at the gentle way in which he took it, half expecting him to crush it.

"I . . . yes. I am Emily. Our little girl, Jennifer, she's inside, with the gentlemen who brought me

208

here." She pulled her hand away. "I'm sorry . . . to intrude upon you this way, Mister Monroe. I am sure you are all very tired. Your man, Dooley, he told me . . . where you have been." She glanced over at Wolf's Blood and swallowed, feeling ill at the thought of what Dooley had explained to her about the Sun Dance and Zeke's son partaking of the sacrifice. She looked back up at Zeke. "You . . . you *are* Zeke Monroe, aren't you?"

His smile was warm and handsome, and when he grinned she could see a resemblance to Danny, although their coloring was totally different. "I sure am. Please call me Zeke." His eyes took a quick scan of her body, and he suppressed an urge to laugh at the thought of Danny diving into a quick marriage just to get this pretty flower in his bed. No wonder they had had problems. This was the kind of girl who probably thought all a husband and wife did was kiss, until she became a wife and found out otherwise.

Abbie was dismounting now. Emily glanced at her. Abbie was dark and beautiful, much prettier than she had pictured, and much more preserved. She had expected a weathered, tired-looking, rather dried-up and overworked woman. The young woman who approached her now was far from any of those things, a woman of radiant beauty and a woman of amazing inner strength. It was one of those things another could sense about her right away, and Emily found herself wishing she could be as strong as Abigail Monroe. Abbie approached them carrying little Jason. She shifted the boy to one arm and walked up to Emily to hug her, thinking to herself how bony Emily felt.

"Emily!" she exclaimed softly. "It's so wonderful to finally get to meet you in person. We've heard so much about you over the years."

Emily blushed, realizing that all they had heard had

209

not exactly been flattering. Now she could understand the beauty and strength of the words in the letter Abbie had written to her nine years earlier, urging a then-spoiled and frightened Emily to be a better wife to Danny. Here was a woman that another woman could call friend, a woman one could turn to for comfort, one who probably had all the right words. For Abigail Monroe had suffered and fought and loved and sacrificed all of her life. Her smile and eyes were warm. She pulled back and studied Emily.

"You're even prettier than Danny said," she told the young woman.

Emily smiled and blinked back tears. "I . . . thank you for your kind words. But . . . you might not be so happy to see me, Abbie. Is . . . is it all right to call you Abbie?"

Abbie suppressed her apprehension over the reason for the woman's presence. "My heavens, of course it is! Come back inside, Emily. I hope you found everything clean and comfortable. We've been gone for weeks, so I haven't been here to keep things tidy. How long have you been here?"

The girl twisted her hands nervously. "About four days." She looked Abbie over again. She was a slender but strong woman, her white skin tanned to a lovely brown but still many shades lighter than her husband's natural deep color. "You're so pretty, Abbie," she blurted out. "I didn't expect . . . I mean . . . you look wonderful. Living out here the way you do . . . having your babies all alone . . . ." She swallowed again. "I don't know how you do it."

Their eyes held. "A woman can do a lot of things she never thought she could do when it's for the man she loves," Abbie replied.

Emily's lips quivered and a tear slipped down her cheek. "Yes . . . I am beginning to learn that." She sniffed. "I . . . . was so nervous . . . about coming here. I didn't know what to expect, and I heard . . . so many things about . . . about how wild your husband can be. And after the way Danny and I started out, I thought perhaps . . . I'd get chased right off your land. I was hoping . . ." She looked up at Zeke. "I need your help, Mr. Monroe . . . I mean, Zeke."

To their surprise she burst into tears and Abbie and Zeke looked at each other in confusion. Abbie put an arm around the girl's shoulders.

"Come inside, Emily, and sit down. It will be all right," she soothed the girl. She gave Emily a reassuring hug and they went into the house, Zeke telling Wolf's Blood to keep the children outside for a while. Abbie was surprised and grateful to see that while Emily had been there she had obviously cleaned the cabin. There was even a pot of stew over the hearth, as well as some coffee. A lovely little girl with green eyes and red curls looked up at them from where she sat on the rough board floor playing with a china doll, and three men sat at the large table in the middle of the room. They all rose when Zeke and Abbie went inside, staring in surprise at Abbie's Indian tunic and in amazed awe at Zeke himself, the biggest, meanest-looking Indian they had ever seen.

Emily dabbed at her eyes and breathed deeply for control. "These three gentlemen are Sidney Bale, Paul Smith and Bernard Randall," she told Zeke and Abbie. "They are all from St. Louis, where I grew up and where I am now staying in my father's house, which he bequeathed to me. These gentlemen were old friends of my father, and were kind enough to agree to accompany me and help me find you, Zeke. My father was a well-respected army general when he died, and was closely associated with all three of these men. Of course you know my father is the man Danny saved down in

211

Mexico all those years ago. That was how he and Danny knew each other, and how Danny and I eventually met. But that was years later. My . . . my father is dead now.'' She turned to the three men. ''This man is Danny's half brother, Zeke Monroe,'' she explained to them, ''the one I told you about. And this lovely woman here is his wife, Abigail. She is also from Tennessee.''

The three men nodded to Zeke and each shook hands with him. ''Emily had a rough idea where you were supposed to be living,'' Paul Smith spoke up. ''So we just headed south and asked at various forts until we found your place. You have some handsome horses out there, Mister Monroe.''

''Thank you. I raise them. Helps feed the mouths of seven hungry children.''

The three men smiled, unable to keep themselves from nothing short of staring at Zeke and Abbie, a most unusual couple. Zeke's friendly handshake and smile did not match his size and appearance. He looked more like the kind of man who would prefer to lift their scalp, and none of them doubted he could take on all three of them at once.

''It's good of you to watch out for Emily this way and give her protection in coming here,'' Zeke was telling them. ''This is quite a surprise. Surely it was a dangerous journey, with the country in so much turmoil.''

Sidney Bale frowned. ''It was indeed. The country is dangerous for everyone right now—Negro, Indian, Federals, Confederates, just about any faction you can name. Things are a mess, and, well, that's partly why Emily insisted on coming here and talking to you in person. And since the three of us are not involved in the war, and were very close to Emily's father when he was alive, well, we agreed to come along and keep watch. It was a long, hard journey for her. But she's had time to

212

rest while we waited for you to get back." His eyes scanned the powerful man before him. "You've . . . . been at some kind of Indian celebration, your friend, Dooley, tells us."

"The Sun Dance. My son took part in a very painful but religious ceremony."

The men smiled nervously, totally ignorant of Indian ways and friendly to this one only because he was distantly related to Emily, a fact that seemed incredulous when looking at him, but not as incredulous as the fact that the beautiful white woman who stood next to him had been married to the man for several years and had borne him seven children, all without the help of a doctor.

Abbie knelt down beside the little girl who was playing on the floor. She smiled and touched her curls. "You must be Jennifer." She looked up at Emily. "She's beautiful." she exclaimed.

Emily smiled. "Thank you. I suppose you know her middle name is Abigail—after you."

Abbie smiled more. "I'm very flattered that you did that, Emily."

Zeke walked toward Jennifer to get a closer look, and the girl's eyes widened. She immediately ran to her mother, burying her face in Emily's skirts. Emily blushed.

"I'm afraid . . . she's never seen anyone quite so . . . so big and dark," she told Zeke. "I'm sorry."

Zeke only chuckled, and the three men made their way toward the door. "We'll give you folks some privacy," Paul Smith spoke up. "Emily needs to talk to you. We'll be outside. Is your son out there? The one who participated in the sacrifice?"

"He's the biggest one of the lot—the one who looks the most Indian. His name is Wolf's Blood."

The three men looked at each other, and Paul Smith

213

looked back at Zeke. "Wolf's Blood?"

"That's right."

"He . . . doesn't have a white name?"

"No. The others do, but not Wolf's Blood. He wants only to be Cheyenne."

The men smiled nervously, fingering their hats in their hands, and Zeke found their attitude humorous.

"He doesn't bite," he told them. "While you're waiting, have him show you his knife throwing. He's very proud of that."

"Knife throwing," Smith replied. He glanced at Zeke's own blade. He had heard some wild tales about this man. "Of course." They all nodded to Abbie respectfully and went outside, and Zeke moved his dark eyes to Emily, losing his smile.

"What has happened to Danny?" he asked immediately. "I've been worried about him for over a year, ever since I learned he joined the Confederates. Why did he do that?"

She blinked and stepped back again. His presence seemed to fill the room and make it seem smaller. "Why, because he's from Tennessee, of course," she replied. "Surely you would understand that."

He snickered. "No, I do not understand that. If you think I have any kind of allegiance to Tennessee, ma'am, think again. I have no ties to Tennessee."

"But . . . your father is there!" she exclaimed "He's old and alone now. Your . . . your brother Lenny is dead, Zeke. He was killed at Wilson's Creek. That was part of the reason Danny went back to Tennessee to fight for the Confederates. Lenny left behind a wife and two children. He was a good man, Zeke."

Zeke closed his eyes and turned away. When he left Tennessee, Lenny was just a child. It felt strange to know he had a grown brother he had never seen and who was now already dead. It brought an ache to his chest, the ache of wondering where all the years had gone.

"What about Lance?" he asked in a strained voice.

"Lance is also fighting for the Confederates. But no one knows where he is or if he is even alive. Your father is all alone on the old farm, Zeke. In his last letter to me, Danny told me how . . . how withered and lonely he is. Lenny was good to him . . . stayed on the farm. Your father has no one now."

Zeke turned, and the look in his eyes frightened her. The hard muscle of his body tensed at the words. "My father is dead, Emily. His name was Deer Slayer, and he was Cheyenne—the man who married my Cheyenne mother and is the father of my Cheyenne brothers, Swift Arrow and Black Elk. I have no father in Tennessee."

"But you do!" she replied, confused by the words. "Your *true* father lives there!"

"I make no claim to Hugh Monroe." he told her in a louder voice. "The man is no father of mine!"

Emily blinked and her lips puckered. Perhaps she had come to the wrong man after all, and now she had offended this favorite brother of Danny's, although she was not quite sure why he was a favorite.

"Zeke, you're scaring her," Abbie spoke up quietly. "You can't expect her to understand all of that, and you have no right talking to her that way. This is Emily—Danny's wife. And she apparently needs our help."

Zeke sighed and reached out. She jumped when he touched her cheek lightly, but his touch was gentle. "I'm sorry," he told her. "Please sit down, Emily. Tell us what it is you want."

She sniffed and sat down, wiping her eyes again and keeping Jennifer on her lap. The girl curled up, looking at Zeke out of the corner of her eyes. Zeke remained standing, while Abbie began pouring some coffee. Emily stared at him as she swallowed and breathed deeply, trying to regain her composure. He was exceedingly handsome, just like Danny, but his coloring so very dark, and the many scars on his hard body revealed a man who had fought many battles. If he was anything like Danny had described him, Zeke Monroe was just the man she needed. She glanced at Abbie, so lovely and soft. She could not imagine how Abbie could lie beneath this man, in spite of his dark handsomeness. He was like a savage. Was it possible such a man could be gentle in bed? To Emily sex had been a frightening thing in the beginning, something that was merely necessary and painful. She wondered what it must have been like for Abigail. And yet there was the beautiful letter, written by a woman who was apparently totally happy and satisfied, totally in love. This brother of Danny's was a most unusual man.

"Did you really . . . kill all those men . . . back in Tennessee?" she asked Zeke. "The ones who killed your wife and son?"

His eyes hardened again. "I did."

She swallowed. She had nearly vomited when Danny told her how the men had been killed. She glanced at the big knife, then back up at Zeke, while Abbie brought the coffee to her.

"I . . . I think you should know . . . that my father was the one who . . . arranged . . . to get you removed from the wanted list in Tennessee," Emily told Zeke. "He did it as a favor to Danny, after Danny saved his life. I don't think Danny ever told you my father was the one responsible."

Abbie sat down to the table. "We're very grateful, Emily. I always worried about someone shooting my husband in the back just for bounty. What happened to his wife and son was a horrible thing. He's part Indian—a vengeful man. What he did to those men was natural for him. Besides that, they were murderers.

They deserved to die.''

Zeke turned away, always hating talking about what had happened to Ellen. He rubbed a hand over his eyes. ''What is it you want, Emily?'' he asked, somehow already knowing.

Emily looked nervously from Abbie to Zeke. She did not want to hurt them—did not want to separate them. And yet she felt this savage brother of Danny's could help her husband. She couldn't let her husband die slowly of his wounds in some filthy prison camp.

''I . . . I know that you and Danny . . . cared very much for one another,'' she told Zeke. ''You weren't close . . . to anyone else in your family. But you were close to Danny. And after you came west, to seek out your Cheyenne family, Danny came west also, searching for you. That's how he got involved with the army in the first place—a way of earning food and shelter out here while he searched for you.''

''So?'' Zeke turned, folding powerful arms in front of him.

Emily swallowed and clung to Jennifer. ''Danny . . . got you cleared in Tennessee,'' she went on. ''And during the years he was up at Fort Laramie, he learned to care about your people. There were many times when he helped them, Zeke, in various ways. When other officers were ordering Indians chased and shot, Danny was working for peace and fair treatment. And I don't doubt that if . . . if you were . . . hurt . . . and needed him . . . he would come to help you . . . even risk his life for you.''

Abbie's heart pounded with apprehension. She looked up at Zeke, but he was watching Emily with a frown.

''What has happened to him?'' he asked her cautiously.

The girl swallowed and blinked back more tears. ''I've learned . . . he was at Shiloh,'' she replied. ''It's

217

a place in Tennessee where one of the worst battles took place. You probably don't know very much . . . about what has been happening in the war. It's been . . . a horrible, bloody war, Zeke.'' She dabbed at her eyes again. ''They say . . . they say that at Shiloh, hundreds and hundreds were killed and wounded. They say it was so bad that . . . that the streams and ponds ran red with blood . . . that the wounded lay out all night in a cold sleet, while . . . while hogs . . . feasted on the dead ones!''

Abbie closed her eyes while Emily cried quietly.

''Damn,'' Zeke muttered. ''Danny?''

''A man . . . who was there and who knew Danny came to tell me,'' she whimpered. ''Danny begged him . . . to come to St. Louis if he ever got away from there . . . and to tell me Danny loved me and to let me know what had happened. Danny was . . . badly wounded . . . and thought he was dying. Then the Federals came . . . and Danny was still alive when they took him away with other prisoners. The other man escaped, and he came to tell me.'' She sniffed. ''And now . . . all I know is that Danny was very gravely wounded, and they . . . took him away to some terrible prison camp! I have never heard another word since it happened.''

Zeke thought about the night he had the bad dream. ''Was it . . . last spring?'' he asked, his chest aching at the thought of it.

She looked up at him. ''Yes. How . . . how did you know?''

He looked at Abbie and sighed. ''I was right,'' he told her. ''It was Danny.'' He turned to Emily. ''I had a dream. Someone I loved needed me.'' He looked back at Abbie. ''It's happened before.''

Abbie closed her eyes and he walked over and put his hands on her shoulders. Emily was beginning to see the

218

deep love, and that this man could be gentle after all. She also saw the weight of the pain she was bringing to Abbie by coming here to literally take Zeke away to help Danny.

"What do you think I can do?" he asked Emily.

Emily dabbed at her eyes again. "I . . . I need someone to try to find Danny and get him away from wherever they have taken him. All of Daddy's soldier friends are Federals. I don't dare ask them to help my Confederate husband. When I married Danny, I never expected anything like the Civil War to happen. I never expected brother to fight brother, or that my daddy's soldier friends would turn on me, just because my husband became a Confederate. When I married Danny, I knew he was from Tennessee, but he was a lieutenant in the Western Army. There was . . . no thought of a war between North and South . . . or of Danny ever returning to Tennessee. He was just . . . an army man. And after . . . after things got better . . . in our marriage . . . I just loved Danny for Danny. It made no difference to me when he decided to join the Confederates. I understood . . . and I didn't stop him." She looked at Abbie. "I have tried . . . to be a good wife . . . to be more like you explained in your letter. I'm so very grateful for your letter, Abigail. I still have it."

Abbie forced a smile, her heart shattering at the thought of what Emily was asking of them. She wanted to hate the girl for it, yet she could not blame her. If the tables were turned, and Danny might be able to help Zeke, she would ask him to do so.

"At any rate," Emily went on. "Danny had told me so much about you, Zeke." She looked back at him pleadingly. "You are so . . . so skilled in fighting. I've heard stories . . . about how you saved your sister-in-law and a missionary woman from terrible outlaws . . . about how brave and skilled you are . . . and the many

219

fights and dangerous situations you have been in in your lifetime. He always told me you were the best at tracking, and that you were very clever at spying and such things. He said there is no man like you with the knife . . . and that you can fight many men at once and win.'' She studied the scars on him again, and Danny's stories about Zeke Monroe made the man seem ten feet tall in her eyes. "I thought . . . perhaps—" she swallowed—"I thought that since you once lived in Tennessee, you would know how to mix in back there. And you obviously know the land there. With your skills and your knowledge of the land, as well as the love you have for Danny . . . . I just was hoping . . . you would consider trying to find him and perhaps freeing him. At the least, you could find out for me if he is even alive.''

Zeke stood rigid for a moment, moving his eyes from Emily to Abbie. He suddenly felt ill, and he began to tremble. "I can't," he told her. "I love Danny. But you . . . don't understand, Emily. I can't go back there. I can't go back to Tennessee. It's impossible for me.''

Her frail body jerked in a sob. "But . . . he's probably sick . . . maybe dying slowly in some . . . some filthy camp with rats licking at his blood!'' she whimpered. "He's your brother . . . and he got you freed from a charge of eight murders. You're the best man to do it, Zeke. You can find him, I know you can! I . . . I don't know what else to do. I sit in St. Louis day in and day out going crazy not knowing where he is or how he is. Please. Please help him!''

His eyes glittered with determination. "No. I'll not go back there! I vowed I would never go back.'' He whirled and stormed out the door, and Emily broke down into resigned sobbing.

Abbie sat there, pity for Emily and sorrow over what had happened to Danny mixed with the terrible temptation to scream at Emily and tell her she had no right coming here and asking Zeke to go away on a dangerous mission. Her heart pounded with dread at the thought of being apart again, for every time he left her, there was always the possibility he would never come back. How could she live without Zeke?

But then the old courage and strength ran through her veins. There was right and wrong. Zeke owed it to Danny to try to help him. And there was more than one reason why he should return to Tennessee. It would not be easy convincing him, but if he did not do this thing, she knew that in the long run Zeke Monroe would suffer a terrible guilt that would haunt him and drain him and keep him from ever again being the strong, vital man that he was.

Abbie rose from her chair and put a hand on Emily's head. "I'll go and talk to him, Emily. Give him a little time to think it over."

The woman sniffed and looked up at her. Then she suddenly grasped Abbie's hand and kissed it and held it to her cheek. "I have never known a woman like you," she sobbed. "All I ever had was that letter . . . and now I've met you for the first time. But I can tell you're a strong and wonderful woman, Abbie. I . . . envy you. I wish I had . . . . your courage."

Abbie pulled her hand away gently. "I'm not as strong as you think, Emily. Sometimes we pretend, because our love for someone else is more important than our own fears and weaknesses." Her throat ached with a need to scream. "I'll go and talk to Zeke. Drink your coffee. I'll send the children in so you can meet them."

She turned and walked outside, walking past her children and saying nothing, forcing all of her strength to come forward and help her do what she must do. She headed for the creek, that little place where she and Zeke often went to be alone when they wanted to talk. She knew that he would go there.

Fourteen

Water splashed musically over gray and white rocks that were scattered throughout the little stream that fed the nearby Arkansas River. This was their secret place, a little alcove that dropped down from the rest of the land and was surrounded by yucca bushes and several young cottonwoods. The grass here was soft and thick, and purple iris bloomed along the creek bank and in scattered spots among the trees and bushes.

Abbie walked quietly toward Zeke, who sat beside the creek, his back to her. Her heart ached at the turmoil she knew he was experiencing. How many times had they come to this place to get away from the children and talk, often to make love? Here was the place she had come to weep when she thought he was dead after he had gone to search for Yellow Moon. But he had returned, just like other times when he had been forced to leave her. Always he managed to rise above the forces against him and return to her.

He had been home for many years now, other than short hunting excursions. She had grown accustomed to having her man around, and he in turn had no desire to leave her. She had hoped that perhaps it could always be that way. But life in this land was seldom kind for long.

"Zeke, we have to talk about this," she said softly, cautiously coming closer.

"There's nothing to talk about," he muttered, picking at some grass.

"Yes, there is. Emily needs your help, and you owe something to both her and Danny. I have Wolf's Blood now and Dooley and we can get more men from Black Elk's village to camp out here if you should have to go away. I would be fine."

He sighed and got to his feet, his back still to her. "I'm not going anywhere. It's Danny's home. Not mine. And Hugh Monroe is Danny's father. It's natural for him to care about the old man, and I don't hold that against him at all. But I don't care for him, and I can't even stand the thought of looking at him again."

"Then just go back and find Danny. You don't necessarily have to see your fa— I mean, Danny's father again." She suddenly frowned disgustedly and put her hands on her hips. "What am I saying? Zeke Monroe, you have to go back east and try to find Danny. And when you do, you'd be making a terrible mistake not to go and see your father again!"

He whirled and glared at her.

"Yes. Your father." she repeated. "It's the simple truth, and one you have to face."

His eyes were fiery with anger. "I've told you before I have no father! Deer Slayer was my father, and since he died I have none."

"Deer Slayer was your Cheyenne stepfather, and he loved you as his own son. But you have a white father by blood, whether you like to admit it or not. It's a fact, Zeke."

The look returned to his dark eyes—that of a small

223

boy forced from the arms of his true mother. The terror of being torn from his Cheyenne mother at a young age could still sometimes be seen there, and the torment and humiliation of growing up a half-breed among whites in Tennessee still haunted him, though it had been better than twenty years since he had left that place and come west to find his Cheyenne mother.

"I hate him!" he growled. "He used my mother and then tossed her to the dogs—selling her to that stinking Crow brute and taking me from her. How can I care about a man like that, father or not?"

"I didn't say you had to care about him. But you left something unsettled when you ran away, Zeke." He turned away again, his breathing heavy with hatred and turmoil. Abbie watched him with pity. "What did he look like, Zeke?" she prompted, daring to provoke his anger by making him talk about the man he thought he hated. "Was he handsome? Surely your looks didn't come totally from your mother. You've never even described him to me, Zeke."

"Shut up!" he growled, his fists clenched. She flinched. Never in all their years together had he said such a thing to her. There was a different tone to his voice, different than when he had ordered her out of Wolf's Blood's *tipi* when the boy was ill. His anger then was not directed at her personally as it was now. She swallowed to control the tears, her mouth tight, her cheeks crimson from the hurt.

"Life . . . is strange," she finally spoke up, her voice wavering. "You hate your father, who is alive. My father . . . is dead . . . and I would give the world to have him standing before me now . . . to see him again . . . tell him again that I love him." A tear slipped down her cheek. Zeke threw back his head and sighed deeply. Again she was the little girl he had befriended on the wagon train. The woman-child who had lost her family and had no one. "There is . . . a place back east called Tennessee," she went on bravely. "I grew up there myself. Your brother . . . loved it enough to join the Confederate Army to defend it. You have a father and two brothers there; and a part of you is there, Zeke Monroe, whether you like to admit it or not. You have more reason to go back than just to help Danny. You have to face a part of your past that you have denied for too long, and there will never be total peace in your heart until you do. You had . . . best think about how you will feel when you find out your real father is dead, and you never made your peace with the man." Her voice broke, and she turned away. She started back toward the cabin.

"Abbie," he groaned. She stopped and turned around, and he still stood with his back to her, his fists clenched at his sides. "I'm . . . . sorry . . . about the way I spoke—"

"I know you are," she interrupted. She saw his shoulders moving in his deep breaths as he struggled desperately to stay in control.

"It isn't . . . just hating my father," he tried to explain. "It's . . . . all of it. All of it. I'd feel . . . suffocated. I'd . . . remember her. Ellen."

An odd jealousy stirred in her soul. His first wife had long been dead, but the horror of the way she died still burned at his insides. The pain was still there.

"Then perhaps that is just another reason to go back. Perhaps you will settle that part of your life once and for all, and there will no longer be those moments when you look at me and see Ellen."

He turned, a shocked look on his face.

"Do you think I don't sometimes feel it?" She sniffed and swallowed, wiping at her eyes. "I know you

225

love me, Zeke. God knows we've both been through enough to never doubt such things. If someone told you to sink your knife into your own heart in order to save me, you'd do it without hesitating. But there have been times when she was there between us. Perhaps if you go back there, you can finally bury her.''

He stepped closer, looking as though he realized something for the first time. He studied her eyes, his own full of terrible apology. ''I . . . never knew you felt this way . . . never knew I had made you think . . .'' He shook his head, reaching out and touching her face. ''Abbie-girl, surely you know how much I love you. My strength lies in you. I love you for you . . . just for Abbie. But . . . my mind is so haunted. And sometimes she just . . . appears out of nowhere. But you've never been a replacement, Abbie. Never. I've loved you for you. I never dreamed I could find this much happiness again in my life.''

She took his hand and kissed the palm. ''I know that. But the fact remains that there is a part of your life back there that's been left hanging for years. You should go to Tennessee, Zeke. Find Danny. See your father. And you should visit the graves of Ellen and your son.'' She felt as though someone were pushing a sword through her at the way he trembled. ''You never even told me your son's name, Zeke. Never in all these years. Perhaps you need to talk about it. Perhaps you keep it too deeply buried.''

He looked at her with the little boy eyes again. ''His name was Tim. Timothy,'' he choked out. ''I . . . didn't like it. But Ellen, she liked it. So . . . we . . .'' He closed his eyes and his body jerked in an unwanted sob. ''Oh God, Abbie!'' He pulled her close, embracing her smotheringly in his sorrow.

He would go. She knew he would go, that he should go. It would be a terrible time for both of them, but it

226

must be done. Fate had come to steal him away from her again, for how long she could not know.

Charles Garvey settled back into the plush leather chair, glaring at the six men who sat opposite him, all of them bandaged in various places, two with arms in slings, two on crutches, one whose face was covered with rips and stitches, and one with a face badly swollen and purple, his jaw wired shut by a Denver dentist so that he could not talk at all. It was obvious his broken face would never be the same.

Garvey turned his eyes to his own son, who sat close by at the end of the man's desk in the large study where they had gathered. His son's ribs were still sore, and his right thumb was still purple and slightly swollen.

"Now that everyone is settled down and you, my boy, can talk slowly and sensibly, how about running through with me again just what the hell happened out there?" Garvey asked his son.

The younger Garvey's eyes glittered with hatred and with the excitement he had found in trying to hurt someone. "We fought with Indians!" he replied eagerly. "I was wounded in the thumb by a stray bullet, and I fought hand to hand with one of them, a young one about my age!" His eyes gleamed. "I gave that scummy bastard a good thrashing, too! It was exciting, Father—my first real fight with Indians!"

Garvey frowned, not the least bit happy that his son had been subjected to danger and had been wounded. He scanned the others again, who all shifted nervously in their chairs, looking guilty. Garvey looked back at Charles again, studying a bruise that lingered on the boy's cheekbone and his tall but spindly build. He suspected that his son was exaggerating his own prowess, for Charles Garvey had no fighting experience, and pitted against an Indian, even a young one, he could not possibly come out victorious. He turned back to the men, directing his eyes to one with an arm in a sling.

"Where and when did all this take place, Ben?" he asked.

The man swallowed. "In Kansas, sir, near the Smoky Hill River. It was about a month ago. We was teachin' the boy here how to track—followed some Cheyenne out of Colorado Territory into Kansas and caught up with them in Kansas. Stopped to question them about bein' off Indian land."

"And where in hell have you been all this time if it happened a month ago?" Garvey growled.

"We had to hole up at Fort Wallace, sir, on account of our wounds. We couldn't ride back to Denver right away. It was just too far."

"Did the soldiers there go after these Indians?"

"No, sir. They didn't have enough men, on account of the Civil War."

Garvey sighed disgustedly. "What started the fight? I told you I didn't want my son involved in any confrontations."

The one called Ben glanced at the other men, then back to Garvey. "Well, sir, we asked them what they was doin' in Kansas—told them we was gonna take them to Fort Wallace under arrest. There was seven of us and only four Indian men, counting the young one. The rest was just women and kids, and they was all hidin' back in the trees. We figured we had it easy. Then, uh, then the young one, he went for your son there, with no reason—called him white trash and such, had no respect, you know? He shot right at Charles with no reason at all."

Garvey gripped the arms of his chair. "Damned, stinking red bastards!" he fumed. "What then? How did all of you get yourselves busted up so bad?"

Ben sighed. "Well, sir, I don't rightly know for sure

how to explain it. Everything kind of happened at once, you know?'' He shook his head. ''The young one, he shot at Charles there and the biggest one, who I think was the young one's father, he dived into Handy. Pulled him right off his horse and ripped Handy's rifle right out of his hands. He smashed the rifle across Handy's face—broke the damned rifle. I went to shoot the man, and next thing I know the young one turns and lands a knife right in my shoulder. In the meantime Joe there jumped on the big Indian man and ended up with a knife in his hip. John was wounded in the foot by another one of the Indian men, after his own gun jammed on him, and Buel, he was attacked by a god-damned big wolf before he could get off a shot. Marty, he got a shot off at one of the Indians, and I know he at least wounded the man, maybe killed him. We ain't sure. But then the big man, he sunk a blade into Marty's side, right under his arm when he raised his rifle again. Marty ripped the blade out and rode off and John rode off after him. Your boy there, him and the young Indian boy went at it for a while. They was already in a tussle while all the rest was happening.'' The man swallowed, seeing the way Charles glared at him warningly. He knew the powerful hand the boy could wield if someone crossed him. ''Well, Charles, he did real good for himself,'' the man lied. Charles grinned proudly. ''But then the big Indian, the father and I guess the leader, he pulled the boys apart and forced Charles to get on his horse. By then they had guns on all of us, and we was all too wounded to object. Even one of the women held a gun on us. Strangest part is, sir, I could swear the woman was white.''

Garvey frowned, and there was a moment of silence while he studied Ben's eyes. ''You sure about that?''

Ben scratched his head. ''Almost. She wore a tunic like any squaw, but—'' he thought a moment—

229

"damn, she had to be white, sir. I'm just sure of it. And some of the kids looked white, too."

Silence hung in the air again for a moment as Garvey pondered the strange story. White. What would a white woman be doing riding around the plains with a bunch of Indians? Was she a captive? Surely not. She fought on their side.

"Father," the younger Garvey spoke up. "The young one I fought with. I have seen him before. I am sure of it. I . . . I never told you, but once when you were in Washington, about, I'm not sure, about three years ago. I . . . I got in a fight with an Indian boy. He was smaller, but he beat me, so I didn't tell you about it because I thought you would be angry with me. I wanted to wait until I beat a boy in a fight before I told you. But I am sure it was the same boy. I could swear it."

Garvey frowned. This was indeed getting more interesting all the time. "You mean the boy was in Denver?"

"Yes, sir. And so was his father. When we were fighting in Denver, a white man grabbed the Indian boy off of me and hit him, and the boy's father began beating on the white man. The father was arrested and taken to jail. But somehow he was freed again. I don't know how it happened. I do remember seeing that prostitute, Anna Gale, help the man's wife. I don't know why she would help a woman who sleeps with Indians. But that doesn't matter. The point is the white woman she helped was the same white woman we saw with the Indians in Kansas. She is the big man's wife. So all of them were in Denver about three years ago. When I told the boy I had seen him before, he looked at me real funny, and he denied ever having been to Denver."

"Did any of you get any names?" Garvey asked.

230

"I did," Charles answered proudly. "One of the other Indians called the big one Zeke. That is the only name I heard."

Winston Garvey paled, and his eyes widened in surprise. "Zeke!" he exclaimed. "Zeke Monroe?"

Charles shrugged. "I don't know. Just Zeke. But he looked familiar. I swear I saw him before Denver, when I was much smaller. But I can't remember. Do you know this man?"

Garvey's mind raced. He must think fast. He must not give anything away, and perhaps he was only jumping to conclusions anyway. At the moment he was totally confused. He needed to sit and think and make notes and try to piece things together. Anna! Anna Gale had seen Zeke Monroe in Denver. Zeke Monroe. The man who had come to his home nine years ago to take the Cheyenne woman, Yellow Moon. And it was just about three years ago that Anna Gale had told him he had a half-breed son. In fact, the more he thought about it, the more he remembered that it was after his trip to Washington.

"They were the damnedest fighters, sir," Buel spoke up. "I never saw men move so fast and sure. And that wolf, he was on me like lightning."

"That Zeke fella, he was one mean bastard," Marty growled.

Garvey scanned all of them again. "Marty, John— you're both fired!" he declared. "You cowards never should have run off like that. My son could have been killed. Get your gear and get out."

The two men looked sheepishly at the floor, then Marty rose. "Yes, sir." He left without another word, and John followed. Garvey looked at the remaining men.

"You fools almost gave away your cover. You never should have been in Kansas. Those Indians knew it,

231

and probably suspected you weren't really Colorado volunteers. I don't want anyone to know I send out my own men on scouting missions. I may be waging my own private war against the Indians, but I don't need anyone else knowing about it! Those red bastards could talk to soldiers or their agent and make trouble. They played it smart by not killing any of you. You'd better believe that if they thought they could get away with it they'd have slaughtered all of you!''

"We're sorry, sir," Ben replied. "But we thought—"

"That's right," Garvey interrupted. "You thought— but you thought wrong!" He pounded his fist on the desk top, his face cherry red with anger.

"Father, do you know the one called Zeke?" Charles asked again.

Garvey turned cautious eyes to the boy. "Did the man speak good English?" he asked.

"Yes, he did. In fact, he did all the talking."

"I think he's a breed," Joe spoke up. "He was too tall and too good-lookin' to be a full-blood. And I never met an Indian who talked that good of English. That might explain the white woman with him."

Garvey rubbed his chin. White woman! Zeke Monroe was perhaps married to a white woman. Yes. This would all take some thought. And he would damned well see how Anna Gale reacted to the name Zeke Monroe. He looked at Charles.

"Yes, son, I think I might know the man. But it was a long time ago. It's of no importance."

"But if you know him, you can go after him for what he did."

Garvey waved him off, trying to seem casual. "I have no idea where the man lives now, and I don't want to stir it up. It might just make the wrong kind of trouble for me. You have to learn when to move and when not to move, Charles."

The boy frowned in frustration. He would love to raid wherever Zeke Monroe lived and kill the man.

Garvey leaned back in his chair again. "All right. Keep this quiet. And the next time you take my son with you any place, take better care of him! I never told you to get into any skirmishes—just to scout around, teach him the lay of the land, that sort of thing." He sighed deeply. "Go on. Get out of here and go nurse your wounds." He turned to Charles. "And you, son. You go to your room and rest. We'll talk more later about your adventures. I'll have your supper sent up to you in bed."

The boy nodded, rising slowly from his chair because of his sore ribs. "Are you proud of me, Father?" he asked.

Garvey grinned. "Of course I am. Now get going."

The boy grinned more. "I'll be the best Indian fighter Colorado ever had, sir," he declared. "I'll count plenty of dead ones some day—dead by my own gun."

The other men looked at each other rather disgustedly. Charles Garvey had been soundly whipped by the Indian boy, and none of them had really minded watching. But Winston Garvey paid their wages, and they were good wages. If they told the truth about Charles, the boy would figure out a way to make sure they were fired, so they kept still, even though all of them thought Charles Garvey somewhat demented.

"I hope you can some day legally wipe every Indian out of Colorado Territory," Winston Garvey was telling his son. "But remember to tread lightly until the laws governing such things are more solid. For now you are fairly safe in assuming you can shoot at any Indian who strays from the reservation, but it's wise to be cautious, son."

The boy nodded, standing straighter and feeling like

a man. He turned and left the room with the rest of the men, and Winston Garvey slumped back into his chair with a heavy sigh. The news he had received was both disturbing and interesting. Zeke Monroe. Denver. Anna Gale. Yellow Moon. Somehow there had to be a connection.

Fifteen

Only about three hundred Sioux raided through Minnesota, the Dakotas and northern Nebraska that summer of 1862, and those few were soon on their way to Canada, fleeing pursuing soldiers. But few whites could be convinced that not all Indians were raiding and ready for all-out war. That summer nearly the entire Nebraska frontier fled to the Missouri River on one wild rumor that the Indians had joined the Confederates and had been supplied with rifles and would raid any day. So frightened were the settlers that many left with hardly more than the clothes on their backs, leaving behind homes and furnishings. The governors of western territories and states pleaded with Washington to send more troops west. But there were none to send, for the Civil War was at its bloodiest height. There was no one to defend the West but their own volunteers, men who already had a hatred of Indians and no inclination to listen to the Indians' plight or to be fair in any bargaining.

Such was the mood of the country as Zeke Monroe packed his gear to leave his family and the people that he loved and go to a place and people he did not love. But he was a man accustomed to doing what must be done, even if it was not what he wanted. Practical, he had called it. It was a word he had used often the first year Abbie met him, and practical often meant terrible sacrifice, even of loved ones.

Abbie rolled fresh biscuits into a cloth and placed them into his parfleche, a parfleche she herself had beaded for him. She fought the terrible agony of his leaving, the need to scream and the desperate wish to make time stand still. They had spent their last night at the creek, in a quickly erected *tipi,* so that they could be alone. In spite of her embarrassment at the realization that everyone knew why they had gone off alone, Abbie stubbornly did not care. Let the three men with Emily think what they would, and let Emily blush. It did not matter. She would spend her last night alone with her man and that was that.

Zeke came through the doorway then. All of the children were outside, saying goodbye to their new-found aunt and cousin, both of whom were already inside their carriage. The three escorts were mounted and ready to ride. They would get Emily safely back to St. Louis first, and had no doubt they would do so now that the "big Indian" would be along.

Abbie looked up at her husband as he came inside. He looked away quickly, his chest hurting so badly he found it difficult to breathe. "Everything is packed but my parfleche," he told her. She handed the article out to him.

"I put fresh biscuits in it."

He nodded, then turned to face her again, running his eyes over her body. "Keep your gun loaded, and don't hesitate to use it, Abbie. Wolf's Blood is practically as good as I am with a rifle and knife. He'll stay close. And there's Dooley. Black Elk said he and some others would be around, maybe camp here as much as possible."

"Tall Grass Woman will come and stay with me also," she told him. Her eyes softened more. "Please don't worry, Zeke. We've lived here for years, survived everything that has come our way. Now we're right in the middle of Indian country, according to the treaty. No whites are going to dare come around here, and they're the only ones I worry about. There's no concern with the Cheyenne, and the Comanches stay to the south. I'm not afraid, Zeke, and I'll not go dragging all my children off to Bent's Fort for who knows how long. I want to be home. You could be gone for—" the words caught in her throat— "for months." She suddenly closed her eyes and put a hand to her mouth.

In the next moment he was there, and she wept against his chest, breathing deeply of the beautiful, manly scent of him, wanting to remember . . . remember. "Oh God, Zeke, I wanted to be . . . so strong for you!" she wept.

He held her tightly, kissing her hair. "Hey, Abbie-girl, remember when I had that dream, about being with you when you were very old and gray? My dreams have never been wrong, Abbie. So you know what that means. It means I'll be coming back, and that you'll be here waiting when I do." He swallowed back a lump in his own throat, and one tear slipped down the scarred cheek. "Don't you see it, Abbie? There's nothing to worry about."

She sniffed and turned her face to kiss the bare skin of his chest that showed through the lacings of his buckskin shirt. "Be careful, Zeke. It's dangerous there." She turned her face up to look at him and he forced a smile for her.

"More dangerous than being out here?" he asked.

She had to smile herself at the remark. "Settle your past, Zeke," she told him, reaching up and touching his cheek. "Settle your past, and then come home to
237

me."

They stared at each other's eyes, and then his lips met hers, savagely, desperately, wishing with all his being that the kiss could last forever. He pulled her so close that her feet left the floor for a moment, as the tall, powerful man swept his small wife into his embrace. He left her lips and kissed her over and over on the cheeks and eyes, then back to her lips before finally releasing her.

"Ne-mehotatse," he told her in a strained voice.

Their eyes held for several seconds before he slowly let go of her completely and reached for his parfleche.

"Ne-mehotatse," she whispered.

He suddenly turned and walked through the door. She forced her own legs to move to the doorway and outside to watch him mount up with the easy grace he always displayed on a horse. He signaled the three men to get started, then turned and nodded to Dooley, moving his eyes to Wolf's Blood, whose eyes registered deep understanding. They had already talked, and Zeke Monroe knew his son would give his life for his mother if need be. He could only pray that both would be alive and well when he returned. He tore his eyes from Wolf's Blood and scanned the rest of the children, to whom he had already given individual goodbyes.

"I love you—all of you," he told them. "Be good for your mother and do your chores. She'll need cooperation from all of you."

"We'll help her, Father," Margaret spoke up. He studied his beautiful eldest daughter. She was another reason to worry.

"I know you will," he told the girl. "You're good children—all of you. I'm proud of you. And I'll be back, that's a promise."

Margaret wiped at her eyes and Wolf's Blood stood with his lips pressed tight, wanting to act like a man this

238

day. Zeke turned his mount and rode up close to Abbie, reaching down for her. She took his hand.

"May the spirits protect you," he told her. "I will pray for you."

"And I shall pray to my God to protect you," she replied.

He gently touched the side of her face. "You'll always be my Abbie-girl," he told her. "No matter whatever happens."

He turned his horse and kicked it into a gallop. If the leaving must be done, then it must be done quickly. She watched him until he was a dot on the distant hill. Then he disappeared over the crest. She stood watching for several minutes, wishing that for some reason he would come riding back down the hill. But she knew he would not. Wolf's Blood was standing beside her.

"He will come back, Mother," he told her. "He always comes back."

She turned to look at her son, a young replica of Zeke Monroe. She breathed deeply and straightened. She must not weep and frighten the children.

"Of course he'll be back," she said flatly. She moved past him and re-entered the house. There were more biscuits in the oven. She must finish her baking.

Somewhere deep in the night a coyote howled, and Abbie stirred. She had slept restlessly, unaccustomed to sleeping alone. When first she woke her stomach hurt at the reawakened pain of knowing Zeke was gone, perhaps for months.

She sat up and put on her robe, going out into the main room to heat some coffee. Perhaps if she sat and read for a while it would help her sleep. She noticed a lantern lit on the table and the door ajar and she frowned. The house was quiet.

"Wolf's Blood?" she called out softly.

There was a moment of silence. "I am out here," he spoke up from outside the door. She wrapped her robe tighter and went to the door, stepping out into the moonlit porch, and the boy turned away to stare out over the distant hills. Far off in the distance he could see the black outline of the Rocky Mountains. Abbie sensed he had been crying, but she knew he would die of embarrassment if she mentioned it.

"You were thinking of your father," she said softly.

He sighed deeply and swallowed. "Except for that time when I was very small . . . we have never been apart. I was thinking, thinking that I will have to go for my morning rides . . . alone."

She watched him lovingly. "Oh no, Wolf's Blood. You know your father better than that. You'll not ride alone. He'll be with you, in his mind. He'll be in the grass and the wind and the sun. Wherever you go in this life, and even after your father is gone in death, he will be with you."

The boy sniffed and nodded. Then he turned to her, and in the darkness it was almost as though Zeke himself were standing there. "Tell me something, Mother," he spoke up.

She stepped a little closer. "What is it?" she asked, grateful for the conversation.

"Why? Why did you marry my father?"

Her eyebrows arched in surprise at the question and she smiled softly. "Why not?" she replied. "I loved him. It's as simple as that. What else can I say?"

"But—what made you love him? I can understand how he could love you. You were young and beautiful and alone, and he must have seen you would be a good woman someday, a good wife," he told her in his forthright manner. It was the Indian in him that made him speak simple truth, with a bluntness akin to most Cheyenne men. "But you are white, and he is Indian in all

240

ways, except that he has a white father. Surely you knew this, and knew he had killed all those men back in Tennessee. Most white women will have nothing to do with an Indian man. They shun them and whisper about them and act as though they are something less than human.''

Abbie stepped even closer, folding her arms and studying the boy's intense, dark eyes. What a handsome son he was, so much like his father. She worried over what lay ahead for this son who was so rebellious.

"Wolf's Blood," she spoke up, glad to have this rare, intimate moment with him, for she had not been as close to him as had Zeke. "When I came west from Tennessee with my father, I wasn't thinking about love and marriage and men," she continued. "But I had a very firm idea of what I'd want in a man when the time came. I wanted someone strong and dependable, brave and sure of himself. I wanted a man I knew would love me forever, who would gladly die for me if need be, who was afraid of nothing and no one. And I dreamed of some kind of prince who would sweep me off my feet.''

She blushed a little and smiled, and Wolf's Blood remained sober and attentive, trying to picture her at fifteen. It was easy, for as she spoke about his father, her eyes were bright in the moonlight, and they danced with love, as they must have then.

"At any rate, I didn't expect to find that kind of man easily," she went on, "especially not one who would be handsome besides." She sighed and dropped her eyes. "And then one night, when we were all waiting at Sapling Grove and arguing about who would lead us and how we'd get where we wanted to go, your father stepped into the light of my pa's campfire to offer his services as scout.''

She sighed deeply. "The minute I laid eyes on him, I

241

knew he was the kind of man I had in mind, and something . . . stirred inside of me—something I had never felt before. I offered him some coffee, and when he took it his hand touched mine for a brief moment.'' She smiled and shook her head, meeting Wolf's Blood's eyes; her own eyes were misty. ''I'll never forget that moment for the rest of my life, Wolf's Blood. Not ever. I looked at him, and he looked at me, and somehow we knew. We knew right then and there.'' She turned and looked out at the distant mountains. ''It took awhile for your father to understand he had a right to love me. After those men murdered his white wife and their son back in Tennessee, he figured he was no good for another white woman. He was afraid harm would come to me if he made me his wife. But I never worried about that. Your father was just the kind of man I wanted, and I was willing to suffer anything to be at his side. Even after I found out he'd been a wanted man back in Tennessee and had killed all those men, it didn't affect my love for him. It only made me feel sorry for him, knowing the hell he must have been through growing up a half-breed back there. And I understood then the loneliness that lay behind those dark, angry eyes of his. I sensed the gentle side of him, the little boy inside the man, who wanted only to be loved.''

She pushed a piece of hair behind her ear. ''Zeke fought his feelings most of that trip, but so many terrible things happened: I lost my family and all, took that Crow arrow that almost killed me. I guess that's when Zeke knew he didn't want to live without me, when he realized I might die and how he'd feel if I did.'' She turned to face her son again. ''So we were married at Fort Bridger, and I recuperated there for the winter. And in the spring, after getting the wagon train the rest of the way to Oregon, your father came for me.'' Her eyes lit up more. ''And that is another moment I will never forget."

Wolf's Blood stooped down to pet Smoke, who had come outside to lie down beside his master. "Were you not afraid to come and live with the people?" the boy asked.

"Afraid?" Abbie laughed lightly. "I was terrified! I knew absolutely nothing about Indians. And your uncle, Swift Arrow, scoffed at me and wanted me to leave. He was not the good friend then that he is now. Black Elk was kind to me, but Swift Arrow did all he could at first to frighten me away."

Wolf's Blood grinned and rose. "I miss my uncle," he told her. "He taught me many things about warrior ways."

She studied the brawny young man who had once suckled at her breast. This was her first, the son she had so proudly presented to Zeke to replace the son he had lost in Tennessee.

"And you shall be a great warrior, Wolf's Blood," she replied. "I knew even when you were tiny what you would choose to do. I saw the fire in those dark eyes, the look I often see in your father's eyes. I saw the courage and the restlessness, and I knew."

The boy shrugged. "I cannot be a bookworm like Jeremy." He sighed and turned. "I tried, Mother. But when I would sit and read, I could feel the wind blowing on me through the window. I could hear the eagle cry and the horses whinny. And I . . . I sometimes felt like I would go crazy if I could not run outside and greet the sun, feel the power of a good horse beneath me."

She put a hand on his arm. "I understand, Wolf's Blood. You are like your father, and I can't say I'm not proud of that, because I am."

He studied the love in his mother's eyes. He swallowed. "Will I know?" he asked. "Will I know . . . like you knew when you touched my father's hand?"

243

She smiled lovingly. "I think perhaps you already know, even though you are still too young to take a wife."

He grinned sheepishly, a rare smile that warmed her heart. "How do you know this?"

She pulled on a piece of his hair. "Because I am a woman, and I have seen how a certain little Cheyenne girl watched you at the Sun Dance. It reminded me of the way I used to look at your father."

The boy smiled sheepishly. "I like talking to you, Mother. We have not talked this way many times. I am glad you came out here tonight."

Their eyes held. "So am I," she answered.

Little Jason was suddenly standing at the doorway. "Mommy?" he spoke up through puckered lips, rubbing at his eyes. "Sleep with me?"

Abbie turned to him in surprise. "What are you doing out of your bed, little one?" she chided. Then she smiled. "Yes, I will sleep with you. Run and climb into Mommy's bed." The boy ran off and Abbie patted Wolf's Blood's arm. "Get some sleep, son. There is a chill of autumn in the air, and you have wood to cut tomorrow."

"Yes, Mother." He watched her go inside. Zeke had told him once that he had made Abigail Trent his woman earlier on that fateful wagon journey, before they were married the white man's way at Fort Bridger. The boy did not want to embarrass his mother by telling her Zeke had confided such a thing to him, but he had to smile at the thought of his mother's dancing eyes when she was talking about Zeke. It made her look like a teen-ager again. He could see that nothing had changed over the years, and it warmed his heart.

He turned and closed his eyes, concentrating on *Maheo*, the Great Spirit, praying for his father's safety. He was not certain he would want to live without his father. But more than that, how would Abigail Monroe go on living without her husband?

Autumn turned to winter, and it would be a cold and hungry one for the Southern Cheyenne, who huddled in *tipis* against the cruel winds of the Colorado plains. The promised supplies had not been sent, nor was game easy to find on the sparse land they were to call their home. Only those who dared to risk being shot by venturing out to the distant mountains and better hunting grounds found enough food to bring home that autumn, and what there was had to be divided among the whole tribe, so that there was never a plentiful supply for any one family.

Abbie gave what she could, creating all kinds of dishes out of leftovers and odd foods such as roots and meat fat that they would not ordinarily eat. With only Wolf's Blood to hunt while Dooley watched the ranch, their own table was not always abundant with food, but she made do, and she kept a happy spirit for the sake of the children.

Zeke had left enough money to tide them through the winter by buying supplies at Bent's Fort, but Abbie chose to use the money as sparingly as possible, always afraid that he might not return at all and she would have to stretch the money farther than originally planned. Dooley, faithful friend that he was, and as he had done many other years, accepted a wage far below that which was due him, always saying just a roof over his head and Abbie's home-cooked meals were all he needed. He was a quiet, loyal man, with few needs other than to find himself a loose Indian woman or to venture to the closest town a few times a year to visit the whores. He was a loner, a man who had once hunted and trapped with Zeke in the old fur-trading days, and one who had never been inclined to settle down to a wife and children. He had come to the ranch before Wolf's Blood was even born, and he had never left; and he was one of the very few white men Wolf's Blood respected and cared about.

It was mid-February of 1863 when the soldiers came. Outside the snow was almost knee-deep from a recent blizzard, and even now the winds howled mercilessly, the air filled with blowing snow but no real precipitation coming from the skies. The little cabin creaked against the icy winds, but inside it was warm, thanks to a potbelly heating stove Zeke had purchased at Bent's Fort the previous spring, swearing to Abbie and the rest of the family that they would not spend another winter shivering in front of the big fire place that seemed to eat up more heat through its chimney than it gave off.

Wolf's Blood added another piece of wood to the stove, and Abbie smiled as a kettle of water on top of the contraption hissed with steam. Here was another gift of Zeke's love. The warmth of the stove was to her representative of the warmth of his arms, and she knew he was with them this night.

"I hope we have enough wood to get us through the rest of the winter," Wolf's Blood lamented. "It looked like so much when I stacked it in the fall."

"It always looks like a lot when it is warm outside," she replied, rocking near the stove as she mended an elkskin jacket for the boy.

It was then they heard Dooley's boots tramping onto the porch outside, and in the next moment he banged on the door. "Let me in quick," he called out.

Abbie set down her sewing and rose, while Wolf's Blood unbolted the door. Dooley came inside, his hair encrusted with snow, and snow blew in through the door before Wolf's Blood could get it closed again.

"There's a lot of men comin', Abbie," Dooley told

her quickly. He had his rifle in his hand, and Wolf's Blood immediately went for his own rifle.

"What men? Where?" Abbie asked.

"Down the north ridge. I was out at the shed checkin' the horses when some of them got skittish, and I thought I heard a shout far off. The wind's blowin' down from the north. Carries a man's voice quite a ways. I closed up the shed and rode out a ways—seen several men between gusts of snow. There must be ten or twelve. I could hear the voices and I seen quite a few lanterns. I heard orders shouted, like maybe they was soldiers."

"Soldiers!" Wolf's Blood stiffened. He had bad memories of soldiers. He cocked his rifle.

"Wait, Wolf's Blood!" Abbie ordered. "We don't know if they're Union soldiers or Confederates. Perhaps they're even Colorado volunteers."

"That would be the worst!"

"If there are ten or twelve then there are too many!" Abbie told him. "We have your brothers and sisters to think about. It's possible they mean no harm at all. Perhaps your father is with them."

The boy paced. "If he was with them he would be here already, riding in fast. You know that."

She sighed, glancing around the room as though something there would tell her what to do. She looked at Dooley. "What do you think?"

"I think we have to wait and see what they want. Wolf's Blood and I will each take a window. You'd best get your own rifle ready. They'll be here too damned fast for us to make any real plans. We've got no choice but to hope they mean no harm."

She breathed deeply for composure, glancing up at the loft where the rest of the children slept snugly, oblivious to the possible approaching danger. Already she could hear the voices herself as the men came close to the cabin. She walked to the corner and retrieved her faithful Spencer. She had used it before. She would use it again if necessary.

Sixteen

The inevitable knock came to the door, and Abbie breathed a sigh of relief. At least they had not tried to storm inside uninvited. Abbie glanced at Wolf's Blood.

"Let Dooley and I handle this, Wolf's Blood. These men are white. We understand how to handle them better than you. Don't act rashly."

The boy's breathing was rapid. "There are many of them, and you are the only woman! I promised Father—"

"Not all of them are like the soldier at Fort Lyon," she interrupted. There was another knock at the door and she gave Wolf's Blood a warning look. "Keep your gun ready, but don't point it," she told him. She glanced at Dooley. "The same goes for you. With that many men we can't afford guns going off in every direction. The children might get hurt."

Dooley nodded, but she knew by the way he looked at her that if one man made an advance, Dooley's shotgun would blow the man in half. She went to the door.

"Who is there?" she demanded.

"I am Major Tilford Mayes, ma'am," came a shouted voice. "We have a man here who's been wounded—several days back in a skirmish on the Santa

Fe Trail. We beg of you to give him a warm place to rest for a few days. My men are freezing. If we could take turns warming by your hearth, we would be deeply grateful.''

The man had a strong Southern accent. Abbie looked at Dooley. "From the sound of his drawl they must be Confederates." She looked back at the doorway, stepping closer so he could hear her better. "How do I know you aren't lying about a wounded man?" she shouted.

The children began to stir then, and Margaret came wandering out to sit down on the edge of the loft where it met the ladder to climb down. She rubbed her eyes. "Get back!" Wolf's Blood ordered her. "Keep the rest of the children up there. Do not let them come down."

"What is it?" she asked sleepily.

"Soldiers! Get back."

The girl's eyes widened, and she scooted back out of sight.

"I beg of you, ma'am, I'm telling the truth!" came the shouted reply. "I will leave the wounded man by your door and the rest of us will go farther away and build a campfire. May we use some of your wood that is stacked outside?"

Abbie closed her eyes in apprehension, struggling with her decision. "All right," she finally spoke up. "Leave the wounded man here and we will see what we can do for him. The rest of you may use some of our wood to build a fire and pitch your tents outside. There is not enough room inside the cabin. You may send in two men at a time, taking turns an hour each by the stove. Go lightly on the wood, and I hope you have food. I haven't near enough to share. How many are with you?"

"Eleven, ma'am. Plus me. Thank you, ma'am. Thank you. We'll bring the wounded man right up."

"Wait!" Abbie called out. "You haven't told me what kind of soldiers you are—Federals or Confederates."

The wind blew wild again and for a moment he did not answer. "Does it make a difference?" he finally asked, wanting to make certain an unknown enemy was not waiting inside.

"No difference," she shouted through the crack in the door. "We take no part in the war in the East. But I am originally from Tennessee."

"Tennessee!" the man exclaimed. "Damn, we came to the right place. We're Confederates—good ole Southern boys! Thank you, ma'am. Thank you!" She heard him leaving the porch, and began to relax a little more. They were Confederates. She looked at Dooley.

"I've never gone back to Tennessee in all these years," she told the man, "and I swear no allegiance to it now. But at the moment I think I am glad I was born and raised there, and it might be wise to let them think we sympathize with the Confederates. It would be safer for me. Perhaps if we are kind to them they'll leave without robbing us of everything we own, and perhaps my being from Tennessee will create enough respect to keep their minds off things they should not be thinking about." She reddened at the words, but they had to be said so that there was an understanding.

Dooley nodded. "Good idea. I'm partial to Georgia myself, so we got no problem there." He looked over at Wolf's Blood. "Take it nice and easy, son, and we'll get through this just fine."

The boy's dark eyes glittered with apprehension. He trusted no strange white men, whether they be Federals or Confederates. There was a thumping on the porch again and a rustling against the door.

"Got the wounded man here," came the major's voice again. "Name's Monroe. Lance Monroe."

251

Abbie's eyes widened in shock, and her body tingled from the thought of how fate acted to strangely twist peoples' lives. Her mind raced and her ears did not hear the major as he told her he was leaving to set up a camp. All she could think of was that Zeke had been gone for nearly five months, and now a wounded man lay on her doorstep that might be his long lost white brother from Tennessee, the youngest one that no one had heard from since first he went off to war. She started to open the door in her excitement, but Dooley grabbed her arm and pulled her back.

"Let me do it," he told her. "Step back out of the way."

She nodded, her breathing rapid. Could it be Zeke's brother? She looked at Wolf's Blood, whose eyes showed the same surprise. "Monroe," he spoke up. "My father has a brother called Lance. He told me."

Abbie nodded. "He does. But it could be a coincidence," she told the boy, praying it was not. Nothing would soothe her longing for Zeke as much as being able to help one of his brothers.

Dooley cautiously opened the door and peeked out. A man lay on the porch, and others were several yards away. He could hear orders being shouted. Dooley opened the door farther and reached down to drag the wounded man inside, bringing him over to lay him on a buffalo skin in front of the wood stove. The buffalo skin still had shaggy fur on it and made a decent temporary bed.

Wolf's Blood quickly bolted the door again, and Abbie was already bending over the wounded man, helping Dooley unwrap woolen scarves from around the man's head and face and unbutton his tattered coat.

"My God!" Abbie exclaimed, looking at what could be Danny Monroe's twin, only with dark hair. His eyes were closed, but somehow she knew they would be

252

brown, not blue like Danny's. Zeke had told her Danny was the only one of the three white brothers who had inherited his white mother's blond hair and blue eyes. His father had been dark, and this man was dark, with the same tall, broad physique of Zeke and Danny. "Surely this is Zeke's half-brother," Abbie whispered. "God has blessed me this night, Dooley. He has brought me Zeke in the form of his brother." She looked at Dooley. "I only hope that if Zeke is wounded, someone will be there to help him also."

"Well, if this don't beat all," Dooley muttered. "Zeke out there searchin' for one brother, and another one shows up at the door."

Wolf's Blood stepped closer to peek curiously at the wounded man who was an uncle. Dooley removed the man's coat and shirt, and Abbie gasped at the crude bandages around his ribs. Blood spotted the bandages on the man's lower right side.

"Wolf's Blood, pour some of that hot water that is on top of the stove into a pan," Abbie ordered right away. "Get me some clean cloths." The boy moved quickly. "Dooley, go outside and find out if this man still has a bullet in him," Abbie continued. "If he does, we have to get it out quickly. This is Zeke's brother. We must not let him die."

Dooley nodded and rose, pulling his sheepskin coat closer around his neck before venturing back out into the howling January winds. The man on the floor moaned, and Abbie put a gentle hand to his forehead.

"You'll be all right," she told the man softly. "We're going to help you."

He reached up and took her hand, his eyes still closed. "Pa?" he groaned. "I promise . . . I'll stay home this time, Pa. I'll help . . . get the corn in."

Abbie looked at Wolf's Blood, who had knelt down beside her with the pan of hot water.

253

"Life is so strange, Wolf's Blood," she told him, dipping a clean cloth into the water and wringing it out. She bent over the man and gently washed his face. "The very man your father hates, this man loves. Surely he was not that bad of a father." She looked back at Wolf's Blood. The boy looked down at the pan of water.

"I do not understand hating a father. It is something my own father never talked about. It is the only thing he would never discuss with me, except that often he told me how cruel life was back in that place called Tennessee."

She sighed and returned to washing Lance Monroe. "Yes. It was cruel, Wolf's Blood. But a man's father is his father and it cannot be denied. It will be very hard for Zeke to go back there. I hope he has the courage to go and see his white father. It isn't good to hate the man who gave you life, Wolf's Blood. It's wrong, no matter how badly the man might have treated you."

Wolf's Blood watched her gently wash this white man who was the product of the white grandfather he had never known and would probably never meet. It chilled his blood to realize how much white blood was in him, for he did not want any at all. He would always hate it. Yet he would never hate the mother or the father who had given him that blood.

Dooley returned, bolting the door and coming to stand over them. "He's still got a bullet in him," he declared.

Abbie sighed deeply. Removing a bullet was never easy, nor was it a pretty sight. "Get your bowie knife, Wolf's Blood," she told her son. "It's the sharpest object in the house. I don't want to do this, but I've done it before." She bent over and began removing the dirty bandages, remembering a day, many, many years ago, when Zeke Monroe lay wounded in a cave after saving her from outlaws. She had removed a bullet from his side, while he lay biting on a piece of leather. It was a traumatic experience for the young girl she had been then. But she had done it. She would muster the courage and stamina to do it again. How strange that the patient should be his own brother, one she had never met in all these years.

Zeke yanked on his horse's reins and pulled back out of the way as an old man and two young women darted past in front of him. One woman slipped and fell in the muddy street, spilling an armload of meat she had just stolen from a nearby store. The windows of the store were broken and the door beaten in. The woman scrambled up again, hurriedly picking up her stolen goods and running off.

Zeke stared in pity and disbelief as ragged, skeletal people hurried here and there, picking their way through the muddied streets of Nashville, the mud made worse by the thousands of wagons that had churned their way through it on their way out of the city, fleeing the oncoming Union soldiers. The South Zeke had returned to was not the South he had left. The South he had left had been quiet and soft, a wealthy land populated by farmers and plantation owners, its people slow and casual, with little care about what the next day would bring.

Now that South was ravaged and burned, a place where danger lay not just in the cities, but on the plantations and in the remote woods and swamps. Every place he turned, hatred swelled and brother fought brother. People who were once proud and gentle were killing and destroying, grasping at whatever remnants they could find to keep them alive. With the fall of Forts Donelson and Henry, and now with the desertion of Nashville by Confederate troops, Tennessee was falling

255

into the hands of the Federals. To the citizens of Tennessee, such a fate was worse than death, a wound to their pride that might never heal.

Zeke had at first thought himself lucky in his search for Danny. After leaving Emily at St. Louis, he had ridden into Illinois and paid a prison official at Rock Island to allow him to visit Confederate prisoners to search for Danny. What he saw there was revolting—tattered, wounded men dying of infections and disease, eating food most animals would not eat. He did not understand this war. He could not believe it was just to free slaves. It had to be more political than that. He had vivid memories of the Trail of Tears and what the government had done to the Indians of the South when they chased them west. Now, mysteriously, the slaves would be freed, which was fine with him. But what would be done for them once they were released from bondage? Would the white men who freed them suddenly find a great love in their hearts for the black man, any more than they cared about the Indian? And why was the white man suddenly so concerned about the Negroes, while at the same time they were considering ways to imprison and destroy the red man?

None of it made sense to him. A man was a man, as far as Zeke was concerned. It was not his color that made him so, or his name. It was merely his human traits, his skill, his courage, his honor. There was no honor in this war, or in what was happening to the Indians. But that was not his problem or concern for the moment. His problem was to find Danny. On that first visit to Rock Island, to his relief, Danny was not there amid the filth and humiliation of that prison. He had come upon one prisoner there who had known Danny at Shiloh. He claimed that Danny had escaped and was probably back with the Confederates again.

But after hearing descriptions of what had happened

at Shiloh, and seeing now what was happening to all of Tennessee, Zeke wondered how Danny could have survived, especially if he was wounded as Emily had been told. His only choice was to cover as much country as possible, searching out Confederates and asking questions. But it was a dangerous chore, for without a uniform he was always suspect, trusted by neither Union men nor Confederates. He had already dodged more bullets than he cared to think about, fired by men who didn't bother to ask questions first.

"Gimme that horse!" a man growled then, grabbing the reins of Zeke's mount and pushing at Zeke. He was a big, bearded man of considerable strength, a man who obviously was accustomed to getting what he wanted by simply taking it. Zeke kicked out at him, sending the man sprawling into the mud. He moved his Appaloosa a few feet back and the man glared at him. "Stinkin' redskin!" he shouted. "What are you doin' here? Get the hell out of Nashville, unless you plan to stay here and join the niggers!"

The man got up and grabbed an old woman who was crossing the street and carrying blankets and a bag of flour. He shoved her down and yanked the articles from her hands and made off with them. Zeke kicked his horse into motion and rode down upon the man, pulling out his rifle and whacking the man between the shoulders with the butt of the rifle. The man sprawled forward, the belongings in his arms flying out in front of him. Zeke quickly dismounted and placed his foot on the back of the man's head, holding his face in the mud.

"Mister, there isn't a war or anything else horrible that could happen to me that would make me push around an old woman. A man with any guts and honor would die of hunger first." He held his foot hard until the man stopped struggling, then picked his way through the mud to pick up the blankets and flour. He walked them back to the old woman to return them to her, setting them down beside her and bending over to help her up. He grasped a thin arm and raised her up, but when he turned her around there was blood on her forehead where she had hit a rock. Her withered face was covered with mud, as was the frayed pink ruffled dress she wore. He knew in an instant that she was dead.

He did not know her. Yet the way she died pierced his heart. She should have died in peace, rocking beside a hearth and enjoying her grandchildren. Seeing her lying there, dead and muddied and skeletal, suddenly brought terror to his own heart, terror for what might lie ahead for his Abbie. Surely such suffering would one day come to his people. Would Abbie suffer for loving them?

He looked around at others who scurried here and there with their loot, people who would not normally even consider robbing and plundering the property of others, but people who were now desperate and starving. No one seemed to notice the old lady. Apparently no one was particularly concerned and surely none of them was family.

In the distance he could hear cannon as the Union soldiers approached. He picked up the old lady and layed her over his mount, then climbed up and rode north into the hills. Someone should bury her. He could not bring himself to leave her lying in the street, only to be shoveled into a mass grave by the Federals.

He headed his mount into the woods north of Nashville, a place that was quiet and overlooked the city. He took a spade from his gear and started shoveling. It would take a lot of time and work with nothing bigger to work with, but he was determined and angry. He shoveled hard and dirt flew as he struggled against tears that he could not explain. Why should he care so much for this old woman he did not know? Was he missing Gentle Woman, his own Cheyenne mother? Yes. He always missed her. Yet somehow that was not what this old woman reminded him of. It was something else. He knew deep in the hidden crevices of his mind what it was, but he refused to believe that he might be worried about his father—his real father. Old and lonely, Emily had told them. *"He truly did love you, Zeke,"* she had said. *"He longs to see you again before he dies."*

He shoveled faster until the hole was finally deep enough. Then he gently laid the old woman inside of it and started shoveling the dirt over her. Soon the pink dress and withered face disappeared. In the distance below, Union soldiers rode into Nashville, followed by freed Negroes who were singing songs of joy, men who would now look to their "saviors" to guide them in their new life.

Zeke fashioned a little cross from sticks, sure the old white woman must have been Christian. Again he thought of Abbie and her Bible and her prayers. She would have wanted him to bury this woman and put a cross at her grave.

He rose and mounted up, watching for a few minutes the Union troops move into Nashville, the Negroes trudging faithfully behind them.

"Don't expect any help from your new white friends," he muttered. He turned his horse and gazed out to the south—south . . . where the old farm was, where his father was. For a moment he considered going there, but then he headed out in another direction. He was here to find Danny and for no other reason. He headed east. He would make his way toward Virginia, where he had heard General Lee and a great Confederate fighter by the name of Stonewall Jackson would carry out major defenses. Finding Danny would be like finding a needle in a haystack. Perhaps the man had died of his wounds after escaping. This was a much more difficult task than he had anticipated, but he hated the thought of going home with no news of his brother.

He headed out into the woods, leaving the fresh grave behind him, trying to not think about the fact that time and weather would someday destroy the little marker, and no one would ever know the little old woman was buried there. He wondered how many other unmarked graves this war would leave through the hills and farmlands of the South. This was indeed a bloody and cruel war.

Abbie sponged Lance's face again, her heart aching at the man's pain. Through the night he had groaned and sweated, but in the early morning he had seemed to sleep well. Now it seemed the pain was returning. Major Mayes stood warming himself by the stove, glancing periodically at a watchful Wolf's Blood and feeling nervous under the boy's defensive gaze. The boy had not slept or put down his rifle since the arrival of the soldiers. The boy's Indian features told the major that it must be true that his father was a half-breed. The possibility of the man being a half-brother to Lance Monroe seemed incredible, matched only by the fact that the beautiful white woman who had removed Lance's bullet and nursed him faithfully through the night was actually married to the half-breed and had mothered the wild-looking lad who watched him now.

"I can't begin to express my gratefulness for giving us a place to hole up and for helping Private Monroe," the major spoke up to Abbie. "We will leave you as soon as Lance can travel."

Abbie looked up at the man. "Will you see that he gets home to his father's farm?"

"I'll do what I can. But we've lost our stronghold in

the West, ma'am. It will be difficult just to get out of here alive. We're surrounded by Unionists. I don't even know where the closest Confederate encampment is. We've lost contact. But if we can just get through to Tennessee, he can go on from there.''

"Is it really that bad, Mister Mayes? The war?''

His eyes saddened. "It's the worst thing I've ever seen or hope to see again. Plantations and cities are ravaged and it's getting worse. The Federals have us surrounded. They come up from the south by sea, down from the north on the rivers, and now they have the West. I've seen battlefields red with blood. Citizen and soldier alike are starving, dying of disease and exposure. Yes, ma'am, it's a terrible thing, with son turning against father, brother against brother, old friends plunging bayonets into one another.''

She sighed and swallowed. "And . . . what about those who do not choose sides, like my husband?''

Mayes twisted his hat in his hand. This woman was alone with seven children to care for, a woman who had lived in this lonely, savage land for many years. "I'm . . . sure he'll be all right, ma'am.''

She smiled sadly. "I thank you for your kind lie, Mister Mayes.'' She looked back down at Lance, who stirred and opened his eyes for the first time since he had been brought to her. "He's awake!'' she exclaimed, putting a cool cloth to his forehead again. "You must lie still, Lance,'' she spoke up softly.

He looked up at her lovely face through blurred vision, totally unaware of where he was and thinking perhaps he was dreaming that he was warm and a woman's soft voice had just spoken to him. In spite of his pain, Abbie could not help her terrible curiosity. She must know.

"Tell me,'' she told the man as he looked around the room, blinking and trying to get his bearings. "Your

261

last name is Monroe.'' The man looked back at her and frowned in confusion. ''Are . . . are you related to a Danny Monroe, and a Zeke Monroe? Is your father Hugh Monroe?''

He swallowed. ''My . . . brothers . . . Danny and . . . Zeke. Lenny. And my father . . . Hugh.'' His body shuddered. ''Am I . . . home?''

Abbie could not stop a sob from jerking at her shoulders. She sniffed and swallowed. ''My God!'' she whispered, bending down and placing her cheek against Lance's. He breathed in her feminine smell and was comforted. ''I am . . . your brother's wife . . . Zeke's wife,'' she told him. ''You're in Colorado Territory. You've lost a lot of blood, Lance. Just lie still.''

She pulled back and Lance stared at her, his vision more clear now. How lovely she was! Had God brought him to this place, to the wife of the brother he had not seen in twenty years? So this was she! The mysterious white woman Zeke had married and who had agreed to live in Indian territory for his sake.

He quietly studied her, his eyes moving over her lovely form. She wore a plain cotton dress, choosing to dress as a white woman around the white soldiers, to ensure they afforded her proper respect. She was shapely and well-preserved, and Lance was surprised, half expecting a weathered, tired woman who had aged before her time. But she was the prettiest woman he had seen in quite some time.

''You . . . you're . . . Abigail?'' he asked.

''Yes.'' She took his hand. ''But I'm sorry to say Zeke is not here. How wonderful it would be if he could see you! It seems so ironic. He has gone back East to look for Danny. We learned that Danny was wounded at Shiloh and taken prisoner. Zeke went to see if he could locate him.''

''Danny? Shiloh?'' He closed his eyes. ''If he was

262

. . . at Shiloh . . . . he can't be alive. I heard . . . about Shiloh."

She squeezed his hand. "Don't worry about Danny," she told him. "You have no idea the kind of man Zeke is. He'll survive, and he'll find Danny and get him back to the farm. And that is where you must go when you're healed. Your father needs you, Lance." She thought about mentioning Lenny's death, but perhaps he did not know yet. This would be a bad time to tell him. "With . . . with all his sons gone off to war, he's a lonely man. You must get back home and let him know you're all right."

He turned his eyes to study her again. "You're . . . truly Abigail . . . Zeke's wife?"

She smiled softly. "I truly am."

"Danny . . . wrote us about you . . . talked about you a couple of times . . . when he managed to get back home. The wagon train . . . how you lost your family and met my brother." His eyes moved around the room, coming to rest on Wolf's Blood. "Zeke! He's right there!" he said in a weakening voice.

Abbie looked at her son then laughed lightly. "I suppose the way you remember him when he left, you would think so," she told the man. "That is Wolf's Blood, our first-born and oldest son. He looks very much like Zeke."

His breathing quickened from the exertion of just talking. "I'll . . . be damned," he muttered.

"We'll talk more when you're better," Abbie told the young man. "You must get some more rest now, Lance."

The major knelt down beside the young man. "We'll wait for a while, Monroe. I hope you get better soon enough to travel with us, but if not we may have to go on without you. The rest of the men need some time to rest up, too, so we'll give it a few days. Mrs. Monroe

263

here has been kind enough to allow us to camp out right here and take turns coming in by the fire.''

Lance met the man's eyes. "Don't let . . . any of the men treat her with . . . disrespect," he told the officer. "She's my . . . brother's wife . . . and she's from Tennessee. When the men . . . come inside . . . make sure they treat her right."

"They do, son," the officer reassured the boy. He glanced at Abbie, aware of how tempting she was to the others, for she was tempting also to him. But there was an air of saintliness about her that made a man back off, as though to touch her would be to burn in hell forever. She was a proud, strong woman who had known suffering. She was not a woman to be taken lightly or toyed with. But he could not help thinking what it might be like for a man to lie close beside her in the night. She was reserved and proper with strangers, but he did not doubt she was warm and responsive to the man she loved. He rose and walked to the door. "I'm sending in two others now, ma'am."

"Make sure they bring no weapons inside," Wolf's Blood spoke up, his eyes dark and menacing.

The major smiled lightly, very impressed by the young man's manliness and his touching defense of his mother. "Your wish is my command, young man," he replied. He nodded to Abbie again and walked out.

"My side . . . hurts awful!" Lance groaned. Abbie's attention was immediately drawn back to the brother-in-law she had never known until now.

"The pain will go away in another day or two. I took a bullet out of you, Lance. But I don't think anything vital was damaged."

He looked at her in surprise. "You?"

She smiled and nodded. "I've done it before—took a bullet out of Zeke, in fact, that first summer we met."

Lance smiled. "Zeke. I bet . . . he's got plenty of

scars. Danny told us . . . about all the things he's done . . . how he can use the knife.''

Her heart tightened at the thought of him. Was he even still alive? Zeke! How much longer would she have to endure the lonely nights? How much longer must she be strong of her own will, without his strong arms around her, his broad shoulder to lean on, his tender words of reassurance, the protection of his mere presence?

"Yes, he has plenty of scars,'' she replied. "But he always tells me he's too mean to die.''

Lance almost laughed, except that he ended up crying out in pain instead. Abbie grasped his hand again. "I . . . bet he is!'' Lance groaned. He clung to her hand. "Hold my hand, ma'am . . . till I fall asleep again . . . will you?''

She took his hand as two more men came inside, their collars turned up against the cold and wind. One was very young, perhaps eighteen, a sandy-haired boy with soft blue eyes. This was his second time in the house, and his eyes roved the room, searching for the fetching young daughter he had seen the first time. He finally caught her peeking at him around the curtained doorway of her mother's bedroom. He flashed a handsome smile, and Margaret quickly pulled back, closing the curtain. Wolf's Blood watched defensively, fully aware of his sister's beauty.

Seventeen

Anna Gale glided away from a roulette table to greet Winston Garvey, who was shaking hands and feigning jovial friendship with several prominent Denver businessmen who dared to frequent Anna's saloon and gambling hall. Most area citizens saw only that; what went on in the upper rooms was passed off as mere rumor. It was true, and most knew, that Anna Gale had once been the most notorious and beautiful prostitute in Santa Fe, the reputation she brought with her to Denver. But in the last few years she had become more conservative in her attire and had built a new gambling hall that boasted the best in decor, a saloon/restaurant/gambling hall so elegant that people found it easy to overlook Anna Gale's past or what might even still be going on in the upper rooms. After all, if one wanted to impress another with a night out on the town at the very best places, Anna's place was one of those on the list, one of the places where most area businessmen wined and dined, perhaps crude by Eastern standards, but plush by Western standards.

Garvey removed his hat and bowed to her, pretending, as always, that he was no more than an acquaintance and frequent customer. Anna gave him a

266

sly grin.

"And where have you been, Senator?" she asked. "Haven't seen you for quite some time."

"Oh, I've had a lot of business to attend to back East, you know." He smiled, his eyes roving her luscious body knowingly. She knew he would end up in her room for the night, and much as she detested this man who had once ruled her like a chained dog, she would oblige. She owed him nothing now, but it was wise to remain on friendly terms with men like Winston Garvey.

"How about a drink on the house?" she asked.

"Never turn one down," he replied.

She turned and sauntered toward the bar, and he watched her walk, her red satin dress hazy from the smoke-filled air. She had a way of walking that had helped make her a rich woman. Men still wanted her. She was in her early thirties now, but one would never guess. Unlike other whores, this one had taken care of her unusual beauty. She was selective of her customers and had stayed away from heavy drinking and smoked only occasionally. She never overpainted her face, and her clothes were not quite as gaudy as most whores dressed. Garvey stepped up to the long, oak bar and stood beside her while she ordered the bartender to pour the man a shot of the best whiskey he had. She turned to face Garvey, her blue eyes vivid and fetching.

"And what dirty deal did you make back East this time?" she asked him with a wicked grin.

"Come now, my sweet, I don't always make dirty deals."

"Oh? Well, invite me the next time you make a fair one. I'd like to see it."

The man guffawed and picked up his glass of whiskey, raising it slightly. "To an exquisitely beautiful woman," he toasted, his eyes dropping for a moment to the ivory skin of her enticingly exposed breasts.

She watched him cautiously. She knew this man too well. He had something up his sleeve.

"You seem unusually happy tonight, Senator," she told the man. "The deals you made must have been exceedingly rotten."

Garvey laughed again. "Now, Anna, you overestimate my evil."

"That would be impossible," she replied, sobering. "And that son of yours is going to give you a run for your money."

He frowned. "Now, Anna, don't insult my fine son. He's a chip off the old block. Actually, that's part of the reason I have been gone. I got Charles settled in college back East. He'll be gone two or three years. He'll be home summers, of course."

She could barely hide the relief on her face. Charles Garvey would not be around to pester her for a while. Even whores had a sexual code, and Charles Garvey went beyond it. She hated the boy and shuddered whenever he came around, reading in his eyes that if she did not participate in some of the odd sexual fantasies he dreamed up, the demented boy just might decide to beat her or scar her for life with a knife. He was not to be trusted, and not to be insulted.

"Well," Anna replied, turning away to hide her pleasure at the news, "it took you a long time to get the boy settled. You've been gone half the winter." She reached for the whiskey bottle and turned back to pour another shot into Garvey's glass.

"Charles was a little bit nervous about the whole thing," he answered. "We are very close, you know. So between that and all the holdings I still have back East to settle, I took an apartment and stayed there for a while, until the boy got used to his new surroundings.''

She nodded. ''I see. And did you get all the loose ends tied up?''

He grinned wickedly. ''I did.'' He looked her hard in the eyes, and she told herself to be alert.

''Good,'' she told him. ''I, uh, suppose you want to go upstairs later.''

The man shrugged. ''Perhaps. But actually, Anna, I came here to ask you about Zeke Monroe.''

The color drained from her face and her smile quickly faded. Garvey grinned at the look on her face, as though someone had just hit her in the gut. She had been prepared for him to pull something, but she never expected him to mention Zeke. She turned away, frantically trying to keep her thoughts straight. He knew something! She had to protect Zeke. How much did this man know, and how had he found out?

''My, my, Anna, I didn't mean to draw such a reaction,'' he told her with a joyous gleam in his eye. ''I dare say Zeke Monroe left quite an impression on you at one time. I must admit I never dreamed any man could make you expose your emotions this way, or that you even had such emotions.'' He chuckled lightly. ''But then I know who the man is, and I dare say he must be quite a specimen in bed. Any man who can shake up an experienced woman like you is quite a man.'' He reached out and traced a finger over the satiny skin of her shoulder. ''However, my dear, the man is married, quite happily, I hear. How on earth did you ever get him into your warm bed?''

She quickly turned back to face him, and he was surprised to see she had tears in her eyes. ''What is it you want, Garvey?'' she hissed.

He smiled like a man who had just won a prize. ''You have already given it to me by your reaction, my sweet,'' he told her. ''You saw this Monroe fellow—in

269

Denver—about three or four years ago. In fact, you even helped him out of a bit of trouble, I'm told.'' He leaned on the bar and rubbed his chin thoughtfully. "Now, isn't it a coincidence that it was just about that same time that you broke the news to me about my having a half-breed son? I wonder who could have given you that information?''

She stiffened, regaining her composure. "I have a lot of sources.''

"I'm sure you do, my pet. But so do I. I'm going to let you sit and wonder how in hell I discovered Zeke Monroe was here in Denver those years back. But the discovery of it began to make a lot of things clear to me. I've been pondering the whole thing over these last several months, making notes, connecting things. And I'll tell you what I came up with. About nine or ten years ago, when I still lived near Santa Fe, and you ran a whorehouse there, I had an Indian slave—an Arapaho woman named Yellow Moon. She'd been married to a Cheyenne man and was sold off to outlaws for whiskey. Her son was murdered by those same outlaws and she eventually was sold to you. You couldn't make a decent prostitute out of her because she was half crazy from the death of her son, so I very kindly took the woman off your hands.''

"I didn't know what else to do with her. If I had just turned her out she would have died. At least with you she had shelter and food.''

He feigned admiration for her concern, shaking his head and pursing his lips. "Oh, Anna, your generosity and kindness overwhelm me,'' he touted. Then he leaned closer. "Well, I was equally kind. I took her in.''

"And made a sexual slave of her, I dare say,'' Anna said quietly, the hatred beginning to gleam in her eyes. "I've changed since then, my dear Senator. I regret

270

giving that poor woman over to you."

"Tut, tut, Anna. Let's not spoil your dirty image. Besides, I want to finish my story."

"I don't want to hear it!" she snapped, turning and walking away. But he quickly moved up behind her, grasping her arm so tightly that it hurt.

"How about finishing this conversation in your office in back?" he told her quietly.

She winced from the pain and did not want to make a scene in front of her customers. She smiled for them as she moved toward her office, her heart racing. Zeke! If only she could hate him! If only she didn't care! The worst part was she even cared about his wife, admired her for her courage and goodness. Abigail Monroe was everything Anna now wished she could be. But there was no hope for that. She walked into her office and Garvey closed the door behind them.

"Let's see now. Where was I?" he goaded.

"You were taking advantage of a poor, mourning Indian woman who was half crazy from the death of her baby boy," Anna replied. "You were taking advantage of her mental condition and planting your fat, stinking body over hers." She whirled. "Something you'll never do with me again."

His eyebrows arched. "My goodness, Anna! Why I truly believe you're in love with Zeke Monroe. Can that be possible? Is that why you're reacting to your old friend this way? Because you consider me a threat to your half-breed lover?"

She stepped closer. "You're a threat to humanity of any kind!" she replied bitterly.

There was suddenly a sharp sting to her face and she found herself on the floor, red finger marks on her cheek where Garvey had slapped her hard.

"You bitch!" he glowered. "You owe me everything! And you owed me this! You should have told me—years ago!''

She blinked back tears, grasping her desk as she got back to her feet. ''Told you what?'' she replied stubbornly. ''I have nothing to tell you.''

''You have plenty to tell me!'' he growled. ''Zeke Monroe came searching for his sister-in-law. And somehow he traced her to my place. He told me it was one of the other girls who ratted on me. But it was you, wasn't it? It was my old friend and confidante, Anna Gale. How did he get you to tell, sweet Anna? Was he so well endowed that he made you gasp out the information so that you could have another piece of him?''

''Stop it!'' she yelled. ''He's not that kind of man.''

''Is that so? Well, my little whore, there is only one way to make a bitch like you talk, and that's to get between your legs and give you a damned good time!''

''I made him do it!'' she blurted out, whirling. ''He didn't want to—''

Garvey burst out laughing. ''Tell me another one, my sweet.''

She turned around again, wanting desperately to shoot this man. ''You bastard!'' she whimpered. ''A hundred men like you wouldn't be worth Zeke Monroe's little finger.''

He watched her, glowing with great pride in his accomplishment and cleverness. ''That depends on what you're judging,'' the man replied. ''But no matter. The point is, it was Zeke Monroe who came to my place and threatened me into giving up Yellow Moon. And it was Zeke Monroe who saw you in Denver later. And after that you came to me with the news that I have a half-breed son floating around someplace. Now my guess is that it was Zeke Monroe who told you that. I don't know what compelled him to do that, but it was a mistake. And now you are going to tell me where the boy is.''

272

She turned to face him, her cheek even redder against her paled skin. "I don't know," she answered, hanging her head. "I honestly don't know one thing about the boy. I only know that he exists. The mother has been dead for a long time. Zeke only gave me enough information to use against you—to get out from under your fat thumb!"

"Well it worked—for a while. You're still free, sweet Anna. I owe you nothing now, and you owe me nothing. We're even. I can get the rest of my information elsewhere."

He turned to leave.

"Where?" she demanded.

He turned to face her, grinning slyly. "Anna, my pet, a man like me has all kinds of ways to spy on people and find out what he needs to know. I dare say that by the time I am through, it will be Zeke himself telling me where that boy is." He opened the door.

"Garvey!" she yelled out.

He looked back at her again, closing the door so no one would hear. She stepped closer, her eyes glazed with hatred. "Go ahead and try it!" she hissed. "I sincerely hope that you try to give Zeke Monroe trouble. And I'll tell you why. It's because I will take great joy in seeing what Zeke does to you in return. You don't mess with men like that, my fat senator. You do anything against that man or his family, and you'll regret it for the rest of your life, only that life won't last very long!"

"The man's a common, dirty half-breed!" Garvey sneered. "Men like that are no threat to men like me."

She smiled then, true joy in her eyes. "I hope I'm around when Zeke Monroe comes after you, Winston Garvey!" she glowered. "It will be the happiest day of my life."

He just scowled and left, slamming the door behind

him. Anna sank into a chair, suddenly enveloped with uncontrolled sobbing.

"Zeke!" she whispered, the old ache returning, the longing to be with him just once more.

Margaret stepped out onto the porch to retrieve more wood for the stone oven next to the fireplace, which her mother used for baking. She loaded up one arm when she heard her name spoken softly. She turned in the direction of the voice, and the handsome young white boy with the sandy hair was peeking at her from around the corner. She could not help but smile, for he'd been smiling and winking at her regularly for the past twelve days, and she could not control the flutter he brought to her young heart.

"Come and walk with me?" he said quietly. "We leave in just a couple of days."

Margaret looked toward the doorway, then back at the young man. "It wouldn't be proper," she answered.

"Proper!" he exclaimed in a near whisper. "You're the prettiest thing I've seen since I left home, and pretty soon I'll be gone for who knows how long, little girl. But I intend to come back, because I intend to see you again. So what's wrong with a little walk? Don't you like me?"

She felt flushed. "I . . . like you very much, Mister Troy."

He winked again. "Call me Billy. I'll be waiting." He darted back around the corner, and Margaret walked back inside with the wood, her mind whirling. She was too enamored and too ignorant of men to wonder why the young man did not simply come inside and ask her mother if he might walk with her. She was caught up in the secrecy of it, and automatically believed it was best not to tell.

274

"Mother, it's warmer today, and there's no wind. There's lots of sun," she spoke up. "I'm so tired of being cooped up in the cabin. Would it be all right if I went for a walk?"

Abbie looked up from the table, where she was kneading bread dough. "I suppose," she replied. "All of your morning chores are done. You've been a very big help with the extra work the soldiers have created for us. I appreciate that, Margaret. And why don't you take one of your brothers or sisters along on your walk?"

Margaret dropped her eyes. "I'd rather walk alone," she replied. Wolf's Blood looked up quickly from the corner, where he sat showing his uncle Lance some Indian weapons, as well as his scars from the Sun Dance. He had noticed the soldier named Billy Troy watching his sister. "I . . . I've been surrounded inside the cabin by brothers and sisters for so many days, I prefer to walk alone."

Abbie studied her a moment. She would herself enjoy the relief of being completely alone for a few hours. "Go ahead then," she answered. "Perhaps later you can stay and I will go walking alone myself."

Margaret smiled. "Thank you!" She rushed up to the loft to get her warmest elkskin coat, then climbed back down, hoping her braids were neat enough. She hurried through the door and Wolf's Blood continued to look in that direction, even after the door closed. Then he rose and excused himself. "I am going riding," he told his mother. "I, too, need to go out for a while."

The boy left, and Abbie looked at Lance and shook her head. "The restless age," she told him.

Lance grinned and rose to walk over to the table and watch her knead the dough. "I was told you were just about the same age when you married Zeke. Were you

275

restless when you married him—marry him out of boredom maybe?''

She blushed and chuckled. "The things that happened on that wagon train could hardly be called boring," she replied.

"And I doubt life thereafter with my brother was boring either."

She shook her head and looked up at him, wiping back some hair with the back of her hand and leaving some flour on her forehead when she did so. "Life with your brother is like being married to the eagle or a wild buffalo," she answered. "There has never been a dull moment."

Lance grinned. "I can imagine." He shook his head. "You're some woman, Abigail. I can't believe all you've been through, and you only a couple years older than me."

She smiled softly and sighed. "I'm so glad you landed on my doorstep, Lance. Having you to take care of has helped the loneliness for Zeke. I can't wait to tell him I actually met you—and took a bullet out of you no less!"

The man picked at a piece of dough and put it in his mouth. "And I can't wait to tell Pa I've met you. Danny has told him about you. Now I can tell him, too. I wouldn't mind staying right here, Abigail. But I've got a hitch in the Confederate Army to finish, and I've got to get back to Pa, now that Lenny is gone. He'll be needing me. You tell Zeke that I intend to come back out here someday."

She nodded. "I'll tell him. I just hope he goes and sees your father while he's that close to home. I urged him to go, but I'm afraid he'll avoid it if he can. His feelings for your father are not fond, I'm afraid."

Lance frowned. "That's too bad. Pa loved him. Talked about him a lot. He didn't like the way Zeke got

276

treated, but he couldn't change those people. It just couldn't be helped."

Abbie broke off a piece of dough and put it in a bread pan. "I suppose not," she said, staring at the dough, her heart aching for the lost little boy that dwelled inside her husband. "But Zeke is very bitter about it." She swallowed back a sudden urge to cry. "I just hope that whatever happens to him there, it will be for the good, and that he'll make it back here to me and the children."

"He'll get back all right," Lance assured her. "You're the one who said he's too mean to die, right?"

She nodded, tearing off another piece of dough then and filling another bread pan. "Of course. I did say that, didn't I? And it's true. Lord knows he should have met his maker a hundred times by now."

He saw the loneliness and fear in her eyes, and decided to change the subject. "Hey, is it true you've killed three Crow Indians?" he asked her.

She filled another bread pan. "It's true. I shot them with my pa's old Spencer carbine. Killed one when Crow Indians attacked our wagon train, and another one was a renegade who ran with the outlaws that captured me—the ones Zeke took care of single-handedly except for the one I shot. I shot the third one the next year, when your father and I were riding into his brothers' village. Crows were after us, chased us right into the village. My horse stumbled and I went flying. When I landed I turned and shot one. I made one grand entrance that day, I'll tell you! But shooting those Crows made me more respected among the Cheyenne, who were enemies of the Crow. It helped get me accepted." She looked up at Lance. "But I'm not proud of it, Lance. I don't condone killing and I pray to God every day that He will accept my soul. It's just that out here, a person has to be practical. There is no law

277

except the law of survival. That's one of the first things I learned from Zeke. How to be practical and survive. It was a hard lesson and I still have trouble with it. But it's been a way of life for Zeke for a long time. I dare say he has no idea how many men he has killed." She broke off another piece of dough and just stared at it a moment. "It's strange to see that side of him, and then to know what a good husband and father he is. He is many different men all rolled up into one body. He can be the gentlest of men—and then again he can be the cruelest, most vicious man you could ever imagine, but only to his enemies, never his loved ones."

"Anyone who knows what happened back in Tennessee can attest to that," the young man replied. "I remember—"

The door burst open then, and Margaret came inside, panting, her lip bleeding. "Mama, I'm sorry!" she sobbed.

Abbie's chest tightened and she rushed over to the girl. "Sorry for what?"

"I . . . thought he was . . . nice." She looked up at Abbie with wide, frightened eyes. "He . . . called me names—squaw names," she whimpered. "Mama, go stop Wolf's Blood. He'll kill Billy! He'll kill him!"

Abbie looked at Lance, putting things together quickly. She ran outside without a coat and Lance followed, himself now almost completely healed. Down near the shed men were pulling Billy Troy and Wolf's Blood apart, but they were having a difficult time with Wolf's Blood, who growled like an animal and fought and kicked with a strength the men found amazing for a fifteen-year-old boy. Abbie hurried to the scene and stepped right between the two fighting men.

"What is going on here!" she demanded, too angry to be affected by the cold.

"He attacked Margaret!" Wolf's Blood growled.

278

"He pushed her down and touched her breasts, the filthy, white bastard maggot!"

"Wolf's Blood!" Abbie snapped. "Watch your tongue!" She saw in that moment the same angry look she had seen before in Zeke's eyes, the wild Indian ready to kill. She turned her eyes to Billy Troy, who jerked his arms loose from the men who held him and stood there panting, his face badly bruised and his lip bleeding profusely. Abbie secretly took delight in the battered face of the young man, while Wolf's Blood had no marks on him.

"She was willing!" the boy spit out. "She's just a damned squaw, so what's the big deal?"

Abbie's cheeks colored with anger and Wolf's Blood jerked viciously at the three men who held him, almost getting away again. Major Mayes, who had made it to the scene of the skirmish and heard Billy's remark, stepped up to the man, his eyes angry.

"Get to your tent, and stay in there until we leave out tomorrow, or by God, Troy, I'll have you shot!" the man growled. "And you will apologize to Mrs. Monroe for that remark. She has shown us nothing but kindness, and we have put her to great extra burden by being here for so long. That girl is no more than a child. Apologize, or you'll get the worst assignment I can give you when we get back!"

The man looked at Abbie, his eyes roaming her with a sneer. She knew what he was thinking, but she had borne such treatment before. It was Margaret she felt sorry for.

"I apologize," Troy said grudgingly.

"And you will see that the wood is stacked good and high at Mrs. Monroe's hearth before we leave out!" the major added. He turned to one of the men. "Accompany Billy to the house and see that the wood gets stacked."

"No!" Abbie spoke up. "Not yet. I wish to go and talk to my daughter first, and I want to be sure she is not present when this snake of a man goes inside."

The major looked at her, seeing an anger and a fight in her eyes he did not expect in such a gentle woman. He could see that Abigail Monroe could also be a scrapper when necessary.

"I'm deeply sorry, ma'am," he told her, admiring her greatly. If he were not so certain she was the kind of woman who had no inclinations toward any man but her own husband, he would have done his best to lure her away from this place and take her for himself.

"I believe you," she told the major. "But I want you and your men to leave as soon as the sun rises in the morning. I will regret seeing Lance go, but I will not regret seeing the rest of you leave. Go and fight your Civil War, Major. I have enough problems on my hands and my own battles to fight. Remarks like the one Private Troy just made don't make my job easy."

She brushed past him and stormed toward the house. The three men who held Wolf's Blood cautiously let go of the boy, and he glared at Troy, suddenly whipping out a huge blade.

"If your friends were not here, I would cut you to ribbons!" he sneered. "And it would be a pleasure!"

He whirled and followed his mother, and Lance glared at Billy Troy, wishing he were not recovering from a wound, for he would dearly love to finish what Wolf's Blood had started.

"You dumb bastard!" he growled. "You're damned lucky my brother Zeke wasn't here, or your guts would be hanging out on the line to dry." He stalked away, heading for the cabin. When he entered, Wolf's Blood sat at the table studying his bloody knuckles. His dark eyes darted up to greet Lance, and Lance sensed that although he was an uncle, he was not entirely welcome

280

because he was white. This boy had little use for whites, and had been defensive and suspicious ever since the soldiers had come.

"You sure look like your father," Lance told him. "Act like him, too."

They both glanced at the loft, where they heard soft crying. Then they looked back at each other.

"My father killed those men who murdered his wife and little boy," Wolf's Blood told Lance. "I will gladly do the same if any man hurts my mother or my sisters!"

Lance sighed and sat down near the stove to get warm. "That I do not doubt, Wolf's Blood," he answered. Smoke lay near the hearth, staring at Lance with the same dark look that Wolf's Blood had.

In the loft Abbie tried to console her weeping daughter, whose humiliation at such a tender age would not easily be forgotten.

Eighteen

"Dear Abbie, You would never believe how bad this war has become," Abbie read, in only the second letter she had received since her husband had left eight months earlier. She sat by the stream in their favorite spot, surrounded by the purple iris that she loved. It was a warm spring day, and the smell of new grass and thawing earth filled her nostrils, while the songs of birds mingled their music with the icy, splashing waters of the stream. She struggled against her tears of loneliness and longing as she read. "I would have written more often, but it is almost impossible to find people who can get letters through, and I have no idea if you will get this one," the letter continued. "I can only pray to the spirits that you will, and I pray for you, too, just as you pray for me. I am glad we are not living in Tennessee, Abbie-girl. I would be more worried about you here than where you are now. Every place I go there is nothing but destruction and starvation, looting and death. I am sure that by the time this war ends, the deaths will be in the thousands, maybe hundreds of thousands. I've visited prisons and hospitals searching for Danny, and what I see there makes even a man like myself feel sick. I have never seen so many men with arms and legs missing or dying from filth and disease. A few months ago in Nashville I buried an old woman who was trampled in the street. I don't even know what her name was. I wonder now if this country will ever again be at peace. It seems this war will go on forever, let alone what is in store for the Indians in the years to come.

"I have searched every camp I can find, looking for Danny. No prison or hospital seems to have him. I travel among both Union and Confederate camps, sometimes at great risk. Right now any man not in a gray or a blue uniform is suspect, even when it's obvious that man is an Indian who has no interest in either side. Everyone is suspect, and there are spies everywhere. If I do not find Danny soon, I will simply have to come home and give up the search. I fear for you and the children. I hate to tell Emily he has not been found, but soon I will have no choice. I wish there was a way I could hear from you and know that you are all right, but I move around so much that there is no one place where you could write to me.

"I miss you and the children so much that it is difficult to sleep. I long to hug my little Monroes, and I don't think I need to tell you how I long to hold you. It is only when I am apart from you that I realize how much I need you for my own strength, and I know it is the same for you. I miss the ranch and the cool mountain air that sweeps down across the land in the spring. It is already hot here. Now I remember one of the things I hated about the South—the hot, wet air and the bugs.

"Tell the children how much I love them. And you know how much I love you, Abbie. Always cling to that. I love you and I will be home by late summer. I promise. I will not let this continue much longer. I know this is a long letter, but it may be the last one I am able to write. Perhaps when you hear from me again, I

283

can deliver my message in person.

"I am headed for Virginia and should be there in just a few days. I am told a very large Confederate army has gathered there under General Lee and a man called Stonewall Jackson. I will be someplace around Fredericksburg and a little place called Chancellorsville.

"Remember that I am with you in spirit. And if I should never return, I will be with you forever. We are never truly apart, Abbie. I take strength in your love, and send you strength in return. I love you. I love you.

"Zeke."

She folded the letter. How many times had she read it? She should know it by heart, yet reading it made him seem closer. She watched the dancing waters for a while, remembering another time when he had returned to her right here in this spot. She kept thinking that if she came here everyday, perhaps he would return again to this very spot, and she would feel the strong arms around her, breathe in his manly scent, feel his warm lips on her own, her breasts pressed against his broad chest. What wonderful strength it would give her to be held by him again, just for a while!

She sighed and rose. She would return again tomorrow, and read the letter again. She pushed it into the bodice of her dress, wishing he had mentioned his father. Apparently he still had not gone to see the man.

Zeke picked his way among the fallen Rebel soldiers at Chancellorsville. Although a victory for Lee, the battle here had cost the South thirteen thousand men, as well as the accidental shooting of their own great commander, Stonewall Jackson, who lost his left arm and died a few days later of pneumonia. His death had brought a dark curtain down on the Confederate troops, who in spite of their victory at Chancellorsville, still felt impending doom. Stonewall Jackson had been of utmost importance as a leader of men.

Zeke walked on foot, leading his horse behind him, as he made his way among the burial detail, looking at each dead body and hoping he would not see a familiar face. Cannon boomed in the distance. The Union Army was still very definitely close by, and an attempt to roust Lee's forces out of Chancellorsville was expected. Confederates sat scattered here and there, looking weary and half starved, many of them with uniforms that appeared to have been worn day in and day out for months. Some chewed on hardtack, biscuits so difficult to chew that men often broke their teeth on them. Most preferred to dunk the biscuits in water or coffee first, which brought the wiggling weevils to the surface where they could be skimmed off before eating the biscuit. Zeke knew that if the Union Army could not win this war by force and tactic, they would win it simply by waiting for the South to starve to death, which would not take much longer.

Suddenly his blood felt like ice and his chest tightened. He spotted the blond curls first, thick, wavy hair that reminded him of Danny's. He told himself he was beginning to see things, but when he bent closer he felt as though a vise were gripping at his heart and squeezing it tightly. His breath did not want to come, for the gaunt face he looked at was surely Danny, even though it was so thin he had to study it hard to be sure.

The body lay among a heap of dead bodies awaiting burial. Those digging the graves paid little heed to Zeke, as he bent down to gently turn the blond-haired man's head to see if there was a scar on his neck where Danny had once fallen against a sharp stick and cut himself badly when a boy. Zeke knew at once by the easy way he could turn this man's head that the man was not dead at all. If he were, he would be stiff. His heart pounded when he saw the scar. He turned the head back again and gently lifted an eyelid. The eyeballs were rolled back, but not completely. He could see the eyes were blue. Zeke quickly felt for a pulse, glancing at the burial detail to make sure no one noticed he'd found this man alive. The pulse was faint and slow, but it was there.

Zeke struggled against his excitement. He did not want these men to know Danny was still alive. If they did, they would throw him into the pile of the wounded who lay waiting for a doctor's help. He might lie for days without that help and die after all. He must take Danny with him and help him himself, find a place where he could heal and then get him back to Emily.

"Hey, what are you doin' there?" someone called out. A tattered sergeant approached Zeke. "Who the hell are you?"

"My name is Zeke Monroe. I've been searching for my brother," he told the man. "I . . . just found him. He's dead. I'd like permission to take his body and bury him myself."

The man looked from Zeke to Danny and back to Zeke. "You don't look like no brother to me."

"I am his brother," Zeke repeated, feeling desperate. "We share the same father. But my mother was Cheyenne. I swear to you, he's my brother. His name is Danny Monroe and he's from Tennessee. I've been searching for him. I'd heard he'd been wounded and taken prisoner, but I couldn't find him in any of the prisons."

The man looked down at Danny again. Then he nodded. "That's Monroe, all right. I served under him when this damned battle here began." He looked back at Zeke. "He was sickly, though. He'd been wounded like you said. When he came to us he wasn't really healed but he wanted to get back into the fightin'."

286

The man shook his head. "Stubborn sort. I remember now. Saw him go down a couple of days ago to a Union sword. Sorry you had to find him dead, mister."

"There are a lot of things to be sorry for in this war," Zeke returned.

The sergeant sighed. "That's a fact," He shrugged. "Go ahead and take the body, mister. What the hell? In this damned war who will know the difference? He's already been listed as dead. With all the bodies we have to bury, one more won't be missed."

"Thank you," Zeke told him, putting out his hand. The sergeant took it hesitantly.

"I ain't never shook no Indian's hand before. Don't seem right. We just got done gettin' most of you out of the South. Now we got the niggers to worry about."

He shook Zeke's hand, and Zeke checked his own anger. He had to get Danny away, and giving this man the punch he rightly deserved would get him nowhere. The sergeant turned, and Zeke dragged Danny's body from the pile and carefully laid him over his mount. Danny's uniform was soaked with blood. Zeke threw a blanket over the body and took his horse by the reins, leading the animal on foot.

Zeke headed south. He had to get past Union lines before he could help Danny. Until he did so, no place that he might stop to make a camp would be safe for them. Deep in the woods of maple and ash he stumbled over the dead body of a Union soldier. His eyes darted around the immediate area, his keen Indian senses telling him there was no one alive close by. He quickly pulled out his big blade, slicing Danny's Confederate coat from his body and then removing the dead Union man's coat, a difficult job because the body was stiff. He held off an urge to vomit at touching the bloated body. Then he threw the Union coat over Danny's

287

body, tying the sleeves around Danny's neck where he hung face down, and tucking the tails under Danny's belly. Then he took another blanket from his supplies and wrapped it around Danny's legs to cover the Confederate pants. If they ran into Union troops, he would have to do his best to pass Danny off as a Federalist.

He proceeded quickly then, ever closer to Union camps. He veered to the west, hoping to avoid the Union soldiers altogether. He moved among the trees and underbrush with the expertise of a man long accustomed to moving like a wild animal, ever watchful, quiet, alert. Sometime soon he would have to stop and give Danny some immediate aid, if the man wasn't already dead. For two hours he kept moving, still walking his horse. Now the cannon were more distant again. So far he had avoided Union forces and the questions they would have for him. He knew that in the town of Orange, only about twenty miles to the west, there was a hospital that served both Union and Confederate soldiers, with no questions asked. In this confusing, unorganized war, he could get help for Danny there with no trouble, and since he was already listed as dead, there would be no Confederate commanders searching for him.

He walked until dusk, sure he could get to Orange before it was too dark to travel any further. He stopped occasionally to pack Danny's middle with more gauze between his body and the horse's blanket. But the gauze was soaked so quickly that it seemed fruitless. The only hope he could take in that was that the man was still alive. Otherwise the bleeding would stop. He spoke to Danny occasionally but got no response.

He came within range of Orange, spotting the lights of the town from a high hill above it. He was almost at his resting point. But then a shot rang out, and pain seared across his back at his shoulder blade. His body

288

spun around and he landed on his back. He heard running feet and saw shadowy figures coming toward him.

"Git his horse 'n' supplies!" he heard a man growl. "And strip the bodies. We need everything we kin git. Hurry it up, boys!"

Through slightly blurred vision Zeke saw a grizzly, bearded man bending over him. Hands started to unlace his buckskin shirt, but in the next moment Zeke Monroe's big blade was out and plunged deeply into the man's abdomen. There was a strange grunt, and with a strength that came only from that inner place not often used, Zeke shoved the man off his knife in spite of the wound across his back. He quickly got to his feet, letting out a Cheyenne war cry and charging with the big blade. It was all a strange blur to him. He kicked a rifle out of one man's hand and slashed the blade across the man's throat. Then he whirled, kicking out again and landing a foot to the side of another man's head. The man went down, and Zeke pulled a handgun from his waist and fired it point blank into the man's face.

"Jesus Christ, it's a wild Indian!" somebody shouted. Zeke turned to see two more men running. He threw the menacing blade, and it landed with a thump between the shoulder blades of one of the men. The man went crashing forward with a cry and the last man kept running. Zeke quickly picked up one of their own rifles and took aim, hardly able to see the man in the darkness. He pulled the trigger, then heard a grunt and a crash.

Zeke threw down the rifle and hurried to the man with the knife in his back. He yanked out the knife, tempted to take the man's scalp. But then he shoved the knife into its sheath, his breathing labored and his back feeling on fire. He knew it was just a graze, or he would not be alive at all, but he could feel blood running down his back beneath the buckskin shirt. Now he had to get to Orange before he himself passed out and was of no use to Danny. He stumbled back to his horse and grabbed the reins, heading down the hill toward Orange.

The forty-five minute journey into the town seemed more like twenty-four hours to Zeke. He struggled toward the makeshift hospital he had already seen on his way to Chancellorsville just two days before, but a man stopped him as he climbed the steps.

"Sorry, mister. We're full up. It's impossible to take any more."

"But . . . my brother . . . needs help badly. And I'm . . . wounded."

"So are a lot of others. You might try down the street, the big white house a few doors down. There's a doctor and a nurse there takin' in more wounded."

Zeke was too weary to argue. "Thanks," he muttered. He stumbled back down the steps and pulled on his horse, the white house seeming six miles away. He finally reached its gate and walked through, pulling his horse with him up to the steps. He tied the horse and struggled up the steps, feeling more and more dizzy. He leaned against the door frame and pounded on the heavy door. He could hear footsteps, and finally the door opened. A lovely woman with light hair and blue eyes greeted him, and for a moment they both stared in utter shock.

"Zeke!" she exclaimed. "It is you, isn't it?"

A grin made its way through his pain. The spirits truly were with him. "Bonnie," he whispered.

Out of sheer joy at seeing someone he knew, someone who would most definitely help him, someone he could call friend, he grabbed her close and clung to her.

"Bonnie Lewis!" he muttered. "Thank God!"

She breathed deeply of his earthy, manly scent. How many years had it been? Too many. Far too many.

Zeke! She let him hold her. For this one brief moment in her life she could share his arms again.

Winston Garvey studied the ugly scars on Buel's face and neck, put there by Wolf's Blood's pet wolf the day Garvey's men made trouble for Zeke Monroe and his family. He moved his eyes to Handy, whose hideous, deformed face had never healed right after Zeke Monroe had smashed a rifle butt into it.

"I have a mission for you two," he told the men. "It's highly secret. I want no foul-ups, understand?"

"Yes, sir," Buel replied, speaking for Handy, who had difficulty moving his jaw.

"I'll pay you well—very well."

Both men's eyes lit up eagerly.

"It's May. Most of the snow has thawed from the plains and you should be able to travel. I'll give you a map my spies have drawn up for me. I want you to take at least ten more men along—good men who can keep their mouths shut and who don't ask questions as long as the pay is good. Can you find them?"

"We can find them," Buel replied, nodding. "Where are we going?"

Garvey leaned back in his chair. "To southeast Colorado, around Bent's Fort. There's a ranch down there in Indian territory, near the Arkansas River. Belongs to a man by the name of Zeke Monroe."

Buel's eyes lit up. "You mean the big guy that headed that bunch we got into that fight with last summer?"

Garvey nodded. "Same one. I want none of the children hurt or taken. There is a ranch hand there. If he's killed it makes no difference. I am told the Indian himself is gone—went back East for some reason. So the woman is there alone. I'd never get any information from Monroe, so I'll go to the weak one—the woman. I want the woman. She has some information I need. What it is makes no difference to you. It's none of your business. Just bring her to me.''

Buel grinned. ''I remember her. She's the white woman. And she's damned pretty.''

Garvey scowled. ''I don't want her harmed or raped. I'll decide what to do with her once you bring her to me—and, by the way, once your extra men help you get her away from there, pay them off and send them on their way. Only the two of you are to know that you brought her to my place, understand? No one must be aware of where she has been taken.''

''You've got it,'' Buel told the fat senator.

''Very good,'' Garvey answered. ''Take your time. Don't move too quickly. Ask around first. Sometimes the Cheyenne camp out around there. Monroe has relatives among the tribe and they watch out for the woman. Make sure you pick a day when there are no extra men there. Sometimes they go off to hunt. And watch out for the oldest kid. He's a mean one.''

''We're already aware of that,'' Buel replied. ''We'll watch out for him. I just hope the father still ain't home when we get there. Him I don't want to mess with again.''

Garvey just grinned. ''Buel, by the time I'm through, that man will be crawling to me on his knees. That bastard will be begging to get his woman back. But there is only one way he will get her. But then perhaps I'll find out what I need to know from her own lips.''

Buel smiled. ''She's got pretty lips, Senator.''

Garvey just chuckled. ''Let's get down to business and study the map,'' he answered, opening a desk drawer.

Nineteen

Zeke's eyes were heavy with sorrow as he watched Bonnie Lewis and her father work diligently on Danny. His handsome, robust, younger half-brother was shockingly thin and pale. His stomach, exposed for surgery and stitches, was sunken; the man's bright blue eyes were closed and hollow-looking.

"He has an older injury that wasn't taken care of properly," Doctor Beaker muttered as Bonnie sponged away more blood.

"He was wounded at Shiloh," Zeke spoke up in a strained voice. "That's all I know."

"Well, that and this new wound have taken their toll. It's truly amazing that this man is even alive."

Zeke smiled sadly. "He's just stubborn like me," he replied.

Bonnie glanced up at him, the trauma of the moment only soothed by the fact that Zeke Monroe had found his way to her doorstep. What ravaged her heart most of all was that he had not changed one bit, except that now he looked so very tired and lonely. There was much to talk about, but it would not be easy talking to him. His reappearance in her life brought shocks of terrible need to her long-sleeping body, needs Zeke Monroe always awakened her to. How strange and cruel was the hand of fate that brought this man to her heroic rescue years ago from the hands of vicious outlaws; for although he had saved her from a fate worse than death, he had also stirred within her womanly instincts she had not known existed in her soul. She had ignored them, for Zeke Monroe was totally in love with and married to another woman; and Bonnie, being a proper preacher's daughter, buried her sinful love for a man she could not have and married a preacher. Now she must struggle to hide her feelings again, but Zeke Monroe knew that she loved him.

"You look tired, Zeke, and we'll have a look at your back as soon as we're finished here."

"I'm all right," he answered. "It's Danny I'm worried about. I'm just glad I found you. I'd have had to work on him myself if I hadn't found help when I did. You can do a better job. You have all the right supplies."

They looked at each other for a moment, then she turned back to her work, feeling warm and excited. "With all of your experience you probably could have done just about as good a job as we're doing," she answered while her father began taking stitches. "I remember how you told me you had to cut infection out of Abbie when she was wounded with an arrow, and even had to burn some of it out. I'm sure you could have helped Danny."

The mention of Abbie's name brought on the old ache. He turned away, walking out into the cool hallway of the huge home that Bonnie and her father had occupied and set up as a hospital. The owners had fled to parts unknown, leaving a good share of their belongings behind, including several beds, all of which were full. A less injured man would have to be moved to make room for Danny. Zeke would be content to sleep on the floor, for he had slept on the hard ground most of his life and hated soft beds. Again, he thought of Abbie, who had given up soft beds for a bed of robes . . . a bed they shared very happily. To lie beside her this night was the most wonderful thing he could imagine. How many months had it been? Seven? Eight? God, how he missed her! He pulled out a pipe and filled it, walking to a parlor and sitting down wearily on a rose-colored love seat. He lit his pipe and puffed it, closing his eyes for a moment, fighting a much-needed sleep. When he opened them, he stared in surprise and pleasure.

Before him stood a boy of perhaps eight or nine, a very handsome boy with olive-colored skin, sandy hair and blue eyes. He wore short pants . . . and a leg brace.

"Joshua?" Zeke asked.

The boy smiled brightly, and Zeke's heart swelled with exceeding relief. They had most certainly done the right thing by allowing Bonnie and Rodney Lewis to adopt this little half-breed. He was obviously happy and looked healthy and robust, in spite of the brace; and as the boy walked toward Zeke, he showed a limp, but not a bad one. At least he was walking. The baby Zeke and Abbie had handed over to Bonnie Lewis all those years ago had been so badly twisted and crippled, they found it hard to believe anything could be done for him. Yet here he stood. And what was most difficult to believe was that this charming boy before him could have been sired by Winston Garvey.

"How do you know my name?" the boy asked.

Zeke frowned. He had no idea how much this boy knew about his roots. He must be careful.

"Your mother told me in the operating room," Zeke replied. "I brought in my half-brother who's been badly wounded. She said if I came out here and saw a young boy, it would be her son, Joshua."

"Oh," the boy answered, stepping cautiously closer, his smile fading. He suddenly took on an apprehensive look. "Are you . . . an Indian?" he asked. "You look like the Indians I know out West in the Dakotas and Wyoming."

Zeke nodded. "I'm only part Indian, though. Half Cheyenne. My name is Zeke Monroe. Ever heard it?"

The boy puckered his lips in thought. "Nope," he finally answered. "Do you know my mother?"

Zeke puffed his pipe. Apparently this boy knew nothing about his past. Perhaps he didn't even know yet that he was himself half Indian, for he had very little of those features, except for the olive skin and rather high cheekbones.

"I, uh, met her once, down in Santa Fe, when she lived there with your grandfather before she went north to marry your father." He would not say anything about the outlaws. Perhaps that was another thing Bonnie had never told him, and perhaps it was something she would never want him to know.

"I haven't seen any Indians since we came here," Joshua was saying.

"That's because all the eastern Indians have been chased west," Zeke replied. "There used to be lots of Indians around here, son—Creeks, Choctaws, Cherokees, Iroquois, Delaware, Catawba."

The boy eased himself into a chair near Zeke. "What happened to them?"

Zeke puffed his pipe again. "Well, the whites came along and wanted their land. And since there were a lot more whites than Indians, and since a lot of the Indians died from the white man's diseases, the whites were able to just kick out the Indians and send them west. Trouble is, the same thing is happening out west now. The Indians are getting pushed into smaller and smaller territory."

The boy thought for a moment, toying with a button on the arm of the chair he sat in. "That's kind of mean. I like Indians—most of them, anyway. Some are kind of mean back, but I think it's because the whites are mean to them."

Zeke grinned. "You're a clever little boy."

"I listen to my mom and dad talk, and my grandfather," he answered very seriously. "They talk about the Indians. They help them sometimes. Grandfather helps them when they're hurt or sick, and I've heard my mother say that most white doctors won't help Indians like that." He sighed, then sat up straighter, feeling more important. "I think I'll help Indians someday, too. I don't know how yet, but I have Indian friends, and I get mad when my white friends won't play with them. They make fun of them and spit at them."

Zeke leaned forward, resting his elbows on his knees. "Well, Joshua, I hope you can help them in some way someday. Something tells me you'll do just that. You seem like a very nice and very smart young man."

The boy smiled. "I'm going to college someday. Have you ever been to college?"

Zeke chuckled. "I'm afraid not, young man. Far from it. My education has been living in the open, with animals for friends and all of nature to teach me about God."

The boy suddenly jumped up, his young mind flitting from one subject to another. "I've had six operations!" he announced proudly. "I walk real good now, see?" He paraded once around the room and Zeke smiled and nodded.

"Very fine. You must be a very brave boy."

He shrugged. "I just want to walk, that's all. Mom tells me when I was born I was all twisted. It's called clubfoot. But I'm a lot better now, and I don't have very much pain."

297

Zeke nodded obligingly. If only Yellow Moon could see this fine son she had birthed! And if only Abbie could see him. How happy and contented she would feel knowing Joshua had turned out so handsome and brave and was so happy.

Suddenly Bonnie was at the doorway, and Zeke rose. Her face paled when she saw that Joshua was in the same room with the man who knew everything about his past. Zeke gave her a reassuring look. "I've just been getting acquainted with your son, here, Mrs. Lewis," he told her. "He's a fine boy." Their eyes held again. "A very fine boy."

"We're . . . very proud of him," she replied.

Zeke flashed the handsome grin she had remembered all these years, and what she felt in her chest was sheer pain. She turned her eyes to Joshua. "You get to bed, young man," she told him. "It's very late, and Mister Monroe is wounded besides. We have to take care of his wounds and let him get some rest."

"Yes, ma'am," the boy answered. He put his hand out to Zeke. "Nice to meet you, sir," the boy told him. Zeke took his hand gently, squeezing the tiny hand in his own big palm.

"I'm very happy to meet you, too, Joshua," Zeke replied.

Joshua felt a strange tingle at the touch of the tall Indian's hand, as though there were something familiar about him. But he was too young to question or worry about such feelings.

"Goodnight, sir," he told Zeke. He turned and limped over to his mother, who bent over and kissed his cheek.

"I'll come and check on you soon. Can you handle the brace by yourself?" she asked him.

"You know I can, Mother," the boy said almost chidingly. He walked off and Bonnie looked at Zeke with a glowing pride.

"You've done a marvelous job with him," he told her. "I never really doubted Abbie and I did the right thing bringing him to you, Bonnie. I can't express how relieved and happy I am at seeing him—so healthy and happy."

She studied the handsome face. Why was her God so cruel as to bring this man of men back into her life? "He's my whole world," she answered. "I apparently am not going to have any children of my own."

She suddenly blushed and looked away. Zeke knew Rodney Lewis, and he strongly suspected what kind of husband the man was. He contemplated the fact that if she were his own wife, she'd have plenty of children by now. She was a fine woman, and it angered him that she was wasted on Rodney Lewis. But that was not his business now, nor was there anything he could do about it. Bonnie Lewis was nothing more to him than a gentle, lovely woman he had helped and befriended, and who now raised his crippled nephew. She had never been anything more than that to him, although he knew she wished he could have been. He had never had any feelings of desire for her in the way that he desired Abbie.

"Some things just aren't meant to be, I guess," he replied, trying to console her. She remained turned away, and he knew she was struggling with her emotions. He scrambled desperately to change the subject. "Well, how about telling me what the hell you're doing here in Virginia," he spoke up. "I figured you were still out in Wyoming."

She turned to meet his eyes again. "I could ask you the same thing," she answered.

Zeke sat back down. "Well, Danny's wife, Emily, she came around last summer and told me Danny had been wounded and taken prisoner, begged me to come

East and see if maybe I could find him." He nodded toward the room she had just come from. "As you can see, I found him. How's he doing?"

"It's hard to say yet. We can't guarantee anything, Zeke. We'll just have to wait a few days."

He sighed and nodded, then relit his pipe.

"How long have you been gone?" she asked him.

He stared at the design in the Oriental rug on the floor. "Too long," he said wistfully. "I just pray to God Abbie and the kids are all right. We have seven children now—four girls and three boys."

"Seven!" she exclaimed. She quickly smiled, trying to hide her burning envy of Abigail Monroe, who had lain beneath this man and taken his seed, turning it into seven little Monroes. What a lucky woman she was! "My goodness, Abbie must be busy."

Zeke grinned. "She has a way of handling everything like clockwork. A very organized woman, and a woman with enough love to give everybody an equal share." He puffed his pipe again. "You still haven't answered my question—about why you're here."

"Oh, I guess I haven't," she answered, coming to sit down beside him. She was rigid and tense. "Joshua . . . needed another operation. And Father, he felt that with this terrible war, there would be a lot of men here in the East who would need his services. He wanted to come and do what he could until the war is over. And because Joshua needed to come again, I came along with Father. Rodney and I . . ." She looked away again. "We . . . agreed . . . that it was best."

Zeke frowned. "Rodney didn't come with you?"

"Oh, no!" she replied too quickly, putting on a defensive smile. "He has a circuit he travels now. He felt he should stay out in Wyoming and continue his practice there. There are so many settlers now, scattered here and there, who have no church to attend. So he goes to them.''

She felt hot and flustered under his all-knowing look. Somehow this perceptive man knew how cold and lonely was her marriage. And he knew she wished her husband had wanted to come along, or had asked her to stay. She twisted her skirt in her fingers. ''We . . . we should take care of that wound on your back, Zeke. And then you must get some rest. You'll be of no use to Danny if you get sick. There is a lot of disease everywhere. You rest, and then we'll talk more.'' She met his eyes again, putting on the unaffected smile. ''I want to know all about what's happening with your family, Zeke—about the children, what they're like. And how is Abbie?''

He smiled softly. ''Abbie's fine. At least she was when I left. I hope Danny heals fast. I can't stay away much longer.'' He reached out and took her hand. ''It sure is good to see you, Bonnie. It renews my spirit to see someone I know. I've seen so much . . . hell. I've been all over the place for about eight months now, visited Confederate camps and all. I've never seen anything to match this war when it comes to filth and starvation and horrible wounds—makeshift hospitals with arms and legs stacked up outside the door. It's the damnedest, bloodiest thing I've ever seen.''

She took a moment of joy at the warmth of his big hand. ''Yes. It's a terrible thing.'' She saw in his eyes the deepest of friendship. Yes. He knew. Of course he knew. ''I'm glad Abbie is fine,'' she told him. He knew that she was sincere. ''Father and I will pray for your family this evening when we retire.'' She rose and tugged at his hand. ''Now, you come and let Father patch up your back. I'll fix up a bed for you.''

''I don't need a bed,'' he answered. ''I'll spread out my bedroll some place on the floor. That's all I need. I'll be fine. Save the beds for the ones in a bad way.''

She sighed. "I had forgotten how much Indian you are, Zeke Monroe. Now I'm remembering that very savage-looking man who did some rather gruesome things to a band of outlaws that had captured me. I remember how frightened I was of you that day."

He flashed the handsome grin again, and in spite of his tired eyes and a face that was thinner from too much travel and worry, he was still the disturbingly desirable man she remembered, still as tall and strong, as hard and yet gentle, as fierce looking and dark. He was still Zeke.

"I . . . still have the necklace you gave me," she found herself saying.

He squeezed her hand gently. "Good. I give such gifts only to those I love and respect the most," he replied.

She blinked back tears. "Go and see Father. I'll get your things off your horse and I'll take your horse out to the shed in back where it can eat. I'm so happy to see you again, Zeke. So glad God sent you here to our door so that we could be the ones to help Danny." She suddenly let go of his hand and hurried out the door. The sight of a lovely, soft woman who cared about him made him long for Abbie even more, and he felt an even stronger urgency to get back to his woman. He loved her. He needed her desperately. And most of all, he needed to know that his Abbie was all right.

It was not until three days after his surgery that Danny opened his eyes for the first time, unaware that he'd been stitched up like a quilt and that water and hot broth had been forced down his throat faithfully by Zeke and Bonnie. The first thing he saw when he came around was an Indian, who stood at a nearby window. The man was shirtless, his long, black hair brushed out and hanging over the bronze skin of his back. For a moment Danny just stared, trying to get his bearings. He thought perhaps he was back at Fort Laramie, and the man he was looking at was one of the Sioux or Northern Cheyenne with whom he had had many dealings. He blinked and quietly glanced around the room, noticing other men were in the room then, all lying on beds and patched up one way or another from injuries. He moved slightly and pain ripped through his abdomen, and it was then the reality of his situation hit him.

He groaned from the agony of it—not just his horrible injury, but also the fact that he must be in some kind of hospital among others who were wounded and dying. Now he remembered the horror of the sword, the ugliness of all the battles, the pain of seeing mere boys gouged and torn and ripped to pieces by shells and shrapnel and swords. Never in his wildest dreams could he have imagined the hell he had seen in this war.

The tall, dark Indian man at the window turned and came toward him when he cried out, and at once a strange new life began trickling through Danny Monroe's veins.

"Zeke!" he whispered, reaching out a shaking hand to his favorite brother. Zeke took his hand and stooped down beside Danny's bed.

"Are you truly awake, Danny?" he asked.

"Zeke," the man repeated, tears coming to his eyes. "How on earth . . . . why are you . . . here? Where are we?"

"We're in Virginia, and you're in a fine hospital where you'll get good care." He smiled, his own eyes watery with tears of relief. "I've been searching for you for months, Danny."

"But . . . how . . . why?"

"Take it easy, brother. You're full of stitches." Zeke squeezed the man's hand. "Emily came to us last fall and told us you had been wounded and captured. She asked me to see if I could find you. I owe you a lot, my brother. I had to come and try. But it was a damned hard job, I'll tell you. And when I found you, you'd already been given up for dead. You're badly wounded, Danny. You've got to stay in bed for a good long time."

A tear slipped down the side of Danny's face. "Emily?"

"Emily is fine. Some good friends of her father escorted her to our place, and I saw that she got back safely before I left to look for you." He winked. "She's one beautiful woman, Danny. A little too delicate, but I can see why you had to marry her."

Danny smiled, but the tears wouldn't stop coming. "My . . . Jennifer?"

"Pretty as a picture—fine and healthy. Don't worry about them, Danny. Don't worry about anything but getting well. That's going to take some time. I'll get word to Emily that I have found you and you've received some help."

Danny closed his eyes. "I'm . . . sorry. I . . ." He put a hand to his face, embarrassed at his tears. Zeke kept tight hold of the other hand.

"I've been bad wounded before myself, Danny. And I've wondered if I'd ever see my woman again—see home again. I know how it feels. When a man's beat down from fighting and wounds, he's got a right to feel bad. If you think I've never shed a tear in such times, you don't know me too well."

"It's just . . . this war . . . Shiloh . . . that filthy prison and the pain when they . . . worked on my gunshot wound. They . . . didn't give me anything . . . for the pain."

"Don't talk about it, Danny. It's over. You'll not be going back into that damned war. I don't even want to know what's happened to you over these past months.

Don't talk about it now. Save it for when you're better."

"I . . . don't know . . . how or why you . . . found me," the man replied, sniffing and wiping at his eyes. "Goddamn, Zeke, you could find a half-buried penny in the middle of the Great Plains if somebody asked you to."

Zeke grinned, releasing the man's hand to dip a clean cloth into a bowl of cool water. He wrung it out and leaned over to gently wash his brother's face. "It wasn't me that found you, Danny. It was the spirits, guiding me. I prayed every day, followed my senses and instincts, acted on what I considered guidance from the spirits within me. And you can bet my Abbie has been praying every day to her own God."

"I've . . . been around the Indians . . . long enough to know there's no difference . . . between our God and your God," Danny replied.

Zeke chuckled. "Maybe not." He sponged around Danny's neck. "At any rate, man doesn't accomplish things all alone. If we didn't have an inner strength and guidance, we'd never make it."

"That sounds . . . strange . . . coming from a . . . knife-wielding, bloodthirsty . . . son of a bitch . . . like you," Danny answered.

Zeke laughed harder. "You're definitely feeling better!" he commented. "Now you're starting to talk like the Danny I know."

Danny reached up and grasped his wrist. "Zeke," he spoke up, sobering then, his eyes pleading. "Take me home."

Zeke shrugged. "To Emily? Of course I will—just as soon as you're well enough to travel."

"No," Danny replied. "Take me home . . . to the old farm."

Zeke lost his smile and stood up, pulling his hand

away from Danny's. "That's out of the question. You'll stay here for several weeks. You're in a very good hospital. Then I'll take you to Emily."

"Zeke . . . please . . . listen to me," Danny answered, his voice growing weaker. "Please, please . . . hear me out."

Zeke sighed and layed the wash cloth back in the bowl. He knelt back down, but his eyes were still hard. "All right. Speak your piece, but you know I can't go back to that farm."

Danny considered telling his brother how lonely his white father was—how much the man loved Zeke and wanted to see him again. But he knew that would only make Zeke angrier, and he didn't want him to walk away.

"You . . . were always the one . . . talking about what's practical," Danny told him. "Be . . . practical now. I'll be . . . weeks recovering. Maybe I'll even die after all."

"Don't talk stupid. I won't let you die."

"It's not . . . your choice. All kinds of things . . . could happen yet. Don't you want to get back to Abbie? My God, Zeke . . . . how long have you . . . been away from her?"

Zeke sighed and rubbed at his eyes. "Eight months —something like that."

"Jesus, Zeke, you've . . . got to get back to her. And me . . . I'd recover a lot faster . . . if I was . . . home on the old farm. I'd have . . . Pa there to take care of me . . . be in familiar surroundings. I'd be safe there . . . and you could go on home where you belong. And . . . if I should die . . . I'd die in peace in a place I love. Lenny's dead, Zeke, and God only knows . . . where Lance is. It's important . . . that Pa see me soon as he can . . . important he knows . . . I'm alive. Tennessee . . . isn't that far, Zeke. You could . . .

306

pack me onto a travois. I'd be all right traveling that way. And you . . . you mean bastard . . . you'd make sure I got there all right."

Zeke stared at his ailing brother. "Danny, I promised myself a long time ago I'd never go back there," he told him. "You don't understand. I'd rather fight ten men than go back there. I'd rather finish this war than to go back there. I can't do it. I can't . . . look at him."

"Would you . . . rather sit here . . . for weeks with me? Wouldn't it be better . . . to risk how you'd feel . . . going back, than to go even longer . . . without seeing Abbie . . . the ranch . . . the kids?"

Zeke stood up and paced a moment, going to the window and then returning to kneel back down beside his brother. "You could just stay here until you're better—then go home on your own."

"My God, Zeke . . . don't you . . . understand?" His eyes teared again. "If you knew . . . what I've been through. Damn it, Zeke . . . I just . . . want to go home. It means . . . nothing to you. But it means . . . so much to me. He's my pa. I love him just like you loved . . . your Cheyenne stepfather . . . and your Cheyenne mother. I'd . . . get well . . . so much faster there. And if I'm to die, I want to die there. Jesus, Zeke, I came here to fight for Tennessee. Doesn't that . . . tell you . . . how much I love it? How much I love that . . . farm . . . and Pa? Why is it so much . . . to ask you . . . to take me there? Just take me there . . . and you can go home to the place you love . . . to Colorado . . . to Abbie. Use your head, Zeke."

Danny's eyes closed for a moment, and he suddenly felt weak and light-headed. He had talked far too much for this first awakening, yet never had home sounded so good to him. He'd risk anything now to get there.

"I'll think about it," Zeke answered. There was no reply. Danny's eyes were closed, and Zeke leaned closer, alarmed. "Danny?"

"Thank you . . . Zeke," the man whispered before again floating off into unconsciousness.

Zeke gritted his teeth in his own inner struggle. "Damn!" he muttered, shuddering at the thought of seeing his father again. "Damn that old son of a bitch!"

Twenty

It was only one rifle shot, but it cracked through the crisp morning air with startling shock, and was the beginning of Abigail Monroe's worst nightmare. Wolf's Blood stood behind the cabin chopping wood, and his head jerked up at the sharp report, just in time to see Dooley, far out in the pasture, slump to the ground. Several men were riding toward the cabin then, their horses thundering fast and hard down the north slope. Smoke leaped to his feet and went charging after them.

"Smoke, come back!" Wolf's Blood shouted. "They will kill you!"

The wolf paid no heed, and there was no time to worry about the animal at the moment. The men charging toward the cabin most certainly had nothing good in mind. For the moment, there was also nothing he could do to help poor Dooley. He slammed his axe into a stump and headed around to the entrance to the cabin, bursting inside to see his mother already loading her old Spencer.

"Load your rifle," she told her son calmly. But he saw how pale she was.

"A lot of men are coming!" he told her, rushing to the corner to grab his own weapon. "They shot Dooley!''

"I know," she replied, her voice a little shaky. "I was at the corner of the cabin, starting to take Dooley some biscuits. I just hope the poor man isn't dead. He's been a good friend for a lot of years." She blinked back tears as Wolf's Blood loaded his gun. The boy walked closer to her.

"I think they are white men," he told her. "They are not raiding Comanches or Apaches. This I know. They must be outlaws. Let them have what they want, Mother. Let them take the horses, if that's what they're after."

She looked so white he thought she might faint. Then his eyes lit up with sudden knowledge, and they turned black with rage, just the way she had seen Zeke's eyes blaze when he was on the defense.

"Our first concern is the children, Wolf's Blood," she told him sternly. "You remember that. Above all else, I want nothing to happen to you or any of my other children."

Several gunshots could be heard in the distance, and a few bullets pinged against the cabin. In the loft, little Jason began crying, and Margaret and Ellen stared down at their mother and brother. Abbie walked over to the ladder while Wolf's Blood bolted the door and the thundering of the horses came closer.

"Don't cry, Jason," Abbie called up to her son. "It's just a game we're playing. All of you must lie flat on the floor and you must not cry or talk, and above all you must not come down or look out of the loft window. Keep the shutters closed," she ordered. She looked at Margaret, her beautiful daughter's dark eyes full of fear. The girl still had not got over the dirty words and the crude pawing of the Confederate soldier, who had told her quite frankly what squaw women were made for.

310

"It will be all right, Margaret. Keep the children down and keep them quiet."

The girl nodded silently, and Abbie turned back to Wolf's Blood, who had just finished closing and bolting all the wooden shutters. "We must do our best to keep them from seeing your older sisters. Do you understand?"

The boy nodded, but his eyes were still on fire.

"Don't do anything rash," she added. "Wait and see what they want. If we're lucky, they'll just ride through and take the horses and leave." She calmly sat down in a rocker, her father's old rifle on her lap. Wolf's Blood walked toward the door and pressed his back against the wall to wait.

The horses were close then, and men called out in yips and yells in the fashion of Indians, but it was only an imitation. He heard laughter, and more shots were fired, as then they seemed to be circling the cabin, shooting at random. More bullets zinged and snapped against the outer walls and the terrifying circling went on for several minutes.

"Wait a couple of minutes. Let them think we won't fight back," Abbie told her son. "Then we will each take a window and get as many as we can. We will have to move quickly and get the shutters closed again. We don't want to risk any of them getting through."

Wolf's Blood gripped his rifle tightly. "Somehow they must have planned this. They must have known that Black Elk and the others left yesterday for the hunt. Things have been so peaceful. I thought it would not matter if my uncle went away for a few days."

"I thought the same," she answered. "Don't blame yourself, Wolf's Blood."

The boy's breathing was heavy with sorrow. He was sure they must have shot Smoke. He struggled not to think about it now. The time for mourning would have

311

to come later.

Abbie rose and walked to a window at the side of the room, and Wolf's Blood positioned himself at a front window.

"Let's show them how the Monroes can shoot!" she told her son.

Wolf's Blood nodded, his teeth gritted in anger. He slammed aside the bolt and threw open the shutters and began firing at the startled men outside, who apparently were not after the horses, for they had kept circling the cabin.

The boy and his mother both began firing at the same time, and for the first time in her life, Abigail was killing white men. But in these situations a woman could not think soft thoughts or worry about whether or not she might go to hell for killing another human being. These men would do the same to her if they got inside, and for the moment, the mother would kill a hundred men if it meant keeping harm from her children. There were at least fifteen men. She managed to hit two of them. Wolf's Blood shot four. But then one of the attackers rode up to Abbie's window from the side where she could not see him. His horse charged past, knocking her rifle right out of her hands, and as he dashed by the window he threw a flaming torch inside.

Abbie screamed and slammed the shutters closed, then turned to run to the bedroom, where she grabbed a robe and hurried back out to throw it over the torch. She stomped and beat on it until the flames finally went out.

Wolf's Blood closed the shutters to his own window, and they looked at each other.

"What do they want? There must be ten or eleven more of them, Mother!"

She closed her eyes and breathed deeply. She must stay calm. "I have no idea what they want. But if they set this cabin on fire, we will have no choice but to go outside and find out. It's the children I'm worried about, especially Margaret and LeeAnn. They must be outlaws—perhaps men who deal in the buying and selling of women. If they don't want the horses, I can't imagine what else they would want."

"Damn!" Wolf's Blood growled. "I will kill all of them."

"There are too many!" his mother snapped. "You could get five, maybe six more. But you can bet you'll be dead before you could possibly get them all. If it were a matter of just waiting here and shooting them down as they ride by, perhaps we could do it. But sitting in here is like being in a trap, Wolf's Blood. That torch tells me that. They'll burn us out if they have to." She began pacing, wringing her hands. "There must be a way. It's the children I'm worried about. Those men aren't stupid enough to keep riding around the house getting shot." She suddenly cocked her head. "Listen."

There was only silence.

"They have stopped circling," Wolf's Blood said quietly.

Abbie looked up at the ceiling, half expecting to see smoke. Then they heard the voice.

"Abigail Monroe!"

She looked at her son in surprise. "They know my name!" she exclaimed. She headed toward a window, but Wolf's Blood grabbed her about the waist.

"Wait!" He pushed her back and went to the shutters himself, opening one just slightly. "Who are you?" he shouted. "What do you want?"

He heard a laugh from behind a shed not far from the cabin. "Your ma, boy. Just your ma. Nothin' else. Send her out, and we'll leave you and all the young ones and the horses alone."

Abbie's heart pounded, her mind rushing with confusion. Why on earth had these men come asking for her by name?

"White belly scum!" Wolf's Blood shouted back. "What kind of cowards are you to ride in and attack a woman and her children? Back shooters! Snakes! You are not men! You are women! *Zetapetazhetan!* Squaw killers! You touch my mother, and your gizzards will greet the sun! My father and I will see to it!"

"You talk big, boy!" He heard more laughter. "But we know your pa ain't here. And with your hired help dead, you're the only one around for protection. How long do you think you'll last against ten men?"

Wolf's Blood closed the shutter, his chest heaving in quick breaths. "If Father were here, he would know what to do. He could get them all!" he lamented. "I wish I knew what he would do."

Abbie walked toward him, her chin held high, pretending to be brave. She calmly put a hand on his arm. "You're a brave and skilled young man, Wolf's Blood. You've done just fine. And I have no doubt perhaps you could go out there and get a lot more of them. But you are my son, and I refuse to let anything happen to you. You have to remember your brothers and sisters, Wolf's Blood. They are the important ones. You must not risk getting yourself killed and leaving them out here all alone. Now calm down and let me make the decisions."

"They will not touch you!" he growled, throwing off her hand and heading for the window.

"Wolf's Blood!" she shouted. "We must be practical. That is your father's first law. Do what is practical for the moment, until you find a way to be the one with the upper hand."

The boy turned and stared at her, blinking back tears. "And what is practical?" he hissed. "To just

314

hand you over to them?''

Their eyes held. ''Perhaps,'' she replied quietly.

''Abigail!'' came a shouted voice again. They both walked closer to the window. ''You have five minutes, woman. If you care about them little lice carriers you've got in there, you'd best come out and leave peacefullike! If you aint' out in five minutes, we're gonna throw a rain of torches on that little ole cabin, and by God we'll shoot every little redskin that comes through the door. If they don't come out, they burn to death. Is that what you want, mama?''

Wolf's Blood turned to the window again, opening one shutter. ''Who are you? Why do you come for my mother?'' he shouted.

''Sorry, boy. Ain't nobody supposed to know where your ma is goin'.''

Wolf's Blood turned to his mother, but to his surprise she walked into her bedroom. He stared after her until she returned, carrying a little jeweled music box, a gift Zeke had bought for her the first year they were married. She slowly wrapped one of Zeke's buckskin shirts around the music box, then raised her eyes to meet her son's.

''Listen to me,'' she said calmly. ''Whatever those men have in mind for me, Wolf's Blood, it could not bring me near the heartache I would suffer at the loss of any one of my children. We could fight these men, perhaps do very well. But in the end we would lose. And it is certain some of my children would die. You must understand a mother's love, Wolf's Blood. I can bear whatever these men have in mind, as long as I know my children are all right.''

''No!'' he hissed, bolting the shutter closed again.

''Yes!'' she said sternly. ''I want you to do as I say, Wolf's Blood. I am going out there. I do not want you taking any chances of getting yourself hurt or killed.

315

The children will need you after I am gone. You will be like a father to them. Now listen, and listen well!'' She stepped closer, agonizing over the pain and terror in her son's loving eyes. ''You go to the Cheyenne village and you wait there for Zeke. He can't possibly be gone much longer. I feel it in my very bones that he is alive and is coming home soon. Don't do a thing until he gets here. Tell him exactly what happened—that these men planned this and they knew my name. That surely means something. Tell him it's my feeling that they are not slave traders. There is some other reason for this. Zeke will know what to do.''

''I cannot let you go out there!'' the boy pleaded, his eyes tearing more.

''You can and you must!'' she ordered. She looked down at the shirt with the little music box wrapped inside. ''I will go with them,'' she said quietly. ''And I will wait for your father.'' She moved her hand over the soft buckskin and actually smiled slightly. ''He will come. I know he will come. He will find me. And until he does, I will have these things to remind me of him and keep up my hope.'' She looked up at her son. ''Zeke and I have been through all kinds of hell, Wolf's Blood. We'll get through this.''

The boy shook his head.

''This is my decision,'' she told him. ''The children must come first.'' She turned and looked up at Margaret, who was peeking down at them and sniffling. ''I love you,'' she told the girl. ''I love all of you,'' she spoke up louder. ''I want you to make me proud by not crying and carrying on. You must learn that in this land we do what is practical. I learned that many years ago from your father, when I was hardly any older than you, Margaret. I will be all right. I promise you that. Your father will come home soon. He will come and find me and we will all be together again.''

She turned and glanced at Wolf's Blood once more, then headed for the door.

"No!" the boy groaned.

"You all fixin' to smell some smoke?" a voice came from outside. "We're ready to use them little redskins for target practice."

"I am going," Abbie told her son quietly. "Let me go, Wolf's Blood. Please. I must do this. Don't make me have to bury some of my children."

Wolf's Blood gazed at his mother for several long seconds. Then he lowered his rifle. "We will find you!" he told her, one tear slipping down his cheek. "Father and I—we will both come for you!"

She forced a smile for him. "I have no doubt that you will." She touched his cheek for a brief moment, then opened the door and walked out onto the porch.

"Well, well, pretty lady. Come on a little farther out. And send that son of yours out where we can see him. Have him throw out his rifle."

Abbie looked back at Wolf's Blood, her eyes pleading again. The boy stepped outside cautiously, resignedly tossing aside his rifle. The ten men began slowly emerging from behind the shed, leading their horses. Some mounted up, while others picked up their fallen comrades and slung their bodies over their mounts to take them back with them.

As two men rode closer to Abbie, Wolf's Blood's heart pounded faster. He had seen them before! He was sure of it. But where? One with several scars on his face and neck leered at Abbie, reaching down and grasping her hair.

"You're about the prettiest thing I ever touched," he told her. Wolf's Blood's fists clenched, and Abbie jerked away.

"What horse shall I ride?" she asked calmly.

"Why, you'll ride right up front here with me, white

squaw woman. It'll make my ride back real pleasant."

She glared at him. "I have seen you before." She glanced at a second man, who rode up beside the first. His face was oddly deformed, as though one side had been caved in and had never healed right. She glanced at Wolf's Blood. "Last year—Kansas," she told her son. "These two men were with those who tried to stop us from going to the Sun Dance. I remember them. You tell your father."

The one with the scars laughed. "Sure, boy, you tell your pa. My orders is to take your ma, and that when your pa gets home and figures out where she is, he's welcome to come after her, understand? You tell your pa that when he comes, he ought to be ready to talk. That's all I can tell you, boy. Your pa will figure it out." The man grinned. "By the way, that wolf of yours is the one that put these here scars on me." He glanced out at the north pasture. "You'll find the son of a bitch out there—layin' beside your hired hand."

He broke into harder laughter, reaching down and jerking on Abbie's hair, pulling her up painfully. Abbie clung to the shirt and music box with one hand, while she grasped the mane of the man's horse with the other and helped hoist herself up. The man grabbed her between the legs and gave her a boost, still laughing, and Wolf's Blood could not control his agony. In a flash his bowie knife was out and slammed into the thigh of the man who had grabbed his mother. The man screamed out and his horse reared and moved away.

"No, Wolf's Blood! No!" Abbie screamed.

In the next instant the man with the smashed face slammed a rifle butt across the side of Wolf's Blood's head, and the boy went down.

"Wolf's Blood!" Abbie screamed, struggling then to get back off the horse. But the man who had been stabbed managed to keep hold of her.

318

"Let's go!" he shouted to the others, who were all mounted then. They moved out at a gallop, hooting and yelling, thundering away just as quickly as they had arrived.

In the north pasture, Dooley and Smoke lay dead. Wolf's Blood lay unconscious in front of the cabin, his knife still in his hand. The doorway stood open, and little Jason, who had run away from Margaret's grasp, hurried out onto the porch just in time to see the men riding away with Abbie.

"Mama!" the boy sniffled. "Mama, sleep with me tonight?"

Bonnie watched as Zeke's body suddenly jerked in his sleep. He had been up all night helping Bonnie and her father with more wounded men and had fallen asleep late in the morning on a blanket in front of the kitchen fireplace. Bonnie watched him lovingly, taking pleasure in his strange Indian habits, wondering how on earth he could sleep on the hard floor. But he had slept there faithfully night after night in the two weeks they had been waiting for Danny to heal enough to travel.

Bonnie sat at the table peeling potatoes. She put the knife down when Zeke jerked again, then rolled onto his back, his breathing heavy and sweat pouring from his face. She rose in alarm, worried he had somehow contracted a fever. "Zeke?" she spoke up softly.

"No," she thought she heard him say, his hand grasping the blanket that he lay on. She jumped back when he suddenly turned on his stomach again and reached out toward the fireplace, groaning. Then he yelled out Abbie's name and suddenly sat up. He glanced around the room, as though confused, then caught sight of Bonnie and quickly got to his feet, standing there before her in all his manly glory, wearing nothing but a loincloth, his hair long and loose and free of ornaments. She quelled the desires he had teased since he had first arrived, for they could be nothing more than friends. She cautiously stepped closer. "Zeke? What is it?"

He glanced around the room and blinked, wiping sweat from his forehead. He began trembling and looked back at Bonnie, staring at her strangely. "Abbie!" he groaned.

She reached out to him. He grasped her hand and startled her when he jerked her close.

"Hang on to me, Abbie!" he moaned.

She rested her head gladly against the bare chest, allowing herself the pleasure of breathing in the scent of him, the ecstasy of his powerful arms wrapped around her. But she was also alarmed. She put her arms around him and pressed tight against him.

"It's all right, Zeke. You've been dreaming."

She felt him tremble and he pulled back slightly and looked down at her. "Bonnie?"

"You had a bad dream," she told him. "You reached out and grabbed me. You spoke Abbie's name."

He suddenly grabbed her close again, hugging her so tightly her breathing was difficult. "Something is wrong!" he groaned. "My God, Bonnie, something is wrong! I have to go home!"

"Calm down, Zeke. Get your thoughts together."

He rested his cheek on the top of her head. "Forgive me," he whispered. "Let me . . . hold you just for a minute. It's like I'm . . . holding her."

"I am the one to be forgiven," she whispered. "For I would let you hold me forever if it could be so." She turned her face up to his, and somehow he thought if he could pretend for just a moment that this woman was his Abbie, it would somehow help the horrible feeling

320

he had inside. How he missed her! How he needed her! He put a hand to the side of Bonnie's face and bent down to kiss her, lightly at first, then more savagely, wanting so much to open his eyes and see that it was Abbie. Bonnie gave no resistance, relishing in his moment of need, knowing it would be only that, a brief moment he was experiencing between being fully asleep and fully awake.

He suddenly released the kiss and pulled back, then turned away from her. "I'm sorry," he groaned. "I . . ." He ran a hand through his hair. "I had a dream. She was . . . calling for me . . . reaching for me. And I . . . reached back. But something kept . . . pulling her farther away. I tried and tried, but she kept . . . slipping farther away!" He shuddered and grasped the mantle of the fireplace, bending down his head. "Abbie! My God, something is wrong! I know it! I've had . . . these feelings before, Bonnie!"

"But it was just a dream."

He shook his head. "No. You don't understand." He turned to look at her, his eyes watery. "I knew . . . way back when it happened. I knew something had happened to Danny, even though I wasn't even aware at the time that he had joined the Confederate Army. And there have been other times, mostly involving Abbie. Our love is so strong, it's like . . . like we're the same person sometimes. When she called out for me in the dream . . ." He sighed and turned away again.

Bonnie seized the moment to drink in the vision of all that was Zeke Monroe. Like the Indian that he was, to stand before her half naked was nothing to him. Why should a man wear a lot of clothes when it was so wretchedly hot? She wished she could be so free with practical thinking. But she was Bonnie Lewis, the preacher's daughter and a preacher's wife, the missionary who had lived by specific rules all her life. She suddenly felt flushed and ashamed at the thought of letting him kiss her only a moment before.

"You must go to her right away then," she spoke up. "Go and build a travois. I think Danny is well enough to travel. You have no choice now but to take him to Tennessee, Zeke. That way you can ride directly west through Indian territory into southeast Colorado. Danny will be in good hands and you can send word to his wife in St. Louis. It wouldn't be safe to take Danny to St. Louis right now. There are too many Northern sympathizers. He'd be safer and rest easier at the farm."

He turned back to face her, his eyes moving over her lovingly. "I'm sorry . . . about kissing you that way. I had no right. I thought for a moment I could . . ." He sighed and bent down to pick up his blanket.

"Pretend I was Abbie?" she finished for him.

He folded the blanket and laid it on a chair, turning to face her again. "I suppose." He saw the pain and embarrassment in her eyes. "You're a good woman, Bonnie Lewis."

Her eyes teared. "No, I'm not. I'm bad. When it comes to my . . . feelings . . . for you, I'm a bad woman, Zeke."

He reached out and touched her cheek gently. "There is nothing bad about you. The trouble with you white women is that you can't tell the difference between bad and just plain normal feelings."

She blinked back tears. "Sometimes our normal feelings can never be shown," she replied.

He brushed at a tear with his thumb. "Thank you for all you've done with Joshua," he told her. "You're a fine woman, Bonnie. We'll continue the secret. Remember how important it is that no one know, not even Joshua for a few years yet, where he really came from. You have to understand the kind of man Winston Garvey is. He'll kill Joshua if he can ever find him."

She nodded. "No one but Rodney and Father know."

"Danny knows. But he's never said a word to anyone, not even his wife."

She sniffed and suddenly grasped his wrist, kissing his palm. "When . . . . will you leave?" she whimpered.

"Today yet, if I can get a travois put together quick enough. I feel an urgency, Bonnie. I must get back. Much as I don't want to see my white father, I'll take Danny there. Then I'll head for Colorado as fast as my mount can go without falling on his face."

She began crying harder, kissing his palm over and over. "Today!" she whispered. "I don't want you to go, Zeke."

"And even if I didn't feel this urgency to go, what good would it do to stay?" he replied. "It is something that can never be, Bonnie. You've always known that."

"I'll never see you again," she wept.

"It's possible. But then our paths may cross again, just as they did here. I hope you will continue to write us about Joshua."

She nodded, raising her blue eyes to gaze into his own. "What must you think of me? A married woman, her husband fifteen hundred miles away, weeping over another man?"

He smiled softly for her. "I think you are a woman who has always done what is right, at the sacrifice of her own desires. You are a good woman. This I have always thought."

She turned away, making a choking sound. "I could have refused to marry Rodney," she groaned. "Not because of my love for you, Zeke. But simply because I knew I didn't love him anymore. But I had made a commitment. I was so . . . so bent on doing what was . . . proper! I might have met another man who . . ." She put a hand to her eyes. "Oh God, Zeke, he didn't even make love to me on our wedding night! He'd never . . . never . . . he was . . . more frightened of it than I was!"

"Bonnie, stop it! You don't need to tell me—"

"I do! Somehow I do need to tell you. I . . . I need you to understand why . . . after all these years . . . I sometimes think of you . . . why I let you hold me a moment ago. Oh, how I envy Abbie, who has a man who is truly a man to her! A man who understands a woman's needs . . . . who shows concern and compassion. And the worst part is he . . . he's good to me in all other ways. He's not a bad husband, Zeke."

Zeke sighed, hesitantly putting his hands on her shoulders. "I'm sure he isn't. Maybe things will be better when you get back. You've been apart for a long time. And maybe you need to tell him more about how you feel, Bonnie. Maybe he thinks that because you had such a sheltered life and are so . . . so reserved . . . perhaps he thinks you aren't capable of passion."

She stiffened slightly and turned to face him, her cheeks crimson. "But . . . that's how I have always felt about him. That he was the one incapable of such feelings."

He gave her a supportive smile. "You might as well tell him how you feel, Bonnie. What harm can it do? You aren't happy this way, so things can't be any worse if you tell him. Maybe they would get better."

She sighed and hung her head. "What kind of woman am I—discussing such intimate things with a half-breed Indian I haven't seen for nine years! What is it about you that always makes me bare my soul and make a fool of myself?"

He took her chin and raised her face to greet his eyes.

324

"You haven't made a fool of yourself." He bent close and kissed her cheek lightly. "I'm glad as hell I saw you again, and especially to be able to see Joshua and know how well he's doing. Surely the spirits sent me to this place." He brushed her cheek with the back of his hand. "I must go now and build the travois. I must get home to Abbie. I am sorry to leave you so quickly, but I can't wait any longer for Danny. Do you truly think he is ready to travel?"

She sniffed and nodded. "You have no choice, and there is nothing more we can do for him here." She took both his hands. "Good luck, Zeke. God be with you. My father and I will pray for Abbie's safety. And if there is any problem at all—if . . . if any kind of tragedy should befall you or your family . . . never hesitate to come to us. You know you can depend on us."

He squeezed her hands. "Thank you, Bonnie." Finally he turned and went through the door. Bonnie looked at his huge knife, which lay on the kitchen table with his other weapons and some clothing. She touched the handle of the knife, remembering the skill with which he had used the weapon when rescuing her so many years ago. And she knew that even if Rodney understood her needs, he would never be able to bring out from her soul the heated passions Zeke Monroe stirred there. But Zeke was Zeke, and only the very best of women, the most understanding, the strongest, could live with such a man. That woman was Abbie.

Twenty-One

Zeke's heart tightened with every forward step of his mount. This June day in Tennessee was unbearably hot, and he slapped at bugs that pestered him as he approached the old farm. He had always hated the humidity of the South, but he knew that if his life had been happy here the weather would not have bothered him nearly as much. The closeness of the day was only enhanced by his own feeling of anxiety, a strong desire to turn and run. Not only did he not want to see this place and his white father again, but being here also brought back memories of Ellen, who had lived on the next farm, just over the hill. Ellen and Tennessee! Visions of his first wife lying in a bloody pool kept flashing into his mind, as well as his little boy lying headless. A terrible pain shot through his chest so that he actually stopped his horse a moment and groaned. He breathed deeply for several minutes, wishing the air were cooler.

He urged his horse forward again, past a sorry-looking cornfield and toward the house. Its weathered wood seemed to be sagging every place, and he wondered for a moment how it was even still standing. His jaw flexed in his own determination to be strong and hard and bear what he must bear. He would simply deliver Danny and leave, hoping he would not suffocate from his own hatred before he could get out of there again.

He wore only a loincloth and apron because of the heat, and in his determination to show his father just how Indian he was and deny any white blood, he had worn nothing that would make one think he was even a half-breed. He wore his hair brushed out long, with tiny braids at one side that had beads wound into them. Two eagle feathers were tied into the other side of his hair, held there by a round, beaded leather hair ornament that Abbie had made for him. At his neck he wore a bone and copper necklace, and a copper band encircled the bicep of each arm. His big knife was strapped to his waist and moccasins covered his feet. He painted his war colors onto his face, for he truly was at war—at war with his own emotions.

Now he was within easy sight of the house. He could feel his own heart pounding as someone came out the door, carrying a rifle. Zeke halted. The man approaching was a younger man, with dark hair. As he came closer, Zeke saw a resemblance to Danny. He was tall and handsome, and for a moment Zeke felt intense hate, for the man looked very much like the father he had left so many years ago. The young man pointed the rifle at Zeke.

"Who the hell are you, mister?" he demanded, glancing at the travois on the back of Zeke's horse.

Zeke looked him over cautiously. "You must be Lance. You were just a little boy when I left home. Is this any way to greet a brother?"

Their eyes met, and the man slowly lowered his rifle, his face beginning to glow with happiness, "Zeke?"

Zeke nodded. Lance just stared at him for several long seconds, absolute awe and admiration showing in his eyes. The stories he had heard about this mysterious half-brother were enough to give a person nightmares. "I'll be goddamned!" he finally spoke up, walking closer and putting out his hand. "Yes, sir, I'm Lance. Goddamn, Pa will have a heart attack when he sees you! Jesus, this is great. Just great. I've only been home a month myself."

Zeke smiled slightly, and Lance started to tell the man about meeting Abbie, but he didn't have the chance before Zeke suddenly pulled his hand away and went rigid, his smile fading and turning to a frightening glare as he stared past Lance toward the house.

Lance turned to see his father coming down the steps of the porch hesitantly. Lance looked from the old man to Zeke, unsure just what might happen. There would be time for talking later. The younger man hurried over to his father. "Pa, it's Zeke," he told the man. "Zeke's come!"

Hugh Monroe's eyes were glued to this son he never thought he would see again. His eyes teared as he walked hesitantly toward Zeke, who still sat astride his horse, his eyes so terribly hard and cold, his posture proud and defensive. Zeke noticed his father seemed to be mere skin and bones, still tall and broad, but most of the meat gone. The man's white wife, the mother of Zeke's white brothers, had been dead for several years. Now Lenny was dead also, the only brother who had stayed close and helped with the farm. The loss of both was reflected in the sad state of the farm and of the old man who owned it. But Zeke would not allow any pity to enter his feelings. Why should he pity this man who had made his early life so miserable for him?

The elder Monroe came close then, staring at Zeke with eyes full of love. He blinked back tears as he took in the fine Appaloosa Zeke rode, and the magnificent specimen of man who was his eldest son. He was so overwhelmed at Zeke's presence that he reached over and clung to Lance for support, feeling faint.

"Zeke!" he finally spoke up. "I . . . never thought the prayers of an old man like me . . . could be answered. God has truly blessed me this day!"

Zeke just glared back at him, unable to find his own voice at first, contemplating taking his fist and sending the old man flying as far as a good punch would carry him. But the old man seemed undaunted by the fiery hatred in Zeke's dark eyes.

"Danny . . . has told us so much about you, Zeke," the old man spoke up. "He was right." He looked Zeke over again. "You did grow into a fine, handsome man. I . . . I guess it would seem strange now . . . to call you . . . to call you . . . son. You're a full-grown, middle-aged man now."

A sneer passed over Zeke's lips as he slid from his horse, standing taller than either Lance or his father. "Why worry about calling me son?" he asked, his voice cold and flat. "I never called you Father."

The old man flinched, and Zeke turned to begin untying the travois, disturbed by his own remark and the pain he had seen in the old man's eyes when he made it. But he let himself take pleasure in the pain. The man deserved some pain. "I'm only here because Danny wanted to come here," he spoke up." "He's on the travois here. He's been wounded."

"Danny!" Hugh Monroe gasped. "You . . . have Danny with you?" He and Lance walked around to the travois, where Danny was just awakening from a groggy sleep brought on by the muggy weather and his own weakness. "Danny! Danny-boy!" the elder Monroe exclaimed, stooping down and touching Danny's face.

Danny smiled. "Pa!"

Hugh Monroe bent down and put his arms around the man, pulling him up slightly and weeping. "If only . . .

329

Lenny could be here!'' the man wept. ''My sons! All here! Surely someone . . . has been praying for this!''

Zeke watched as he finished untying the travois, thinking for a moment about Abbie. He was almost angry with her, for it was probably her own prayers that had created this moment.

''I'll carry him inside for you,'' he told his father. ''He was wounded pretty bad at Shiloh and again in Virginia. It's a long story. Emily asked me to see if I could find him. I've been away from my own wife and children far too long. I've brought him here to mend and I'll be on my way in the morning.''

All was spoken matter-of-factly as he bent over and scooped Danny into his arms as though the man were a child. Lance hurried into the house to prepare a bed and Zeke started to follow Hugh Monroe, but the elder man stopped and turned.

''You go on. I walk kind of slow now. You hurry in with Danny,'' he told Zeke.

Zeke stood there a moment glaring at him. ''Did Danny tell you that my mother is dead now?'' he asked.

The old man nodded.

''And did you shed any tears?'' Zeke sneered.

The old man looked away and sighed. ''Get Danny inside,'' he said quietly.

Zeke headed for the house. Neither man noticed that another man watched them from the bushes, a neighbor who had come to see Hugh Monroe but had held back when he saw the Indian man there. There was no doubt about it. The Indian man was Zeke! Zeke Monroe!

''I'll blow your guts out, you goddamned half-breed!'' the man muttered to himself. ''If you hadn't married my sister, she'd still be alive today!''

The man headed back to his own farm, his mind reeling with hatred. Zeke Monroe had come back to

Tennessee! He had come back to the old farm. "And he'll be buried here!" the man growled.

Abbie tugged at her bindings, but such efforts over the past three weeks had been useless, only reopening the scabs at her wrists where the leather ties had rubbed her skin raw. She had given up screaming for help. There was no one to hear her in this Godforsaken place—a damp, dripping, smelly mine shaft, at a gold mine long deserted, one of those discoveries that had proved to be only a fluke. Now the shaft held a woman who had been beaten and starved and kept from her children in an effort to make her tell Winston Garvey something that she stubbornly refused to tell. The crueler Winston Garvey was to her, the more determined she was not to tell him who had taken Joshua. The thought of the poor boy in the hands of the sadistic ex-senator gave her the strength she needed to hang on; and that strength was only enhanced by the determined belief that Zeke would come for her. Somehow he would find her and help her.

Every two days Garvey came to see her. She dreaded his visits—for the man seemed to take delight in hurting her. He never did enough to kill her, for he wanted her alive. She knew his idea was to wear her down, through pain and starvation and her own longing for her children. Each day she grew weaker. Each day she missed her children more. Each day a little more hope faded from her soul. She prayed that she would not lose so much strength and hope that she would give up and tell Winston Garvey what he wanted to know. But she was not certain how much longer she could hold out.

In between Garvey's visits to the mine shaft, she lay with her arms tied over her head to a stake in the floor of the shaft, her ankles tied to two more stakes. She was freed only two or three times a day so that she could go to the bathroom. The two men who had been with those who had attacked them in Kansas were her guards, taking turns sitting with her. She hated and feared both of them. They had not touched her wrongfully, but she knew it was only on the order of Winston Garvey. Both of them watched her with hideous leers, Buel's scarred face and neck and Handy's smashed face both revolting to look at.

She had had a lot of time to think, and one thing she knew was that Winston Garvey wanted no one, not even these two men, to know about his half-breed son. After she had been captured from the ranch, all the men but Buel and Handy had split up, and only Buel and Handy had brought her to this place. Apparently Winston Garvey did not want the rest of the men to know anything about where she had been taken. And when Garvey came to question her, even Buel and Handy were ordered to leave. Garvey always questioned her alone.

She closed her eyes and prayed again, her stomach growling from hunger, her lips dry from thirst. In the distance she heard the carriage again. He was coming. "God give me strength!" she prayed.

The minutes it took for the man to come inside to where she lay passed too quickly, and then he was there, looking down on her where she lay on a damp mattress. "Pretty day out there, Mrs. Monroe," he spoke up with a smile. "Wouldn't you like to see some sunshine? Wouldn't you like to hear the birds, see the blue sky, see your lovely children?"

She glared at him. "Go to hell," she said weakly.

Garvey chuckled, putting his thumbs into the pockets of his vest. He wore a white suit, obviously expensive, and several rings on his fingers. "Now, now, sweet lady, is that any way for a nice woman like you to talk?" He knelt down. "It would be so easy, Mrs.

332

Monroe," he continued, grasping her jaw tightly. "So easy. You simply tell me where that boy is, and you can go home."

"It's too late for that," she answered. "Whether I tell or not, my husband will still come after you, Winston Garvey. You are a dead man."

He put on an air of unconcern. "I am too well protected," he announced. "Your husband tries to harm me, and he'll hang from the highest tree in Denver, with all of its fine citizens coming out to watch. We'll make a holiday out of it."

She watched him smugly, her hatred of him giving her renewed strength. "You don't know my husband!" she sneered. "What a fool you are, Winston Garvey! You could have left us alone, and no one would ever have known about your half-breed son. Why couldn't you have left things as they were? Now there will not be anyplace in this country . . . where you can go and be safe from Zeke Monroe! You don't know him . . . . the way I know him. You think . . . power and money . . . can keep you safe. But there are other powers, Garvey—stronger powers . . . stronger than all the money you might have . . . all the people you might own."

The man leaned closer. "Must I remind you again that we can go back at any time and begin killing off your children—one by one?"

She stared back at him, undaunted. "My children are with the Cheyenne by now. If you want to send your men to the village and try to take them from the Cheyenne warriors, go ahead and try!"

The man chuckled. "All I have to do is send in soldiers."

"Oh? And what excuse will you give?" she answered. "How would you explain it?" She glared at him in stubborn defiance. "You were too much of a coward to face my husband man to man, or even to raid our ranch when Zeke was there! Are you that afraid of him that you had to wait until he was gone? And how do you know if he will even come back? He could be dead.''

''That, dear lady, is your problem, not mine. If you choose to lie here this way for another month, perhaps six months, maybe forever—you will just lie here. Unless you tell me what I want to know. It's your decision whether or not you will ever see your children again. You can demand your own fate, my dear. Just say the words.''

''Why should I? As long as I say nothing, and until my husband comes, you have to keep me alive!''

The man's face darkened with anger. This woman was smarter than he had figured. He had thought, since she was a white woman married to a half-breed, that she must be ignorant and slutty. But she was beautiful and intelligent, amazingly perceptive, and worst of all, she had incredible strength and courage. He had not expected the kind of woman that was brought to him, and her own character had foiled some of his plans. He had expected her to fold and weep and tell him where he could find his half-breed son within a matter of days. But she had held out for three weeks, and every threat he had used had been to no avail.

Abbie saw the worry in his eyes, and she smiled through her pain and weakness. ''What you don't understand, Mister Garvey,'' she spoke up haughtily, ''is that I have it figured out.''

''He grasped her hair and pulled. ''Shut up, bitch!''

She winced with pain but just got angrier. ''You won't kill me—or harm my children!'' she spit at him. ''Your only hope is to keep us alive. You brought me here in the hopes . . . I would tell you where that boy is. But you figured . . . that if I wouldn't tell . . . you

334

would get your answer from my husband when he returns. You think that just to get me back, he will tell you what you want to know. But if I am dead, why should he tell you anything? There would be no purpose. So you dare not kill me—or harm our children. Because you know Zeke Monroe will come for you if you do. You think that by having me as your captive . . . you have power over my husband. But I will tell you now, Winston Garvey . . . that this is the biggest mistake . . . . you have ever made! My husband won't tell you . . . anything. He will simply . . . kill you. And then he will find me on his own.''

''You talk cocky for a woman who's looking for a beating!'' the man snarled, glowering.

''And you're supposed to be an intelligent man,'' she sneered. ''You fool! You could have left it all alone and never suffered. But men like you . . . aren't happy unless they have their finger . . . on everything and everyone. Is your hatred of Indians so terrible . . . that you need to kill an innocent little boy who is the product of you and an Indian woman? Or is it just that you fear your own demented son will one day find out his father slept with a squaw! That he's related to an Indian!''

Garvey backhanded her hard and she tasted blood in her mouth. Then he stood up and began removing his clothes.

''I am Winston Garvey!'' he growled. ''I own a good share of Colorado and the people in it! I own gold mines and banks! One lice-infested half-breed Indian does not frighten me, Mrs. Monroe. And one thing I know for certain. If that man of yours fought outlaws and all other odds to come and find that sister-in-law of his years back, he'll most certainly come to find his own woman. But there is just one way he will get her, and that is by telling me where that boy is. He can't get you back any other way, and I'm too powerful and too well

335

protected for him to try to come after me himself. And if he kills me, he'll never find out where you are, so that would do him no good. No one comes around this place. You'll die of starvation and be eaten up by rats before your husband ever finds you here!''

She spit at him and he slapped her again. He removed his shirt and shoes, then unbuttoned his pants. Her eyes widened in horror, and he began to smile.

"I've decided pain can't make you talk, woman. You're too proud. So I thought that perhaps injuring that pride would make you talk faster than injuring your person.'' She looked away when he stood before her then, completely naked. Her mind raced. Surely he wouldn't do this! She belonged to Zeke. To Zeke! No other man had ever touched her. He was right. This was worse—much worse—than being beaten. She felt his fingers untying her tunic and he pulled it down to expose her breasts, then jerked it up from the bottom to her waist. He grinned at her sudden quiet desperation, her sudden loss of haughty dignity and strong determination. He bent over her, grasping one of her breasts in his fat palm, his ugly, wide lips and double chin close to her face.

"Tell me, bitch,'' he told her with a lurid grin. "Just tell me where that boy is, and I won't take my pleasure in your lovely body. I won't even send in Buel and Handy and let them have their turn. Is that what you want, white squaw? Would you really go so far as to let other men touch you? Is that stinking little half-breed worth it?''

She met his eyes, a tear slipping down her cheek. "Please don't do this,'' she said quietly. "Isn't there even . . . one ounce of decency in you?''

He only chuckled, and she could feel his fat belly touching her stomach. Her head reeled and she felt vomit in her throat. "No, Mrs. Monroe. A man doesn't get ahead by being decent." He ran a hand over her breasts again, taking pleasure in her tears. "You'll talk. When Buel and Handy come in here for their turn, you'll talk."

She turned her face away, looking at the buckskin shirt and the little music box nearby. Zeke! She belonged only to Zeke Monroe. No matter what these men did to her, they could not change that. Zeke! She would think only of Zeke. But was she truly strong enough to bear this? Yes. She would be strong for Zeke, and for the little crippled boy. She would not betray a child. She would think only of Zeke. He would come! He would come, and somehow they would live through this. She heard Garvey, somewhere in the distance, calling for Buel. She felt an ugly heaviness on her body, and she wondered if she had fainted, for it all seemed far away, as though it were taking place in a nightmare and not in reality.

Zeke paced inside the farmhouse, looking like a panther needing to get out of its cage. His father came out of the bedroom where Danny had been put down, and Lance followed. Hugh Monroe walked up to Zeke and put a hand on his son's arm, but Zeke jerked it away.

Hugh Monroe sighed. "I know how you feel about me, Zeke. But before you run off again, I have to tell you that no matter what you think of me, I thank God you were forced to come here . . . thank God I've seen you again. And I want to thank you for searching for Danny like you did . . . bringing him home."

"Home! Maybe it's home to Danny, but not to me!"

"Zeke!" the elder man snapped. Zeke whirled and faced his father. "I'll say it now because I'll never have the chance again. I love you. Why can't you understand that? I never wanted you to suffer."

"Then why didn't you leave me out there with my mother where I belonged?"

"Because you were my son. My *son!* I wanted you with me. *You* have sons. If you had to go away, would you leave them behind?"

Zeke's eyes momentarily showed a hint of understanding. He thought about Wolf's Blood. But then he hardened again. "If you loved Tennessee so damned much and missed it so much, fine. I can understand that. All men have a place they need to call home. But, goddamn it, why didn't you bring *both* of us back with you? Why did you have to leave her behind and take me from my mother? Why did you sell her to that Crow bastard, you goddamned son of a bitch?" His fist clenched. "God, how I'd love to hit you!" he hissed.

The elder man stood straighter and did not move or flinch. "Then hit me," he dared. "You've been wanting to all these years. Go ahead. A man of your strength would probably kill an old man like me with one punch. But so what? You hate me anyway. I give you permission to hit me and take the chance. Perhaps I do deserve it."

They stood there glaring at each other for a long, tentative moment, and Lance watched in terror. He did not want his father hurt, nor did he dare to try to stop his brother. But then Zeke suddenly turned away.

"You can't do it!" Hugh Monroe challenged. "You can't do it because deep down inside you have to face the reality that I am your father—your *real* father. You can't hurt your father. It goes against everything that is Zeke Monroe. And if you dig deep enough, you just might even discover there is a small bit of love buried down there somewhere for me. Tell me it isn't so, Zeke!"

Zeke whirled. "It isn't so! I won't hit you, old man, only because you sired me. But that's the only reason.

338

There is no love in my heart after what you did to my mother!"

"Use your head, Zeke. How do you think Gentle Woman would have survived here in Tennessee? How do you think the white women would have treated her? Leaving her there was the kindest thing I could have done for her. I didn't want to do it, but I wanted to come home."

"You never loved her! She was just a squaw to you."

"Yes, she was! I can't help that I am white, Zeke. I can't help what I grew up on—being taught it was all right for a white man to go out West and hunt and trap and take a squaw to care for his needs while he was there. Damn it, Zeke, that was the way it was. What else can I say? Thousands of men did it! That was a way of life for a while. And I thought if I had any children by her, I could leave them when the time came that I wanted to come back to Tennessee. But I . . . I didn't expect to have such . . . such strong feelings. You were my son—my little boy. I wanted to bring my son home. He was so handsome, so strong, so intelligent. I loved you. I loved you so much. But I couldn't bring her here. It would have been terrible for her. So I had to make a choice. My choice was to come home and bring you with me. I can't change any of it now. It's over. And don't think I haven't had some regrets. I can't count all the times I have wept over you."

The old man turned away, and Zeke stood there breathing heavily. He suddenly felt closed in, smothered. "God, I've got to get out of this stinking house," he growled. He turned and stormed out the door.

Lance quickly followed. "Zeke," he called out. "Wait!"

"Leave me alone!" Zeke fumed. "I'll not wait till morning. There's still some daylight left. I'm leaving tonight, soon as I repack my gear."

"Zeke, he's an old man!" Lance begged, grasping his brother's arm. "He's waited all these years to see you again. Can't you stay one lousy night?"

Zeke stopped walking and glared at his brother. "You don't understand, Lance, because you were too young to remember. You were just a baby when I was growing up here—listening to constant insults, fighting my way through school because every day other kids picked on me and started fights with me. I was called every name in the book, whipped by teachers, forced to sit in the back pew in their churches, hated by my stepmother. The only time I was even close to happy was when I would go off to the swamp alone. Danny understands, because he was old enough to remember. Danny was always good to me, always understanding. That's why I searched for him. I owe him a lot. But I don't owe anything to that old man!"

"You owe him your damned life!" Lance growled. "His blood runs in your veins."

Zeke's eyes blazed. "And how I wish I could drain myself of that blood!" Lance sighed resignedly and Zeke turned away. "It isn't just that, Lance," he spoke up, his tone of voice softening. "Being here makes me think of Ellen. You can't know . . . what it was like for me. She was . . . so special—this . . . sweet, young, pretty white girl who was all goodness and tenderness. She used to come and meet me in the swamp . . . and we'd talk, just talk. And before we realized what we were getting ourselves into, we were doing more than just talking, and we knew we loved each other. But we also knew what the people would say . . . and that her father would never allow it. So we ran away—found an old preacher who agreed to marry us. No one knows it but . . . by then Ellen was already pregnant. If I had been . . . older . . . wiser, I never would have let any of it happen. But I was just a kid myself then, and crazy in love with that pretty white girl who was so sweet to me. Then her father sent those men after her to bring her back. But when they finally caught up with us, they raped and killed her and our son instead, out of pure meanness and terrible prejudice. All of them had known her—and they learned to hate her just because she'd married a half-breed." He whirled. "I had a right to kill those men the way I did. If I could do it twice over, I'd do it."

Lance signed. "Ellen's brother still lives over the hill, you know."

Zeke stared off into the distance, his eyes filled with terrible pain. "I know," he said quietly.

"He never believed those men killed Ellen. They were all friends of his. He thinks you turned wild and killed her and your son yourself, and that you killed all those men out of pure meanness."

Zeke met his brother's eyes. "And what do you think?"

Lance smiled a little. "I think it's the way you tell it. That's because I've met your wife, Zeke, and any man who can make a woman like that glow with love and happiness the way she does, and can sire all those beautiful kids, has to be a damned good man. He can't be as mean as they say."

The mention of his family wiped away all of Zeke's hardness and hatred. He grasped Lance's shoulders. "Abbie? You've . . . seen Abbie? When? Where?"

Lance laughed lightly. "Last winter. I was with a troop of Confederates that got cut off by Union soldiers as we were headed back East from New Mexico. We had been part of the South's unsuccessful attempt to take and hold the forts along the Santa Fe Trail. At any rate, I was wounded pretty bad. We rode to this little ranch along the Arkansas River. The snow was so damned deep we couldn't go any further. The place

341

turned out to be yours. I didn't know it till I came to a couple of days later and found out it was your own wife who took a bullet out of me. She's a hell of a woman, Zeke. God works in mysterious ways sometimes. I hadn't seen you since I was ten years old, and there I was in your house being nursed by your wife.''

Zeke's eyes teared. "My God! You saw her? You truly saw Abbie?''

"I just told you so, brother. And I sure can see why you married her.''

Zeke turned away, and Lance knew the man didn't want him to see the tears in his eyes. "How . . . was she?''

"Fine. Just fine. They were all fine, Zeke. And your son—Jesus, he's as Indian as you. When I first looked at him, I thought it was you. That's how I remember you, because you were so young when you left here.'' Lance sobered then. "I will say, the boy is the same kind of scrapper you were. He got into a fight with one of the soldiers who, uh, insulted your daughter, I'm sorry to say.''

Zeke stiffened and turned, his dark eyes cautious and concerned. "What do you mean?'' he almost growled.

"Don't go getting all excited, brother. My commanding officer took care of it, and everybody is fine.''

"Took care of what?'' Zeke asked, his anger building. Could this be the event that had alarmed him in his sleep? But how could it be? The dream had only been two weeks ago. Lance had been at the ranch during the winter.

"Took care of the fight and the insult,'' Lance was saying. "You have one hell of a beautiful daughter, Zeke—two of them, in fact—Margaret and LeeAnn both. And who the hell would believe that LeeAnn even belongs to an Indian? She looks more like she belongs to Danny than to you, with that blond hair and those

342

blue eyes.''

Zeke's mind raced in confusion. How he hated Tennessee and this farm! Now here was Lance telling him he'd seen Abbie, seen his ranch, seen his children. And there had been trouble! He had not been there to help. His anxiety to get home made him feel as though he could not breathe. ''What happened, Lance?'' he asked, grasping the man's arm firmly.

Lance sighed. ''I probably shouldn't even have mentioned it. It was just one of those things, Zeke—you know, a pretty young girl, a lonely soldier. Your daughter—the dark one, Margaret. She had an eye for one of the men, that's all. The bastard was nice to her—till he got her alone. Then he got fresh—scared her some, that's all. He didn't hurt her or anything like that. But he insulted her pretty bad, I'm afraid. Called her squaw—you know. I'd have landed into him myself, but I was still recovering from my wound. Besides, that son of yours got to him first.'' Lance grinned and shook his head. ''The kid would have killed him if they hadn't been pulled apart. That boy is the strongest fifteen-year-old I've ever seen.''

Zeke turned away, his heart heavy for poor Margaret, but full of pride for his son. So Wolf's Blood was doing a fine job of protecting his mother and sisters. That was good. ''He's sixteen now,'' he told Lance in a strained voice. ''And he's as much a man as you and I.'' How he missed his son. How he missed all of them. And Abbie. ''Are you sure my daughter wasn't harmed?'' he asked.

''She's fine, Zeke. Really. Just hurt pride. But your wife talked to her. I think she made the girl feel better. Your wife has a way with words. She's a hell of a woman, Zeke. I envy you, brother. If I could find somebody like that, I'd settle down, too.'' He put a hand on Zeke's arm. ''Hey, they're OK, Zeke, really." He sighed deeply. "I probably shouldn't even have told you. That's no way to get you to stay."

Zeke turned. "It isn't that, Lance. I'm sure they were all right when you left. But . . . I've had this feeling. I had a bad dream. I've had them before. I can't help thinking something else has gone wrong. Something much worse than what you've told me. I feel it in my bones and I don't like it. I've got to get back to them—as fast as I can ride without killing my mount."

Lance frowned and nodded. "Sure. A man gets those feelings sometimes. And I guess if I was married to a woman like your Abbie, I'd be anxious to get back, too." Lance wished he'd known Zeke in his growing up years. Here stood the man who had been the subject of stories and rumors in Tennessee for years. Here stood the long lost brother. Looking at him now, Lance could not imagine the gentle white woman named Abbie lying beneath this tall, broad, fierce-looking Indian man who had probably killed so many men he had no idea of the count. He smiled. "Thank you, Zeke, for finding Danny. Someday I just might come on back out West. I expect Danny will return to Fort Laramie when he's able and this damned war is over—if the army will take him back, that is."

Zeke forced a smile, but his eyes were watery. "They'll take him. He's a damned good soldier—one of the best." He looked at his younger brother. "I'm glad to see you, Lance—see how you turned out and all. You're a good man—a lot like Danny."

"And so are you a good man," Lance returned. "Doesn't that tell you something about our pa? We all came from the same seed, Zeke. Pa is a good man, too. You just could never see it in him." He saw Zeke's eyes hardening again, but he was determined that Zeke make some kind of amends with his father before leaving. "Look at it this way, brother. Your kids are all

344

half-breeds, too—maybe a little less Indian than you, but they still have Indian blood in them. How will you feel if one or more of them someday turns and blames you for all their misfortunes, just because you fathered them? Wouldn't that hurt a hell of a lot?''

He saw a flicker of understanding in Zeke's eyes. ''I know what you're saying, Danny. But I have kept my children in a place where it's easiest for them to live.''

''You kept them there partly because you love it there yourself. Pa loved it here. That's the only difference.''

Zeke sighed. ''I'm going to pack my gear.'' He turned away, and Lance started to speak up again. But then someone yelled from the bushes.

''Zeke! Zeke Monroe! Halt where you are, half-breed!''

Zeke stopped in his tracks, and both men turned to look toward the voice. Neither man had a gun in his hand, but Zeke wore his knife at his waist. A man emerged from the underbrush, and Zeke's heart froze. The man had not changed much. There was a resemblance to Ellen. Ellen! This was her brother! It all happened quickly then. The man came toward Zeke, holding a shotgun on him.

''I'm gonna blow your guts out, you goddamned, murderin' half-breed!'' the man swore. ''You forced yourself on my sister and run off with her. Then you killed her, you damned savage—tried to put the blame on those poor men you murdered.''

''They murdered Ellen, not I,'' Zeke returned. ''I loved Ellen!''

''You lyin' half-breed scum!'' He raised his rifle. For the first time in his life, Zeke Monroe hesitated. He could easily kill the man by landing his knife in him before he could even pull the trigger. But the fact that he was Ellen's brother caught in Zeke's heart and he could

345

not make his hand move for his weapon. Suddenly Hugh Monroe was shouting at the man from the porch, running down the steps and wielding his own rifle.

"Terrence Huett, you son of a bitch, put that shotgun down!" the elder Monroe shouted, a new spring to his step. His defense of his son suddenly put added life in the old man's veins. "You pull that trigger and I'll shoot you myself."

The moment of anger and hatred was too intense for any of them to think rationally. Terrence Huett turned at Hugh Monroe's shouting, and in his own bitterness he fired. He would not let Hugh Monroe stop him from killing the half-breed who had ruined his sister's life. Zeke stared in shock as a hole exploded in red blood in the middle of his father's chest. Hugh Monroe took two more steps, then slumped to the ground.

"Pa!" Lance gasped, running toward the man.

Zeke's eyes widened, and he stood in torn confusion. The very man he hated the most had come to his defense, as any father would do, and in that moment he realized he loved the old man after all. Ellen's brother turned his eyes back to Zeke, as he fumbled with a jammed gun. It was the only time in his life that Zeke suffered from indecision in a moment when quick action would have normally been his response. But this man was a part of Ellen. He could not bring himself to make a move toward the man right away. Everything happened in only seconds. He glanced back at his father, lying on the ground covered with blood. His father! His last words to the man had been cruel and hateful, and now the man was dying because he had come to Zeke's defense. Zeke gripped his knife as Ellen's brother raised his shotgun again, but then another shot rang out, and the man's body flew backward, his neck and face instantly shattered and bloody.

Zeke whirled to see Lance standing near his father

346

holding his father's smoking gun, tears on his face. There was a long moment of absolute silence until Zeke managed to make his legs move toward his father and brother. He came close to Lance.

"I couldn't . . . let you kill him," Lance said in a choked voice. "After what happened . . . before . . . Tennessee would never have let you leave this time, Zeke. They'd bring it all up again—hang you. It had to be . . . somebody else. I . . . I won't even tell the authorities . . . you were here."

Zeke's heart swelled with love for this brother he hardly knew. "I . . . don't know what to say, Lance."

"It was easy," the man replied, his body jerking in a sob. "He killed my pa."

The terrible pain of regret stabbed at Zeke's heart, and his own eyes filled with tears. He turned away and knelt down beside his father, whose eyes were open and still had a flicker of life in them. The old man was covered with blood, and his eyes looked at Zeke pleadingly. Zeke shuddered with overwhelming memories and almost unbearable regret. He bent closer, bringing his lips close to the old man's ear.

"I love you, Father," he groaned. "Damn you! You . . . wanted to hear it. You're hearing it. I love you." He broke into sobbing and cradled the old man in his arms. For a brief moment Hugh Monroe reached up and patted his wayward son on the shoulder. Then his hand slid down and the life went out of him.

Danny sat in a chair and watched while Zeke and Lance pounded in the cross at the head of their father's grave. Then Zeke came over and knelt in front of Danny, reaching up and tucking the blanket around the man's neck.

"You want to go back inside?" he asked.

"Not yet," Danny replied, his blue eyes sunken and

tired. "Life sure takes strange turns, doesn't it, Zeke?"

Zeke nodded and sighed. "I have to go, Danny. I've sent word to Emily. You should be safe here. I've got to get back to Abbie."

"I understand." He reached out from under the blanket and they grasped hands. "Thank you, Zeke. What else can I say? I'll be indebted to you forever. If you hadn't come along, I probably would have been buried alive with those other bodies. It's over for you now, isn't it? You finally got your past out in the open and really looked at it?"

Zeke squeezed his hand. "That's true. A man can keep so much hatred and emotion buried that he chokes on it unless he throws it up. I was choking to death. All of a sudden I feel . . . I don't know . . . free for the first time, I guess. Free of the past. Free of my love for Ellen. It's like I can finally let go of her. Now all I want is to get back to my Abbie."

Danny grinned. "What man wouldn't want to get back to Abbie? You're a lucky man, Zeke."

Zeke smiled. "You didn't do so bad yourself. A little spoiled and delicate, but she's coming along."

Danny chuckled. "I intend to get well as fast as I can. And then we're both coming back out West. Since I've been back here, I've discovered I, too, have a past to leave behind. I learned to love the West, Zeke. I'm coming back out."

"Good." Zeke rose and looked at Lance. "Maybe I'll be seeing you out there also sometime, little brother."

Lance looked at his father's grave, then scanned the old, battered farm. He met Zeke's eyes. "I just might come out," he replied. "There's nothing left for me here now. Maybe I'll come out and help you run the ranch. I don't know."

"Well, I've got one good man. But I can always use

another—especially when he's my brother.''

They shook hands. ''Take good care of that woman of yours,'' Lance told him. ''She's a fine lady. And that's a fine brood of kids she mothered.''

Zeke nodded, his hunger for Abbie suddenly intensified to near painful proportions. Never had he missed her more! Never had he loved her more! Home. How good it sounded to be going home. ''Take good care of Danny,'' he told Lance.

''You know I will.''

Zeke glanced at Danny once more, love in his eyes. ''Be seeing you, brother.'' He walked to his mount and eased onto its back with graceful quickness. ''As the Cheyenne would say, my brothers, *nohetto*. That is all. It's over.'' He looked from one to the other, then at his father's grave and around the old farm. He looked at his brothers again. ''*Maheo* be with you.'' He whirled his horse and kicked with his heels. ''*Hai! Hai!*'' he shouted, getting the mount into a fast gallop. He left the old farm, and he was leaving Tennessee a free man at last. He headed West—to Colorado, to his woman.

Twenty-Two

Anna glanced up from her desk when Winston Garvey walked inside her office, irritated at the way he sometimes barged in uninvited, as though he still owned her business. "How did you get in?" she asked. "We aren't open."

The man closed the door and heaved himself over to a chair, slumping into it and smiling at her. "You forget that I am an important man, my dear. People see my face at the door—they let me in."

She scowled. "I will have to talk to Benny about that. He shouldn't let anyone in without my approval."

"Tut, tut, dear Anna. You have certainly become haughty and snobbish of late. Ever since you thought you got the better of me with your news about my half-breed son, you have walked around with your nose in the air." He took a handkerchief from his pocket and wiped sweat from his brow. "But we both know the real Anna, don't we?" he added. "Her nose belongs in the mud. She's nothing more than a common slut who happened to fall into the good fortune of meeting a senator in Washington who gave her a start in her illustrious career."

Anna leaned back in her chair, picking up a thin cigar she had been smoking. She puffed it once, then put it out. "What the hell do you want, Senator? I'm trying to balance some figures here. I don't have time for this."

He raised his eyebrows. "So much money that you have trouble keeping up with it?"

She smiled. "My girls and I come high—let alone the gambling table earnings. But you know all that. Did you come for some kind of cut perhaps? I paid you off a long time ago."

"Oh, no, dear. I only came to gloat."

"Over what, pray tell?"

He shifted in his chair. "Well, I just wanted to see the look on your face when I tell you I will soon have Zeke Monroe where I want him."

She watched him cautiously, deciding that this time she would show no emotion. "A man like you could never get the better of a man like Zeke."

"Oh, but I already have. Your, uh, ex-lover has gone off to the Civil War, you see. And while he has been gone, some of my men paid his ranch a little visit. Now I have his woman. Don't you think a man like Zeke will come for his woman?"

Anna paled slightly, feeling a sudden pity for Abigail Monroe, but she kept her composure. "Of course he will." She feigned unconcern. "What's that to me? It's your problem, not mine."

"Of course it is. But, well, since this whole thing is kind of a secret between me and Handy and Buel, and since you were so sure the last time we talked that I could never get the upper hand on Zeke Monroe, I just thought I'd come and tell you about my success."

She snickered. "You brag too soon, my dear senator. Has the man come for her yet?"

"He will come. I have a man waiting down at Bent's

351

Fort. He'll know when Monroe has returned, and he will come to tell me.

We'll be ready for him."

She laughed harder. "You truly amuse me, Senator. You'd better hire yourself an army, because that is what it will take to stop Zeke Monroe."

"I have plenty of men. You realize, of course, the position you are in. Monroe will think you ratted to me. He'll probably come for your hide before he comes for mine. And if he doesn't kill you, I will—just as soon as I get my information from the man. I have played along with you long enough, my dear Anna. Once Zeke is dead, you will be the only one left who knows anything, other than the people who took the boy, of course. But they will die, too."

She refused to act frightened, knowing he would only take pleasure in it. "I don't understand you anymore," she spoke up, her smile fading to a sneer. "I always thought you were an intelligent man. But kidnapping that woman is the dumbest thing you've ever done. You should have let it all lie sleeping, you fat fool! What if that woman, or Zeke himself, does tell you where the boy is? What would it accomplish to kill the boy? How many people must you kill to hide the filthy life you lead behind closed doors, Senator? You might as well kill half the people you do business with."

His face darkened. "That is not the point, my dear. A lot of people know I am ruthless and underhanded. That doesn't bother me. It has made me rich. What bothers me is that I have a half-breed son walking around someplace. Perhaps those who know would let it lie. But that isn't enough for me. The fact that the boy exists at all is utter horror for me. I cannot allow it. I want that boy dead. D-E-A-D. Dead! I have only one son—my Charles. I would do anything, including risking my own life, to stamp out that half-breed boy and make damned sure my own son never finds out about him.''

She just stared at him, a look of shock on her face. "You're crazy!" she said quietly. "You're flat out crazy. It's really that important to you?"

"It is."

She shook her head. "You could have just let it go, and no one would ever have known."

His eyes turned to slits of hatred. "I would know!" he growled. "I can't bear the thought of being the father to half-breed scum."

Silence hung in the air for a moment as Anna rose, moving around to sit on the edge of her desk. "What have you done with Mrs. Monroe?" she asked cautiously.

The man snickered. "Now wouldn't you just love to know that?" He leaned back again and put his arms behind his head. "Well, my dear, I can't tell you that, except that she is *not* at my estate. I will say one thing for her, though. She's one stubborn woman. My original plan was to get my answer out of her by taking her from her children and making her my prisoner. I thought that beatings and starvation and separation from those little brats of hers would make her talk. Then I would kill her and go find the boy and his family and get rid of them also. Then I would stage another raid on the Monroe ranch and get rid of the rest of them—make it look like an Indian attack. That would be easy for the public to believe, considering all the raiding that is taking place."

"But she messed up your plans when she wouldn't talk," Anna added for him, cautiously trying to find out all that she could.

His face darkened again. "The damned woman is smarter and stronger than I figured."

"I could have told you that."

"But there's no hurry. As long as she won't tell me anything, I'll keep her alive and wait for her husband to come for her. And if he wants her back, he'll have to tell me what I want to know. I merely have to keep the woman alive. If I kill her, Zeke Monroe will never talk."

"He'll never talk either way. Why should he? If he talks to get her back, you'll still have him killed."

He shook his head. "I will very quietly have the 'evidence'—the boy and his family—disposed of. They will simply disappear. That isn't hard to accomplish in this Godforsaken country. Then let Monroe yell all he wants. There will be no evidence. And who will believe him: the word of a stinking half-breed against a prominent businessman like myself? I suppose even with the boy alive, Monroe would have a hell of a time convincing the public he is mine, but there is always the chance. Once he's dead, the threat is gone. And Zeke Monroe will have nothing to hold over me. No good citizen in his right mind would believe such a story."

Anna folded her arms. "It all sounds very smooth, Senator," she told the man. "And when Zeke gets back from the war, just how is he supposed to know where to go to look for his wife?"

"Oh, he'll know once he thinks about it for a while. He'll figure it out."

She shrugged. "And what if he never comes? I hear the war back east is a damned bloody one. It has even affected us here. Maybe he's been killed."

Garvey chuckled. "So be it. The longer he is away, the more his wife will wear down until she finally gives up. She will tell me sooner or later. She can't go on forever in her condition."

Anna's heart raced. "What condition? What have you done with her?"

Garvey smiled. "I always got a certain pleasure out

354

of hitting a woman," he told her. "Pain and starvation can work wonders in changing someone's mind." He rose from his chair. "But in her case, that wasn't enough. She was too proud. You've seen the sort. So Buel and Handy and I decided to break her pride."

The horror of what he was saying made her her feel ill. "You pig! You slimy, fat, stinking pig!" she hissed. "Abigail Monroe is a good woman—a woman of virtue and . . . and . . ."

"And everything you are not, I dare say," the man sneered. She started to slap him, but he grabbed her wrist. "It is far too late for you to be thinking about being the kind of woman Abigail Monroe is, my worthless whore! Or should I say the kind of woman she *was?*"

Anna jerked her wrist away and moved back, feeling nauseous at his closeness and wondering how she had ever allowed herself to put up with him all these years. "You misjudged one thing," she told him.

"And what, pray tell, is that?" he asked pompously.

Her eyes glittered with hatred. "You figure Zeke Monroe to be like most other men—a person you can bully with your money and your power, a person beneath your false dignity, someone of the lower class to be used and abused and threatened and bought off. Your power has gone to your head, Winston Garvey, so that you think you are invincible, invulnerable, your estate impregnable. But one day you will awake to find Zeke Monroe's knife at your throat. Your pompous love for yourself has caused you to do something you never should have done. You have dug your grave, Winston Garvey! You can't threaten or buy off a man like Zeke. You have met your match this time."

The man merely chuckled and walked to the door. "Think what you wish, my dear. I only came to tell you because I have a feeling the man will pay you a visit before he comes to me. I wanted you to be ready for him. You may tell him whatever you wish. Lead him right to my door. I'll be waiting with open arms. In fact, why don't you come along with him? I could take care of everything at once." He snickered at the hatred on her face. "I just wish he would hurry. With my wife and son gone in the East, this would be the ideal time to tie up all these loose ends."

"And what makes you think I won't go to the authorities myself?" she returned.

"Be my guest. Send them out to my place. They won't find anything. How far can the word of a slut like you go? This is Denver, dear. We're even considering laws against prostitution. Cooperate, dear Anna, and I just might spare your life. That's your only hope. Fight me, betray me, and your body will be lying at the foot of the loneliest mountain in the Rockies—or I can easily arrange to have you put in prison for the rest of your life. I'm sure I can think of any number of matters that would put you behind bars. No, Anna dear. You aren't brave enough or strong enough to go to the authorities. I'd break you in half, and you'd be the common homeless slut I picked up off the streets all those years ago in Washington. You don't realize it, but even today you are still dependent on the old senator. You'll never really get away from me, you know. I've only played along with you this long because you didn't know the whereabouts or identity of the half-breed boy. As soon as I get that information, you will be back under my thumb, my pet, to do with as I please." He stepped closer and suddenly grabbed the bodice of her dress, ripping it open and exposing her breasts. "This is what you are and what you always will be, Anna Gale! It's a little late to be thinking of doing good deeds!" He looked down at her breasts, then spit on them. "Don't ever, ever try to threaten me again!" he hissed.

He turned and left. Anna stared at the closed door, her body jerking in silent, unwanted sobs. But she did not cry for herself. She wept for Abbie Monroe. She hoped Zeke would come soon. Zeke was one man Winston Garvey could not threaten or control. She pulled her dress back over her breasts and bent over, wishing she was brave enough to kill Winston Garvey herself.

Zeke crested the hill and looked down at the cabin. He felt as ecstatic as a young lover anticipating making love to the woman of his dreams for the first time, as excited as a little boy planning a wonderful surprise. He breathed deeply of the air that he loved and patted his horse's warm, moist neck. He had ridden the animal harder than he would ever normally run a horse. But he had to take the risk. He had to get back here. Each mile had brought a little more life to his lonely soul, a little more urgency to the gait of his horse, a little more happiness to his heart.

But it was only a few seconds before that happiness and excitement began to fade, and he felt an odd pain in his stomach. There were no sounds of children laughing and playing, no horses running in the corrals or out in the pasture. The ranch looked lifeless and empty. He frowned, heading his mount down the hill, his dread mounting as the cabin came closer. He stopped and looked around cautiously, pulling his rifle from its casing.

"Abbie!" he called out. There was only the sound of a soft wind. "Dooley! Wolf's Blood!"

Still no reply. He trotted the horse around to the front of the cabin and dismounted, his rifle ready as he walked up the steps to the front door. The door was padlocked with the lock they always used when they would be gone. He turned to walk back and get his key from his parfleche. It was then that he noticed the strange markings all over the front of the house. He walked closer, running his finger over one of them.

"Bullets!" he muttered. He inspected a few more, finding some bullets embedded in the thick logs. "Jesus!" He ran to his parfleche and rummaged for the key, hurrying back and unlocking the padlock and charging into the house. "Abbie?" he shouted. He stared around the main room. It looked as though no one had occupied it for a while. Dust was settled on the table and on the fireplace mantle. Abbie would never let dust collect. He walked to the fireplace and touched the black embers in the hearth. They were cold. Abbie was perpetually cooking. The coals were always warm.

He forced back the thoughts of horror that wanted to come to his mind. He climbed up quickly to the loft, but there were no children there, and some of their quilts were gone. Then he walked hesitantly into the bedroom where he and Abbie slept. The bed of robes was there, neatly made. Everything was in place. He tried to understand how the outside of the cabin could be so riddled with bullets, yet nothing inside seemed wrongly disturbed. If someone had attacked the cabin, there would have been a struggle once they got inside. There should be blood and broken articles.

He felt sweat beading on his forehead. He told himself he should be glad there was no sign of blood or struggle. Perhaps things were not as bad as he might think. Yet the fact remained his family was not there, his horses were gone, and there were ominous bullet markings on the cabin.

He turned and ran outside, shouting names again, checking the sheds and Dooley's soddy. The silence, broken only by the distant rush of the river and the soft wind, almost hurt his ears. Abbie! Wolf's Blood! Where were they? He would not be so worried if not for the bullets that peppered the cabin. Bullets! He breathed deeply. He had to think. He ran back toward his horse, and it was then he saw them in the distance, at the back of the cabin. They were two fairly fresh mounds of dirt, one with a cross at its head, the other with two notched stakes that held something.

At first he froze in place, afraid to find out who the graves might belong to. Yet he had to know. And there were only two. Whoever they were, there were surely more Monroes left some place who needed him. Whatever had happened, it had to be devastating. Nothing else would have made Abbie leave the ranch. He felt his legs moving, but they suddenly weighed a hundred pounds each as he forced them to walk toward the graves.

"Nothing lives long. . . . Nothing stays here. . . . Except the earth and the mountains," he chanted softly to himself, reminding himself of the Cheyenne death song. He must prepare himself. Gradually the graves came close, and he fell to his knees, staring at the cross. "Dooley—a good man," it read. His eyes widened. "No!" he whispered to the wind.

He cautiously moved his eyes to the other grave. The two stakes at its head were notched to hold a necklace—one made of wolf's claws. He stared at the necklace in disbelief. What else could it mean but that the grave held his son? It was the necklace the shaman had given Wolf's Blood at the Sun Dance.

A horrible, black shudder surged through Zeke and he bent over, so much pain in his chest he thought perhaps his heart was giving up and he was dying. A terrible groan exited his lips and he grasped his stomach. He rocked on his knees that way for nearly an hour, groaning, the horrible black pain ripping through his stomach and chest without mercy. This could not be! Always when he had gone away before, he had come home to his woman and his family. What had happened? The bullets! The graves! The emptiness! He would weep for his good friend Dooley, but his utter horror at the thought of his first-born son being dead was too overwhelming to have any room left for Dooley.

He sunk his fingernails into his cheeks and threw back his head, raising his arms and screaming out a long, savage wail, blood streaming down his face. He screamed out the names of his Cheyenne gods, begging for help, for an answer, for comfort. And then as he sat there with the hot sun on his face he felt a sudden peace, and a small yellow bird flitted down and perched on one of the stakes, singing and hopping from one stake to the other and then to the top of the grave.

Zeke lowered his arms, his own tears mingling with the blood on his cheeks. He looked down at the bird, and suddenly his senses returned. This bird was a sign. A sign of life. There would be a time for the terrible mourning that must come, a time to face the ugliness of reality. But for now he must be strong, stronger than he had ever had to be. He must remember that the rest of his family was somewhere. Abbie was somewhere. And in his great love for his son, he felt deep inside that the boy's spirit was not dead. He could not be dead. Not Wolf's Blood. Not his son! And Abbie. Where was Abbie?

He got to his feet and the pain shot through him again. But he must put on hardness and put off feelings. He must be hard and strong until this terrible nightmare was over. Something horrible had happened, that was certain. But he could not sit in this place and wonder. He must go and find them.

His legs felt weak and cramped as he headed toward the front of the cabin. He walked inside, clinging to the walls and the furnishings as he half stumbled into the bedroom, the terrible pain still in his chest. He went to the old chest of drawers where Abbie kept some of her belongings. He took out a flannel gown and held it to his face, kissing it, breathing deeply of the light scent that was his woman that still lingered in the material.

"Abbie," he whispered. "Be alive, Abbie. Be alive!" He walked back into the main room, clinging to the gown. "All of you . . . be alive!" he groaned, looking up to the loft. "Wolf's Blood, Margaret, LeeAnn, Jeremy, Ellen, Lillian, Jason! All of you!" Somehow it felt better to say their names, as though he was truly speaking to them and they would answer.

He charged back outside then, putting the padlock back on the door, then going to his mount to place Abbie's gown into his parfleche, the parfleche she had beaded for him herself. He traced his fingers over the beads, then looked to the heavens again, the blood beginning to dry on his face, making him look like the fierce savage he could sometimes be.

"Give me strength, *Maheo!*" he prayed. He mounted up. He would go to Bent's Fort and see if anyone knew anything—then to Black Elk's village. And if someone had harmed anyone in his family, he would bring them more horror and pain than they could possibly imagine. There would be hell to pay!

Settlers and traders alike gawked at the dark, menacing Indian who rode into Bent's Fort. His long, black hair was dusty and dull, his face crusted with blood from deep gashes on his cheeks. His eyes were bloodshot, his lips tight, his whole being radiating fierce anger. He looked at no one as he approached the drinking room and dismounted. One young white woman who was passing took one look and gasped in fright, turning and running away. Zeke turned and watched after her, thinking of Abbie. Then he walked into the room that was the general meeting and drinking area for traders

361

and male settlers.

Patrons glanced up and stared and stopped talking. The man approaching was tall and broad and hard. He wore many weapons and anyone could tell he knew how to use them. Zeke walked directly to the bar, amid the screech of scooting chairs and frightened whispers as men moved out of his way. A white man serving drinks turned and saw Zeke approaching, and he quickly picked up a bottle of whiskey and a glass. "Zeke!" he exclaimed. "Thank God you're back!"

Zeke glared at him. "Where is my family, Smitty?" he asked, his voice icy.

Smitty frowned. "We were all hoping you'd show up soon, Zeke." He poured a shot of whiskey. "Drink this. You look like hell, and you'll need it, my Cheyenne friend."

Zeke took the small glass and quickly downed the whiskey. "What's happened?" he asked. "I just came from my place. It's empty. I've been gone ten months, and I come home to nothing but two graves behind my cabin!"

Smitty sighed. "The Cheyenne say your white woman has been taken by some kind of outlaws, Zeke. That's all I know."

Zeke felt the horrible sickness and pain again, but he let his savageness win out and forced the hardness to stay. To let go of it would be to go insane. "The rest of my family?"

"They're with Black Elk, Zeke. They're all right. But your hired hand, Dooley, he was shot in the back. They didn't give him a chance."

Zeke gripped the glass. "Wolf's Blood?" he managed to choke out.

"He's all right. He took a good whack on the head when he tried to help his mother, but he's all right now. That wolf of his was shot, though. It's all been hardest

362

on him, I hear. The Cheyenne say he's broke up real bad about the whole thing.''

Zeke struggled against tears. ''But . . . he's alive?''

''He is.'' Smitty poured more whiskey, aware that Zeke Monroe was struggling not to break down. ''What happened, Zeke? Where have you been?'' the man asked.

Zeke swallowed the second drink. ''It's a long story. I have to get to Black Elk's village. Has anyone tried to find my wife?''

Smitty shook his head. ''No soldiers, anyway. They refused to try.''

''Why?'' Zeke asked, his eyes glittering. ''Because she's a white squaw?''

Smitty met his eyes. ''I'm sorry, Zeke. They said it was because there aren't enough of them to go chasing after elusive outlaws. All their good men are back East fighting the war. A few men and myself, we looked for a few days. But the bastards rode to the river and must have had boats waiting or something. Their trail just disappeared into nothingness.''

Zeke shoved the glass back toward the man. ''I appreciate your trying.''

''I wish I could tell you more, Zeke. But your children can probably fill you in better than I can. Your brother and the other Cheyenne men couldn't go after your wife because they simply didn't know where to look, especially since it was white men that took her.''

Zeke's eyes grew to narrow slits. ''We live right in the middle of Indian country, and it's her own kind that brings her harm,'' he hissed. ''It figures!'' He buried the gnawing fear that she had already been sold to outlaws or Mexicans. He had to hope for the best. He started to leave, but Smitty grabbed his wrist. ''Zeke!'' He leaned closer. ''Come in back with me a minute. You look like a man who needs some good whiskey to

363

take with you."

"I don't have time."

"Make time," Smitty told him, his eyes hinting at some kind of message. Zeke frowned and nodded. He walked around the bar and into a room full of kegs and bottles in back. Smitty closed the door.

"There's a man out there," he spoke up. "Calls himself Hank Lund. He's been asking about you, wanting to know if you ever show up around here, what you looked like and all. He's been around ever since the tragedy at your ranch. He's out there right now, and he was watching us. He had on a blue shirt, and he has a big mole on the left side of his face and a mustache. I think he might know something, but whenever I talk about what happened, he acts as though it's news to him—acts real interested, says it's too bad, things like that. But I think he's been watching for you. I just thought you'd want to know."

Zeke put out his hand. "Thanks, Smitty. I appreciate that."

Smitty shook his hand. "Out here a man like me grows to like the Indians as much as the whites—men like me and Bent and some of the other traders. There's good and bad in all kinds, Zeke. Remember that."

Zeke nodded. "I've known mostly the bad."

Smitty sighed. "I'm sorry about that. And I'm sorry about your woman. She was something real special to everybody who knew her—even to the Cheyenne. I hope you find her alive, Zeke."

Zeke let go of his hand. "If I don't, whoever has harmed her will be sorry he was ever born!"

Smitty studied the savage eyes. "I'm sure they will."

Zeke turned and walked out, scanning the room. But the man Smitty had described was not there.

"He's gone," Smitty commented. "You'd better find him, Zeke."

Zeke hurried out into the open courtyard of the fort. Someone was riding out at a fast gallop. Zeke quickly mounted up and whirled his horse to follow. He rode hard, whipping his already tired horse into a run again. It was a good horse, one of his finest Appaloosas.

He rode over the dried earth around the fort and continued on into soft prairie grass, charging hard, his horse beginning to gain on the other rider. The fort began to fade into the distance, and there was only the sound of panting, snorting horses, clinking bridle and the soft thud of hoofs. The harder Zeke rode, the more certain he was the man ahead of him knew something. He had left too quickly once Zeke arrived. He had probably not expected Smitty to say anything to Zeke. Now he glanced back occasionally to see the big, dark Indian gaining on him.

He whipped his horse even harder, but the animal simply could not outrun Zeke's bigger, stronger mount. Moments later Zeke landed hard into the man, and both went crashing to the ground.

The other man, much smaller than Zeke, tried to scramble up, but Zeke grabbed him about the waist and slammed him down again, and in the next instant his big blade was at the man's throat.

"Who are you?" he growled. "Why were you asking for me at the fort?"

"I . . . I don't know . . . what you mean!" the man panted.

"You damned well do!" Zeke hissed. He quickly cut a deep gash from the man's temple to his chin, along his left cheek. The man screamed in terror. "Do you understand better now?" Zeke growled.

"Garvey!" the man yelled, beginning to cry, unable to move beneath Zeke's big body and strong hold. "Winston . . . Garvey! I've been waiting . . . for you to return. I was . . . supposed to warn Garvey. . . .

365

when you got back!''

Zeke's eyes widened. ''Garvey!'' He held the tip of the knife to the man's eyes. ''Does Winston Garvey have my wife?''

''Y-yes!'' the man whimpered. ''I . . . I didn't have anything to do with that . . . I swear! My orders were just . . . to come here and wait till you . . . showed up . . . or until the Cheyenne traders mentioned you were back!''

''Why? Why does Garvey have my wife? What does he want?''

''I . . . don't know! I swear to God, I don't know!''

''That's too goddamned bad, isn't it!''

There was no hesitation or regret. The big blade plunged into the man's eye, and the savage side of Zeke Monroe only smiled at the man's screams, which he quickly ended with a swift jerk of his blade from the man's abdomen up to his throat.

Zeke wiped his blade on the man's clothing, then shoved it back into its sheath. He dragged the body over to a ravine and shoved it down the short bank, where it landed with a thud in the soft earth of a nearly dried-up stream. He unsaddled the man's horse and threw the belongings down onto the body, then slapped the horse and sent it running. In this land it was still not unusual to find a dead body here and there. There were outlaws and renegade Indians everywhere. Let the soldiers wonder. Smitty would never tell on him. Smitty was a good man—one of the few. He kept nothing that would serve as any evidence, even leaving a hefty money belt on the man's body untouched.

He mounted his horse. He had an advantage now. This man would never make it back to warn Winston Garvey that Zeke Monroe was back. That was good. That was his edge.

He headed west, toward Black Elk's village. He would need men. The Cheyenne would help him. And he needed to see his children and let them know their father was all right, before he could go after poor Abbie. But he most certainly would go for his woman, and Winston Garvey would meet his match.

Twenty-Three

Even from the distance Zeke could hear his Indian name being shouted.

"Lone Eagle! He comes! Lone Eagle is back!"

It seemed the entire Cheyenne village of two hundred that was camped at Sand Creek had turned out to greet him, but there were few smiles, for all knew by the wild eyes and the scratches on Lone Eagle's face that he already knew about the raid on his home and the capture of his woman.

The excitement suddenly quieted as he rode silently into the village, his lips hard set. Tall Grass Woman broke into an eerie wail as she watched the tortured look on Zeke's face. She had wept daily for her good friend Abbie, who she feared she would never see again. Some of the other women joined her in the chilling cries of Indian women in mourning. It was the only sound. Even the many dogs in the camp did not bark.

Zeke moved his horse through the circle of *tipis*, where a few of the men just sat, some drunk on white man's whiskey. Many of the women and children looked hungry, and where an abundance of meat should be hanging for drying and smoking, only a few meat racks boasted game. To Zeke the worsening state of this proud people who once rode free and wild, following the seasons and the buffalo, was fuel to his hatred for men like Winston Garvey. The capture of his Abbie was the final spark that brought the explosion to his soul.

He spotted his horses in the distance then. His people were caring for them. Then he saw Margaret, and he felt a small wisp of hope that they could be family again. The girl was running toward him from Black Elk's *tipi*, where she had been sitting outside helping Black Elk's wife, Blue Bird Woman, mend some worn moccasins. Finding enough hides for new clothing was becoming difficult.

More Monroes came running then from other directions throughout the camp. "Father!" Margaret cried out, reaching him first.

Zeke slid from his horse and embraced his beautiful eldest daughter, not caring about the taboo of showing affection publicly. Just to see his children alive was a most wonderful, uplifting experience. He hugged the weeping daughter tightly, as the rest of the children— all but Wolf's Blood, who was not among them— hugged him and climbed all over him.

Zeke gloried in the touch of small hands, the feel of soft cheeks against his face. None of the children were frightened or hesitant about their father's wild look. They had seen it before. That look was for his enemies, not for them.

They all began babbling at once, some of them crying, most of them trying to tell their own version of what had happened in the raid, all of them begging him to go and find their mother immediately.

"You can find her, Father!" LeeAnn whimpered. "You can do anything!"

"Those men took Mama!" Lillian wept. "We thought you were dead and were never coming back!"

"You have to find her, Father!" Margaret told him. "Two of the men were those who attacked us last year in Kansas. One was the one you hit in the face with a rifle!"

"They killed Smoke!" Jeremy lamented. "They killed our brother's wolf!"

"And Dooley! Poor Dooley!" Ellen cried. "He's dead, Father. Dooley's dead!"

Some of the other Cheyenne there began putting in their own comments, and Black Elk hurried then to the scene. Zeke hugged each child, totally silent while the rest of them chattered. Their babbling was welcome noise to his ears, their voices like music.

Black Elk came close then, and Zeke set little Jason down. Zeke saw the remorse in Black Elk's eyes. "We needed food," he told Zeke apologetically. "We were only gone two days. We . . . did not know. There had been no trouble. I am sorry, Zeke."

Zeke reached out and grasped the man's wrist. "There is nothing to be sorry about. I was not there. I am the one who is sorry. Save your apologies, Black Elk. I may need you and a few more men."

Black Elk nodded. "We will help in any way we can."

Zeke squeezed his wrist. "Where is my son? I want the whole story from him. Where is Wolf's Blood?"

Black Elk frowned and pointed past the village. "Out there. He sits beyond the village at the creek. He speaks to no one. He just sits."

Zeke stared at thick cottonwoods for a moment, understanding the pain and guilt Wolf's Blood was suffering. He turned his gaze back to his children, taking them in one sweep of his eyes, checking their condition. They all looked healthy but tired and mournful.

"I will find your mother and bring her home to you," he told them flatly. "That is a promise." They all smiled and stared at him through tears. "I am going now to talk to your brother. All of you wait for me right here."

Margaret nodded. "Yes, sir." She wanted to tell him about her own terrible experience with the Confederate soldier, but she was too ashamed and embarrassed, and for now her mother was the only important topic. Her father must concentrate all of his powers on that one subject.

But then Zeke looked at her as though he saw her for the first time as a budding woman and not a little girl. He put a hand to the side of her face. "I have seen my brother Lance," he told her. "He told me about the soldier."

Her eyes quickly teared and her cheeks felt hot with shame. He took her hand and led her away from the others, and she walked with her head hanging, embarrassed that her father knew she had walked alone with a man. Perhaps he would chastise her firmly. Perhaps he was most angry because the man had been a white man. But when they were away from the others he only put an arm around her shoulders.

"You know, Margaret, that some white men call your mother a squaw woman," he told her gently. "Some take it for granted she's loose and worthless just because she is married to a breed. But what do you think of her?"

She raised her eyes and looked at him curiously. "Mother is the finest person I know. She is good and honorable."

He met her eyes. "That's right. And when men insult her, she doesn't hang her head and feel like she's a bad person." Their eyes held, and he stroked some of the long, dark hair from her face. "You remember your own honor, Margaret. You did nothing wrong, and no matter what kind of names they call you, you
371

are not what they say. You are Margaret Monroe, a very beautiful young woman. But you must understand the way some men are, and you must be careful, because men will want you. It is the white ones you will have to watch. I know you had no bad thoughts when you went with that soldier, but some men think differently. If you have an interest in a young man, tell your mother and me about it. Don't be embarrassed to tell us."

She dropped her eyes again. "I will," she replied quietly.

He hugged her again. "And I will tell you a secret, Margaret. Your own mother was not much older than you when we met. And she was just as innocent as you are, yet she did everything she could to get herself alone with me, which could have been just as unwise a decision as yours was. What you did was natural, Margaret, not bad. Your mother wasn't bad, just in love. The only difference is I had respect for Abbie's innocence and for women in general. That soldier was the kind of man who has respect for no woman. So don't go hanging your head. You're a good girl, Margaret, strong like Abbie. And you have been a big help to her, almost as much a mother to the little ones as Abbie." He gave her a squeeze. "Now, go back to the village. I need to go find Wolf's Blood and talk to him alone. I will find your mother, Margaret, and we will all be together again, and all the bad things that have happened since I've been gone will be put behind us."

She hugged him tightly around the middle. "I love you, Father!" she whispered. Then she turned and ran off, and Zeke watched with an aching heart. Life was not easy for a beautiful girl of mixed blood.

He turned sad eyes toward the grove of cottonwoods in the distance. He had soothed his daughter's troubles. Now he must turn his attention to his son. Once his children were settled and comforted, he would find their mother and they would be family again.

He walked toward the place where Black Elk had pointed, moving quietly, his heart pounding with pity for his eldest son, who surely felt he had failed in protecting his mother.

He reached the thick grove of young cottonwoods and ducked through them, then spotted the boy sitting in soft sand beside the creek, throwing pebbles into the water. Wolf's Blood! He was alive and well! He sucked in his breath in a moment of utter joy, his hope mounting faster that he would truly find his Abbie. For the spirits had spared all of his children, and this precious first-born son was alive. Alive! Somehow just being told he was alive had not been enough. Relief surged through him at truly seeing the boy himself.

He moved around to the boy's side and called out his name softly. Wolf's Blood's head turned quickly at the sound, and he jumped up, pulling out his knife in quick defense, but his eyes widened when he saw that it was his father.

He slowly put the knife back into its sheath as Zeke came closer, Wolf's Blood consumed by conflicting desires to embrace the precious father he thought might be dead and to run away in disgrace. He trembled as Zeke came close enough to touch, but he stood rigid and speechless.

Zeke's pity was enhanced by the fact that the boy had lost weight, and his eyes held a look that was begging for some kind of forgiveness. "I saw the grave," Zeke spoke aloud in a strained voice. "The necklace. . . and I thought . . . it was you." His eyes teared. "Thank God you're alive, Wolf's Blood!"

A tear slipped down the boy's cheek as he struggled for words. "I. . . failed her!" he finally choked out.

Zeke shook his head. "Things happen, Wolf's

373

Blood. They just . . . happen. I felt the same way . . . when I was away and the outlaw Arapaho woman attacked your mother years ago. Remember that? You were there then to help her, and you tried, even though you were little. And I know you helped her all you could this time, too. I have failed her more than once, Wolf's Blood. It's all right. We'll find her. Both of us. We'll find her and bring her home.''

The boy stared in surprise at the remark. "You . . . will take me with you?''

Zeke grasped the boy's shoulders. "I want only the best at my side.''

Wolf's Blood's dark eyes lit up with new pride. The two of them embraced then, both weeping quietly for a moment.

"Father,'' the boy whispered. "You are alive! Mother said you would come. She never lost faith.''

They pulled away from one another and Wolf's Blood quickly wiped his eyes. He ran his hands over Zeke's arms and smiled through tears. "Father!'' he repeated. They both hugged again for several long seconds. "She demanded that I let her go and do nothing to stop those men,'' Wolf's Blood groaned, pulling away again. "There were . . . so many. I shot four of them, and mother shot two with her old Spencer.'' The boy turned away. "But still there were . . . many left. I wanted to fight them all—but they said if Mother did not come out, they would burn the cabin and shoot each child as he or she came running out. Mother . . . did not want to risk harm to the children, and she was afraid for them to see Margaret and LeeAnn. So she . . . she . . . went to them.''

Zeke watched in sorrow as the boy's shoulders jerked in a silent sob. "When they . . . touched her, I felt . . . crazy. I stabbed one of them, but then another one hit me in the head . . . and everything went black.

When I woke up, Mother was gone and there was nothing I could do." The boy wiped at his eyes again, and Zeke's heart swelled with added love for his woman, who had literally sacrificed herself for her children. "They killed Dooley, Father . . . and Smoke."

Zeke sighed. "I know. I also know who they were and who has your mother."

Wolf's Blood whirled, his eyes on fire. "Who!"

"Winston Garvey."

The boy's eyes saddened. "Garvey! He is the bad man who you said is powerful and dangerous."

"That's right. The man who fathered Joshua." Zeke thought about the happy, handsome boy with the brace on his leg. There was so much to tell his children about where he had been and what he had seen. But there was no time now. First they must find Abbie.

"But . . . how do you know this?" Wolf's Blood was asking him.

Zeke put an arm around the boy's shoulders. "I will explain at the council tonight. I want all of the warriors to meet. I need to talk to all of them, and to the priests. I have an idea, and I need their advice and their blessing. We will have Black Elk call a council. We will pray and smoke the pipe and ask the spirits for strength and cunning. We will need both if we are to go after a man like Garvey. But we will go, and we will find Abbie, and you will be by my side. No more sitting here pining. I know where she is and we're going after her."

The boy dropped his eyes. "Are you sure you want me to go?"

Zeke squeezed his shoulders. "Look at me, Wolf's Blood." He moved around to face the boy, and Wolf's Blood raised his eyes to meet his father's. Zeke's own gaze dropped for a moment to the scars on Wolf's Blood's chest and arms from the Sun Dance sacrifice. "Of course I'm sure I want you along," Zeke told him.

375

"Just as sure as I am that you are man enough for it, and sure that you did everything you could to help your mother and would have fought to the death for her if she would have asked you. But I know Abbie and I know why she made the choice that she made. You just remember that it was her decision, a mother's decision, a practical decision. She would have had it no other way. So stop blaming yourself."

The boy swallowed. "But what if . . . if she is . . . dead?"

Zeke's eyes hardened. "Winston Garvey isn't that stupid. He'll keep her alive, thinking I'll tell him about Joshua to get her back. But I'm telling him nothing. I'm getting my woman, and once my hands are on Winston Garvey, he will find out he is just an ordinary man, capable of pain and death like all men!"

Wolf's Blood stood straighter at the words. "I want to kill the one with the scarred face who hurt my mother when he pulled her onto his horse," he said coldly. "I need to kill him myself!"

Zeke grinned with the joy of impending vengeance. "Then that one is yours, my son. For the next few weeks there will be no white in us. We will be the savages that Winston Garvey and the other whites say we are!"

Drums beat rhythmically, and Cheyenne men danced the war dance. They had obeyed the treaties and caused no trouble. Yet harassment, disease and starvation had been their only reward. The men, even those who had become drunk and lazy because of their disillusionment and despair, joined in the dancing, most agreeing to riding with Lone Eagle to the mountains near Denver, where they would await instructions before raiding the ranch of the man called Winston Garvey. They were friends to Lone Eagle. They would help

376

him get his woman back. It would be like the old days, when they raided Ute or Pawnee camps to recapture their own women who had been stolen from them.

Zeke and Wolf's Blood sat side by side. And as Zeke had commanded, there was not a white person alive who would have thought there was any white blood in the veins of either father or son. Both had pierced their chests and let blood in sacrifice to the spirits for the loss of Abbie, in accordance with the custom of suffering physical pain to relieve the emotional pain. They wore only loincloths and bone necklaces, their bodies and faces painted in their war colors. Zeke wore his eagle feathers, the sign of an accomplished warrior, his body much more fierce looking than his son's because of the man's many battle scars. The years had not softened the hard muscle or the swift movements and keen alertness of the man.

Father and son shared the pipe with a priest and with Black Elk. Black Elk's acceptance of the pipe from Zeke signified his agreement to take his Dog Soldiers to Denver. It would feel good to ride and raid and be a man again, to fight back at least once against the forces that were against them. Winston Garvey represented the worst of the white man.

"Wait in the hills," Zeke told his brother. "We must be silent and cautious. Soldiers must not see us. I will go first to the woman called Anna Gale. I know that she will know about this thing. And I know that she will help me. When I know all that I need to know, I will come to you and tell you what to do. It is important that you stage a good raid. Steal horses—kill as many men as you can. Make it look as though it is an Indian raid and nothing more. Ride off with the horses. Then they will think all the Indians have gone, and they will send out more men to come after you and get the horses back. Lead them on for many miles, then let the horses go. The men will quit the chase then and bring the horses back. And you will have none of the horses with you, so the soldiers cannot come to your camp later and accuse you of being the ones who raided the ranch. I want no blame to come to you. But your raid will give me time to get into the house and get Winston Garvey out. From then on it is my risk. Your job is to get as many men away from there as you can."

Black Elk nodded, and Wolf's Blood's heart pounded with great anticipation. This would be his first true Indian raid, his first real mission of vengeance. He was ready.

"There is the chance that the soldiers will ride down on the village, Black Elk, or on another village, hitting out aimlessly in retaliation," Zeke told his brother. "I will be very sorry if this happens."

Black Elk waved him off. "It does not matter. They ride through our villages even when we are peaceful, threaten us, bother our women. These volunteers, they are the worst, just citizens who have an excuse to ride around are shoot at us." He frowned and took out a tomahawk, fingering the blade. "The runners came to us not long ago—told us that the leader of this Colorado, called Evans, wanted all of us to gather and meet with him and put signatures on that worthless treaty. But we did not go. The whites are settling on our land, claiming it for themselves. But talk at Bent's Fort is that the men who award the land in Denver will not file the claims because there are not enough names on the new treaty that takes all that land from us and gives it to them. So some say the land is still ours. At the fort they say the whites have written to their father in Washington. Now we wait to see what will happen next. We try to wait peacefully, but every time we go out on a hunt, we are shot down. White men steal and rape our women. Whiskey traders come into the camp and ruin good men with their bad spirits. Our own men are giving up, Zeke, some selling their wives and daughters for whiskey and food. Especially for food. We cannot go out and hunt, and there is no game on this little piece of land they have given us. Other land is fenced off and is dangerous because we are shot at. We starve, we die of disease, and we sit here going crazy, trying to decide how we are to survive."

"It will get worse, Black Elk. I am afraid for all my people. But as long as there is a way to fight, you should fight. I ride the terrible road in the middle. You cannot understand the pain of walking that road. But I am happiest when I am Cheyenne. Never have I felt stronger than at this moment! I have great faith that we will accomplish our mission." He reached out and touched his brother's shoulder. "But I don't want to bring you pain and death. It would go hard on me."

Black Elk grinned. "The spirits are with us this time. I feel it." He sat straighter. "Now it is not like the days of freedom, when we followed the seasons and the buffalo, when we rode as far as the sun sets, or far to the north or the east or the south, and we knew that all that we saw belonged to us. In the north the Sioux fight, and the soldiers ride down on them and bring them harm. Here we try to keep the peace, and still the soldiers ride down on us. It does not seem to matter which we do. We are blamed for anything that happens, whether it is Comanches or Apaches or the Northern Cheyenne. Sometimes even the white men dress like Indians and fool the stupid settlers and raid them, so that the settlers say that Indians are raiding again and shout about how bad we are." He tossed his head. "I spit on them! If they are going to blame us for things we do not do, then let them blame us for a good reason! We will go with you and raid this man's place. We will get your woman out of there. She is one of us. She is my sister. She is

Swift Arrow's sister. She saved Tall Grass Woman's little girl from the deep waters. She has killed three Crow and been wounded by a Crow arrow. We wish to help your Abigail. She has been our friend, nursed our sick ones, helped with the skinning and meat curing and the sewing of *tipi* skins. She has been a good friend.''

Zeke nodded. He turned to the priest with questioning eyes. The priest nodded. ''The men of Black Elk's warrior society have voted to help you,'' he told Zeke in the Cheyenne tongue. ''The sacrifices are good. The signs are good. You are a man pure in thought, true to the Cheyenne in your heart, a warrior of respect in spite of your white blood. The council has voted. When the sun rises, you will go to Denver.''

Zeke's heart raced with fiery vengeance and an eagerness to get his hands on Winston Garvey. He could almost taste the man's blood. He rose and pulled out his knife, feeling as though he was exploding, as the beating drums and jingling bells and frenzied whooping and chanting of the dancing men penetrated to his soul and made him feel wild and strong and fearless. He left the council to join in the dancing, shouting the chants in the Cheyenne tongue, his long, black hair hanging straight and loose, framing his painted face and burning eyes. His handsomeness was marred this night by his almost hideous wild look. The gentle side of the man was nowhere to be seen. It was as though Zeke Monroe had totally disappeared and had been replaced by the fierce warrior called Lone Eagle. And soon, behind him, his son also began to dance, and other than Zeke's more mature, filled-out manliness and the lines of hard living on his scarred face, there seemed to be little difference between the two.

The rest of the Monroe children sat with the women of the camp in the shadows of the huge campfire around which the men danced, watching the frenzied preparation for battle. Jeremy watched Wolf's Blood, knowing in his young heart he could never be like his brother. He liked the Cheyenne, yet deep inside he wanted to be white. He liked books and learning, and he wanted to go to a white school when he was older. But he kept the thoughts to himself for now. He was not ashamed of his Indian blood, but he was fast learning that to be Indian was to face starvation and insults. To be white meant being respected and educated. To be white meant not being shot at and called names. Little Jeremy was not so sure he wanted to be Indian at all. He did not look Indian. Why should he say that he was? It was something to think about.

LeeAnn watched with the same doubts. She of all the Monroe children looked the least Indian. She was white in every way, always feeling out of place in the village with her blond hair and blue eyes. She turned to her beautiful sister Margaret, whose dark features were such a contrast to her own, both of them beautiful in opposite ways. Margaret was like Wolf's Blood, looking all Indian, but bearing the exquisite beauty that comes to women of mixed blood.

"What will we do if Mother can't be found?" she asked her sister. "Will we live here in the village, Margaret?"

Margaret looked at her in surprise. She had not even considered such a thought. "I don't know. When I look at Father tonight, I see only an Indian. I think he would like to always live with the people."

LeeAnn blinked back tears. "But . . . I don't want to live with the people," she answered. "I mean I . . . I love them. But I want to live in the cabin, Margaret. I'm white. I don't belong here."

Margaret turned back to watch the dancing. "You are lucky that if you want to be white, you can be, because you look white. I have no choice." She looked at her sister again. "I am Indian. I do not want to be white. But I am afraid, LeeAnn. I am afraid because of what that white soldier told me when he . . . touched me. I was proud to be Indian . . . until he told me what white men think of Indian squaws." She blinked back tears. "I am not like that. But they think it. It will be hard being Indian."

"But . . . what will we do, Margaret?"

Margaret took her hand. "We will be ourselves. And until our mother comes, we will help our father. He loves us. I think he would understand, LeeAnn, if you told him how you feel. He would not make you live the Indian way if it is not what you want. You see how Mother lives. She has her cabin and her oven and her potbelly stove. Father understands the white ways, and his white woman's needs. He will understand yours also. We will all be different, because of our two bloods. Don't be afraid, LeeAnn."

LeeAnn looked back at the wild dancing, wishing she were at home in front of the fireplace knitting or reading. "But look at Father! He looks so . . . so mean!" she said in near awe. "Tonight he has no white blood at all. I've never been afraid of him before. But tonight it's like . . . like he's not my father, but someone else—a fierce warrior come to kill me and take my scalp!"

Margaret just smiled. "Don't be silly." She watched her father. "Look at him! He is our father. He is Cheyenne and he loves being Cheyenne. And he looks mean because he is pulling all his meanness from his soul so he can go after that man who took Mother from us. I like the way he looks! It means he will win his battle, LeeAnn. He will find Mother and bring her home. I know it! You should be glad he looks that way. Mother will come home and we'll all be together at the cabin again. We'll be happy and safe, LeeAnn.''

Margaret turned to the rest of the children, feeling suddenly mature and motherly. ''All of you pray for Mother.'' Little Jason crawled onto Margaret's lap. ''Mother is coming home. Father and Wolf's Blood will bring her,'' Margaret announced.

''Mama sleep with me?'' Jason asked his sister.

''Yes,'' Margaret replied with confidence. ''Mama will sleep with you. And she'll bake and sew and read to us. You'll see. Our father will bring her.''

The campfire raged, its flames lapping upward into the dark sky. But its flaming roar could not compare to the rage that burned in the soul of Lone Eagle.

Twenty-Four

Anna brushed out her lustrous, dark hair, studying her still firm, silky body in the mirrow and adjusting a ruffled nightgown around her breasts, pulling it down so that they were enticingly exposed. In a half hour a very prominent banker would be paying her a call. He paid well, and he was kind to her. She leaned closer to the mirror to put a touch more color on her eyelids. It was then she heard the soft tapping at her door.

She frowned. Apparently her customer had come early. She sighed disgustedly. She was not ready. She walked to the door and flung it open, and immediately she paled to a ghostly white, feeling weak and suddenly sweaty with shock. "Zeke!" she exclaimed, her livid blue eyes wide with surprise and sudden fear. He looked wild and ready to kill.

He just glared at her, faint scratches on his cheeks that she suspected were the remnants of self-inflicted wounds out of sorrow. She had lived in the West long enough to know something about Indian ways. Her fear was suddenly mixed with the old, burning love and desire for this man of men, and she stepped back to let him in, not even caring if he meant her harm. Just to see him again, to be close to this man whose masculinity permeated the very air, was a thrill.

But the fear came back to overwhelm all other feelings when he grasped her hair painfully tight in his hands as soon as she closed the door. "Traitor!" he growled. He backhanded her hard, knocking her to the floor. She lay there a moment, half expecting to feel his knife slice into her, but he only came and stood over her. Her gown had fallen away from her legs, exposing slender, milky thighs. He took his foot and stepped on one of her legs, pinning her down. "How much did Garvey pay you to find out we were the ones who knew about his half-breed son?" he demanded, no sign of remorse in his eyes for the huge red welt that was forming on her cheek.

She blinked back tears and put a hand to the hot skin. "Nothing," she replied calmly. "I never told him a thing. He figured it out for himself, Zeke."

He smiled in a sneer. "Slut! You told him!" He reached down and jerked her up by the arm and she winced as he slammed her close to him, holding her in a viselike grip with one arm while he grasped her chin with his other hand. "Say it again, Anna Gale. Look me in the eyes and tell me you had nothing to do with this. You helped us once. I owe you. I do not want to hurt you, but I know when someone is telling the truth. If I see you are lying, I will slice up your beautiful body so that no one recognizes it."

She gazed into his dark, hypnotic eyes. God, how she loved this man! How she wanted him! But that could never be.

"I didn't tell him," she said with confidence. "He came and told me. Somehow he . . . he figured it out, Zeke." Tears began to form in the blue eyes. "I love you," she whispered. "Why would I betray you?"

She watched the hardness in his eyes battle with a softness that lay behind them somewhere. "If you are not a traitor, Anna Gale, then tell me what you know. Help me find her!''

He released her, and for a moment she could not talk as she struggled against the tears that wanted to come. She walked to a dresser and dipped her hand in a bowl of water, pressing its coolness to her cheek.

''He . . . found out somehow,'' she told Zeke. ''I swear to God I don't know how. But he discovered you had been to Denver four years ago. He put it all together. And he hit me with it unexpectedly. Then he . . . he gloated about it. There was nothing I could do, Zeke. And later . . . I found out he'd taken your wife. He gloated over that, too.'' She turned tear-filled eyes to him. ''If I even knew where he had her, I'd have tried to help her, Zeke. But he says she's not at his place, and he won't tell me where she is! God, I'm sorry, Zeke! I'm very fond of your wife. I swear to God I'd never bring her harm if I could help it. I know how you feel about her. I'd never do that to you!''

He watched her, walking closer then. ''Where is Garvey's spread?'' he asked.

''West of here. There's a valley called Tumble Rocks. He owns the whole valley. His house is a big, gaudy thing, made of granite—two stories. His bedroom—'' she looked away— ''his bedroom is on the second floor,'' she continued quietly, ''on the right end as you face the house.'' She turned back to look at him. ''His son is off to college and his wife has gone east for a visit. He's there alone. If you could find a way to get to him, you could make him tell you where Abbie is. The man's a stinking coward. He'll tell you in an instant.''

His eyes glittered with the taste of vengeance. ''I have no doubt that he will tell me,'' he hissed. ''I can make a man sell his own mother!''

Her body surged with passion at the sight of him, tall and broad and dark, wearing the sweet-scented buckskins and the array of weapons. Never had she forgotten the one night she had spent with him. Her eyes moved over him longingly. She wanted to remember every feature, every weapon, every scar. "How did you get up here, looking like that?" she asked.

"I am quiet. And I can climb."

She nodded, smiling sadly. "I don't know why I even asked." Pain suddenly filled her eyes, and she turned away then, her heart heavy for his sorrow and what she must tell him next. She swallowed for courage. How she hated to hurt him! But he should know. He should be prepared. "Zeke, he . . . he . . . raped her. And I don't think he was the only one. He has two men helping watch her. The way he talked, I think they also . . ."

She waited, but there was only silence. When she cautiously turned, he just stared at her, his jaw flexing, his eyes blazing. "I expected no less of such a man," he answered. "But Abigail Monroe belongs to me. For another man to touch her is to touch a stone. They have not touched her at all!"

Her eyes teared more and she stepped closer, reaching out hesitantly to put a hand to his side. "I'm so sorry, Zeke!" she whispered. "I can at least tell you the two men watching her are called Buel and Handy. I know them. Buel has scars on his face and neck, and Handy is a big dark man with a deformed face. They're the only ones who know Garvey has Abigail. And even they don't know why. If you can kill the three of them, there will be no one but myself who can link you to Garvey's death. You would never be traced."

He studied the blue eyes. "And can I trust you, Anna Gale?"

She held his eyes steadily. "You know that you can. There is nothing I want more than to be rid of Winston Garvey. I hate him! And with Garvey gone, I don't

387

need to do business anymore with that vile son of his."

Her eyes teared, and she turned away. "The boy is sadistic," she added. "He makes my skin crawl."

Zeke watched her. For a woman like Anna Gale to be brought to tears of shame by a customer could only mean the Garvey boy was truly cruel and demented.

"He sends his son to you?" he asked quietly.

She nodded, and he put a hand on her shoulder in a sudden urge to console her. He squeezed the shoulder, thinking to himself again what a wasted woman she was. But there were some things in life that could not be changed. She turned and looked up at him for one brief moment of remembrance before his eyes changed again to ice.

"I know the two scarred men," he told her. "They were part of a party of men who attacked us last year in Kansas. Garvey's son was with them and recognized us from Denver. We are the ones who put the scars on those men. And right now I regret not killing the Garvey boy. I am not a man to kill one so young, but that one is different. He is dangerous."

She shivered and rubbed her arms. "When he told his father he had seen you in Denver—that must be how Garvey figured it all out. Someone must have mentioned your name, and Garvey remembered you from Santa Fe."

Zeke nodded, struggling to ignore the screaming inside his soul at the thought of his woman being touched by other men. Abbie! His sweet Abbie! The woman whose virginity belonged only to him, whose body and soul and heart and all her private places belonged to Zeke Monroe! Anna felt his rigidness building, and she knew he was battling to stay hard and strong, not allowing his emotions to overwhelm him and make him weaker. She stepped back.

"Garvey will be expecting you, Zeke. He had a man

waiting at Bent's Fort—''

"I killed him," he answered flatly. "Garvey does not know I am back."

Her eyes lit up and the smile returned to her lips. "Wonderful!" she exclaimed, looking delighted. "God, how I'd love to see the look on his face when he sees you and feels that big blade at his throat!"

"How many men does he have?" he asked.

"An army. I don't know how you'll ever get in there. He must have forty men working for him."

"That isn't so many. I have a plan."

She breathed deeply, catching the earthy scent of him, feeling the excitement of his power. "I hope it works, Zeke."

"Don't worry about me. When I am thirsty for vengeance, I do not die easily. And I have help—Cheyenne. We will raid the ranch. Once I get my hands on Winston Garvey, I will discover what he has done with my Abbie."

She stepped closer again, touching his arm. "On Tuesdays and Saturdays the maid is there. With his family gone, they don't need a maid every day. Go when she isn't there, then you will have only Garvey to worry about inside the house and you won't risk witnesses." Her eyes saddened. "I'll worry about you, Zeke."

Her eyes were glassy with love. It would be easy to take her now. She was soft for him—wanted him badly. And he had not had a woman for many months. But all of his manly desires were gone, replaced by nothing but the awful hatred and vengeance. And even if he could find those desires, they could not be awakened by any woman but Abigail Trent Monroe, the little girl he had claimed in the foothills of the Rockies so many years ago.

"Be careful, Zeke," she told him softly. "God be

389

with you.''

He reached out and touched the welt on her cheek gently, then bent down and lightly kissed the cheek. "I love her so," he whispered. He pulled back and she saw tears in his eyes. They suddenly embraced. He held her for a moment, then quickly pulled away. "Thank you, Anna. You will be free of Winston Garvey. This is a promise.''

For a brief moment he saw what she could have been. "Your secret is good with with me, Zeke. Surely you see that. Surely you know that I love you too much to ever bring you harm. Tell me you believe me. Tell me you trust me. Give me that much.''

He studied the blue pools in which so many men had been drowned. All but Zeke Monroe. "I believe you," he finally answered. "I believe there is a goodness beneath your harlot eyes, Anna Gale. Before I came, I thought—'' he bent down to kiss the puffy cheek again— "I'm half crazy with grief and worry, Anna. I should not have hit you.''

She looked up at him, the fires of desire almost bringing her pain. "It's all right.'' She stepped back, surprising herself with this new-found strength he seemed to give her, for she wanted nothing more than to throw herself at him and beg him to sleep with her once more. Perhaps she could have tried using his body again as a price for giving him the information he needed. But looking at him now she knew it wouldn't have worked. His condition now was not one to toy with. He would have killed her. This was no time for playing games with Zeke Monroe.

But she did not want to play games. That first time was before she had slept with him—before she had fallen in love with him. She no longer wanted to tease him and hurt him. She took his hand and kissed the severed little finger that he had cut off years earlier in per-

390

sonal sacrifice for having betrayed his wife in order to get information out of the harlot Anna Gale. That kind of love was far above the likes of herself.

"Good luck, Zeke," she said softly, squeezing his hand. "I hope you find her. But . . . if you don't . . . and you need a woman to hold you—"

He shook his head. "Without Abbie, I'll have no desires left." He turned to leave.

"Zeke," she called out. He hesitated at the door and looked at her. "Try to get word to me, will you? Try to let me know when Garvey is dead and if you find Abbie and she's all right."

He nodded, running his eyes over her sensuous body. "I will try."

He ducked out the door, and she hurried over to get a last look, but he had already disappeared. She ran to the open window at the end of the hall, leaning out. But she saw nothing. He had vanished as quickly and silently as he had arrived.

She slowly returned to her room, closing the door and walking to the bed, where she sat down and wept. She no longer had any desire to see the banker who was to come and do business with her. She suddenly wanted no men at all, save one. And that man she could not have. But at least she had seen him once more.

Two days passed, and on the night of the second day, there was a restlessness in the air. The animals felt it, and even the wind felt it, for it stirred fitfully in impatient gusts. There was a chill to the darkness. And like all wild things that sense impending changes, Swift Arrow sat awake that night, praying alone near a campfire deep in the Black Hills of the Dakotas. The news that the runners had brought from Zeke, that Abbie had been stolen away by white men, burned in his Indian heart. He ached for his half-brother's agony, but most

391

of all he ached for Abbie herself—the white woman he loved but could not have. His deep hatred for most white men was now engraved deeper into his soul, for it was white men who had killed his half-brother's first wife and son; and now whites had taken Abbie.

Abbie! He threw back his head and prayed to the spirits for the beloved white woman and for Zeke. His arms bled where he had let blood in sacrifice to bring strength to his prayers. It would be easier now to continue leading Northern Cheyenne warriors in riding with the Sioux against the white settlers. Wherever a white man walked, trouble seemed to follow. It was not enough for another white to have the same color skin. Just to associate with an Indian meant insults and condemnation. Now those terrible things had come to Abbie, and if the white men had touched her wrongly, they must suffer.

Swift Arrow looked into the flames, his eyes wild with vengeance. How he would love to be along with those who would ride against those who had wronged the white woman. But by the time the runners came, Zeke would already be at that place called Denver, and would be ready to act. There was nothing to do now but wait until another message came—one that would tell him Abigail Monroe had been found alive and was all right. He breathed deeply, satisfied that if anyone could save Abigail, it was Zeke—Lone Eagle. Of this Swift Arrow was certain—just as certain as he was that no man was as skilled with a knife. And the boy, Wolf's Blood, would have his turn also. Yes! He was a fine warrior. Swift Arrow himself had helped train him when he was very small. Now he would get his chance at warrior ways by helping his father avenge his mother's abduction.

Wolf's Blood! Zeke! Abbie! How he missed all of them—and the others: the children and his brother,

Black Elk. How he would love to be riding with them against those white men! But the North was his home now—the Sioux and Northern Cheyenne his people. He had made this his home so that he would not have to be near the white woman he loved, for stronger than that love was his respect for the much greater love the woman shared with his half-brother. The impossibility of having her was something he had accepted many years ago, and living at a distance made it easier to bear.

And so he stayed in the North. He would pray very hard for Zeke and Abbie and Wolf's Blood. He would ask the spirits to guide Zeke this night, for he knew in his very bones that this was the night. It was in the wind. Tonight vengeance would be tasted, and it would be delicious. Zeke was the supreme master of vengeance. He had proved it in that place called Tennessee, against the white men who had wronged his first wife. He would prove it again. And it would be tonight.

"Wagh!" Swift Arrow muttered. "It is a good night to die. But it will not be my brother or his son who die. It shall be the white men who took my brother's woman!" He closed his eyes. *"Ho-shuh,* Abigail. Do not be afraid," he spoke into the darkness. "Your man will come, and the strength of my own spirit will be with him. I shall ride with him this night, and you shall not suffer again."

He rose and stretched out his arms and blood streamed down toward his elbows. "Take my strength, Lone Eagle!" he shouted, using Zeke's Cheyenne name. "I shall ride with you this night, and glory in your vengeance!"

The moon hung quietly over the distant peaks, huge and bright. It was a good night for raiding and stealing horses. Cheyenne warriors moved in on foot, the first

393

silent attackers who would pave the way for those who held back in the foothills on swift mounts, waiting for the signal to ride in.

Like creatures of the night they crept among the shadows, soundless, stealthy, wild things stalking their prey. First they must kill the men riding night watch, those few who rode the perimeter of Winston Garvey's ranch, keeping guard and watching horses and cattle. They were easy. A man could aim his silent bow well in the bright moonlight. And these men were unsuspecting. Most of the Indian trouble was to the north, not this close to Denver. In the South there was a little trouble with the Southern Cheyenne, and a lot of trouble with the Comanche and Apache. But Winston Garvey's spread was situated in a peaceful valley protected on one side by the mountains, and on the other by the city of Denver, only five miles away. Indians did not bother him.

Garvey himself sat before a marble fireplace, puffing an expensive cigar and writing a letter to his son, telling the boy about new telegraph lines coming into Denver and what progress the city was seeing.

"With the new supply company I have purchased," he wrote, "I can triple our income. Nebraska Supply carries food, tools and merchandise from Omaha to the miners in the Rockies. The miners pay incredible prices for the simplest items, Charles. Remember that. Those men are desperate for goods, isolated from the rest of the world, willing to pay anything for good whiskey and potatoes that aren't rotten. They also pay well for pretty women. Prostitution is another lucrative operation you should consider. If you want to get rich, then serve men who are desperate for food, whiskey and women, and you can't go wrong. Just charge a certain price and then stick to it. They'll pay it.

"We are still concentrating on the Indian problem.

Governor Evans is trying to get the Cheyenne to put more signatures on the Treaty of Fort Wise, but I say if they don't do so soon, the hell with them. We'll put them in their place by force and starvation. The Indians are really the only fly in the ointment out here. I don't understand why Washington doesn't do more about it. Evans needs help and so do the settlers who want the land. It can't be much longer before the treaty is deemed valid, at which time I am ready to buy up considerable properties myself, Charles. I-foresee the day when the Indians will be placed behind fences and told to stay there. I would like to see them all shot myself, but some of the fine Christian people of Colorado can't seem to go that far. They prefer to try to educate them and reform them—cut their hair and put them in white man's clothing. I suppose that isn't all bad. If you take away their basic way of life, you are still destroying them—but just doing it indirectly and legally. The key, Charles, is to break their spirits. Remember that. You can't just move in and kill them off, although a raid on a camp here and there will go unnoticed. You simply have to be clever and quiet about it.''

He put down his pen and looked toward the window. He felt restless and uneasy, but he shrugged it off, attributing it to the full moon. The night was perfectly quiet, except for the howling of wolves now and then. If anything was wrong, one of the men would come and tell him. He returned to his letter, while outside a tenth arrow silently found its mark and another ranch hand fell from his horse.

It was all taking place quietly, without even disturbing the animals. No dogs barked, no horses whinnied, no cattle grew restless. Shadowy warriors moved ever closer, those in front using silent weapons— knives, tomahawks, arrows and lances—to eliminate their opposition. The ranch had been watched for two days. The Indians knew their targets and destination well.

A tall, silent warrior who had waited in the shadows gave a soft, trilling call, and on that signal, more warriors moved in, those in the second group leading their mounts quietly by the reins, their well-trained animals as quiet as the men. This second group waited just beyond the corrals and out buildings, while the first group moved in even closer. Eight more men went down without a sound, their throats slit or arrows in their backs, while Winston Garvey continued his long letter to the son that he missed so much. Charles would be home soon on a break, at which time he would join the Colorado volunteers and get some more experience in the field. The Indian problems were coming to a head. Charles should be involved, and the boy was anxious to kill some Indians himself. Besides that, his father had promised him a high position in the volunteers, a rapid move up to at least lieutenant. He would be not only rich and prominent, but a respected officer in the Colorado volunteers, where he would learn the guts of politics and get some leadership training, hone his keen sense of brutality and authority.

But outside there crept a breed of man who could be more brutal than even Winston Garvey could imagine. The sort of brutality Garvey envisioned toward the Indians was now creeping ever closer to him, as he sat in those last hours giving his final directions to his cherished son. And while Cheyenne bucks swarmed onto the Garvey ranch, a half-breed named Lone Eagle made his own way on quiet moccasins toward the big stone house, his own cherished son at his heels.

Another call went out, sounding like the eerie cry of an owl. Garvey glanced at the window again as the sound was cried twice more. Then there was an explosion of yips and hoots and war cries, mingled with the thunder of hoofs.

"Indians!" the man muttered. "Goddamned sons of bitches! What the hell are Indians doing this close to Denver?"

The man rose and stormed to the front door, where two men came running toward him. "Indians, sir!" one of them shouted. "We just found three men dead. Don't know how many others they got, but if they're this close, they must have got a lot of the outer guards! They're after the horses, Mr. Garvey."

Garvey's face was red and puffy with anger. "Well get the hell out there and stop them!" he fumed.

"Sir, it's dark out there! We can't see them. I don't like fighting Indians in the dark."

"You stinking coward! I'll give you twice your pay, if that's what it takes. Round up some men and chase them off!"

Buel rode up then, leading some other men. "Indians are riding down hard, sir. I think they're after the horses and cattle."

"I know that, Buel! Send some men after them. Take as many extras as you need. Chase those red sons of bitches until they drop! I want to know if they're Utes or Cheyenne or Comanches, and by God every last one of them will pay for this, and so will their women and children!"

The men were excited then, and even the first one who had been afraid ran for his horse.

"Buel!" Garvey called out, stopping the man as he turned his mount to leave. "Stay here with me, will you?"

Buel frowned. "I wouldn't mind gettin' me a few redskins, sir."

"You'll have plenty of other chances for that. Some of those bastards might stay behind and break in here for food and supplies. You and Webster and Deacon stay behind, and leave a few men outside.''

The air was filled with Indian cries and pounding horses. Now the cattle were also sounding off, stirred up by all the commotion. Garvey ducked back inside as warriors came even closer. An arrow thudded into the door, and Buel turned and shot, but missed his elusive target. It was as though the arrow had come from the very air. Buel leaned over and slid from his horse, literally crawling to the door, pounding on it and calling for Garvey to let him in. The door opened and Buel ducked inside, Garvey nearly slamming the door on his foot.

Outside there was nothing but confusion and pandemonium, as cattle began breaking loose and charging through a fence. Garvey men quickly organized, some circling the cattle to keep them within close boundaries; but the horses were already headed south, urged on by victorious Cheyenne, who had so far suffered no injuries or deaths. Lone Eagle's plan of careful watching and surprise attack was a good one. They had killed many Garvey men, and now more were organizing to chase after them. That was good. The Garvey ranch would be unprotected. Winston Garvey would be unprotected.

Black Elk screamed out a victorious war cry as he chased the fine Garvey steeds toward the southern foothills, glorying in the excitement of being chased by Garvey men. He and his warriors would give the white men a good run for their money. They would lead them many miles away, while Lone Eagle and Wolf's Blood took care of Winston Garvey. The feel of the wind in his face and the taste of white man's blood and the smell of the stolen horses made him cry out again. It had been a long time since he had raided and fought and lived the way a Cheyenne man was supposed to live. He yipped and howled and rode on into the darkness, leading Garvey's men ever farther from the ranch.

Twenty-Five

Garvey paced in his study while Buel watched from where he sat in one of the leather chairs, puffing on one of his boss's fine cigars. The night had quieted again, as Indians, stolen horses and pursuing men thundered off into the night.

"I feel spooked," Garvey muttered to Buel. "It gives me the chills the way those bastards can sneak up on you and then hit and run so fast. They're like a mountain storm: One minute it's peaceful and then—boom—there they are."

"Tricky devils," Buel drawled, studying the fat cigar in his fingers.

Garvey stopped pacing and watched him. "How's the woman?"

Buel shrugged. "Hangin' on, like always. She ain't so high and mighty anymore, though. We broke her good. That man of hers better be comin' pretty soon. She's sick—pneumonia is my guess. She won't last much longer this way. She's got so thin me and Handy can't even have any fun with her any more. Handy's up there with her tonight, bitchin' and moanin' about havin' to throw water on her to wash away her messes. And she's got that bad cough—feverish, you know? If you ain't careful, the white squaw is gonna die on you."

Garvey frowned and walked to the window, opening it and leaning out to get some fresh air. The house suddenly felt close and hot. "You out there, Joe?" he called.

"Yes, sir, right here," the one called Joe replied from the veranda. "Can't hear the horses and Indians no more. Must be givin' Jess and the others a good run for their money. But they'll get them horses back, sir."

"They'd by God better!" Garvey fumed. "I'll not be outdone by those uneducated savages. What the hell are Indians doing so close to Denver anyway? They must be crazy!" He turned back inside and paced again, removing his suit jacket. "I wonder why we haven't heard from Lund yet? Isn't Monroe ever coming back from that damned war? The man should be coming home to his family by now."

"Lund's a good man. If he hears that the man is back, he'll be here to tell you, Mr. Garvey. You can bet on it."

Garvey sat down in his big leather chair, pulling out a drawer and removing a flask of whiskey and a small glass. He poured himself a shot and drank it down.

"You look nervous, sir," Buel spoke up. "You got no worry about that Monroe fellow, if that's what you think. There's plenty of men left here. Besides, it was just an Indian raid. Big deal. Happens all the time. The men will chase them down and get the horses back. Then we'll tell the soldiers and they'll take care of the bastards—hang a couple of them—and that will be the end of it."

Garvey sighed. "What bothers me is the raid being right here. There's something strange about it."

Buel grinned. "You worry too much."

Outside the one called Joe lit a pipe and puffed it casually, scanning the darkness with keen eyes, his rifle tilted against the support post right beside him. The night had suddenly grown quiet again, as though the Indians had never been there. It was hard to tell how many men might have been killed, but he doubted it was many. They would have to wait until morning to go out and look for bodies. Fifteen men had ridden after the Indians, and he knew that there were four men in one bunkhouse. The second bunkhouse was empty. But the raid was over and the Indians involved were well on their way with the stolen horses. They would most certainly not be back or even come anywhere close, because by morning the soldiers would know. The cattle had scattered. They would have to be rounded up in the morning. He and the few men left could do that.

In the bunkhouse, four men plunked down on their bunks, cussing, about having had to get out of bed to go running out in the darkness after damned Indians. Two of them had run out in their long johns, strapping on guns without even putting on clothes. Now they removed their weapons and tossed them aside, one of the men taking out a bottle of whiskey and swallowing some.

"What a night," one of them grumbled. "If Garvey didn't pay so well I'd say the hell with his damned horses. Let the redskins have them. I had a long day today. I'm beat."

"Well, you'd better get some sleep," another replied. "We'll spend all day tomorrow buryin' bodies and roundin' up them beef, let alone probably havin' to go after the rest of the men if they don't show up tomorrow." The man stretched, then froze, his arms still outstretched, his eyes wide. A stranger had emerged from a partitioned section of the bunkhouse, the fiercest looking warrior the ranch hand had ever seen—and the

401

biggest.

There was no time to think first. The ranch hand reached for his gun, but a huge knife instantly landed in the man's chest with a thud. The other three men whirled, none of them near their guns, all of them standing there in their underwear. Before they knew what was happening the big Indian was landing into them with a growl, literally knocking all three of them to the floor at once. The Indian moved with a swiftness that overwhelmed the three ranch hands, his size and strength amazing, his movements leaving no room for hesitation or doubt. He rolled off the three men and yanked his knife out of the first man's chest, quickly ramming it into the stomach of one of the other three men, who had lunged at him.

He shoved the man off his knife, and only four or five seconds had passed since first he showed himself in the bunkhouse. The remaining two men, shocked, were just getting to their feet. The Indian kicked out at one, hearing the crack of ribs as his foot landed in the man's side. The man grunted and crashed over a table, and the fourth man went for the door. But the Indian, his eyes maniacal, his strength comparable only to that of the insane, slammed hard into the man with his shoulder, aiming for the lower back and ramming the man against the door hard. There was a crunching sound as the man's spine dislocated, and the Indian's hand was quickly over the man's mouth as he tried to scream out in his pain. He bent the man farther back before the man could get any kind of fighting stance, folding the man in half and breaking the spine, first at the neck and then at the lower spot where he had first dislocated the back.

The Indian stepped back and let the man fall to the floor, while the man he had kicked in the ribs stared in disbelief, still on the floor.

At the house Joe looked out at the bunk house in the distance, thinking he had heard some kind of scuffle. But it was not unusual for the men to get into fights. It had happened before, usually over gambling debts or women. This time it was probably an argument over who had been dumb enough to let the Indians sneak up on the ranch. Joe just grinned and shook his head. He puffed his pipe more and paid no attention.

Inside the bunkhouse the fourth man lay with his throat cut. Zeke moved to a back door, opening it to let in Wolf's Blood. "Take a look," he told the boy. "Any of them the ones who took your mother?"

Wolf's Blood studied the bloody, broken bodies, on fire with pride at his father's strength.

"No, sir," the boy finally replied. He met his father's fierce eyes, seeing now what the man must have been like when he went after the men who had killed his first wife in Tennessee. "When do I get my turn, Father?"

"Soon as we find the right ones—and Garvey," Zeke replied. "Stay in the shadows. We already got the two outside. I'm going to check around the house now. When I give the signal, you come. There's a lamp on down on the first floor. My bet is it's Garvey's study. It won't be long now, son. By tomorrow we will have found your mother."

They ducked through the back door and made their way toward the main house. Joe stood on the veranda smoking his pipe, still noticing nothing unusual. A horse whinnied in the distance and he stood straighter, then moved to the railing of the veranda and tapped out his pipe, knocking the small embers into the dirt beneath the railing and shoving the pipe back into his pocket. He stared into the darkness, trying to see something. All was quiet now at the bunkhouse. Apparently the minor scuffle had ended. But now everything seemed too quiet. He told himself he was just spooked from the raid. Indians always rode in bunches. They had got what they came for: the horses. He chided himself for feeling so uneasy. He had lived in this land for a lot of years, knew how the Indians usually conducted a raid. Yet there was something strange about this one, and the more he thought about it, the more he wondered. Indians seldom ventured out at night—something about evil spirits. So why had these Indians chosen the night, and why this place, so far from their normal stomping grounds? He started to reach for his rifle, then heard a board creak behind him. He turned to say something to Buel, who he thought had come outside, but he stared dumbfounded into the face of an Indian, a wild-eyed, powerful-looking man who was painted for war. He opened his mouth to call out to Buel, but his voice was cut off by a huge blade that slashed across his throat. The man no longer had to wonder what was different about this night.

Zeke caught Joe's body before it could hit the veranda floor and make any noise. He dragged it into the shadows, then crept to the window where he had seen the light. His heart exploded with rage and vengeance when he saw Winston Garvey sitting at his desk, and a badly scarred man sitting across from him. The scarred man! Surely he was one of those who had taken Abbie!

Zeke moved back into the shadows and gave out a soft hoot. A moment later Wolf's Blood was at his side. The boy knew by his father's eyes that the man he wanted was inside. The boy gripped his own knife, but Zeke held up a finger, warning him not to move too quickly. Zeke motioned for the boy to follow him around the back side of the house.

"I don't want to kill them inside the house," he told his son quietly. "We could end up leaving some kind of evidence. I want them out of the house and in my own territory—out in the open. Do as I say. You'll get your turn with the scarred one."

The boy nodded. Zeke removed his rifle from where it was slung around his shoulder. "I'm going to find a way in the back side," he whispered. "You go back around to the window. When I get inside the room, come through the window. The maid won't be here tonight. It's down to just Garvey and the scarred one. We have to get them out of there quickly now, before some of the men start coming back." He cocked his rifle. "Remember, Wolf's Blood, if anything goes wrong, never hesitate. Hesitating can cost you your life. Let the other man hesitate. Always follow your instincts. You have good instincts and you're fast."

The boy's eyes glittered. "I am ready!" he whispered back. "I will not forget how that man touched my mother!" Their eyes held for a moment in the moonlight, both feeling the same fear that Abbie might not even be alive any more. Zeke pushed the horrible thought to the back of his mind and turned away, heading along the back of the house and looking for an open window. Wolf's Blood moved back around to the front window, where Winston Garvey sat lighting another cigar.

"I suppose we'll have to start feeding the bitch if we want her to live," Garvey was telling Buel.

"What if she needs a doctor?" Buel replied. "How do you explain that?"

"I'll think of something," Garvey answered. "All men can be paid off one way or another, even doctors."

"I'll say one thing—the woman's a stubborn bitch. I figured she'd have talked a long time ago. I can't figure it. I think even I would have talked under her circumstances."

Garvey rose. "I think it's time we saw about getting hold of one or two of the children. The father just might have got himself killed in that war. If he did, I'm back to zero without a way to make that woman talk. She'll have to see one of her children in pain. Trouble is, we'd have to get them out of the hands of the Cheyenne. I could always come down on them with the new law they're trying to get through mandating that all Indian children must be shipped off to white schools to be educated. That could be my excuse. I'd just send in some soldiers and haul a couple of them away.''

''When we was spyin' on them, before we attacked, we saw a couple of older daughters that would make your mouth water, Mister Garvey. You grab one of them and tell that woman you'll make prostitutes out of them, and I'll bet you she'll talk. Let me and Handy break in one of the little girls under the woman's nose. She'd tell you quick enough whatever it is you want to know. If the man is dead, she's totally helpless, and so are the children. We have free rein with them. And I can tell you I wouldn't mind my turn at either one of them older daughters.''

Garvey chuckled. ''That doesn't sound bad to me either. Maybe we can—''

His words were cut off when the door to the study suddenly burst open. Buel whirled, going for his gun, but he hesitated when he saw the big Indian standing there with the rifle.

''I wouldn't make a move!'' Zeke growled.

Garvey paled to a white that almost matched his white shirt. He sat speechless, his throat constricting as though someone had just poured sand into it. He stared in disbelief at the huge, painted Indian, who stood before them nearly naked except for moccasins and a loincloth, his bronze body striped in war colors, his nearly waist-length hair hanging loose and wild. Zeke's fiery eyes moved to Garvey.

''It's been a long time, Senator,'' he hissed. ''I

406

should have killed you nine years ago in Santa Fe, but I didn't have the advantage then. Now I do, and this will be a very exciting night for all of us.''

Garvey's face was already drenched with sweat. He put a hand to his throat, opening the top button of his shirt so he could breathe better, and Zeke hoped the fat man wouldn't die of a heart attack from shock before he got the information he needed.

''Relax, Senator,'' he said with a smile. ''You have a few more minutes to live. Maybe even an hour.''

The senator whirled his chair, thinking perhaps he would have time to dive out the window. Buel went for his gun then and Zeke swung the rifle, ramming its butt into the man's chest and knocking him to the floor. He aimed the rifle at the man while Garvey remained in his chair, never getting the chance to try to duck out of the window. He had been greeted by a young Indian buck who held out a huge, menacing blade. The senator had no place to turn. Wolf's Blood came through the window and glanced at his father.

''Get that gun off, mister!'' Zeke growled to Buel. ''Throw it aside and let's get going. We're taking a little trip—the four of us!''

''How did you . . . get in here?'' Garvey finally managed to choke out. ''Where are my men?''

Buel groaned as he got to his feet, holding his side where he was sure some ribs were cracked.

''Half your men are out chasing the Indians,'' Zeke replied. ''I had to figure out some way to lead them away from here, and it worked. The other half of your men are dead. When they're discovered, the authorities will simply think it was an Indian raid. I don't like risking my people getting in trouble, but there was no other way.''

Garvey's eyes turned to slits of hatred. ''I knew there was something strange about that raid. You half-breed son of a bitch! You'll not get a word out of me!''

Zeke only grinned, the evil in his eyes chilling Garvey, who suddenly wondered if this man could perhaps be more ruthless than himself. "What a fool you are, Garvey!" Zeke sneered. "None of this had to happen."

"You underestimate my power, Zeke Monroe!" Garvey tried to bluff, standing straighter. "You'll never get away with this. And don't forget that Anna Gale knows about you and me. She can make a lot of trouble for you."

Zeke stepped closer, while Wolf's Blood moved to hold his knife on Buel, anxious now to spill the man's blood.

"I have already seen Anna," Zeke told Garvey with a grin. "She is the one who helped me find your place and told me what to expect. She looks forward to your death." He laid the tip of his rifle barrel under Garvey's nose. "You are the one who misjudged, Senator," he sneered. "You are the one who underestimated things. I have a power of my own, and it does not involve money or my station in life. It is my own power—the power from within, the power that can master all odds, even men like Winston Garvey. Now start walking! We will leave the house nice and tidy —no blood, nothing broken. Your men left some horses mounted outside. We will ride to a place where my son and I have our own mounts waiting. Then we are going to take a little ride through Cash Creek so that our trail disappears. And then you will tell me, my fat senator, what you have done with my woman. And once you are dead, I will make sure your body is never found, and people will always wonder whatever happened to the fine Senator Winston Garvey, the prominent, respectable citizen of this new Colorado. And there will be no one to connect you with me, because even the men who helped capture my wife do not know she was brought to you. And the only two men who do know will be dead. You have caught yourself in your own trap, Senator!"

"Have I?" the senator replied, reminding himself of who he was and telling himself he should not be afraid. Surely it was a bluff that all his men were dead. Surely someone would come and save him. "And why should I tell you where your wife is? It will only mean my certain death. You need me alive to find her, you stinking half-breed! Threatening to kill me does you no good!"

Zeke punched his rifle barrel into Garvey's belly, knocking the man back into his leather chair. He moved the rifle to his left hand and whipped out his knife, laying the big blade against Garvey's cheek just under his eye.

"I did not say you could live or die, my friend," he sneered. "If you choose not to tell me, you have that right. But it will not mean that you will live. I will tell you your choice, Senator. Your choice is whether or not you want to die quickly by telling me right away—" he lightly nicked a tiny cut under the man's eye so that it stung, and Garvey swallowed— "or slowly." Zeke lowered the knife and shoved it back into its sheath, then took up his rifle and put it under Garvey's chin, pushing upward so that the man was forced to rise. "Now move, fat man! My thirst for your blood burns hot in my mouth." He motioned for the man to move toward the door, and Wolf's Blood, who stood grinning at Buel, waved his knife in the same direction, signaling the man to follow Garvey.

They exited the study of the prominent ex-senator, moving through the hallway to the front door. With every step the senator felt his legs getting weaker and heavier, his breathing becoming labored. Could it possibly be true that there were no men to help him? Was this really happening? It could not be. He was Winston Garvey. Half of Colorado knew who he was. Men in Washington knew who he was. And Charles! What about Charles! What would the boy do without his father? He was not ready yet to be on his own. He stopped at the steps of the veranda, gasping at the sight of Joe lying with his throat slit. The reality of the moment was beginning to sink in. He grasped a post for support, feeling faint.

"Look, Monroe," the man spoke up. "Listen to me. I—I'll tell you where she is, if you just let me go. I know that isn't enough . . . but I can make it up to you. I can make you a rich man. You name the price and it's yours. I—I admit I shouldn't have done it. But . . . why can't we just make an exchange? You tell me about the boy, and I'll tell you where your wife is, and we'll call it quits. And I will hand you whatever sum of money you name. You'll never be a rich man, Monroe. You have a big family. I can give you enough money to support them the rest of your life."

Zeke smiled. "How touching," he said coldly. "But there is no amount of money that could make up for what you've done, Garvey! I am the one who paid the price—and my Abbie! Now you shall pay, but not in dollars, my friend. No. The price will be higher than all the money you can get your hands on. Now mount up!"

Garvey swallowed back tears of fear then, making his way down the steps in shear agony, enveloped with fear. Buel followed toward the horses tied at a hitching post near the bunkhouse. They reached the horses, and Buel kept holding his side, turning to look at Zeke when he reached his horse.

"Wait," the man spoke up. "I don't want to die! I can tell you where the woman is."

"Shut up, Buel!" Garvey ordered. "Don't tell the

half-breed scum anything! He means to kill us either way, you fool!''

''Then I don't aim to die slow!'' Buel shot back, his voice beginning to squeak from fear. ''Don't you know the Indian ways? Do you really want to die that way?'' His breathing was coming in short gasps then. ''Dead Canyon—north of the ranch,'' the man said quickly. ''There's an old mine shaft up there. She's inside it.''

Zeke grinned. ''How easily cowards talk!'' he sneered.

''He's lying!'' Garvey growled. ''He's just trying to get out of this.''

Zeke suddenly kicked Garvey between the legs and the man crumpled. ''We shall soon learn what is the truth!'' he hissed. He slung his rifle over his shoulder and bent down, jerking the man up, surprising Buel with his strength, for Garvey was a hefty man. The senator groaned and held himself between the legs, feeling faint from the pain. He heard someone ordering him to mount up, but he couldn't make his legs work. ''Mount up or I'll drag you out of here!'' Zeke ordered.

Garvey grasped the saddle horn and got one foot in a stirrup, then cried out from pain again. Zeke pushed him up but Garvey could not get his right leg over the saddle. He lay flat over the horse, clinging to the saddle horn. Zeke quickly removed the rope from the saddle gear and began looping it around Garvey's ankles.

''What are . . . you doing?'' Garvey moaned.

''I'm tired of dallying with you, Garvey,'' Zeke replied. He ducked under the horse and came up on the other side, jerking Garvey around so that he was completely sideways bent over the horse. He began tying the other end of the rope to Garvey's wrists and shoulders, pulling tight.

''No!'' Garvey begged. ''I can't ride this way. My God, all the blood is going to my head! My stomach! It's smashing my stomach! I can't breathe this way!''

"You touch my heart, Garvey," Zeke sneered.

"Mount up!" Wolf's Blood was ordering Buel. "For the next few hours you will regret you ever touched my mother."

Buel wished he had killed the boy the day of the raid, but his orders were to harm none of the children. That had been a foolish order. Now it was too late. He had to think and think fast.

"It's too dark!" he protested. "We can't ride through Cash Creek at night time."

"Don't you know that Indians can see in the dark?" Wolf's Blood sneered. "Now get on your horse!"

Buel obliged, his only hope now that Handy might somehow see them. But Handy was at the cave, and it wasn't likely he would leave it. Their orders were to stay at the cave when it was their turn and not leave it. But surely something would happen to help them. To fight now would mean certain death. He would ride. At least that meant a few more minutes or hours of life, and as long as he was alive, there was hope. He mounted up, and Wolf's Blood quickly began tying the man's wrists to the saddle pommel.

"Let's go!" Zeke told his son. "Some of those men might start coming back."

Wolf's Blood nodded, taking Buel's horse by the reins, as Zeke did with Garvey's horse. They led the animals away from the ranch, and the great stone house sat empty, all its comforts and fine furnishings of no help to Winston Garvey. For he had dared to challenge Zeke Monroe.

Twenty-Six

They made their way along Cash Creek, four men alone in the early dawn, with nothing but the wolves and the eagles to know that they were there. When they had followed the creek long enough that Zeke was sure their trail would be hidden, he brought the horses to a halt and dismounted. He walked back to Garvey's mount and began slicing the big blade through the ropes that held the man on the horse. He shoved Garvey's body off the horse and it fell with a splash into the creek. The man groaned and drank some of the water, rolling to his back so that he could finally breathe better. Zeke nodded toward Wolf's Blood to untie Buel's wrists and let the man down, while he himself began looping his rope around Garvey under the man's shoulders.

"What . . . what are you doing?" Garvey asked weakly. Zeke tightened the rope and deftly ripped open the man's shirt, slicing off the material quickly with his knife, then continuing down, removing all clothing so that the man was completely naked. Wolf's Blood followed suit, his young heart on fire for revenge after hearing how these men had talked about his mother in the study when he was outside the window.

"What are you going to do?" Garvey screamed this

413

time, as Zeke tied his end of the rope to his horse. Still Zeke did not reply. He looked at his son.

"Keep the clothes. We will burn them later. Leave nothing, Wolf's Blood. We want no signs left. We must make certain nothing is found."

"*Ai,* Father."

Buel panicked. He would rather be shot than dragged! He shoved at Wolf's Blood and began running before the boy could tie the rope around his mount. Moments later a powerful man crashed into him, slamming him to the ground. Zeke quickly rolled the man over and kicked him hard between the legs, his thirst for vengeance beginning to consume him now in maniacal proportions. He grabbed the rope and dragged the screaming man back to Wolf's Blood's horse, tying the other end. He walked back to Garvey, who had started to cry. Zeke just stared down at him.

"How many times did she cry?" he hissed. "How many times did she beg you to leave her alone and take her home? You made a foolish choice, Garvey. You should never have touched my woman, or any member of my family. Now we are going for a little scenic ride. And when we are through, you will tell me if Buel is telling the truth that my wife is at Dead Canyon in a mine shaft. You will know great pain, Garvey. And you will tell me—beg me—to let you die quickly. My wife needs me. I do not have time to waste."

He mounted up, taking Garvey's horse beside him by the reins. "I hope my horse is strong enough to drag all your blubber!" Zeke shouted, a gleam in his eyes. He kicked the mount into a gentle run, and Wolf's Blood followed, dragging Buel behind him. The men screamed and struggled, trying to get to their feet. But Zeke and Wolf's Blood rode just fast enough that it was impossible to get up and run. Dawn was just beginning to show its light then, and Zeke chose the rockiest part of the land over which to ride, deliberately searching out small cacti that grew close to the ground.

The screams of Garvey and Buel were music to his ears, and he rode faster, caught up then in the glory of revenge. He kept an eye on the bodies, not wanting to go so far that the men might die before they could talk. After a mile or so he stopped, dismounting and looking down at Garvey's shredded skin and badly bleeding body. He kicked the fat man over onto his back.

"Where is my wife?" he growled.

"You stinking . . . bloodthirsty half-breed," Garvey groaned. Zeke just grinned and bent close, removing his knife.

"You may choose to tell or not to tell. I am good at prolonging death, Senator. How long you choose to lie here and suffer is your decision." He laid the knife against the man's face. "Which shall I take first, Senator, your eyes or your privates?"

The senator's eyes widened more. In his sedate, pampered life, he had not considered that a man could do such bloody, vile things. But then this man was Indian. Blood and violence were as natural to him as breathing. "You'll never . . . get away with it!" he tried to argue. "You'll be hung! My . . . son . . . will find you and have you hung!"

Zeke just grinned. "No one will ever know what happened to you, Garvey," he sneered. "And I doubt your bastard son will even care. With you dead, he owns the empire. But I will at least have my woman back." He traced the knife lightly down over Garvey's cheek and chest, just enough to make a sting. Garvey began shaking violently as the knife wandered toward his privates. "You raped my wife, Garvey!" Zeke hissed. "So we both know what I will take first from you!"

"No! No, wait!" the man screamed, starting to kick. But Zeke straddled the man, sitting on his legs just long

415

enough to grab the man and whack off everything that made him a man. He laid the organs on the man's chest. Garvey's groans and weeping only made him smile.

"How long shall we continue, Garvey?" he asked. "Your eyes are next, my friend. Then your fingers— one at a time."

"Dead . . . Canyon!" the man wept. "Buel . . . told you . . . the truth. Oh, God, finish me! Finish me if that's what you . . . intend to do!"

Zeke just smiled. "You can lie there and look at your own privates, Senator, and think about how good life might have been for you if you had never touched my woman." He walked back to Wolf's Blood and Buel. Buel tried to scramble to his feet, his eyes wide and frightened over what had just happened to Garvey. His body was badly torn and bloody. The man crawled away from Zeke and Wolf's Blood, but he could only go so far before the rope stopped him. "It's your turn, Buel," Zeke told the man. "Who else is at the canyon? Is there a guard?"

The man crouched on his knees, his breathing quick and frightened, his eyes wide. "Yes!" he replied in a squeaking voice. "Just one man—Handy! That's all, I swear! The mine shaft . . . is about a mile into the canyon . . . on the north side! Please . . . let me go! Please!"

"You raped her, too, didn't you?" Zeke growled.

"N-no!" the man replied. "Please! I swear . . . I didn't touch her!"

Zeke just walked over and kicked the man in the jaw, sending him sprawling. He grabbed the man's ankles, and in his broken, torn condition, Buel was too weak to fight back. He lay there dizzy and filled with horrible pain. Zeke looked at Wolf's Blood. "He raped your mother," was all he said.

The boy's eyes glittered as he pulled his own bowie

416

knife and walked over to Buel.

"No! He's . . . just a kid!" Buel protested. "He . . . wouldn't . . . ."

Wolf's Blood reached down and sliced at the man, then stood up and held the organs in the air while Buel lay screaming and crying. At that moment, the boy never felt more savage or more victorious. This was proper punishment for what they had done to his mother. The whites would not have punished these men at all. White man's justice made no sense to an Indian. An Indian had to deal out his own justice. He turned to his father with gleaming eyes.

"Do what you want with him, son," was all Zeke told him. "Let him suffer first. There are many ways with the knife that can bring pain but not death. I will take care of Garvey." He looked around the maze of boulders and rocky crevices into which they had ridden, at the base of the towering Rockies. "We'll bury the bodies deep and roll boulders over them. We'll burn the clothing so that if the bodies are found there will be no clothing on them to help identify who they might be. Then we'll find your mother." He turned and Wolf's Blood called out to him.

"I heard them say she was sick, Father," the boy told him. "We have to find her quickly now. She might be dying."

Zeke nodded and turned to walk back to Garvey, knife in hand. Screams of agony could be heard out of both men, who lay at the mercy of men who dealt their own form of justice. But there was no one to hear—nothing but the eagle and the coyote and the jack rabbit. But the animals were kin in spirit to the Indian. They would not tell.

It turned out to be a warm day. Birds sang and wildflowers bloomed everywhere. It was difficult to imagine that in a mine shaft someplace amid this beautiful canyon there lay a woman beaten and raped and dying. Zeke and Wolf's Blood had led Garvey's and Buel's horses with them until they were a great distance from the site of the two men's deaths. They had turned the horses loose then, not far from Garvey's own ranch. By the time the animals wandered home or to someone else's ranch or were found by Indians, there would be nothing left but for people to wonder what had happened to the men who rode them. The third man at the mine shaft would be buried deep in the shaft once they finished with him, and the three men would never be found or heard from again.

Zeke's heart pounded now with anticipation. It mattered little to him that other men had touched his wife. She was still his Abbie. He would hold her and hold her forever, until she learned to forget the horror the three men had inflicted on her. He would make her forget. He must make her forget and reclaim her for himself. His body raged with a need to be one with his woman again, to take back that which belonged to Zeke Monroe, to lie beside her and know that she was alive and they were together again!

But he knew Abbie. It would be a long time before she could be a wife to him again in that way. But he would be patient and move slowly. First there would have to be a physical healing. Yet no matter how badly she might be injured or how sick she might be, he knew the physical healing would be easier than the emotional and mental healing. That was the healing he worried about. Abbie! Poor, sweet, beautiful Abbie! His mind reeled with the reality of it. The very thing he had feared might happen to her just because she was his wife had happened. Memories of Ellen spun around in his mind. Would he find Abbie dead also? How would he live after that?

He stopped Wolf's Blood not far from the place where he thought the shaft should be. "Tie your mount and we'll go in on foot," he told the boy. "We'll climb up the ridge of the canyon here and search from above."

The two of them dismounted and began making their way quietly through rocks and coarse bushes, climbing and moving like mountain goats, their dark skin and buckskin clothing matching their surroundings so that they were difficult to spot. They ran along the top of the ridge for several hundred yards until finally they spotted a horse tied below. From their vantage point, they could not see the shaft entrance several hundred feet below them, but the horse told them they were at the right place. Zeke motioned for Wolf's Blood to follow him down until they finally spotted the entrance. Wolf's Blood started forward, but Zeke grabbed his arm and shook his head.

"Let him come out first," he whispered. "If we trap him inside, he might shoot Abbie out of meanness."

Wolf's Blood nodded and Zeke picked up a large rock and threw it, trying to make a noise outside the entrance and arouse the man inside. The man's horse whinnied and father and son crouched and waited.

"That you, Buel?" a voice called out. "Where in hell have you been? I'm gettin' tired of watchin' this smelly bitch!"

Zeke motioned to Wolf's Blood to get his knife ready, pointing to the boy that the kill was his. There must be no sound. A gunshot in a canyon could echo for miles. So far everything had been done silently, and this must also be done silently.

Wolf's Blood pulled out his big knife, realizing he must be accurate the first time, or the man might turn and shoot. His young heart pounded with glorious revenge and the joy of showing his father what he had learned.

"Buel?" came the voice again. A man finally emerged from the shaft, a man whose face was caved in on one side, the remains of what Zeke Monroe had done to him the year before in Kansas. Wolf's Blood rose and let out an Indian war cry. Handy turned at the sound, and in the next moment a huge blade pierced the man's heart, square in the middle of his chest. Handy fell backward and it was over.

"Good work!" Zeke told the boy. "Go back and get the horses. Use his horse to go. No sense walking back." They moved down to the shaft entrance and Wolf's Blood started to go inside to his mother. Zeke grabbed his arm. "Wait," he said, the pain now beginning to show on his face. "Let me go. You stay out unless I call you to come in. Just go get the horses, Wolf's Blood." The boy glanced at the cave entrance, then back to his father, realizing the agony his father must be suffering now. He nodded and bent down to yank his knife from the dead man's body, then went to Handy's horse and mounted up.

Zeke glanced around to be sure no one was about, then dragged Handy's body just inside the shaft entrance so that it would not be lying out in the open. Then he walked farther back into the shaft.

There was no sound, save the quiet dripping of water here and there. He picked up a lantern that Handy had left so that he could see his way through the dark cavern, his heart already screaming at the thought of poor Abbie lying in this dark, damp shaft for weeks.

"Abbie?" he called out. There was no reply. He kept walking, searching with the lantern. Finally he thought he heard a raspy breathing. "Abbie-girl?" he called out again. Someone coughed, a deep, ominous cough that bespoke sickness, perhaps pneumonia. He ran toward the sound until finally the lantern shed its

420

light on a soiled mattress and a woman's naked body lying tied to stakes. His eyes widened, and at first he had to turn around and struggle to keep his composure. What he had seen could not be his Abbie. What he had seen was more like a skeleton, white skin on bones, sunken eyes, a bruised body lying in its own waste, the beautiful hair tangled and stringy. He threw his head back and breathed deeply for control, begging the spirits to give him the strength he would need now for her. The horrible pain was in his chest again, and his breathing was labored.

He set the lamp down and turned back around, a groan exiting his lips from somewhere deep in his soul. He went to his knees, bending over her and touching her bony face. "Abbie-girl!" he whispered. At first there was no reply, and she seemed dead. He whipped out his knife and quickly cut the leather cords that held her, gently kissing each wrist and ankle and lightly massaging them to get the circulation going. He looked around and saw a blanket hanging from a peg nearby. He quickly ripped it down and threw it over her. Then he noticed the little music box and his shirt lying beside her. His heart wrenched with pain. She must have brought the things with her when they first took her, faithfully believing her husband would come for her. He leaned over her and carefully wrapped the blanket around her, not caring about her soiled condition or the way she looked—not caring about anything but that it was his Abbie and at least she was still alive. And deep down beneath his initial remorse and horror lay a secret pride that his Abbie-girl was still the stubborn, strong woman he had married. She had suffered all of this and had never told Winston Garvey where his half-breed son could be found.

"Abbie! My Abbie!" he groaned, pulling her frail body into his arms. So small! Surely she was even smaller than the fifteen-year-old girl he had fallen in love with so many years ago! "Don't you die on me, Abbie-girl," he whispered. He held her close, sitting on his knees and rocking her gently. He kissed her cheek, her eyes, cradling her in one arm while he smoothed back her hair with his other hand. She was hot and damp in spite of the cold shaft, and fear gripped him. Her body convulsed and she began coughing, a deep, dangerous cough that shook her whole body. He held her tightly until it was over, and the coughing seemed to rouse her.

She cried out and pushed at him then, a weak, futile effort, no strength in her movements, just fear and a lingering stubborn pride. Her blanket started falling away and he grasped her arms tightly, wrapping the blanket around her again and holding her tight against himself as she let out a pitiful wail of surrender.

"It's all right, Abbie. It's over. I'm here. Zeke's here and we're going home to the children."

She heard the words somewhere in the distance. Surely she had finally died and now Zeke's spirit called to her. Perhaps he was dead also. Yes, she must be dead and perhaps in heaven, for she was warm, and someone was holding her gently, not beating her or doing vile things to her. She began to relax, and her breath came in choking sobs. "Zeke," she whimpered. "Where . . . are you? I . . . can't . . . see you."

"I'm right here, Abbie. It's all right now. We're going home."

The words sounded closer now, and when she breathed the scent was familiar, the smell of the earth and leather, the light scent of sweet sage that he sometimes rubbed through his soft, clean hair or that got on his moccasins when he walked in it. Now it all began to become more clear to her. Zeke! Could she truly be alive, and could he truly be here, holding her in his arms?

She forced her eyes to open. She was still in the hated cave, but she was warm, and someone was holding her. The long, soft hair was against her lips.

"Zeke! Zeke!" she whimpered then. "Oh God, it's you! Sweet Jesus! Oh, thank God!" The words came out in gasps and she started coughing again. He held her tightly while the terrible coughing gripped her, his heart crying out for her, his throat aching with a need to weep.

"Hang on, Abbie. Don't talk any more," he told her, pulling her back into his arms. "I'm taking you home and making you well."

The horror of it hit her as she became more alert, roused now from the hopeless stupor she had allowed herself to fall into, her body's own way of protecting her from the reality of her condition and the rapes. But now he was here, and in spite of her joy at his presence, the awfulness of what had happened to her made her wish she was dead. How would her husband feel about her now? How could anything ever be right between them again? And she could smell her own soiled condition, realizing she had not been bathed since being brought to the mine shaft; lately she hadn't even been untied to go to the bathroom. Yet Zeke was holding her, even kissing her face now, her hair, her eyes.

"Let me . . . go," she whimpered. "Don't look . . . at me. Leave me here . . . to die."

"Don't talk foolish, Abbie-girl," he told her gently. "We're going home. Don't you want to see the children again? They're all waiting for you, Abbie. All of them. They want their mother back."

She choked in a sob and met his eyes for the first time. How beautiful he looked! How utterly savage and handsome. She did not have to ask how he had found her or managed to get to her. She knew her husband,

and she knew instinctively that Winston Garvey must be dead, as well as the two men who had kept her captive in the shaft. There would be time for explanations later. So much to talk about! So much! Where had he been? What had happened to him back East? That didn't matter now. He was here! He had come just like she knew he would come. How wonderful he looked! Zeke! Her Zeke! And yet . . .

A terrible shame filled her eyes as she looked at him, mixed with a strange panic. "I'm not . . . just yours . . . anymore," she whispered. His grip on her tightened.

"Don't ever say that again," he told her. "You're too sick to even worry about that now. We'll talk about it, Abbie. When it's time." He put a hand to the side of her face. "You remember one thing and one thing only while you are healing, Abigail Monroe! I was your first man, I am the only man to whom you have ever willingly surrendered. To them your body was just a thing. They never truly touched you at all."

Tears spilled down the sides of her face and into her ears, and she broke into pitiful sobbing, a terrible, moaning wail that racked her body painfully, the kind of tears that came from the deepest fathoms of the soul; and if cutting out his own heart would change what had happened to her, he would do it.

He reached over and picked up the music box and his shirt, then lifted her in his arms. "Let's go out into the sunshine, Abbie. That's all you need. Just the warmth of the hot sun on your skin and fresh air." He kissed her hair. "Stop your crying now, Abbie-girl. You need your strength, baby. Don't let them win by making you cry this way. Come on. Wolf's Blood is on his way back with the horses. It's all right now. Everything is all right."

"No! Don't let . . . him see me this way!" she wept.

"Don't you worry about that. We'll get you away from this damned place and then I'll clean you all up, Abbie-girl. I brought all the things I need. I brought soaps and creams and a nice clean flannel gown. We'll fix up a travois and we'll go find a nice, clean stream where I'll get you all cleaned up. And I have liniment and some laudanum. We'll doctor you ourselves, and once you get some sun and fresh air you'll start feeling better. You'll see. We'll go home and we'll all be to-gether again."

She was too weakened to argue any further. She tried to stop the crying, but the tears just kept coming. She nestled her head on his shoulder, breathing in the scent that was Zeke Monroe, allowing herself to glory in the strength of his arms. Zeke! He was truly here, holding her, talking to her. Surely she could never be a proper wife to him again. But for now she would just be glad that he was here and that the war in the East had not claimed him. Whether or not they could overcome the horror of the things that had torn into their great love while he was gone was yet to be discovered. For now she must cherish the moment, and she must cling to life for the sake of her children. Even if he never wanted her again, she must think about the children. The children!

Soon she felt the wonderful warmth on her face, smelled the sweet, clean air.

"Father!" she heard Wolf's Blood calling. Wolf's Blood! The last she had seen of him was when Handy had hit her son over the head before they rode off with her. How long ago was that? Two months at least. But she had lost all track of time, lying in the shaft with no idea whether or not the sun was out. She had often wondered if her eldest son had been killed that day. Now she could hear his voice. How she wanted to look at him! To hold him! Yet in her shame and her misera-ble condition, she could not bring herself to even turn her head from Zeke's shoulder to look at her son.

"Mother!" she heard him saying then, standing close. She felt his hand on her hair and she cringed, curling up more into Zeke's arms.

Zeke met his son's horrified look, seeing that the boy could hardly believe that the skeletal woman with the gnarled hair that he held could truly be his mother. The boy turned away and made a strange choking sound.

"Get rid of the body inside the mine shaft, Wolf's Blood," Abbie heard Zeke saying. "Let's get the hell out of here and find a decent place where I can bathe your mother and get her settled onto a travois. I'll ride with her in my arms until we find a place."

Wolf's Blood only nodded, then went into the shaft. Zeke sat down on a large, flat boulder, cradling Abbie in his arm and letting her head rest in the crook of his arm so that the sun shone down on it. Beneath the dirty, sunken face and tangled hair, he saw his Abbie was still there, that her beauty would return with her recovery and the pounds he would put back on her bones by making her eat. She opened her eyes and met his again, seeing the little boy she always saw when he thought something that had happened to her was his fault.

"My Zeke," she said lovingly. "You're alive." Her eyes pained. "How I . . . must look! I'm so ashamed . . . that you should come home and . . . see me this way." The tears started coming again, and he gently brushed them away with his fingers.

"You're the most beautiful thing I've ever seen," he told her. "You've never looked prettier, Abbie-girl." He closed his eyes and pulled her close again, hugging her as tightly as he dared. "Abbie, God I love you, Abbie! I missed you so! When I came home and learned they had taken you . . ." He rubbed his cheek against her face and hair. "I've been half crazy ever since. I never should have left. I never, never should have left! Why do I always leave you? God, forgive me, Abbie."

"I told you to go," she whispered. "Tell me . . . you saw him . . . your father," she added, growing weaker again. "Tell me, Zeke. Please tell me you saw him."

He broke into his own quiet tears. He would not tell her all of it yet. It would be too much. "I saw him. It's all right, Abbie-girl. And I found Danny and took him home to the farm."

"I'm . . . glad," she whispered. "Now if only . . . you and I . . . can be husband and wife again. But I . . . can't . . . and you won't . . . want me . . . even if I could."

He rubbed his cheek against her own, their tears mixing. "How wrong you are, Abbie! I've never stopped wanting you from the moment I first saw you. And I want you now, more than I have ever wanted you."

Twenty-Seven

There followed days and weeks of fever and fear of death, and the initial worry over living at all helped buffer Abigail Monroe's deeper, unseen injuries. For weeks she knew nothing but terrible nightmares in her sleeping hours and spells of dangerous coughing in her waking moments. But each time he was there— her Zeke—holding her, soothing her, ever patient, ever gentle.

A lamp was kept constantly lit so she would not awaken to darkness and think she was back in the cave. Once when it went out and Abbie woke up screaming, Zeke scolded Margaret so harshly that he made the girl cry and later had to apologize to her.

They were tense weeks, the joy of having both mother and father back dampened by fear of Abbie's illness and the shadow of her mental state. Their immediate fears were accompanied by a deeper, unspoken fear—that somehow someone would trace the raid on the Garvey ranch to Zeke Monroe and his son. The newspaper in Denver spewed out bold headlines for days and weeks about the disappearance of Winston Garvey and two of his men. There seemed to be no valid link between their disappearance and the Indian raid, and no particular Indian settlement could be blamed, with any tangible proof, for the raid on the ranch, except that the arrows found in Garvey men were Cheyenne. Yet no Cheyenne seemed to have any idea about the raid, nor were any Garvey horses found in any Cheyenne camp.

After several weeks the excitement and rumors dwindled, and Charles Garvey came home to take over his empire, not nearly as upset over his father's disappearance as some thought he might be. It was generally accepted that Winston Garvey must be dead, but no bodies were found.

Soon thereafter, trouble began to explode with the Northern Cheyenne and the Sioux again in the North, and people began to forget about Winston Garvey. Some of the Indian raids were led by a Cheyenne warrior called Swift Arrow. The whites, and even the warriors who rode with Swift Arrow, would have been astonished to know that the warrior who led so many raids against white settlements was himself in love with a white woman, his raids in part a retaliation against whites who would harm one of their own for being a friend to the Indian. And when Zeke heard about the new raids to the north, he knew secretly that the ones led by Swift Arrow were his brother's way of drawing attention to the north, away from Zeke, until the speculation over Winston Garvey's disappearance settled to a less dangerous level. Zeke had found his white woman. Now she needed time to heal.

Through all the headlines and the raids, the Monroe family kept quietly to themselves, and no woman could have been more pampered and loved through a sickness than Abbie. Each child did his share of chores and took turns feeding his mother and doing everything he could for her. None of them showed one sign of shame or disrespect for what had happened to her, and the younger ones did not understand. They only knew that their mother was sick and the men who had taken her had hurt her.

Often Tall Grass Woman came to help with Abbie's care, fussing and clucking over the harm that had come to her good white woman friend. Her humorous attempts at speaking English and at trying to keep up a white woman's house helped Abbie through the painful memories; the love of her children, and Zeke's strong arms and gentle patience, gave her the strength she needed to hang on through the nightmares and the sickness. When the children or Tall Grass Woman brought her food, she ate more to please them and satisfy their worried hearts than because she had any appetite. But her motive for eating brought the same desired end. She began gaining back some weight as well as strength and color.

By mid-October Abbie was up and dressed, slowly taking over her motherly and wifely duties—save one. Zeke had not touched her sexually since bringing her home, but eventually his need to be a husband to her again and to reclaim her became so intense that he stopped coming to their bed when her nightmares finally began to leave her. To lie beside her just to hold her was impossible, and so he did not sleep with her at all, knowing that if he did so, he would want to make love to her, and she was not ready for such things. But his absence in the night and the business of just getting well and getting back to normal had kept them from talking about the one matter that most needed discussion, the one element of their marriage and their love that each needed from the other for strength.

Everything else had been discussed—the coming of the Confederate soldiers, Lance, and all the things that had happened to Zeke back East. Abbie's heart ached for him when he told what had happened to his father, but at least there had been a final reunion and the chance for Zeke Monroe to face his past and the reality of it. But when he had mentioned seeing Joshua, she had stiffened and paled.

"Don't ever tell Bonnie . . . about . . . about . . . what happened," she said quietly. "She must never know. She might feel badly about it."

"I think she should know," Zeke argued. "She should know the kind of woman you are—know that you allowed yourself to suffer to keep that boy's identity hidden."

Abbie shook her head, her breathing quickening. "No! If we . . . tell her . . . she might find out about . . . the other. I could never face her!"

"Face her!" Zeke exclaimed in astonishment. He reached out and touched her hand. "You can face anyone you want! You did nothing wrong, Abbie. Why should you have to worry about facing people?"

She shook her head, tears spilling down her cheeks. Zeke grasped her chin and forced her to look at him. "My woman doesn't go around hanging her head. Not my Abbie!" he almost growled. "The woman I married is proud and strong and honorable. She is Abigail Trent Monroe, and the only thing that could make me or our children ashamed of you is if you allow what those men did to come between us, Abbie, and let it destroy us and destroy you. Then all I went through to come for you will have been in vain."

He stood up then, taking her Bible from the mantle and shoving it into her lap. "You have not looked at that since I brought you home, Abigail. Before when you needed strength and help, you always turned to that book. It is not my religion, but it is yours, and I know you need it. I tell you now what I think of you. You are the most honorable woman I know or have ever known! You are that same, stubborn little girl I

431

married—that little girl who withstood the loss of her family and bravely asked me to end her little brother's life because he was dying a slow, terrible death. You are still the same Abbie who rode with me against outlaws to find her sister and who shot a Crow Indian and saved my life, then turned around and dug a bullet out of me. You're the same Abbie who came to live with a people she knew nothing about, and who bore all of her children alone on the plains with no doctor to help her, who nearly died in childbirth but fought to stay alive for her family." He knelt down and took her hands. "Now you must fight again, Abbie. You must overcome this terrible thing that has happened to you and be our Abbie again—and be my wife again. We have both known horror and things worse than death, Abbie. We survived, and we shall continue to survive. I love you more than my own life. And if you truly love me, Abbie, you will understand my own need to reclaim you—to remind you that you still belong to me and have never belonged to another. And there is only one way to do that!"

He had kissed her cheek and left her there, the Bible still in her lap. That had been in late October. Now it was nearly Christmas, and she had barely spoken to him in all that time. Zeke felt out of his mind with his need of her. It was over a year now since he had first left to go search for Danny. In all that time he had been unable to make love to his woman, and his desires made him feel crazy, so that he began being absent more than he was home, in spite of the fact that he adored her and wanted so much to help her. She had become like a closed door, and he had not tried to turn the lock, for fear he would frighten her and she would hate him. It had to be her decision. There was no other way.

He worked harder than ever, spending most of the autumn cutting and hauling wood and adding another room to the cabin so that the children would have a place to sit and study without being under their mother's feet in the kitchen. Any free time he had was spent riding, sometimes with Wolf's Blood, sometimes alone. The distance between mother and father had turned the initial household happiness at having their mother returned to a lingering pall over the entire family. Abbie's health and color continued to improve, but her spirit did not return, and there was little laughter in the house. Wolf's Blood continued to suffer a trace of guilt himself, and became more remote and difficult to talk to, often standing on the porch at night and listening to the wolves, pining for Smoke.

Christmas neared, and Abbie sat sewing a new pair of moccasins for her husband. He had always allowed her to celebrate her Christian holiday by baking and exchanging gifts, although they had never had a tree. But this Christmas of 1863 would be the most unhappy Christmas she had ever experienced. She looked up when Wolf's Blood came barging through the door.

"You would not believe where I have been!" the boy spoke up, shaking his head.

Abbie put down the sewing. "And where is that?" she asked, her eyes showing the same dull spiritless gaze the boy had grown accustomed to seeing.

"Out in the east pasture. Father and I went there to check on some horses that strayed over there, and there was this big, painted wagon stuck there where the ground had thawed some and mixed with the snow. The wagon was bright red, and two men drove it. When we went to help them, three ladies opened the door and looked out. It was a strange wagon—all enclosed like a house. The ladies were all white women, those painted kind like Anna Gale. Those silly women were so scared, and they all talked at once and laughed too much. It was funny to watch them." The boy snickered. "You should have seen the way they looked at father when he put his shoulder to their wagon and helped push. I never saw women act so silly. They gave father some whiskey. He is still over there with them. He told me to come and get some potatoes for the ladies. They are out of food."

Abbie looked away, her emotions awakened for the first time since her attack. Painted ladies! How long had it been since Zeke had had a woman? More than a year! Why had he sent Wolf's Blood back to the house? It was a good twenty-minute ride or better one way. It would leave plenty of time. She looked back at Wolf's Blood.

"Painted ladies?" she asked. "What were they doing out there?"

Wolf's Blood shrugged. "They got lost. Father told them which way to go. They are headed for Independence and strayed off the Santa Fe Trail in the snowstorm we had last night. They are going to keep going today now that Father has shown them the right direction. They want to get to Bent's Fort as soon as they can so they can rest up there and get supplies."

"I see," Abbie replied. She walked to a corner where she kept a crate of potatoes, taking out a dozen and putting them into her apron. She held the potatoes in the apron and told Wolf's Blood to get a gunny sack from the wooden cupboard in the corner of the room where she kept her pots and pans. He brought her the sack and she dumped the potatoes inside. She looked at Wolf's Blood. "Tell your father to . . . to please come back soon," she told the boy.

Wolf's Blood frowned. He had not even considered that his father would do anything wrong with the painted ladies, but he suddenly realized his mother thought that he might. "He is just helping them," he said, feeling awkward then. He sensed there had been

434

nothing between his mother and father since Abbie had come home, and now his mother reddened slightly. Perhaps it was good she knew about the painted ladies. She had a new look in her eyes, a new life he had not seen there in a long time. "I will send him right home," he told her. He felt compelled to lean down and kiss her cheek. "I think I should tell you, Mother, that . . . that Margaret and Jeremy and the others— and myself—we miss you. You are here with us, but you are not really here. We wish you could be the mother that lived here before those men came. Jason asked me this morning if you were ever going to smile again. It was then that I realized I don't remember seeing you smile since you came home. I wish you would smile, Mother. Just that much would gladden Father's heart."

He turned and went out the door. Abbie stared after him, then walked to the door and looked out at the children playing, listening to their squeals and laughter as they threw one another down in the snow. It was the first time they all seemed to be enjoying themselves in many months. Wolf's Blood mounted up and rode off toward the east pasture and Abbie watched after him. She fought the hot jealousy that the boy's news had stirred in her heart. So afraid! She was so afraid to lie beneath a man again—even Zeke. What if he didn't even truly want her any more? What if he secretly looked at her as a used woman, one that no longer belonged just to him?

Yet he had done nothing to make her think such a thing. On the contrary, he had been warm and gentle and constantly patient, his eyes showing love and need, two things she had pushed aside. They had been distant, but she knew it was her own fault. She had deliberately allowed the wall to build between them so that she would not have to face being a woman to him

435

again—would not have to make love again, even though somewhere in her own soul she wanted it just as much as Zeke did. Yet somehow her rape had left her feeling guilty, as though it was now wrong to enjoy sex with her own husband. How could the same act be so vile and ugly on the one hand, and so sweet and right on the other? Somehow she could no longer separate the two. It was all vile and ugly.

She looked out at the children again, and it suddenly hit her. The children! Her beautiful children! They had been conceived through making love to Zeke Monroe. He had planted his seed in her belly and the children had come forth—a product of their love, a beautiful result of their beautiful relationship. The children! What could be wrong and ugly about something that had produced her precious children? What could be wrong and ugly about giving the man she loved, the man who had so many times risked his life for her, pleasure in the arms of the woman that he in turn loved and needed? To deny him that right was to bring him continuous pain, for he needed emotional healing just as much as she did. What had happened to her had left scars on both of them. There was only one way to begin a healing of that wound, no matter how frightening and traumatic it might be. She had given up many things for her man and had braved many things to be with him. This was just one more.

It was like Zeke had said—if they went on this way, then Winston Garvey would win after all. She could not let Winston Garvey win. She was Abigail Trent Monroe. She was Jason Trent's daughter, the fiesty young girl who had come west with her family and met the man she would spend her life with. She had made that man promises that she was now breaking.

She looked off to the east, her heart burning, the thought of Zeke being out there with the prostitutes bringing on a jealousy that helped surmount her fears. After all, Zeke Monroe was a man, and a man had needs. And the fear of making love was mastered by the terrible jealousy at the thought of Zeke turning to another woman for the things his wife would not give him. Besides that, she had to face her own needs, and the fact that she would never be really strong again until she could absorb the strength she always found in her husband's arms. How she longed to feel them around her in the night again, to be held that way again! She knew why he had not held her much—knew how difficult it would be for him. He had stayed away from her out of respect, doing everything he could to help her but staying out of their bed at night.

She closed her eyes and swallowed back tears. "God help me!" she squeaked. "Just don't let me see shame in his eyes!"

It was an hour before Zeke and Wolf's Blood made it back again. Both father and son slowed their horses to a slow trot when they saw the unexpected sight. Abbie was playing in the snow with the children, and she was laughing as they buried her and washed her face. Father and son looked at each other in surprise and Wolf's Blood smiled.

Zeke rode closer then, dismounting and walking over to help Abbie up out of the snow. "You shouldn't be out here like this," he told her. "You'll be sick again, Abbie."

She just laughed. "I want to play with my children," she announced. "I haven't played with them and laughed with them since . . ." She looked away and shook snow from her elkskin coat. She breathed deeply, fighting the terrible fear. Now that he stood so near—so tall and strong, so much man—she was afraid again. She looked back up at him, tears in her eyes but a smile on her lips. "Zeke, I want a tree."

He frowned. "A what?"

"A tree. You know, a Christmas tree. Some kind of pine tree. Anything."

He grinned, his heart taking hope in the new light in her eyes and the strange new attitude she seemed to have. "There's nothing around here but cottonwoods, Abbie," he protested.

"Then have Wolf's Blood go and find us a pine tree. There must be one that would do. Load up the children and have them go find a tree."

Zeke watched her closely. Was she saying she wanted to be alone with him? A tear slipped down her cheek.

"Please?" she said quietly. "I want a tree for Christmas. I know it means nothing to you, but for some reason it means everything to me. I want us to laugh again, Zeke. I want to bake and make presents and I want the children to use their imaginations in making things to decorate the tree. I want us to be a family again."

Her lower lip quivered and he touched her face. She had not mentioned the painted women, and he sensed she was not going to ask. "Abbie," he said softly. *"Nemehotatse!"*

She rested her head against his chest, and he wrapped his arms around her. He turned to Wolf's Blood. "Your mother wants a tree," he told the boy.

"A what?" the boy asked with a frown.

"A tree. A Christmas tree. Some kind of pine tree."

"You mean—in the house?" the boy asked.

Zeke chuckled. "Yes, in the house. Take the children and go see what you can find. Cut down something small enough to—no, cut the biggest one you can find. We have the extra room now. We'll put it in there."

"A tree in the house?" the boy asked again. "Why?"

438

Zeke petted Abbie's hair. "Because it's a Christian tradition, Wolf's Blood—one of the white customs I will not deny your mother. Now just do like I say and go find one. And take your brothers and sisters along." He met the boy's eyes. "All of them."

The boy suddenly grinned. "Yes, Father."

The next several minutes were spent rigging up horses while Abbie sat warming herself by the potbelly stove. Suddenly the minutes seemed like hours until Zeke finally came inside and they were alone. He walked over and sat down in a chair near her, removing his winter moccasins and his coat. He stood up then and removed his buckskin shirt. "It's too cold out there and too warm in here," he spoke up. "At least it seems too warm sometimes when you first come in with all these clothes on."

He shook out his long hair, and he suddenly seemed twice as big to her as he really was, standing there tall and dark and broad, scars of battle on his chest and back and face, a man capable of untold violence. Could he still be as gentle with her in their bed as he had once been? He saw the strange fear in her eyes and knelt in front of her, taking her hands.

"Abbie, are you all right?"

She nodded.

He grinned. "It was so wonderful to see you smiling out there, to hear you laughing." He suddenly felt like a nervous young man taking a woman for the first time. "Abbie, it can wait."

"No," she replied softly. "It can't wait any longer. We are either husband and wife, or we are not. It's time to know." He felt her trembling. "Zeke, I'm so scared! Perhaps . . . perhaps you don't even want me!"

He sobered, fire in his eyes then, his eyes moving over her still-too-thin body lovingly. "I want you so

439

badly sometimes I feel like I'm going crazy," he replied. "There is something I must do, and you know it." He kissed her lightly, their first real kiss since he had left her over a year before. How good it tasted! How sweet and delicious and tender! The kiss lingered, becoming more hungry, more demanding. She knew that she had started something that she would be unable to stop if she changed her mind. To stop him now would be the cruelest trick she could play on him.

He released the kiss, bending down to remove her own winter moccasins. He ran his fingers along her legs, his heart aching at how thin they were, hoping he would not frighten her or somehow damage her emotionally by moving too quickly. He reached up and unlaced her tunic at the shoulders, and she reddened as it fell away from her breasts. He closed his eyes and breathed deeply, leaning forward and gently kissing the whites of her breasts.

"Abbie! Abbie!" he groaned, resting his face between her breasts. She stroked his hair and began to softly cry. He moved his lips over her neck and back to her mouth, kissing her tenderly and moving his arms under her to pick her up out of the chair. He carried her to the bed of robes and laid her on it.

He pulled the tunic the rest of the way off and she lay there in short woolen underwear, teasing him in her half-nakedness. She curled up and he laid down beside her, taking her in his arms.

"You are mine, Abbie. Mine. I was the first to take you, and I am the only man you have ever willingly given yourself to. That is all there is to remember. Nothing can change that. Nothing. Do you understand?"

"You aren't ashamed? You truly aren't ashamed?"

His eyes teared. "Oh, Abbie, how could you think such a thing? There is no woman alive who can equal you." He kissed her gently. "I need to take you, Abbie. I need to reclaim you for myself. You are my Abbie—mine! You are my property, my woman, my beautiful, sweet Abbie-girl."

He gently removed her woolen panties and she began to cry more. He kissed her tears. "God, don't cry, Abbie. Please. Don't be afraid." He kissed her mouth then, groaning with his deep passion and joy. He would have her! He would finally have his woman again! He would be gentle. He would move slowly. He would do nothing that might frighten her or make her think ugly thoughts. He would be careful how he touched her. He would save exploring secret places for another time, when she was ready. For now it would be enough to simply be one again, to enter this woman and mate with her like they used to do and remind her there was nothing wrong in wanting her man that way.

She curled up against his chest as he quickly removed his leggings. He pulled a blanket over them and enveloped her in his arms, kissing her over and over until finally he felt a response.

He kissed her harder then and she whimpered, moving her arms around his neck. The fire in his veins was so hot that he felt a burning sensation.

He moved his lips to her neck. "Let it happen, Abbie," he said softly. "It's all right. There is nothing wrong in loving your own husband. It's good and right and natural."

"Oh, Zeke, I was so proud that it had only been you!" she wept. "I've never wanted another man to touch me! I tried to fight them. I could have . . . stopped them if I had told! But I couldn't tell that man . . . where that poor little boy was! You have to believe me! I had . . . no choice! I would rather die . . . than to be touched by anyone but you!"

"Hush, Abbie-girl," he moaned. "Do you really

think you have to explain such a thing to me? It's over, and by this act it is ended. We will never speak of it again. They never touched you. They never touched your heart or soul. They never touched your desires. Those things belong only to me. I took them years ago and no one else can touch them. They are mine! Lone Eagle's! You are my woman, and nothing changes that! Nothing!''

He moved on top of her then, feeling her panic build as he moved between her legs. She cried out when he entered her, her tears flowing harder. He moved gently. "God, I love you, Abbie!" he groaned. "How I love you! For so long I have dreamed of doing this again!''

Their lips met, and he could taste the salt of her tears. Finally she arched up to him, responding to the only man who could bring such response. Her tears were tears of joy! How she wanted him! How she loved him! It could be right again. It was good and beautiful, just as it had once been. Perhaps they truly could pick up the pieces and find the wonderful, special thing they had once shared.

He surged inside of her, his life suddenly pouring into her. It was impossible for him to prolong anything. It had been too long since he had been able to experience being one with his woman. He kissed her over and over, whispering words of love, laughing and crying at the same time.

"I want to do it again," he told her, feeling like a much younger man. "I must have you again, Abbie, before the children come." He kissed her more, moving his lips down to her breasts and gently tasting the taut nipples. These belonged to him. Every part of her belonged to him. Nothing had changed. Nothing at all! She was still his Abbie, and mating with her was still the thrill it always was.

He felt her relaxing more, and when he looked at her face her eyes were closed, her lustrous dark hair spread out on the robes. "Look at me, Abbie," he told her. She opened her eyes and blushed, feeling on fire then beneath this man of men. He flashed the handsome smile. "Tell me who your man is."

"My man is Zeke Monroe," she replied softly.

"And when and where did he claim you?"

She smiled a little, reddening more. "Somewhere in Wyoming—one night when I needed him most. I was only fifteen." She traced her fingers over his dark skin, following the hard muscle of his arm and moving up to gently touch the thin scar on his cheek. She saw the fire in his dark eyes, and again she was overwhelmed that she had this strange power over a man that others feared greatly—this man who could take on many men at once, this man who could break her in half in one quick snap, this man who feared nothing and no one, except for his fear of losing his woman. "I belong to you, Zeke Monroe. No other man has ever touched me."

He ran a big finger over her lips. "And I have wanted no other woman," he replied. His mouth covered hers again, and soon they were one again, sharing a joy greater than any they had known before.

Far in the distance seven Monroe children rode along the banks of the Arkansas River in search of a tree.

"There is one!" Ellen yelled. She pointed to a scraggly pine tree and Wolf's Blood dismounted. It was not much of a tree, but he suspected it was the best one they would find. He took his hatchet from his mount and bent down to chop at it, shaking his head over his mother's strange religious customs.

"Wolf's Blood, look!" Margaret shouted. He frowned

443

and stood up, looking out in the direction she pointed. Farther down the bank of the river stood a small, trembling wolf cub. The children quieted as the wolf stared at them. "Shoot it, Wolf's Blood!" Margaret whispered, thinking how dangerous a wolf could be.

The boy stepped toward the cub. "No. Do not move. I am going to him."

"But the mother might be close by! She will attack you!" Margaret argued.

Wolf's Blood shook his head, walking slowly closer. "Look at him. He is shaking and thin. He is alone. Perhaps someone has killed the mother."

"Wolf's Blood, stay back!" LeeAnn warned.

"Be still!" he ordered, putting up his hand. He dropped his hatchet as he walked even closer. "Hello, my friend," he said gently. "Did Smoke send you to me?" The cub sat perfectly still as the boy came within reaching distance while the rest of the children watched with terrible fear. Margaret pulled her rifle from its casing, ready to shoot the mother if it should come charging at her brother. But there was no sign yet of another wolf.

Wolf's Blood crouched down. "Smoke sent you, didn't he?" he said softly, reaching out to cautiously allow the cub to smell the back of his hand. "Smoke's spirit has brought you here. Perhaps his spirit lives in you. Is this so? Have you come to replace my loneliness for Smoke?"

The cub began licking the boy's hand and Wolf's Blood grinned more. "We are one in spirit," he told the animal. Then he bravely reached out and grasped the cub, lifting it up to see that it was a male. Then he held it against his chest, rubbing his cheek against its head and burying his hands in its thick fur. "Thank you, wolf spirit," he whispered. "This is a great gift you have given me. It brings me new power, new hope.

I will take good care of your little son, and he will take good care of me."

He turned to the others, tears in his eyes. "You see? Smoke has sent him to me. The cub means no harm. It shall be my pet, a gift from the wolf spirit!"

He ran back toward them, and Jeremy watched in awe. No. He would never be like this brother of his. Wolf's Blood was a wild thing, as wild as the wolves he was named after. There was no doubt now that there was only one path the boy would take in life.

Wolf's Blood shoved the pup into his parfleche so that only the animal's front paws and head stuck out. Then he let out a long, Cheyenne war cry, gazing out into the distant gentle hills and thick cottonwoods beyond. From the cottonwoods there came the long, lonesome wail of a wolf, and Margaret felt chills run down her spine. Her brother truly seemed one with the animal. Wolf's Blood cried out again, and the unknown wolf howled again in reply, while the pup in the boy's parfleche yipped excitedly. Wolf's Blood laughed and picked up his hatchet, walking back to the tree.

"This is a good day!" he told the others. "This is the best day I can remember!" He chopped briskly at the tree until it fell, then tied it to his horse and mounted up.

"Do you think Father will play his mandolin for us when we get back?" Lillian asked Wolf's Blood. "It's been such a long time since he played his music." She held little Jason close, and the boy's eyes were beginning to droop sleepily.

"Sure he will, if we ask," Wolf's Blood answered. "Mother likes to hear him play."

The seven Monroes rode off toward home, Wolf's Blood dragging the tree and the pup gazing out from the parfleche, wondering just where its new master was taking him. A half hour later found them near the cabin. It was growing dark and the cabin looked warm and inviting, a lamp lighting the windows, smoke curling out of the chimney of the potbelly stove. Wolf's Blood turned to Margaret.

"I think perhaps this time we should knock before we go inside," he told his sister.

"Why?" she asked.

He frowned. "You figure it out," he told her. "Just do like I say." They headed for the cabin, and Wolf's Blood's heart sang with happiness, something he once thought could never be his again. He would take the silly tree to his mother, if that was what it took to make her happy. And he was anxious to show the wolf to his father. Zeke would understand. He would know the pup was a gift from the spirits. His father was half wild, just like Wolf's Blood. He would know.

In the distance wolves began howling then, unseen wild things that dwelled in an untamed land.

HISTORICAL ROMANCES BY EMMA MERRITT

RESTLESS FLAMES   (2203, $3.95)
Having lost her husband six months before, determined Brenna
Allen couldn't afford to lose her freight company, too. Outfitted
as wagon captain with revolver, knife and whip, the single-
minded beauty relentlessly drove her caravan, desperate to reach
Santa Fe. Then she crossed paths with insolent Logan Mac-
Dougald. The taciturn Texas Ranger was as primitive as the surrounding Comanche Territory, and he didn't hesitate to let the
tantalizing trail boss know what he wanted from her. Yet despite
her outrage with his brazen ways, jet-haired Brenna couldn't sup-
press the scorching passions surging through her . . . and suddenly she never wanted this trip to end!

COMANCHE BRIDE   (2549, $3.95)
When stunning Dr. Zoe Randolph headed to Mexico to halt a
cholera epidemic, she didn't think twice about traversing Comanche territory . . . until a band of bloodthirsty savages attacked
her caravan. The gorgeous physician was furious that her mission
had been interrupted, but nothing compared to the rage she felt
on meeting the barbaric warrior who made her his slave. Determined to return to civilization, the ivory-skinned blonde decided
to make a woman's ultimate sacrifice to gain her freedom—and
never admit that deep down inside she burned to be loved by the
handsome brute!

SWEET, WILD LOVE   (2834, $4.50)
It was hard enough for Eleanor Hunt to get men to take her seriously in sophisticated Chicago—it was going to be impossible in
Blissful, Kansas! These cowboys couldn't believe she was a real
attorney, here to try a cattle rustling case. They just looked her up
and down and grinned. Especially that Bradley Smith. The man
worked for her father and he still had the audacity to stare at her
with those lust-filled green eyes. Every time she turned around, he
was trying to trap her in his strong embrace.

*Available wherever paperbacks are sold, or order direct from the
Publisher. Send cover price plus 50¢ per copy for mailing and
handling to Zebra Books, Dept. 3006, 475 Park Avenue South,
New York, N.Y. 10016. Residents of New York, New Jersey and
Pennsylvania must include sales tax. DO NOT SEND CASH.*